"A well-plotted mystery . . . Past hurts and current passions come into play in a riveting way that simply won't allow you to put the book down." —*The Tampa Tribune Times*

"A strangely exhilarating delicacy . . . It's almost a disappointment to get to the end of the book."
—*Milwaukee Journal Sentinel*

"In his latest southern Florida thriller, we're introduced to some of Hall's best creations." —*Rocky Mountain News*

"Hall fans will be more than reimbursed by his poetic imagery in the landscapes and love scenes. Alex is a heroine with enough endearing attributes to sustain yet another long-running character series."
—*Publishers Weekly* (starred review)

"A double-barreled actioner set apart from the pack by Hall's virtuoso control of tone, which can shift you from giggles to gasps with a single well-trimmed phrase."
—*Kirkus Reviews*

"Suspense and forensic detail with a near-flawless grasp of character." —*Booklist*

"Hall is back in top form . . . A high-priority purchase for thriller fans." —*Library Journal*

ALSO BY JAMES W. HALL

Also by
Mark T. Sullivan

THE FALL LINE
HARD NEWS

Coming Soon in Hardcover

GHOST DANCE

P THE URIFICATION CEREMONY

MARK T. SULLIVAN

AVON BOOKS ◆ NEW YORK

AVON BOOKS, INC.
1350 Avenue of the Americas
New York, New York 10019

Copyright © 1997 by Mark T. Sullivan
Excerpt from *Ghost Dance* copyright © 1999 by Mark T. Sullivan
Inside cover author photo by Chris Booth/Bartlett Studio
Interior design by Kellan Peck
Map by Dan Osyczka
Visit our website at http://www.AvonBooks.com
Library of Congress Catalog Card Number: 96-44565
ISBN: 0-380-79042-4

First Avon Books Paperback Printing: July 1998
First Avon Books Hardcover Printing: June 1997

AVON TRADEMARK REG. U.S. PAT. OFF. AND IN OTHER COUNTRIES, MARCA REGISTRADA, HECHO EN U.S.A.

Printed in the U.S.A.

WCD 10 9 8 7 6 5 4 3 2 1

For Connor and Bridger

ACKNOWLEDGMENTS

I am in great debt to ethnologist Ruth Holmes Whitehead, author of the remarkable work *Stories from the Six Worlds*. Ms. Whitehead's insight into Power and the mind of the Micmac was a constant source of inspiration.

I am similarly indebted to anthropologist Barbara G. Myerhoff, for her haunting study, *Peyote Hunt, the Sacred Journey of the Huichol Indians*. Her descriptions of the rites of the *Mara'akame* fired my imagination.

Thanks also to white-tailed deer hunting experts Sean Lawlor, David Lawlor, Nick Micalizzi and Gordon Whittington for their advice. I am grateful to Joanna Pulcini and Damian Slattery for their patient reading and rereading of the various drafts, as well as to Ann McKay Thoroman, my editor, for prodding the work to its final shape.

Above all, however, my gratitude goes to Linda Chester, whose skill as an agent fashioned for me every writer's dream—the freedom to work.

"We are murderers and cannot live without murdering. The whole of nature is based on murder . . ."

—MARIE-LOUISE VON FRANZ

"In the end, the hunter really hunts himself."

—HUICHOL INDIAN SAYING

BRITISH COLUMBIA

To Barna

Logging Camp Four

Sticks River

Western clearcuts

N
W E
S

The lodge

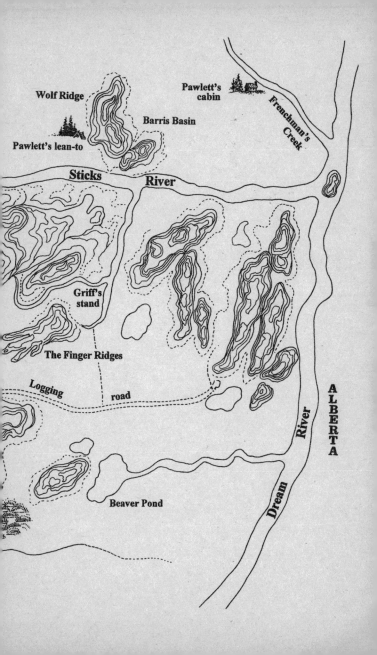

The
Purification
Ceremony

EARLY AUTUMN

HERE LIVES MY STORY.

My name is Diana Jackman, but I think of myself these days as Little Crow, which is what I was called as a child. I am a mother and an environmental software writer. I am also a hunter: a deer hunter, to be precise; a tracking deer hunter, to be more precise still. You might ask how, in this day and age, a woman comes to be a tracking deer hunter and I'd answer: my mother and father and great-uncle. You might ask why I did not track for nearly fifteen years and I'd give you the same answer. And you might ask how I got involved in the terrible events of that November and I'd tell you to sit down and listen.

The facts of what happened in the months before I arrived in British Columbia are thin, and I've been forced to rely on my imagination for much of what must have occurred before I entered into the course of the story.

1

But these few things I know: Pawlett had read the signs accurately. The approaching winter would be early and cruel. The webs of brown spiders hung broad and complicated from the eaves of his cabin. Geese arced south the Tuesday before Labor Day. And the ermines, the best hunters Pawlett knew, had become inordinately vicious in their autumn pursuits.

This last had evidently bothered Pawlett, for he had a strange encounter with an ermine mid-September near Frenchman's Creek, and he was a superstitious man. That morning he grouse-hunted in an aspen regrowth above fresh logging slash. The birds were plentiful and he had shot several. He was on his way back to his cabin about eleven o'clock when he spotted the hare.

I see it plump from a summer feeding on green shoots, the rabbit's fur just beginning the change toward winter white. It crouches at the root end of a blowdown aspen, nervous, its nose pulsing for scent.

The gaunt woodsman scratches at the itch of the skin sore under his gray beard. He flicks off the safety on his battered 12-gauge pump and takes an easy step forward, preparing to shoot. He freezes the gun midway to his shoulder. An ermine, twelve inches long, with a chocolate back and a snow belly, crawls out onto the log. Pawlett smiles. He is a trapper by trade. Come November, the ermine's fur will turn the color of fresh cream. Ermine pelts, despite the efforts of animal rights activists, are still worth their weight in gold. He decides he'll be back with traps in a few months.

Then the weasel does something that makes the old trapper shiver. It turns and stares at him condescendingly, as if it has been aware of his presence all along and doesn't care. The ebony BB eyes roll with blood intent. The animal arches up on its tiptoes and pours toward him. Pawlett has never seen an ermine display such boldness in the presence of a human and he finds himself retreating.

The ermine smirks at Pawlett's distress. When the trapper reaches the bend in the logging road, the animal turns its back on him and slinks into the root system above the hare. The rabbit is twice the weasel in weight, but without hesitation the predator drops onto the neck of its prey. The high-pitched cry of the hare as it leaps away, trying to shake its aggressor, is like the noises I used to hear in the night when one of my babies would suffer night terrors.

Pawlett waits five minutes after the cries have stopped, then creeps forward. When he rounds the root stem, he swallows. The entire throat of the hare has been torn out. For a moment Pawlett thinks the ermine has heard him coming and fled. Then the torso of the hare shakes, and from the throat itself, the ermine pokes its head out and hisses at him.

Pawlett did not return to the woods for nearly a month after the encounter. He believed in nature's ability to presage the future with signs. He got it into his head that the hare's death foretold his own demise; and he did not hunt, or fish, or grease his traps that October. He spent his time splitting kindling. He ate from berry preserves he'd put up in August. He swilled cocktails of Sterno diluted in branch water to mask the memory of the weasel.

One morning in mid-October, a man named Curly arrived outside Pawlett's cabin in a brand-new, red four-wheel-drive

Dodge pickup. Curly always came this time of year. He was chief of security for Metcalfe Timber, the company that owned or controlled logging rights on much of the vast terrain in which Pawlett eked out a living.

The way Curly tells it, Metcalfe Timber had camps throughout this part of British Columbia, hard by the border with Alberta, some of them in constant use, others on a sporadic basis. Because Pawlett was one of the few people who ever ventured into the deep wilderness after the first of November, Curly hired him to make regular checks on the various outbuildings and logging camps not currently occupied. In return, Curly gave Pawlett five hundred pounds of provisions and the right to trap on the land.

"Ain't going out this season," Pawlett said when Curly came through the door hauling a fifty-pound sack of flour and a box of .30-.30 rifle shells.

Curly said the interior of the cabin looked as it always did. Two rudely crafted stools stood next to a battered Formica kitchen table. A hand pump jutted from the sink piled high with dirty dishes. Traps hung from the walls. Under them, the shelves were stocked with golden liquids in pale bottles—Pawlett's trapping tinctures of urine and God only knew what else. Abandoned birds' nests in the rafters. A potbellied woodstove glowed red; its damper begged for repair. The door clung to the cupboard by one fractured hinge. Inside were mason jars stuffed with vegetables Pawlett grew in his summer garden and tins of trout and salmon he smoked in a shed outside. The wall above Pawlett's bunk bed was decorated with a moth-eaten bear skin.

Curly said the man himself rarely bathed. His oily hair was plastered to his head. Scabs poked through his beard.

Not to mention the sick stench of his clothes. Curly hated going to Pawlett's cabin.

"Not going out this winter, eh?" Curly said.

"I had a bad vision last month," Pawlett replied. "I stays here this winter, Curly, wait till it passes."

Curly smiled. "Not here, old-timer. The company owns this cabin and we let you stay here by the goodness of our heart. We need someone making the route this winter. Doesn't matter to me if it's you or someone else. If it's someone else, there's no need for us to keep this dump in its present state. Now, do I bring in the rest of your stuff, or do I radio out to bring in a bulldozer and raze your rathole, eh?"

Pawlett screwed up his face and forced his eyes to focus on the lumberman. The set of his lips did not offer hope. "But everything I own is in here, Curly."

"A damn shame," Curly agreed.

Pawlett rubbed his throbbing temple and forced his brain to consider the options. After a few minutes he sighed. "Okay, bring it all in. Maybe I read the sign wrong, eh?"

"I'll bet you did," Curly replied. He went back to the truck and brought in the rest of the things Pawlett had requested early in the summer: fifty pounds of dried milk, one hundred pounds of dried fruit, shotgun shells, six gallons of rye whiskey, a new wool mackinaw, a set of those modern alloy snowshoes, a pair of deerskin mitts, a new leatherman tool, and oil, gas and a starter motor and carburetor for his aging snowmobile.

Before letting Pawlett sign for the goods, Curly reviewed the terms of their contract. During the course of the winter, beginning at the end of October, Pawlett would check each of the buildings three times. In those buildings with a working radiophone, he was to call in to the main office and report on his progress.

When Pawlett asked if he should check in on the estate, Curly told him not until December at least; an outfitter had leased the property for a whitetail deer hunt in mid-November.

"Be good hunting, seeing how no one's been in there the three years since the old man disappeared," Pawlett observed.

" 'Cept you, of course."

"I never shot no deer on the estate," Pawlett protested.

"A law-abiding citizen, you're telling me," Curly said, almost laughing.

"Ya always said it was off-limits, Curly. I pay mind to what's told me."

"Be sure you do, eh?" Curly said. His lips set thin and hard again. "Someone'll be in here mid-January, check on you and get your furs."

Everything else I will tell you of Pawlett is based on what was left behind. But since I became an integral part of it all, I'm sure you'll allow me my version.

November arrives mild with easy breezes, weather that helps Pawlett to put the weasel behind him. He sobers up. And three weeks after Curly's visit, he's fallen into the daily rhythm of scouting the perimeter of his hundred-mile trapline.

At the end of the first week of November, he decides to make the trek through Barris Basin and over Wolf Ridge onto the series of flats and peaks toward Metcalfe Logging

Camp Four, which abuts the Metcalfe Estate. He shoulders his pack, annoyed that the lack of snow makes it impossible for him to use his snowmobile.

Near the end of the first day of hiking, during which he covers twelve of the twenty-five miles, the wind shifts from south to north, bringing with it blue clouds and the heaviness of increasing humidity.

Pawlett studies the sky and shivers. "Sure enough, we're in for it now."

Wildlife activity picks up in anticipation of the approaching storm. Scrub jays caw. They swoop through the tag alders of a swamp he skirts. He glimpses a moose crashing away at the far side of a clear-cut. A fat whitetail doe feeds on a flat near one of the lean-tos he maintains for his winter work. He shoots it.

Pawlett cleans and skins the deer as the first snowflakes appear. He quarters it, then salts the meat and wraps it in cheesecloth. He hangs the quarters high in the branches of a tree next to a lean-to where it will cool and eventually freeze. If the bears do not get the meat, it will be there when he returns by snowmobile later in the month. When darkness comes, he builds a fire, roasts the deer's liver and eats it. Snow falls.

When I think of Pawlett at this point, I always pray that he sleeps peacefully.

There are six inches of powder snow on the ground by morning, which dawns blustery and cold. Pawlett eats more of the liver with a cup of black coffee and moves on.

At two o'clock that afternoon, Pawlett catches sight of his destination. Active logging at Camp Four was abandoned nearly ten years earlier. But the company still uses it to store spare parts for the skidders and to act as sleeping quarters for the old logging crews called in to perform small clear-cuts for the benefit of the deer on the estate. It's also where supplies too large to be flown into the estate are brought for final transport during the summer, when the two-track road is passable.

Pawlett wipes his nose on his sleeve, then trudges down the hill through the fresh snow that has blown in among a sparse stand of ponderosa pines. He enters an overgrown meadow. At the far end stands an Army-surplus Quonset hut that once served as office, kitchen and bunkhouse to the loggers. Beyond that are three prefabricated metal storage sheds.

The wind picks up. The sun breaks through the clouds, forcing the trapper to squint at the glare thrown off by the snow and the metal walls of the storage units. He stops halfway across the yard. Human footprints? He frowns and kneels. Judging from the depth of the prints and their angle, whoever made them has been carrying a heavy load. And the wind marring along the rim of the tracks tells him they'd been made sometime earlier that morning.

Pawlett glances all around him at the surface of the snow, blazing like millions of diamonds in the sun. No other sign save this line heading off in the direction of the logging road that leads southeast toward the estate. I believe he considers the possibility that the outfitter Curly had spoken of has traveled the thirty-odd miles out from the lake—where old man Metcalfe had his hunting lodge—looking for parts. But where are the tracks of the snow-

mobiles Pawlett has seen around the lodge during his clan-
destine hunting trips in previous falls?

He drops his pack off one shoulder and slides the lever-
action rifle from the side compression straps. He stands and
shouts, "Hello! Hello the camp!"

Behind him, the wind causes a clacking of branches
against the sheds, but no voice raises in response. He calls
again and waits. Again nothing. Two crows drift through
the far tree line.

He looks back at the track. One of the paying hunters?
Curly said the outfitter's clients weren't coming until the
middle of the month, when the rut, the whitetail mating
season, would peak. A resident hunter? Pawlett probably
dismisses the idea. This part of Metcalfe terrain is off-limits,
and besides, it is nearly sixty miles to the nearest town by
some of the roughest two-tracks Pawlett knows. Too far and
too much of a hassle to come hunt here, even if the estate
is home to some of the biggest deer in the world. Besides,
most locals Pawlett knows are interested in meat, not big
antlers.

Maybe the outfitter or one of his guides spent the night
after scouting the perimeter of the estate and kept his vehi-
cle back there in the forest? That would seem the most
logical solution, and I believe Pawlett adopts it.

He holds the gun level with his hip. He follows the
blurred tracks to the door of the Quonset hut and prepares
to kneel to fish the keys from behind the wooden stoop
when he sees that one of the windowpanes in the door has
been broken and patched over with cardboard and duct
tape. He climbs the stoop and tried the knob. It turns. Pawlett lets the door swing open on the wind.

"Hello?" he calls into the dim interior. "Anybody here?"

The air inside rolls to Pawlett. He smells stale smoke, cooked meat and a musky, animal smell. He steps over the transom. The floor is plywood. The tread of his boots makes scratching noises as he moves past a busted table and lets his eyes become accustomed to the feeble light.

On his left is a door he knows leads to the bunkhouse. He goes by that and into the main room. Here the logging foreman used to have his office. And the crews ate at picnic tables and lounged in a couple of sprung couches that had been hauled in years ago. Nothing has changed since Pawlett's last visit.

Except, perhaps, the dust. The cobwebs that normally crisscrossed the thin windows have been cleared to let in more light. The tables have been swept clean. The floor, too. Pawlett crosses to the woodstove and holds his hand above the surface. Still warm. He goes into the kitchen. He turns the knob on one of the stove burners. A muffled cough greets him; someone has turned on the gas. He opens the door to the cold pantry and, to his surprise, finds a deer carcass hanging. The tenderloins have been cut from around the backbone. The head of the deer, a spike buck, has been left on. No hide. Probably skinned it outside. Against the wall, however, stretched taut within a circular hoop of alder wood, is the skinned-out cape of a timber wolf. Pawlett squats and fingers the fur. A professional skinning job. He sniffs his fingers and recognizes the musky smell out in the main room.

I think he returns through the main room then, and, with the gun before him, nudges open the door to the bunkhouse. He waits for a moment, then goes inside. The light is worse than in the main room. He strains to see, and strains again to make sure he's right.

Pawlett finds enough gear in there to support a man for at least a month in the wilderness. Dozens of freeze-dried meals held together in stacks by rubber bands. Four two-gallon water containers and a filtration kit. A down sleeping bag. A bivvy sack. Several clear plastic tarps. Three wool shirts. Two pairs of wool twill pants. Twelve pairs of wool socks. Two complete sets of expedition-weight long under-wear, including the balaclava hoods. A black knit watch cap. One pair of leather boots similar to his own and a second pair of deep-snow pac boots with a fur cuff. A gray camouflage outfit in fleece. A flashlight with ten sets of batteries. A camping lantern and two gallons of white fuel. A folding pack saw. And more equipment stacked in the corner where the light is worse.

As I see it, Pawlett tries the flashlight, but it doesn't work. He's about to tear open one of the battery packages when he notices the faint outline of two white candles that have been set up on a table on the far side of the room. He leans his rifle against the wall. He shrugs off his knapsack. He sets it on the floor. He fishes a matchbook from his pants pocket and weeble-wobbles over the gear. He strikes a match, holds it to one candle and then to the other.

In the wavering light, Pawlett beholds a shrine: the hide of the spike buck has been nailed to the plank boards above the table. The wolf's skull has been boiled free of flesh and affixed to the bloody deer skin. Attached around the skull, in a fanlike formation, are the red tail feathers of a hawk, the white wing feathers of an owl and the oily spine feathers of a raven.

But I know it is what Pawlett finds on the makeshift altar below the fetish that makes him panic. Pawlett's heart catches and snags, as if manipulated by a force outside his capacity to understand. The urge to flee overcomes him. He stumbles over the gear and through the door, forgetting in his haste his gun and his pack.

He explodes into the outer room. He slips on the plywood floor and crashes to his knees, trying to keep down the bile that climbs the back of his throat. He tells himself to calm down, to get to the generator room, gas it and start it so he'll have electricity to run the radiophone. He'll call Curly. He'll be all right.

Pawlett gets to his feet and runs to the door to the generator room. Locked. The keys are under the stoop. Pawlett curses and races out the door of the Quonset hut, barely giving attention to an outer world that has been made anew and powerful and evil in the confrontation of the shrine.

He digs through the snow and reaches in behind the stoop. He strains for the coffee can the keys were kept in. And then the keys are in his hand. He is laughing, telling himself he'll be all right, that he'll be all right.

The generator argues with Pawlett for what seems an eternity until he checks the oil, sees that it is low and fills the reservoir to the brim. Three tugs on the cord and the machine wheezes to life.

Pawlett has time now. He lowers his head and moves straight back through the main room toward the nook where the logging foreman had kept track of the operation. There, on a metal bookshelf, the radiophone glows.

He picks up the phone and is about to dial in the Metcalfe frequency when his heart catches again, only this time he feels the presence of a manipulator, and a shaking takes hold of his entire body. Pawlett turns to see that the outer door is open. A thick shaft of sunlight cuts across the floor and in it, dressed head to toe in a camouflage suit the color of fresh cream, is a man whose eyes shine like ebony.

Pawlett sees the primitive weapon the man holds and realizes he has no recourse. He feels the predator's intent like a claw in his chest. The old trapper drops the phone and begins to cry like a baby stricken with night terrors . . .

The rest of what happened that fall, I know for certain.

NOVEMBER SIXTEENTH

Long before i ever speculated about Pawlett, the chill fore-winds of a gathering storm raked the surface of the lake and the heavy chop spit white foam onto the dock. A twin-engine Otter floatplane bucked and strained against lashes. And the spruce trees on the far side of the inlet cowered.

The wind gusted. The metal Coca-Cola sign above the ramshackle provision store clanged against its braces. I flipped up the collar of my **green** plaid wool coat and turned my back to the storm. I stepped around the two canvas duffel bags and the aluminum rifle case I'd stacked on the dock to be loaded into the floatplane. I shoved my hands deep into the sheepskin-lined pockets of the coat, and for the fifth time that hour, I went to the phone booth in the gravel parking lot.

Inside the booth, I allowed myself a moment of quiet from the chatter of the others who were gathering themselves and their equipment for the flight into the Metcalfe Estate. Then I dialed. Three thousand miles away, at what used to be my home in Boston, the line engaged and the phone rang. It sounded thirteen times. I made to hang the receiver in its cradle.

On the fourteenth ring, my husband answered. "Hello?"

"It's me."

For a moment I thought Kevin had hung up. But over the wind, I caught the faint beat of his breath.

"I'm glad I caught you," I barged on. "I wanted to talk to the kids . . . before I go."

"They're already outside in the car," Kevin replied curtly. "Off to Mom's for dinner."

"You could get them for me."

"I could," he said. "But I won't."

"Are you trying to destroy me, Kevin?" I'd told myself I wouldn't yell at him anymore, but I couldn't help it.

"You've already done a pretty good job of that yourself," he said calmly.

I took a deep breath and tried to be civil. "I just want to say good-bye. This separation is hurting them more than us."

"They're in the car," he said again. "I'll say good-bye for you."

I pressed my forehead against the chill glass of the phone booth. "Why do you have to be so cruel? Haven't you punished me enough?"

"Diana, you punished yourself."

I didn't want to get angry again. I knew I had to keep

my lines of communication open, but it boiled over again. "That's a lie. You're a shit for doing this."

"Judge didn't seem to think so."

"You know I'm a good mother."

He laughed. "And you show it by going on this trip?"

I looked out at the windswept lake. Tears welled. I whispered, "I have to."

"So you've said." There was a pause. "The way I look at it, you lost your mind. Everybody can see it but you."

"I suppose sympathy would have been too much to expect."

"Used up," he replied. "Gotta go."

"Kevin, please . . ."

"Call when you get back, Diana."

The line went dead. I closed my eyes and listened to the static as if it were a wild thing moving electric and purposeful through dry leaves.

Someone rapped sharply on the door behind me. I hung the receiver up, wiped the tears from my eyes and turned to find a vaguely familiar man, short, stocky, bald, early fifties, wearing a long red Pendleton coat that had been woven to affect a Navajo blanket design. He stuffed a stick of gum in his mouth and chewed at it, creating the illusion of a brick smacking a boulder. He was looking at me with a vague sense of hunger.

I say this not to draw attention to myself. Like most women in our culture, I have learned the subtle lessons well. We may be competent. But we may not boast. We may not see ourselves as something more than a part of a community. But here, to tell this story true, I must abandon convention. I must describe myself honestly.

If you were to see me, you would think—a tall, handsome woman in her mid-thirties with a duskiness to her skin that suggests diluted Indian blood. Despite carrying two children, she has kept her waist, her legs and her lungs. Her black hair, flecked silver at the temples, is cut functionally short. My mother, in one of her rare moments of lucidity at the end, said Little Crow's eyes were the color of shale, intent, roving and yet, somehow, sad. My mother always knew me best.

When I opened the door, the man said, "If this phone booth was a john, sweet thing, I'd swear you had the trots, you been here so many times."

The accent was mesquite and cactus and quail and bourbon. "Trying to call home for the kids," I apologized. "First time I've been away from them for a holiday."

"Kids, huh?" He chuckled. "I'm checking in one last time with my broker before we head out. Can't believe they won't let you call out 'cept in an emergency."

I shrugged. "I'm kind of looking forward to the solitude."

"Solitude?" He chuckled again. "Sure, I guess."

I moved by the man, ignoring the way that, despite the heavy coat I wore, he stared at my chest. I suppose I would have found it stranger if he didn't, but I went off toward the dock, past the fly-fishing dories that had been pulled up on land for the winter.

There, the pilot broke off a conversation with a woman perhaps five years younger than I. The pilot got inside the plane. The woman turned and gave me a look of appraisal. I gave her one in return. She could have been called glamorous, but for the hardening influences of an oilskin drover coat, a cowboy hat, an overly precise makeup job and an indifferent expression. She balanced the weight of one leg on the heel of a black, hand-tooled boot and raised her right hand to brush back hair dyed the hue of dried goldenrod. A chunky gold bracelet dangled from her wrist. A four-carat diamond glittered on her left hand. She gestured with the diamond toward the phone booth.

"He figure out whether you're traveling alone yet?" she asked in that same South Texas drawl.

"Excuse me?"

"Earl," she said. Her gaze did not waver from the phone booth. "He likes to hunt women as much as deer. I'm his latest trophy wife, Lenore."

"Look, Lenore, he said he was calling his stockbroker. I was calling my children."

Lenore seemed to think that was funny. "Stockbroker? More likely his secretary or the gal that does his fingernails." She gave me a closer look. "You got looks, honey, but I figure you're a bit too easy for Earl. He likes his game tough to handle."

"What are you—his wife or his bedroom guide?"

At that, Lenore leaned back and laughed. She pointed at me. "You're all right, honey! I come on a little strong, I know. But it helps me tell what people are made of. I can see you're tougher than I thought. No hard feelings?"

She stuck out her hand. I admit she had me confused now. But I could see she genuinely meant the apology. I took her bony hand and shook it. Earl called out behind her. "See you two huntresses have met. Didn't catch your name?"

"Diana, Diana Jackman."

"Earl Addison. Addison Data Systems, Forth Worth."

That was where I knew him from. "Your company's getting lots of press in the trades these days, Earl."

"Yeah, you in the computer bus—?"

Before Earl could finish, another man's voice called out: "Jackman? You're not Hart Jackman's daughter, are you?"

I froze at the mention of my father's name, then forced myself to turn. Within the cluster of duffels and weapons cases stood someone seen in pictures on the walls of my father's office, a man of about fifty-five or sixty with a startling white beard and a tangle of equally chalky hair that ran off his head in thirty directions. He wore a green camouflage vest, jeans and heavy leather boots. His skin was mottled red, the kind of skin you see on open-water fishermen. His eyes were rheumy, but intelligent.

Then the name came to me—Michael Griffin. He owned a store outside Nashville from which he dealt fine shotguns: J. Purdey & Sons, Holland & Holland, A.H. Foxes. But when it came to big game, if I remembered, he hunted strictly with the bow and arrow. He was also a writer who had made a name for himself discussing the more philosophical aspects of the hunt, a trait which had endeared him to my dad.

"Yes, Mr. Griffin, I was Hart's daughter."

He got around the equipment and thrust out his hand. "Then you are Little Crow."

I smiled. "No one's called me that in years. Please call me Diana."

He smiled in return. "Only if you'll call me Griff."

"All right, Griff."

He turned to Earl and Lenore. "Could I have a minute

with Diana here? She lost her dad a little while back. I'd like to make my condolences."

Earl's jaw flapped in annoyance. He was the sort who didn't like to be told what to do. "Sorry, Diana," he said finally, "uh . . . cancer or something?"

"No, Earl," I said softly. "Much worse."

"Oh," Earl said.

"You toad!" Lenore said, grabbing him by the shoulder. She thrust her chin at me. "I apologize. Earl's a genius with computers and business, but his people skills leave something to be desired. Come on."

When the two of them were out of earshot, I said, "I hope Metcalfe's as big as they say it is."

"Thirty-three miles by thirty-three miles," Griff replied.

"Sounds a little small," I said, gesturing in their direction.

"We'll make the best of it," Griff said. His expression turned sober. "It's real nice to meet you. Your dad used to say that, besides himself, you were the best tracker he ever saw."

"It's been a long time. I'm way out of shape for the woods."

"Shape! Young lady, you look like you could run twenty miles."

"That's gym shape," I said. "I haven't been in the big woods in eighteen years. I've been sitting behind a desk, writing software—waste management, pollution control, that sort of thing. You might say I've been living as far away from nature as a person can."

"Then this will be a good place to reintroduce yourself," Griff said. "Isolated country, spirit country, your dad's kind of country."

I found myself looking at the ground.

The pilot called out to us then. The chatter on the dock died, replaced by an awkward entry as we all tried to board the pitching plane. Inside the Otter, I took a seat mid-cabin. Besides Griff and the Addisons, there were three men in their mid-thirties chatting familiarly. And then another guy in his late twenties, overly lean, almost sallow, with curly red hair and a mustache. He took the seat opposite mine. There was something strange about him. I studied him out of the corner of my eye until I figured it out. Everything he wore, from the pile jacket to the wool pants to the pac-style boots, was brand new. Not that I hadn't bought new equipment for this trip. But everything?

He caught me looking and smiled. It was a confident, attractive smile. He said, "More women than I expected on a trip like this."

"I guess," I said.

"Just that you don't expect to see women going on a wilderness hunt."

"I started hunting when I was five," I said, crossing my arms. "And there are more women in the field every year. Threatened?"

"Just intrigued," he said. He held out his hand. "Steve Kurant."

"Diana Jackman."

Kurant craned his head around. "Your husband?"

"Not along," I said. "Doesn't believe in it."

He smiled that smile again. "Really? Now that's an interesting twist—"

The twin engines belched, interrupting him. They wheezed, then thundered to life, sending a vibration down

the plane's interior. The pilot's voice came from an overhead speaker: "Weather Canada has issued a storm warning
for early this evening, so the turbulence could be rough.
In fact, weather's gonna be nasty off and on the next ten
days. Keep to your seats and your belts fastened. I'll try to
make this as painless as I can."

A row behind me, Arnie Taylor, who turned out to be a
pediatrician from eastern Pennsylvania, shook his head and
grabbed the arms of his seat. He gritted his teeth and stared
across the aisle at his friend Phil Nunn, a muscular black
man with a shaved head, thick brow ridges and skin so
scarred by acne that it looked sand-blasted. Nunn owned
a string of auto-parts stores.

"I hate this kind of stuff, Phil," Arnie said. "I don't know
how I let you talk me into this."

"What's your problem, Doc?" Phil snapped. "I been lis-
tenin' to you whine since we left Philly. We'll be up and
down in forty minutes, tops."

Arnie reddened. The man next to him looked like a hippie. Sal "Butch" Daloia had long brown hair, a full beard
and pouty lips perpetually twisted in amusement. He sold
expensive music recording equipment for a living. He said,
"Lighten up, Phil. You know Arnie hates to fly."

"Well, what's he want, Butch, a frigging limo to the
wilderness?"

"Horses," Arnie complained. "You said go out West to
hunt, I figured horses."

Phil made a dismissive gesture. "We'da gotten to the trail
and heard you bitching about being allergic to ponies. You
been like this since we was kids, Arnie, always complaining
about being sick. I been thinkin' lately that's why you be-

came a doctor, so you could figure out new stuff to be bitching about."

Arnie chewed on the inside of his cheek, but didn't reply.

Butch said, "And what about you, Phil? I think you became a grease monkey just so you could keep that pimpish old Cadillac of yours on the road."

The black man laughed. "I admit I got a certain style, Butchy-boy, but c'mon—pimpish? You can do better'n that old stereotype."

Arnie said, "That *was* a little lame."

Butch shrugged. "He takes the fuzzy dice off his rearview mirror, I'll take it back."

"Uh-uh, me and those dice go way back," Phil said, holding up crossed fingers. "Had 'em in my first Caddy before I opened the shop. I'll have 'em in my last."

Butch reached inside his jacket and drew out a silver flask. He took a swig, then motioned to Arnie. "This'll help. I'm in these damned short-hoppers all the time and it's the only way to deal with them."

Arnie attempted a smile. "I'll be okay."

"Think of it as a toast," Butch insisted, shaking his long hair from his eyes. "Then do what *I'm* gonna do—dream about what's waiting for us inside Metcalfe's tomorrow morning."

The pediatrician took the flask, sipped the liquid and shuddered.

I shuddered with him, thinking of the dream I'd had the night before. In it, I had been cooking in my father's hunting cabin in the shadow of Mt. Katahdin in northern Maine. I carried a bowl of water from the sink to the oven and tripped, falling facedown on the floor of the cabin. The spilled water turned to blood and soaked the white clothes I wore. I had awakened sweating and shaking from the vision. In the world I was raised in, blood dreams foretell violent death.

The plane came free of the dock. The lake roiled now, gray and ominous with the approaching storm. We headed into the oncoming waves for several minutes, gained speed finally, bumped twice, then rose. The first wisps of cloud caressed the ridge tops. Snowflakes fell.

Around me, the talk was of the hunt to come. I tuned it out and looked down, trying to identify the various trees by their crowns: Red pine, poplar and, in the wetland bottoms, ash and willow. Where the leaves had fallen I could make out the faint lines of game trails and my eyes became hazy, closed, then opened and shut again as I thought of being in the big woods again, slipping quietly after a deer, after a memory.

It was the day after Thanksgiving, almost two years prior to the flight. I was home at our town house in Boston's Back Bay, preparing leftover turkey sandwiches for my kids. Though I had willed myself over the years to rarely think of my father, when I did, it was of the eventuality of his passing and how I'd react. I used to tell myself that the time apart would lesson its significance. But, as is often the case, the stories we tell ourselves disintegrate under the hammer of reality.

"This Diana Jackman?" the man with the Down East accent asked.

"Yes."

"Been hard to find you. Got bad news. Your father's passed on. Been dead two days up in the woods there nor'east a Baxter Park. Hunters found him laying next to a giant twelve-pointer. Biggest deer I've seen in years. The boys drug it in to show everybody."

I had already faded into the shadow world that comes after someone you know dies. "Heart attack?" I asked.

"No, ma'am, sorry to say, but appears a suicide," he said. "And, sorrier still, but the coyotes been at him. We need you to identify the body."

I summoned all my strength, got directions and hung up. Kevin looked up at me from the kitchen table, where he was trying to get Emily, my younger child, to stop playing with her sandwich. He still had the lank blond hair I remembered from college. He still had that long, slender body that begged for fashionable clothes.

"I have to go to Maine," I said.

The shock must have shown in my face, because Kevin got up fast and walked toward me. "Why? Did someone die?"

I answered without thinking. "My . . . my father."

"Your father?" His bewilderment was total. "I thought your father died years ago. Diana?"

The room around me whirled, but I managed to make it stop. "He did die years ago. At least to me. And that's what counted."

Now Kevin's angular face twisted from puzzlement to anger. "You've lied about this all these years?"

"Mommy lied!" Emily yelled from the table. "She doesn't get her allowance."

"Shut up, Em!" said Patrick, my firstborn, and the worrier in the family. He could see how off balance I was.

"Diana, why would you do this?" Kevin demanded.

The room whirled again and I stuttered. "I don't know. I have to go to Maine."

"I'm coming, too," he said. "I'll call my mother. She'll baby-sit."

I shook my head. "You never knew him and neither did the kids. I'd like to keep it that way. I'll explain when I get back."

You'll be surprised to hear that my father was a doctor, a good one, which in some ways, makes our story all the more tragic. But I'm getting ahead of myself. Suffice it to say, he knew where the vital organs lay. And I believe he knew I'd be the one to come to identify him. Who else? I was his only child, the last of his line. I'm sure he put a bullet through his chest to do the job correctly, and yet to lesson the impact a head wound would have had on me.

My father's face had not been touched by the scavengers, and I know this sounds awful, but I almost wished it had, for when they drew back the sheet I saw how old he'd become in the intervening years, and despite my effort at steely detachment, I began to choke. His once-bushy black eyebrows had gone sparse and white. His hair was pale, too, and longer than I remembered it. His flesh was creviced with wrinkles. His cheekbones stuck out and made me wonder how much he'd been eating lately.

And yet I couldn't bring myself to place my hands on him, to stroke his skin, to call him Daddy. I just nodded my head to identify him, then walked out of the coroner's office where the wind picked up and swirled until the road grit got into my eyes.

*   *   *

After making the funeral arrangements, I drove to the big white Victorian north of Bangor that my parents had raised me in. I stood on the porch for a long while, getting the strength to enter. I looked down the hill to the ice forming on my mother's heart-shaped pond and I choked again; she'd been dead fifteen years and yet he'd kept her precious gazebo repaired and freshly painted. A memorial to her.

My father's lawyer, a young preppie named Wilson, pulled into the driveway and made it easier for me to go inside. We walked through the house together the way you would walk through a furniture store, seeing but not seeing. So much of my life here I'd locked away in closets, hidden from my husband, hidden from myself. I was determined not to let my father's death open them again.

Wilson and I reviewed the papers my father had left behind at the dining room table. I got everything. The house, the cabin up by Baxter, the land, the securities, the money, everything. I told him to sell it all and place the money in a trust for Patrick and Emily.

"You want nothing?" Wilson asked, incredulous. "There's a lot here."

"A few minor things, but nothing important," I said, knowing that Kevin would be enraged; my husband, despite his many admirable qualities, was a spendthrift, always looking for new infusions of cash to keep up with the lifestyle we led but couldn't afford. But in this instance, Kevin's needs would have to be subordinate to my own.

"Are we done?" I asked.

"Almost," the attorney said. From his pocket he drew an

envelope. It was addressed to "Little Crow" in my father's handwriting.

My head came up with a snap.

The Otter lurched from side to side, then dropped fifty feet through a vacuum pocket in heavy turbulence. The plane shook and rolled right and fell again, this time for two hundred feet. Then it leveled and the horrible vibration lessened.

"Oh, God!" Arnie yelled. He dug through the pocket on the seatback in front of him, got out the plastic bag and retched.

"There you go. What'd I say?" Phil said, pointing his finger at Butch. "Fan belt starts to whine, the doc falls to pieces."

Over the speaker, the pilot yelled: "Hold on, now! It's gonna get tight."

The vibration returned and got worse as we descended through the clouds. Arnie groaned. I gripped the arms until I could no longer feel my fingers. Kurant, the redheaded guy, was staring at the ceiling. Lenore Addison was cool, working at her red fingernails with an emery board while Earl gritted his teeth. Finally, when I thought I couldn't take it anymore, the bouncing and dropping stopped and we broke free of the clouds.

There was a long, narrow lake and, beyond it, a broad expanse of ridges, parks and flats extending for miles in every direction. The highlands were mostly coniferous, spruce and pine varieties. And to the north there were dozens of openings in the forest.

Griff yelled to the pilot: "It's been logged."

"For the deer, eh?" the pilot responded. "Some are clear-cuts. Others are fields old man Metcalfe had planted for the deer—clovers, oats, alfalfa, rye grass, winter wheat and a bunch of other exotic high-protein stuff."

He held up his hand before Griff could ask him another question. He pressed forward on a lever to the right of his seat. The engine grumbled in protest and then we were whizzing down over the lake. The snow fell heavier here. Blue fog from the cooling water hung in the trees on the shoreline. Beyond, a flat of several miles. And beyond that, like inverted thunder clouds, opaque, mutating and dangerous, the shadow of ridges.

The plane made the final ten-foot drop, then heaved into chop that spun the Otter sideways. The wing tip cut waves and threatened to dive. The pilot fought for control, righting the wing at last and straightening the fuselage. He trimmed the throttle. We coasted in a slow, undulating taxi through the rough water. We all sighed with relief.

Now I could make out a dock jutting into the lake and, beyond it, a multistory log lodge with a front gallery set back in a grove of ponderosas. A set of elk antlers hung above the stairway. Stretched along the shoreline were eight smaller renditions of the great lodge. Smoke puffed from every chimney.

"Welcome to Metcalfe," the pilot said as we pulled up to the dock. "Sorry for the ride, but I figured it was better than sitting back in town, eh? Given the weather forecast, there's no way I would have got you in here for at least another week."

"Just get me out of this thing," Arnie said, sweat running down his pink cheeks.

"Not before me," Earl croaked.

I got to the plane door to find a wiry fellow with a close-cropped beard holding his hand out for me. He wore a denim jacket and pants, a down vest and a fluorescent orange cap that read "Metcalfe Trophy Hunts." He introduced himself as Mike Cantrell, outfitter and lead guide. I was somewhat surprised that he had an American, not a Canadian, accent.

Out on the dock, Cantrell called our names and gave us cabin numbers. I would take Cabin Four. Dinner was at five-thirty, but Cantrell wanted us all in the main lodge a half hour early to go over logistics. He jerked a thumb toward a young man stooping on the shoreline next to five wooden handcarts. "Grover will show you where you're bunking. He's a little slow upstairs, but he's been here for years and is about the kindest guy you'll ever meet."

I moved to one side as the others hustled toward shore. After the flight, I wanted to be still for a moment or two. I closed my eyes and breathed in the spicy pine smoke wafting from the cabins and wondered at the tingle of new snowflakes on my skin, not knowing that in the coming days I would grow to fear the sensation.

The pilot, who had been checking the struts, called out to Cantrell, "I'm gonna be moving along now, before the storm sets in and I end up trapped."

"See you in ten days, then," Cantrell said.

"Yeah, I'll try to be out here around nine A.M. on the twenty-sixth. Oh, before I forget: I got a message from Curly, the security guy with Metcalfe Timber. Says if an old trapper named Pawlett wanders in, to have him call out. He keeps tabs on the logging camps for the company this time a year and was due for a check-in nearly ten days ago."

"Will do," Cantrell promised.

The pilot got back in the plane, waited until Cantrell had thrown off the dock lines, then taxied away. By then, the Addisons and the three Pennsylvania hunters had gone behind Grover toward their cabins. I lugged my bags to shore, where Griff gave me a hand loading them on one of the carts. Kurant was snapping photographs of the floatplane taking off, with a camera mounted with a large telephoto lens. Cantrell came up toting a big brown canvas bag.

"Here's your bag, Steve. But I can't seem to find your weapons case," Cantrell said.

"Because I haven't got one," Kurant replied.

Cantrell set the bag down hard on the last of the carts. "I don't understand."

"Actually, I'm not here to hunt, Mr. Cantrell," he said. "I'm working on a story about the culture of hunting for *Men's Journal.* Since whitetail deer hunting seems to be the only portion of the hunting community in America that's growing, not shrinking, and the late Mr. Metcalfe was one of the world's greatest whitetail hunters, my editors and I figured what better place to profile the subculture than his estate as it opens to the first paying customers."

Something unspeakable came over Cantrell's face. His lower lip bunched. The quiver in his voice betrayed great effort at control. "Couldn't you have been up front about this? You posed as a regular client . . . booked a hunt . . . aw, pinch my nuts!"

"Calm down, now," Kurant said, his own face reddening.

"I, we . . . the magazine . . . wanted to be treated like any other guest, so we just booked it straightforward. You have no reason to be upset."

Cantrell growled, "Some goddamned reporter sneaks in here, looking to do a hatchet job on hunting, like that's unusual, and I have no reason to be upset? You're right— look at me—I'm cheery!"

Kurant pointed at the outfitter. "Mr. Cantrell, I don't do hatchet jobs."

Cantrell threw up his hands. "Tell it to the trees. You writers are all the same: lackeys for knee-jerk feelings. No connection to nature."

"Think any way you want," Kurant replied. "I've paid my seven thousand dollars to be here. You've cashed the check. I expect to be treated like any other guest."

"My other guests hunt."

"Fair enough," Kurant said. "I'll hunt with my camera, sit in a tree perch, or whatever you call them, all day."

Somewhere in the clouds over the lake, the floatplane banked south. Cantrell searched the sky for it. The buzz of its engine faded, leaving nothing but the wind and the snow and the slap of the lake against the dock.

Cantrell stared hard at the writer. "What other choice do I have now? But I'll tell you something straight: you start upsetting the others, I'll confine you to camp. Clear?"

Kurant forced a smile. "Perfectly."

"Good; now, I've got a lot to get done before nightfall." Cantrell strode off, shaking his head and muttering to the sky.

Kurant looked at me and then at Griff. "Guess I won't be getting *his* perspective."

"Wouldn't expect so," Griff said. "And you won't get it from me or anyone else here if you go on being sneaky. Understood?"

There was a moment between them and then Kurant said, "Understood."

Grover shambled down the hill, whistling. He'd turned his orange cap backward on his head, exposing a doughy, contented face. He had smooth pink skin and ears that stuck out from the sides of his head. His jacket was unzipped to reveal gray wool pants too big for his waist; he'd cinched them to himself with a wide black belt.

"Hello, hello!" Grover said.

"Hello, hello yourself," Griff replied. "You're a happy guy."

"Grover's always happy at the lodge, eh?" He beamed and tugged at his earlobe. "Three years not hearing the loons sing or the wolves howl or watching the big deer run. Sure Grover's happy now; he's home! Come on, then, let's show you the cabins."

Grover tugged at his earlobe again and let loose with another of those beaming expressions. You knew something wasn't right with him—the way he always referred to himself in the third person and that faraway cast to his gentle eyes—but like a yellow lab puppy, he made you feel as if you knew him the second you met him, that his heart was good, that there was nothing contrived about him.

He gently pushed me aside, got behind the handle of my cart and urged it up the embankment. I hurried after him. Kurant called out, "Cantrell said you've been here a long time. How long, Grover?"

The cabin boy's face bunched up as if that question had

an obvious answer. "Born here. Momma was Mr. Jimmy's cook. Grover and Momma spent six months, ice-out to end of deer season, here. Mr. Jimmy fished in the summer and hunted bird and deer in the fall. Grover listened to the loons."

"And what else?" Kurant asked.

"What else what?"

"What else does Grover do?"

"Hauls the wood to the cabins and ice from icehouse to kitchen and bags from the dock to the lodge. He unloads the supply plane. He helps peel potatoes and tends the summer garden. At night he watch the moon. The lodge is a happy place to be."

"Does your mom still cook here?" I asked.

The beam dimmed. "Momma died the year before Mr. Jimmy disappeared. So Grover spent all the time in the apartment the company rented him in town. Till Mr. Cantrell come looking for him last summer. Now Grover's home."

He was radiating goodwill again.

"Disappeared?" Kurant said. "I thought Metcalfe died up here three falls ago."

Grover's head bobbed. "Must be, eh? After Momma died from the stomach cancer, Mr. Jimmy got a big ache in his stomach all the time, too. He never ate much anymore. His eyes got all black and dull, you know—like they do on the big deer when they hang 'em on the meat pole? One day in early December, after all his friends went home and the deer, they headed to the wintering yards. Mr. Jimmy gave Grover a long hug and walked out on the ice. He never came home."

Kurant stopped and looked back at the lake. "They never dragged it, looking for the body?" he asked.

Grover gave him a queer look. "Mr. Jimmy loved the lake. Why disturb him when what he loves is giving him a big hug, eh? Besides, I figure he's with Momma now."

Grover stopped in front of a little log cabin with a front porch loaded with split cordwood and kindling. "This one's yours, Miss Diana. Them next two are for you sirs. Now listen up. We got no electricity in the camps, just the lodge. All the lamps are gas, so you got to light 'em. They make a pop and a *hooooo* before they light. And don't worry when you're out hunting, eh? Grover keep the stoves going. And remember: meeting's in an hour."

"We won't forget," I told him.

"Okay, now," Grover said. He waved and left.

Griff and Kurant pushed off toward their cabins. The screen door to mine sagged open. The inner, hardwood door had an iron latch system that squeaked when I thumbed it.

It was murky and fire-smelling inside, warm with the dry heat of the Ashley stove on the far side of the main room. I drew back green drapes at the front window and surveyed my home for the next ten days. Oiled spruce logs shone in the dwindling light. A finely crafted wooden table and two chairs pressed against the wall by the window. An over-stuffed leather chair and ottoman occupied the corner below one of several gas lanterns. A good whitetail buck with eight long antler points peered down from the rear wall. Below the deer head was a gun rack and to the rack's right was a still-life painting of a game dinner: a pheasant stiff-legged in death, grapes, a shank of venison arranged on earthenware with potatoes and carrots, a half loaf of bread on a board, apples in a wicker basket and a bottle of wine. All set on a wooden table against a black space that seemed infinitely deep. I didn't know the painter, but the work struck me as vibrating between desire and denial, between mortality and the chill breath, a synergy approaching the sacred. I couldn't look at it for long.

I inspected the bathroom, found it clean, then moved into the bedroom, a spare affair with a bed, an end table and a small closet. A dozen pegs had been driven into the logs from which to hang clothes. I went back outside and returned with my bags and gun case. I found matches and lit two of the gas lamps, savoring the textured glow cast across the room.

I unpacked my two sets of wool clothes, hanging them on the pegs. Beside them I hung the tooled leather and porcupine quill pouch my great-uncle Mitchell had given me and which I always wore around my neck when hunting; it was where I kept my maps and compasses. I liked to think of it as my good-luck charm.

I put a framed photograph of Emily and Patrick on the bedstead, then stored all else save my binoculars, knapsack and rubber-bottomed boots on the shelves in the closet. Last I unsnapped the case and brought out my rifle, a pre-1964 Winchester model 70 in the .257 Roberts caliber. Other girls' fathers gave them pretty dresses or jewelry for their sixteenth birthdays. I got this rifle. It was one of the few tangible connections I had to my father, and before I left his house I had taken it, despite the strange look Wilson had given me.

I sat on the ottoman and ran the bolt several times. It

slid clean on the new oil I'd coated it with after my last practice session. I shouldered the gun and peered through the low-power telescopic sight at the buck on the wall, then dry-fired it to reacquaint myself with the trigger weight.

Satisfied, I put the gun in the wall rack, checked the stove and added wood. I went to my parka and fished out the envelope, my father's handwriting wrinkled to a scrawl from being handled so often. I sat in the leather chair and stared at the envelope, thinking of all that the words inside had set in motion.

I had not allowed myself to open the letter before the funeral, which was well attended by all the families he'd cared for over the years. Most of them could not hide their surprise when I showed up at the riverbank to take him across to the burial island north of Old Town. There, he was laid to rest between my mother and his beloved uncle Mitchell.

When I got home that night, Kevin was waiting up for me. He'd had a few drinks and was feeling sorry for himself. "You going to tell me about it? Now? After fifteen years?"

I stared at him. This man I'd spent a second lifetime with. Suddenly a stranger. "If you love me, you won't make me," I whispered. "I want to leave it where it should be. Buried."

"Diana. I'm your husband."

"I know," I said, crossing to him to put my arms around him. I laid my head in the crook of his shoulder. "My father was a very disturbed man. I don't like to think about my childhood with him at all. When I met you, I believed I could leave it alone forever because you were all I needed. I still want to believe that. I want to go on like before."

I started to cry. And I heard him say, "Okay. Like before."
But there was no strength in his hands around my back.

A week later, I read the note and had to go outside to
walk for hours. I never showed Kevin the letter, never let
on that it even existed. I stuffed the note at the back of my
bra drawer. I told myself it would remain there like a scarf
too soiled to wear again, but too precious to give away.

For a year after my father's death, I was able to convince
myself, my family and the world that I had moved on. Kevin
tried to bring up the subject a few times, but I'd managed
to stop the conversations before they started. He'd get this
hollow expression on his face and I knew a gap was opening between us. There was nothing I could do.

Then, just before deer season the following November, I
began to wake up at night, nauseated and sweating.

The insomnia eased into melancholy. I seldom left the
house except to work, habits that turned into the first degrees of separation as my husband continued with the pace
of the social life that accompanied his role as director of
marketing at H.D. Krauss, a prominent Boston publishing
house.

Even my kids noticed the change. Emily would tug at
my arm for attention while I gazed out the window of my
bedroom at the activity on Marlborough Street. It took all
my strength to take them on their normal Saturday outings.
The zoo especially was liable to trigger a fit of anxiety
and depression.

"If you won't talk to me about it, there's this guy, Tim
Dunne—you know, the grief therapist we're publishing,"
Kevin suggested. "He might help."

"I'll be fine," I said.

Kevin turned and walked away.

One Sunday evening in February, the deer appeared to me in a dream. The ten-point buck raced through a snowy logging slash against a peculiar blue sky. It stopped on a knoll and glanced back, its tongue lolling out the side of its mouth and the fur on its flank matted with sweat. It stood panting for several moments, then curled back its lips, moistening the air to better capture scent with its flanged nostrils. It grunted. It urinated down over its hocks and tossed its rack around as if to challenge its pursuer. The buck turned and disappeared over the hill.

The way I was raised, when an animal comes to you in a dream, you follow it. But I told myself I had left all that behind me.

I had the dream every night for a month, however, and at last I relented. On a Monday morning in March, I bypassed the exit that would have led me to my job and kept going up Route 95 all the way into southern Maine. By midmorning I'd found the right clash of field, brush and tall timber that marks deer country.

I left the car door ajar and, in my leather dress boots, walked the edge of a cornfield that a farmer had left standing. Several hundred yards in, I found a large track in the snow. I knelt, running my finger along the internal ridgeline of the cloven print, and knew from the relative softness that it was fresh. I followed the tracks, slipping through the briars for a half mile until I came to a pine thicket on a south-facing hillside.

The deer was probably bedded somewhere above the thicket to take advantage of the winter sun. But where? It had been years since I'd gone one-on-one with a whitetail.

Yet, like an athlete who remembers how her muscles felt at the peak of her form, I decided to try one of my father's most subtle and ethereal hunting tactics. I sought to abandon control over my heart until it sought a new rhythm, the rhythm of the closest living thing around it. As a woman's heart will try to echo her lover's pulse.

It had been years also since I had attempted the joining of spirit between what is seen and unseen, and even in my most sensitive moments as a teenager, I'd managed to achieve only a fluttering in my breast in anticipation of a buck moving before me. But I crouched anyway, closed my eyes and let the tension drop from my shoulders.

After five minutes, I felt my breath come and go like water. Another ten and I could track the push and draw of blood through my arteries and veins. But try as I might, I could not find in my heart the watchful, intelligent spirit of the deer.

I opened my eyes finally and chastised myself for arrogance. It had been fifteen years. This was like starting all over again. Starting over began with humility. I had to return to basics.

I skirted the pines until the breeze blew directly in my face. A deer will distrust its eyes and its ears, but never its nose. To close on a deer, you must not let it smell you. Slowly, tasting the wind with my nostrils, I threaded my way through the brittle understory. Every few moments I stopped to peer ahead through the branches, hoping to catch sight of the animal.

I snapped a twig. The deer broke cover, a bounding white flag that crashed off to my left. It bolted like flickering light through a beech glen, cinched all four legs together below its stomach to leap off a ledge, then bore pell-mell into a stand of thorn trees. I raced after the animal, ignoring the scolding squirrels overhead, the spines that tore at my cheeks and the roots under the snow that snatched at my ankles.

The deer doubled back upon breaking free of the thorns. Halfway to the pine thicket, it coursed downwind toward an unfrozen stream bed and took to water. I reached the stream, gulping air, trying to still my heart, to anticipate the animal's movement. I tried desperately to recall what my father would have done. But the memories were like a language practiced, then abandoned.

I finally arrived at work that day about noon. The engineers who worked for me gave me inquiring glances that I did my best to ignore. I settled before my computer as if nothing had happened. I typed in several codes that brought up the new software program I was charged with developing. Ordinarily, the challenge of devising a system that could three-dimensionally demonstrate environmental change on rivers and estuaries would have consumed me.

That day, however, I dimmed the screen to see my own reflection. Bloody scratches scored my face and forearms like the cicatrices of primitive tribeswomen. I picked at some of the caked blood with a fingernail and brought it to my nose. The dull metallic odor reminded me of childhood.

A sharp rap came at the cabin door. Griff called out, "Hurry up, Diana, or you'll miss the meeting."

"Be right along!" I yelled back.

I put my father's note down and went into the bathroom.

In the mirror was the face of a woman I almost didn't recognize. I wondered whether Kevin was right after all: had I lost my mind?

They were all gathered in the great room of the lodge having cocktails when I arrived. Two men I didn't recognize stood before a granite-faced hearth in which a pine fire roared. Overhead, a chandelier formed from shed antlers bathed the room in soft light. Rust-and-blue kilim throw rugs covered a plank floor. The furniture was the same Mission-style leather and oiled pine I had in my cabin. Expensive works of sporting art, including several Remingtons and Curtises, graced the walls. A spiral log staircase rose at the end of the room to a second level. Above the landing was the lodge's most striking feature—a huge, circular, stained-glass window depicting two mature stags locked in combat. Smaller stained-glass windows to either side of the centerpiece showed does and lesser males watching the battle. With money like that, I thought, you can do anything you want.

I decided to be social and chatted with the Pennsylvania hunters a bit at the bar.

"So how did you three come to be friends?" I asked.

Phil's biceps and pectoral muscles strained against the blue long-underwear shirt he wore. The muscles popped when he grunted, "Vinny the hunter."

Seeing my puzzled expression, Butch plastered a big grin on his Mick Jagger lips. "Vinny the hunter, my old man," he said. "Everyone in the old neighborhood in Philly called him that. He ran a retail appliance store. We lived upstairs over the place. Dad used to go outside the city, hunting every weekend during the fall. He'd bring back what he got—always deer, usually pheasants and rabbits—and butcher them in the garage in the alley out back. He'd share the meat with everyone in the neighborhood. Vinny the hunter."

"Vinny'd give you the shirt off his back," said Arnie, nodding. "What's it been, Butch, five years?"

Butch nodded sadly. "This past May."

Phil said, "My dad moved up from Mississippi just after the war and worked in a garage across the street from Vinny's store. Dad and his brothers always hunted deer down there, but he'd gotten away from it once us kids started coming. The story goes that he was taking a walk at lunch, comes around the corner and finds Vinny skinning this big buck with an apron on over his sales clothes. They got to be talking, realized they were both crazy about it. Next thing you know, they were hunting partners."

"And my dad ran the hardware store around the corner," Arnie said. "He never hunted as a kid, but Vinny convinced him to go along one year. Got a six-pointer. He was hooked and bought in to their camp. Vinny and Phil's dad, Carlton, built the camp in the mountains west of Wilkes-Barre in '58, I think."

"Your dad bought in '60, so that sounds right," Butch said.

Phil's features hardened. "Vinny had to buy the place first in his own name, then sell shares. That was before civil rights, you know. But Vinny was a tough guy. Even when he took some crap about my dad and then me going to the camp, he told those SOBs where they could stick it. My dad worshiped Vinny."

"So you three grew up hunting together, that's nice."

"From the time we were eight or nine, anyway," Butch said. "Every fall, no matter what."

"No matter what," Phil and Arnie repeated almost in unison.

"Sounds like a promise you've all made to yourself," I commented.

"We've gone our separate ways, but we make it a point to do something like this every November," Butch said.

"Hunting's about the only thing I have in common anymore with this aging hippie," Phil joked and punched Butch in the arm.

"If you don't mind me asking," I said, gesturing at his hair. "You know—Butch?"

Arnie spit out his drink and guffawed. "We've been busting him about it for years."

Phil smirked. "Vinny the hunter was this real strict Italian, been in the Air Force and had this thing about keeping a military cut. Butch hated it, but didn't do a thing about it until he was sixteen."

"Seventeen," Butch said. "I went upstate for a music camp I won a scholarship to. I just refused to cut it when I came back. Vinny was pissed."

"Worse when you started protesting," Arnie said.

"He got over it," Butch said. "But anyway, he started calling me Butch when I was eighteen. It was just to bug me about my looks. These guys picked up on it and it's been Butch ever since."

"You got kids?" Arnie asked.

"Two," I said, hoping I could keep a cheerful expression. "Boy and a girl."

"We have two girls," said Arnie. "They're off to Disney-land with my wife."

Phil took a swig of his beer. "So what's the deal, a woman hunting by herself?"

"I just like to hunt," I replied. "I grew up with it, too. Tracking, I mean."

"Kind of a tough way to hunt," Phil said. "You sure you wouldn't take a nice heated stand where you can read one of them romance novels?"

I smiled sweetly. "I figure I'll leave that to you city boys, Phil."

"Aren't you gutsy?" He laughed.

I stared at him. "No, Phil, just good."

He laughed again, but it was halfhearted and he excused himself and headed to the bar for another beer.

Butch put his hand on my arm. "Don't mind Phil. Deep down he's a good guy, just macho."

Cantrell called for our attention then. Without his coat on, you could see the outfitter was wiry, the kind of guy you'd struggle to keep up with in the woods. Cantrell welcomed us all again and introduced the two strangers: Tim Nelson and Don Patterson, the guides. Nelson leaned against the mantelpiece of the fireplace and gave us all a hearty hello. He was past forty. Cold winds had damaged his skin. From the bulging forearms that emerged from the maroon Henley-style shirt he wore, I figured he'd spent part of his life doing construction. Cantrell said Nelson had worked three seasons for Metcalfe and knew the property and the animals well. He was the hunt strategist.

Don Patterson had a beard but no mustache and his whiskers were wispy and blond. His features were equally fair. I had a tough time believing he could be in his late twenties with a master's degree in wildlife biology and five years' experience guiding in Alberta. Cantrell said Patterson had an uncanny ability to read signs and draw disparate pieces of information into a coherent pattern that could be used to decipher a big buck's travel pattern in order to set up an ambush.

Cantrell went on to give a brief history of the estate. Purchased by James Metcalfe in 1954, the 227,000-acre parcel had a resident deer population from the beginning. But Metcalfe was an early student of modern game management. In the early 1960s, about the same time such practices were adopted by Texas ranches, he began applying the techniques to the estate's herds. Since then, more recordbook whitetails had been taken off the Metcalfe Estate than any other piece of property in the world. And all of them had been taken by members of Metcalfe's family, close hunting buddies or business associates.

The hunts had meant so much to Metcalfe that he had stipulated in his will that they continue or his heirs would forfeit the land. His son, Ronny, had returned once to hunt, but hadn't come back in nearly two years. Metcalfe's daughters, who feared losing the property, had offered it up for lease through their attorneys. Cantrell won the outfitting rights through a competitive bidding process.

"You're the first public hunters to see this magnificent property," Cantrell said, rubbing his hands together. "The rut is upon us after three mild winters and three falls with no hunting. The chance to kill a world-class deer here in the next week is probably higher than anywhere else at any other time."

Butch and Arnie threw each other high fives. Lenore smiled. Griff raised his beer in my direction. I tipped my orange juice in return.

Cantrell led us all to a giant topographical map and an enlarged aerial photograph of the estate mounted under glass on an oak table at the rear of the room. He explained that the way to think about the estate was as a chunk of land divided by a minor mountain range running west to east. The lodge and the lake lay in the southern zone. The Dream River flowed north out of the eastern headwaters of the lake through an interruption in the ridge line, then out the northeastern corner of the property. The Sticks, a second river, divided the northern zone and joined the Dream near the estate's eastern border, almost to Alberta.

I pointed to a tiny circle on the map, smack in the confluence of the rivers. "That little island: is it in British Columbia or Alberta?"

"Alberta, technically," Nelson said. "Never been on it myself, but you can see most of it from the river's edge. Just a pile of rock and brush. Big, though, eh?"

Cantrell changed the subject. Each of us, he said, would be entitled to take two deer during our stay, though he urged us to hold out for a minimum of one hundred sixty Boone & Crockett points.

"One Boone and Crockett point equals one inch of antler, right?" Kurant asked, scribbling in a notebook.

"Roughly," Cantrell said.

"And how many inches of antler to make the record book?"

"One hundred and seventy inches as a typical," Earl piped in. "One ninety-five as a nontypical. Typical's a symmetrical kind of rack. Nontypicals, the antlers go in a bunch of different directions, kind of like Griff's hair."

Griff chortled and made a show of smoothing his mop.

Kurant asked, "What are the odds of making the book?"

"A million to one back home," Butch said.

"And here?"

Cantrell said, "One in five."

"That's what I like to hear!" Arnie cried.

The Addisons and Arnie said they wished to take stands in the woods between the clear-cuts that had been made along the base of the central ridge of mountains. Cantrell would be their guide. Nelson would work with Phil, who wanted to rattle antlers near the western clear-cuts to imitate bucks fighting; and with Butch, who was a bow hunter. Griff, of course, was bow-hunting, too. He'd take a tree stand close to a winter rye field. Because I wished to track and still-hunt, Patterson would take me toward the confluence of the Dream and Sticks rivers, drop me off and return at dusk.

"What about me?" Kurant asked.

"Nelson will take you here," Cantrell said, pointing to the corner of the westernmost green field. "There's a box blind with a good view. You want pictures, that's where you'll get 'em without bugging anyone else."

"You act as if I'm going to thrash around in the woods, screaming, 'Run for your lives!' or something," Kurant protested.

Cantrell shot him a withering glance. "Wouldn't surprise me."

A mousy-looking woman with short brown hair, glasses

and an apron came through swinging doors to the left of the fireplace. "Dinner's ready, Mike."

Cantrell broke away from Kurant and gestured in the woman's direction. "Like to introduce my wife, Sheila. Also our cook. Damn good one, too."

Sheila smiled awkwardly. "I'm glad to meet you all. The dining room's through here."

Earl went in first and gasped. "Would you look at this!"

We all crowded in behind him. Gas lamps lit the room. Another fire burned in a hearth beyond a pedestal table. On every wall hung gigantic whitetail bucks, bucks that dwarfed the deer in my cabin. The biggest one, a twenty-two-point nontypical with matching twelve-inch drop tines, occupied the place of honor above the mantelpiece. Cedar-shafted arrows in a leather quiver and a primitive longbow were attached to the wall just below the buck's head.

"I'll be goddamned," Griff whispered. "They said it would be good, but I had no idea . . ."

"Now you see what I was talking at you about, Mr. Addison?" Cantrell said, slapping Earl on the back. "Makes your blood rise, don't it?"

Despite the conflicting emotions I had endured back in my cabin, my spine tingled; I was thirteen again, sharing a cabin with my father the night before the season opened in Maine.

"Whose bow is that?" Butch asked.

"Mr. Metcalfe's, all he used in the last years," Nelson answered. "He shot that buck with it, the biggest nontypical taken in modern times with a longbow. Unofficial, of course. Made the bow himself. Arrows, too. He was a particular bugger, eh? But a regular shaman when it came to hunting."

I winced at the reference, but said nothing. As we took our seats around the dinner table, the doors to the kitchen blew open and a short, large-breasted woman with braided black hair burst into the room carrying a tray of soup. "You gotta hunt, you gotta eat!" she announced. "I'm Theresa, your table-and-scullery slave. You got praise, whisper it in my ear. You want to bitch, tell it to those dusty old stuffed heads on the wall!"

Patterson, who had been stroking his wispy blond beard, broke into giggles at the stunned expressions at the table. He pointed at Nelson. "You got Theresa for ten days. This poor bastard's been married to her fifteen years."

Theresa sniffed, "Poor bastard, eh? As Timothy will tell you, he thanks the spirits of the forest to have found such a wood nymph to keep him warm at night."

"Wood nymph?" Patterson cried.

"Mmmmm," she said. She threw back her braid, leaned down and planted a big kiss on Nelson's forehead. "And here sits my satyr."

We all broke up at the expression on Nelson's face. Theresa squinted at us. "You doubt my powers? Any of you?"

Almost as one, we shook our heads. She cocked her chin in Patterson's direction. "See? Thirty seconds in my presence and the animals eat from my hand."

Theresa placed bowls of steaming leek soup in front of us and disappeared back into the kitchen. She returned with bottles of white wine. The soup was followed by a main course of steamed salmon, carrots and new potatoes.

Lenore Addison gulped from her wineglass. She pointed

up at one of the deer heads and nudged her husband. "Maybe you'll do it here."

Earl became red-faced. "Give it a rest, sweet thing."

"C'mon, little man, those are the stakes, admit it." She waved her hand at Kurant. "Now here's part of your story: tycoon, perpetually miffed because his wife's a better deer hunter, spends years and tens of thousands of dollars in pursuit of a record-book whitetail. Only the two times he's had the monster right in front of him, he shook so hard, well . . ."

"Buck fever, that's what it's called, right?" Kurant asked.

"Earl gets a variation of it I call Ebola Buck Fever, temperature above a hundred and five, muscles in convulsions, basic breakdown of the entire system."

"And you don't get the fever, is that what you're saying?" the writer asked.

"Well, some would say it's luck. But the last one I shot scored one seventy-seven clean."

From the other end of the table, Phil whistled. "That's a buck! In Texas?"

Lenore nodded. "Off the King Ranch. One of those ghost deer the locals call *Muy Grande.*"

"One seventy-seven makes the book, right?" Kurant asked, scribbling.

"The second time I've made it," she answered cheerfully. She patted her husband's arm. His attention was on the china that dinner had been served on. "Now, to be fair, Earl's come close. One sixty-eight typical three years ago. One sixty-nine and a half last year in Kansas. But he never manages to cross that fine line."

Lenore paused for effect. "You know, I shot a book buck

the first time I went hunting with him. I think that's why Earl loves me so much."

"Shit luck." The little businessman seethed.

"Now, now, hon, some of us are just born in tune with nature."

"Well, that's true, you certainly grew up in the great outdoors. Folks, don't let the diamonds and gold fool you. Lenore here spent most of her life crapping in an outhouse before she met me. Wasn't for yours truly, she'd still be grazing beers in the joint I found her in down in brush country. She speaks real pretty only because she's spent the last two years with one of those speech pathologists who helps you try to kill your accents."

Lenore managed a sour smile. "You say the nicest things, little man."

"Only when I got one of your hundred-dollar fingernails in my back, sweet thing," Earl replied.

The awkward silence that followed their spat was broken finally by Theresa's arriving with apple pie and vanilla ice cream.

Kurant tapped his pen on his pad. "What's this obsession you all have hunting bucks with big antlers?"

From the far end of the table, Phil said, "You get better, you want a bigger challenge."

"You're saying these big-antlered deer are more difficult to hunt?"

Patterson laughed and gestured to Cantrell. "You were right, this guy doesn't know squat, eh?"

"Well, then, teach me," Kurant said.

Patterson said, "Once a whitetail buck survives past three years, he might as well be a different species. The older bucks have an extra sense about them. They can see you blink at a hundred yards, hear you scratch your butt at two hundred and smell you a quarter mile away. They know every inch of their terrain and they notice anything out of place. They are the craftiest game animal in North America. To harvest a book buck is a big deal."

"A sad deal, too," Arnie commented. "I always feel bad about it. Not harvesting a book deer—any deer."

"Yet you do it?"

Arnie shrugged. "Can't explain it, but sure, I shoot."

"The rest of you feel like Arnie?" Kurant asked.

"No, siree," Earl said. "When I've got a big buck down I sure don't cry. I feel like I've . . . well, it's probably not politically correct to say it . . . but like I've conquered."

"The way I'd put it is I fooled him on his own turf," Phil agreed.

"Not me," Butch said. "I think when you get one it's mostly luck. They have to make the mistake. So, like Arnie, I feel happy and sad when I've killed a deer."

"So why not photograph them instead?" Kurant said.

"Then it ain't hunting, hon," Lenore said. "It's taking pictures. To hunt, you got to kill."

"What do you think, Griff?" Kurant asked.

Griff massaged the skin below his left eye. "For me the kill is not the point. I go into the woods not caring at all whether I shoot a deer. I hunt for the process, the thinking, the becoming attuned with one of God's great creations. The means, to me, are more important than the ends. How I hunt is more significant than what I take home."

"Yet you are a committed trophy hunter?" Kurant asked.

Griff shook his head. "I hunt big bucks, not trophies. To

hunt a big, mature buck is to engage in my art at its most demanding level. Requires all of my skill, hones my concentration, pulls out my best. It's a process of self-refinement, like Zen archery."

"You make it sound spiritual."

He nodded. "In the hunt we celebrate our role in the beautiful and yet vicious cycle of life. I'm rejoicing in my predatory ancestry."

"You agree with that?" Kurant asked me.

I felt dizzy. "That sort of thinking can go too far."

"Really? Why's that?" Griff asked.

I shrugged, unwilling to open that door. "It's just how I feel."

From the far end of the table, Cantrell said, "Used to be people just loved the thrill of the hunt and the sight of a big buck in the woods."

"That's what I hunt for," Butch said. "I'm pretty liberal, but . . ."

"He's Gandhi, for Christ's sake," Phil interjected. "Except for the hunting."

"It hits me at a gut level I can't explain," Butch said. "Always has."

Kurant wrote all that down. He thought for a moment, then looked at Griff. "But if the process is the most important thing, what do you think about the Ryan incident?"

Phil groaned. "That went down six years ago. Old news."

Cantrell stood up abruptly from the table. "I've had enough of this jabber. I'll see about getting your lunches set."

As Kurant watched the outfitter disappear through the

kitchen door, he said, "It's not old news to me. I mean, Lizzy Ryan was killed by a trophy hunter just like you."

Lenore slurred her words. "Wasn't she the one out in her backyard during deer season . . . ?"

". . . wearing white mittens!" Earl finished. "Must have looked just like a deer's tail twitching."

"The guide, what was his name?" Arnie asked, snapping his fingers.

"Teague," Kurant replied. "He and J. Wright Dilton, the hunter, testified they saw a huge buck running over the ridge. They followed the tracks, came over the rise and said they saw the deer's tail. Teague said shoot. Dilton shot. Lizzy died in her backyard. And both men got off scot-free."

"Yeah, I read something about that," Patterson said, stroking his beard. "The state's fault. There were no laws then in Michigan making it a crime."

"She should have known better," Lenore said. "I mean, didn't her husband hunt?"

Kurant nodded. "Devlin was known as one of the best."

"He must have lost his mind when they got off," Arnie said.

Kurant shifted uncomfortably in his seat. "I heard he had a tough time of it."

"Wouldn't you have?" Griff demanded. "First thing I was taught was never to shoot unless you're sure of your target. If that had been a panel of ethical hunters, neither man would have walked out of that courtroom free."

"You trying to say we're not ethical because we think Lizzy Ryan had some role in her own death?" Earl demanded.

I said, "If you think because that woman wore white

mittens in her backyard during hunting season, her killing was somehow excusable, then you stay at one end of the estate for the next ten days, I'll stay at the other."

Cantrell came back in the room and glared at Kurant. "That's enough. These people have a big day ahead of them. Breakfast's at five. I advise you all to get some sleep."

I went out into the darkness through the fresh snow toward my cabin. Behind me, Earl was angrily talking to Lenore. I heard my name mentioned, followed closely by ". . . probably a dyke!"

I heard the water lapping at the lakeshore and walked to it. I peered out into the gloom, wondering what Metcalfe must have thought about as he walked out onto the ice. Did he anticipate the water taking him? I was assuming here, but did he love Grover's mother so much that he couldn't live without her? My thoughts wandered to my own mother and I told myself to stop. I wasn't ready.

I was about to head back when I noticed the snow had ceased and a vent had opened in the cloud cover. I looked up into a starry night and a crescent moon. A hunter's moon. My father would have rejoiced at the sight. But to me, the moon seemed a thing of many threads, some known and others best forgotten, all of them pulling me toward something I could not avoid. I ran to the cabin. I slammed the door shut behind me. The envelope still lay on the table. I went to it and got my father's note out.

My Beloved Little Crow,
It is not the seasons that haunt us, but how we see
ourselves in those seasons. We are at the whim of
the six worlds and the invisible Power that flows

through it. But because we are humans, not animals,
we understand our fleeting time of awareness and the
terrible decisions we must make in the handling of
Power, and this is our curse. And yet we can still take
hope in such a chaotic world. There are other forces
at work capable of cleansing the things that soil us,
and I hope you learn to sense them. I miss you terri-
bly, Little Crow. Think of your mother and me when
you see rivers. Think of us when you smell autumn
leaves in the rain. Think of us when the seasons turn.
                                        Love, Daddy.

It was dated nearly three years before his suicide. Some of his old friends at the funeral told me he was obsessed with that big buck, and I believe he'd decided long ago to take his life once he'd killed it. I put the letter back in the envelope. His cryptic words echoed around me and bounced off the conversation at the dinner table.

In my mind, I was suddenly eleven again, struggling to keep up with my father as we tracked a deer across a ridge top in central Maine. We had been after the deer for hours in three inches of snow when he noticed the buck's tracks stopped, then jumped sideways: a sure sign the animal became aware of us and was beginning an evasive action.

"He's going to circle us, Little Crow," my father whispered. "Go east!"

I ran in the direction he pointed, through spruce and into a stand of hickory where pale grass jutted from the snow. When the hickory gave way down slope to a meadow choked with wild apple and white pine, I threw myself down behind a stone wall, waiting. Without looking back, I knew my father watched behind me. And then the buck came, working his way up the ravine, his cedar-rubbed antlers swinging in the wind.

I hardly remember shooting. But I did and the buck took off, then staggered and dropped. I turned to Father, unbelieving, "I . . . I got him?"

He leaned forward and kissed me on the forehead. "You sure did."

I remember being unable to look at the deer as I came up to it. There was this feeling inside me, like a river eating away a new channel until I didn't seem like the young girl who'd left the cabin that morning, but a liquid that reflected all that had been part of the day: the forest, the swamps, the snow, the tracks and this deer.

I stood over the buck and the trembling in my hands carried through to my arms and into my knees. I dropped next to the animal and cried. I was angry at myself for crying, as if that weren't the way I should feel; as if I would have acted differently had I been a boy. But my father understood. He knelt and hugged me and said that his uncle Mitchell, who had died the summer before, always believed that those who don't feel great sorrow at the death of an animal should not take to the woods. He crooked my chin with his finger and brushed away my tears.

"Taking life is as profound as giving life, it is the transfer of spirit or Power, which is what our ancestors believed was everywhere around us," he said. "You'll feel this same way when your children are born, because it is all part of the same endless cycle of Power. When you kill, you are accepting the Power of the animal as your own and as part of the greater Power around us. When you kill to end the hunt, you are acknowledging your own death, too; and the fact that one day your spirit will leave your body to meld with all that has come before and all that will come."

He took his knife from his sheath and cut a lock of my hair and handed it to me.

"Leave a part of yourself here in the woods because you are taking part of the woods away with you," he went on. "Say a prayer of thanks to the buck for giving himself to you so that you may eat and live. Then wrap your hands about his muzzle and take in the air that remains in his lungs. All that made the deer lives in that last breath."

As if in a trance, I took the lock of my hair and cast it into the wind. I prayed then, not to some white-bearded man—that seemed ridiculous—but to that river inside me. I went forward past the antlers and took the buck's muzzle and cupped my hands around it. The air in the deer's lungs had the mustiness of earth turned over in springtime. I held it until spots danced before my eyes and I heard all the sounds of the forest in my mind.

I lived in that forest for years and took comfort there. Then there was tragedy and I left. And the only things that ever gave me that kind of comfort again were my husband's arms and the gentle night sounds my children made sleeping.

I went to the bedroom in the cabin and picked up their photograph. It was the new one from school. Kevin had sent it, the one kind gesture of late. Patrick needed a haircut, but his smile was like small arms around my shoulders. Emily? She reminded me of my mother, strong and yet softhearted.

I gave them life, I thought. And it was as my father had predicted: I had sobbed with sorrow and joy when they slipped from me bloody and warm.

And yet here I was, separated from them by court order and thousands of miles, preparing to chase a wild animal through the woods.

What kind of woman was I?

NOVEMBER SEVENTEENTH

BEFORE DAWN, SNOW bowed the conifers alongside the skidder road, creating in the headlights of the Piston Bully the illusion of a tunnel, still and close and white. Gusts spun the snow before us in bodiless waves. The rumble of the diesel machine filled all the space around me. Patterson wrestled to keep the snowcat on the track. I held onto a handle on the dashboard, gripping the forestock of the rifle between my knees, the anxiety of last night held at bay by the anticipation of being at last in deer country.

Breakfast had been a quiet affair. At Lenore's prodding, Earl had mumbled something about "going overboard" the night before. For the sake of peace, I acted the role of demure tribeswoman and asked his forgiveness as well. I told him I hoped he got his record-book buck that morning, and meant it.

I'd forced down my breakfast, then returned to my cabin to retrieve the last of my gear. Griff came to the truck in a suit of snow camouflage. A quiver with six arrows hung from his hip. He carried a recurve bow. We waited for Patterson.

"Are you ready?" he whispered. I don't know why, but you always end up whispering before you go out into the woods to hunt, the mind's instinctive reverence to the gravity of the endeavor to come.

"As much as I'll ever be," I said.

"I hear doubt in there," Griff said. Up close, he was a looming presence, but not threatening.

"That's why it's hunting, isn't it?"

"I suppose," he said thoughtfully. He hesitated, then said: "You know, I lost my wife a few years back. When your father heard, he called. And he helped me, being a widower himself."

It took all that I had to remain in control. Patterson was coming across the yard. I said coolly, "I'm glad he was of help to you. I didn't see him much in his last years."

I walked around to the cabin of the Piston Bully and climbed in. We rode in silence for several miles before Patterson dropped Griff next to a line of bright yellow surveyor's flagging tape that marked the trail leading to a winter rye field and a portable tree stand.

"Be careful now, Little Crow," Griff whispered to me. "The woods can be an unforgiving place." He looked directly into my eyes and I nodded warily.

Griff was at least three miles behind us now, probably climbing up his tree.

Patterson's beard was caked with snow. He yelled to me

above the roar of the snowcat engine. "The Sticks and the Dream meet up about five and a half miles north by northwest of where I'll drop you off. There's flats and ridges that run parallel to the Dream all the way north. The deer love it in there, especially now. The big ones are prowling for does with the rut coming on."

"Okay." I turned on my flashlight and tugged my copy of the Metcalfe map from the pouch around my neck.

"What's that, native or something?" Patterson asked, looking at the pouch.

"My great-uncle's mother made it," I said. "It's Micmac quillwork on leather. Very precious to me. I've always worn it hunting. It's brought me good luck."

"There you go, then," Patterson stated. "Gonna be a good day for you."

I inspected the map, checked the compass pinned to the front of my green-and-black wool jacket, then got out my binoculars from the fleece backpack.

"When you cut a track, I wouldn't press it too hard!" Patterson advised. "These deer haven't been hunted in three years, give or take, and you might find yourself right on top of them before you know it."

He paused and looked at me sheepishly out of the corner of his eye. "Here I am trying to tell you how to run a deer. And, to be honest, I've never done it."

He was a boy in his manners and that made me smile. "I haven't tracked in years. Probably lost my touch."

"Nah. You get out there in the woods, you'll be right at it again, eh?"

"I can hope. You work for Cantrell long?"

It turned out this was his first season with the outfitter. Most people thought Tim Nelson, Theresa's husband, would get the outfitter's lease; he'd worked for Metcalfe three seasons. The word was Cantrell had secured the lease through one of his wife's relatives, who was an attorney representing the Metcalfes.

"Like most things in life, it was rigged," Patterson said. "Tim's pretty easygoing about it, but Theresa thinks the whole thing stinks. Way I see it, Mike's an okay sort. From back East somewhere. And doesn't talk much about what he used to do. Knows deer, though, that's for sure. And he's paying me well, which helps."

"And Sheila?"

"Couldn't ask for a better person," said Patterson. "She's got a kid sister back in Ontario who's sort of a quarter shy of a buck. That's why she's so patient and good with Grover."

"He's . . ."

"Just kind of miswired, eh?" Patterson said. "That's all. He's real smart at some things and clueless on others."

"But nice."

"Yeah, unless he's forgotten your suitcase on the dock and it's fallen in the lake," Patterson said. "Which has happened. Several times. Say, did I tell you I got a new baby!"

"No," I said, feeling the heartache well in me again. "How old?"

Patterson fished in the top pocket of his wool jacket and pulled out a snapshot of an infant in a pink jumpsuit holding a stuffed lamb. "She'll be six months when I get back. Name's Laura, after my wife. You got kids?"

"Boy and a girl."

"Bet they think it's pretty cool you coming out here, eh? Mom a hunter and all."

I bit at my lip. "I wouldn't know. I don't live with them these days."

He heard what was inside me. "I'm sorry. Must be tough."

"Worse."

He downshifted again and turned the rig into what used to be a landing zone for loggers to stack their tree trunks. The snow wasn't falling as hard here. With daylight coming on, I could make out the ridges ahead of me. Patterson pointed to yellow flagging tape on the other side of the clearing. He recommended I take the trail for some distance before breaking off into big country. He'd return to the area about three o'clock to hunt himself. We'd rendezvous about four-thirty. I shook Patterson's hand, got out and shut the door.

The rig rumbled away. From my pants pocket I got out five bullets and loaded the rifle. From the front jacket pocket I took a cigarette lighter. I rolled the mechanism to study the flame. The wind was out of the northwest and my plan was to walk into the wind or quarter to it in a great loop to learn the terrain. If I cut a big track, I would follow it. If not, I would learn the land. That would help as the rut intensified in the coming days.

I slung the knapsack across my shoulders, then set out through eight inches of fresh snow. I wore the minimum to stay warm while moving: running tights under a pair of green wool pants, soft-sole rubber boots with leather tops, zip-neck polypropylene top under a fleece vest under a red chamois shirt and a green-and-black wool jacket. Snug wool gloves. A red felt hat. In the pack I carried extra clothes, a flashlight, a rope, a canteen, knives and survival gear.

The first light became more light and I was walking through the falling snow, through chokes of serviceberry and poplar. The trail steepened after a quarter mile. I climbed to an open bench, almost like a park, down which I could see for some distance. Nothing moved. No sounds were made.

For an instant I had the creepy feeling someone was watching me. I glanced around, nervous. Then, as quickly as it had come, the feeling faded. I looked down at the gun. The years fell away. I could have been a girl again. It's a hard thing to describe, but having the gun with me changed everything, made my every action alive with purpose.

The wet snow helped to soften my footfalls. Still, I set my toe first, then let my weight roll back toward my heel to let me feel under the thin sole of the rubber boots for any twig or stick that might snap the woods alert to my presence. I changed the focus of my vision so it was more wide-angle, a little fuzzy, yet sensitive to movement. I pinched my nostrils shut and blew softly to open my Eustachian tubes to allow all the sound that might be made to come to me. As I moved I became aware of the slight *tat* of snowflakes on browned leaves still hanging from trees, and the scratching of a red squirrel on a fallen log, and now, in the distance, the rush of the Dream River flowing north.

The first tracks I cut were those of a doe—narrow, heart-shaped with a delicate pattern, different from the blunt-toed, dew-clawed, bullish quality that says buck. She had fed on brush and meandered in circles before heading east up the hill. I pulled off my glove. I squatted to touch around the edge of the track. "Twenty minutes ago, no more," I said to myself.

In the next hour I cut more tracks of doe, small bucks and yearlings, and finally those of a good buck. From the depth of and the gait between the hoofprints, I decided the prints' maker was of medium weight—perhaps one hundred fifty to one hundred sixty-five pounds—unlikely to be mature and carry a decent rack. For the sake of practice, however, I followed them.

The deer tracks crossed a small stream, then ambled across a flat. They arced around a rock outcropping. They dropped downhill and ran true north.

I had been traveling in a straight line after the deer for almost half an hour when I noticed the tracks snake and break pattern. Buds on the brush at waist level had been nipped clean. I froze, and, heart pounding, investigated the sidehill above eye level to my left. I feared I'd been scented. Nothing. Then the faintest flicker. I brought up the binoculars and trained them on the spot and soon made out the head of a buck, a spindly-racked eight-pointer. The animal was bedded, chewing its cud.

I studied the area around the deer, found two doe below the buck, but none others. I whistled. He stood up, intent on me. I laid the crosshairs of the scope on his chest and said, "Bang!" He turned ends and bounded off, the does behind him.

Sweat dampened the lining of my cap. My breath came hard. A cramp threatened in my thigh. But overriding all this was the elation that I had not lost all of my skills. Rusty, oh yes, they were rusty. But they were still a part of me. I sipped from my canteen, rested for a few moments, then took another compass reading and headed on.

Within the hour I had climbed a ridge a half mile above

the river bottom. The map indicated I had traveled three and a half miles from the log landing. And now I felt for the first time in so long what it was to be in a wild place. It had not to do with the old-growth trees that towered around me, though there was that. Nor with the ebb and flow of the snowstorm. Nor with the faint boil of the river, though there was that, too. How can I explain? It was the sensation of being small, of being outside myself, a stranger and yet comforted by alienation. I got out a down vest from my pack. I put it on and sat with my back to a snow-covered log on the ridge, reveling in the idea of being, after so many years, at nature's whim.

I could hear the Dream plainly now. I closed my eyes and felt the water's rushing energy flow up the hill. It surrounded me and made me think of my mother, or Katherine, which is what I always called her at her insistence. I remember being four and sitting on the banks of the Wasataquoik Stream with my father and Mitchell in the June sunshine.

"Watch how I do it now!" Katherine called to me. She brought the fly rod in a smooth arc back and then forward. Her full brown hair billowed out from under the silly straw hat she always wore when she took to rivers. She moved sure and powerful among the rips and eddies, casting to runs along boulders and to the deep water that cut under banks. A swirl came on the surface near the fly. She brought the tip of the rod high to set the hook. As she fought the trout into the shallows, she motioned to me to come closer. I slid down the bank and waded into the chill water.

"Go ahead," she said. "Wet your hands and feel her belly."

I slipped my hands underneath the fish and cradled it, inspecting the emerald speckles, the rose hue and the spots of night along its lithe back. When Katherine unhooked the fish, it flashed off into the riffles. From that point on, I believed that the brook trout contained all the colors that were my mother.

Katherine had an undergraduate degree in chemistry, but like her father, she had gone to law school and entered politics. By the time she met Hart Jackman, my father, already an accomplished young surgeon and an activist for Native American rights, Katherine was a rising star in the State House of Representatives for her work crafting water-purity laws. Growing up, I remembered a steady parade of Maine's high and mighty who came to call on Senator Katherine Jackman, powerful chairwoman of the Interior Committee, at our home outside Bangor.

In the late summer afternoons Katherine held court next to the trout pond below the house. I smiled, recalling the expressions of lobbyists on their virgin trip to see her. She made them take off their shoes and socks in the gazebo, then roll up the pant legs of their suits to stand in the shallows and plead their cases while she practiced her cast.

The summer I was eight, Katherine gave me my first fly rod. I waded into the cold spring runoffs with her to cast nymphs.

"The idea is to present yourself, through your fly, as a part of the river," she told me. "Then the trout will accept your offering."

Try as I might, I could not get the fly line to unwind

properly. So every day that summer before leaving for work, she took me to the shallows of her pond. She stood behind me, arms around me, and let me feel the rhythm of her cast. Mitchell would rock on the porch watching us, saying nothing. Even after I'd learned and become an angler, we continued the daily habit of morning casts, April to October, rain or shine. That time was our time. Some mornings we would work out one of the problems all young girls have. Sometimes we talked about her life in Augusta. But the memories I cherish most are the silent mornings when we just shared the waters. Even now, almost two decades after her passing, I will smell rivers or see an older woman's cheeks blush with water-reflected sun and I will feel a desperate need to be nestled in the crook of a neck that smells of wild hyacinth.

Katherine and my father were made for each other. Though I never saw it, their early life must have been difficult. My father was half Native American at a time when prejudice against Indians still ran rampant in Maine. But my father managed to bridge both worlds, practicing as a surgeon in a hospital in Bangor and as director of the medical clinic on Indian Island, the Penobscot Reservation north of Old Town. For many years, Katherine's family did not speak to her. But she never bent and in the end her parents came to realize how good my father was for her. It's funny: they each had their own busy lives, but they found meaning for their lives in each other. Despite all that happened, I know they loved each other and me deeply.

Perhaps that was the source of our final conflict. Growing up, I never thought them different from any other parent. Yet they were. They each rejected Catholicism at an early age. They followed a personally crafted religion based on Mitchell's teachings about the old ways, passed down from his Micmac and Penobscot ancestors, as well as ceremonies and prayers the woods and the rivers suggested to them. Distilled to its essence, the moral underpinning of their days was one of living in accord with the laws of nature: take only what you need, when you need; adhere to the seasons and their fruits; try to live as simply as possible, as if you were a primitive hunter and gatherer. Of course, given their respective careers, this wasn't fully possible. It was an ideal to which they aspired. The hunting of bird and deer, the casting for trout, the tending of gardens, the gathering of berries and nuts, were the rituals they celebrated. As a child, I thought it a blessed way to look at the world. I would learn, however, how harsh it could become.

I must have dozed, for my watch said eleven-thirty when I heard the first shot. It came with a pop, followed by an expanding wind, like a gale coming down a chimney toward me, out overhead and away toward the Dream River. And then another, perhaps eight, ten miles away. And finally a third. All from the same rifle.

In the fallaway echo of that last crack, the hairs on the back of my neck stiffened. I was being watched. I was sure of it now. I made myself settle down enough to create a mental grid on the terrain in front of me, which I dissected sector by sector. A raven hopped along the ground. A chipmunk chattered. But nothing strong enough to make me feel like this.

I craned my head around, studying the lines and shades within the forest behind me. A doe fed farther up the ridge, but her tail ticktocked and her head was down, facing the other way; she felt secure. I looked for almost twenty minutes, the vague threat growing until my heart stammered and an aluminum taste crept up the back of my throat. And then, as suddenly as the rifle shot had come, the threat ebbed and left me quivering inside with the brackish water that lingers after an adrenaline flood.

Right then I caught elastic movement in my peripheral vision. A coyote crept along the top of the rocks above the doe. She winded the dog. Her eyes bulged in terror. She bolted. The coyote ran behind her, its mouth open and salivating. I considered shooting him, then lowered the rifle. The coyote had as much right to hunt as I had. Perhaps more. I had been taught not to alter the order of things unnecessarily.

When the coyote and the deer disappeared, I ate the apple and sandwich Sheila and Theresa had packed for me and drank again from the canteen. I unbuckled my green wool pants, squatted and peed. Relieved, I gathered my things and dropped toward the river.

At a quarter to one, I found what I had been searching for on a flat before the water's edge. The track sank deep into the snow. The gait was long, the rounded hooves slightly splayed. Where the snow drifted, I discovered a furrow from the buck's breastbone and delicate hairs between the tracks. And then a tree six inches in diameter debarked by antlers. From the smell and the trace of sap ooze, I figured the buck had come through here no more than an hour before.

I settled the gun in my right hand and recalled some of

what Mitchell had taught me before he became too sick with cancer to go into the woods to hunt.

"On a track, stick to the downwind side," Mitchell said. "Keep one eye on the deer's direction and the other on the land ahead."

For fifty years my great-uncle had been one of the best trackers in the North Maine woods. It was said that he could read a deer's mind, tell you its character and predict what it would do miles ahead just from following its tracks four hundred yards. It was true. I had seen it. My father could do the same.

Three-quarters of a mile from where I cut the track, the buck mounted a knoll and encountered a rival. The snow was slashed where legs had driven hocks and hooves down and back, searching for purchase. Tufts of gray-black hair lay humped at the center of the circle. Where horn had met flesh, there were tiny specks of blood.

Two sets of tracks left the knoll. One limped east toward the soothing waters of the river. The other, the one I was after, swaggered north again, meeting almost immediately a second track, a doe's. Her urine was pink. She was ready to breed.

I moved harder now. Within a couple hundred yards I found where they had mated before splitting up again. The buck's tracks were fresher, perhaps a half hour ahead of me. I shed my jacket, switched the compass to my red fleece vest and strapped the jacket to the pack. Almost unconsciously, I snapped off a spruce twig and placed it inside my shirt next to my skin. It was something my father had taught me; Penobscot hunters believed that when running after game the spruce twig would prevent pain in the side. I ran now and as I ran, it was as if my father raced beside me.

Mitchell had taught me to track, but my father had taught me to run. He'd weighed more than two hundred pounds, but he could stream through the woods in total silence, as if he were not on his feet but swimming through liquid air. I felt him around me now, coaching me to scan the woods as I moved, to consider how the wind brushed my face and how the rifts in the snow warned me of fallen limbs.

The tracks broke east after another half mile. I stopped, studied the map and figured that within minutes the buck would reach the confluence of the Sticks and the Dream. The water would be rough there. No way to cross. The deer was ahead, close. Cornered.

The open timber shifted to thick spruce growing along the base of a ledge that rose in places to thirty feet or more, a cliff in some spots. I pictured the hands of a clock. I made myself the clock's hands, creeping forward so slow you might not have seen me move, searching between the trees for a vertical line, a white patch, a round black nose, anything that might give the deer's position away. I eased around the front of a blowdown and *BRRRRRRR!* a grouse flushed from beneath the dead limbs, and I jumped back. My knees jellied and I sat down hard on the tree trunk.

I closed my eyes for several moments, then opened them and followed the line of the deer's tracks ahead for several yards. My heart sank. He was circling!

Until now, the deer had run with his attention into the wind where his nose might warn him of danger. He'd stopped here, however, and turned to check his back trail.

Then he'd made a tremendous leap up onto the ledge and gone south.

I sprinted along my back trail, ignoring the spruce limbs that clawed at me, stopping to search the cliff top at every opening that afforded a view. I was passing through a small clearing when, up on the ledge, dark, wide antlers spilled snow. The buck gathered his legs underneath him, the muscles of his haunch and shoulders twitching like springs coiled too tight.

I went to one knee, the safety off and the rifle coming in one motion to my shoulder. I floated the muzzle, searching for him in my scope. The buck bounded just as I got a sight picture.

And then there were only trees and snow trailing in the air and mystery where the buck had been. I'd had fur in the sights, but not the high shoulder shot, the shot of instant death that I wanted. I owed the animal that. I eased the safety back on, unable to rise; that was one of the biggest deer I had ever seen. When I had my wits back, I told myself I would follow him again. Yet I knew he was alert now, running hard; I doubted I'd see him again today.

Sure enough, he had gone out from the dark growth in jumps of twenty feet and more. He'd halted once as he returned to the open timber, checked his back track, then lit out again, traveling almost due south at a trot. I jogged his tracks for almost an hour, trying to learn the cadence of his moves. I'd had my best chance already. But if I could keep the pressure on him, I'd begin to learn his reactions, his way. He might make a mistake.

The buck backtracked twice, once coming full circle right in my boot tracks. At two o'clock I heard more shots in the distance. By two-thirty I began to see the deer's pattern: he circled only when he had the opportunity to take to higher ground, almost as if he wanted to get above me to watch me come by. Indeed, once I found where he'd lain behind a log, his head thrust into a branch where his antlers would fit in. I laughed at his audacity: he'd been watching me pass him not fifty yards away.

I abandoned the track at three-fifteen, figuring to return to the area the next morning. I had nine days left and had come close already. I was in no hurry.

From the map, I figured I was about two and a half miles from the rendezvous point. I moved in a lazy zigzag pattern across the flat, keeping the faint buzz of the Dream on my left. I felt golden inside. Gradually, as I'd engaged in the dance with the deer, my thoughts of home—of Patrick and Emily and Kevin—had faded until they were but shadows behind me. I walked within the world of ghosts now. My parents and Mitchell had given me the skills to move freely in the wilderness, to sense a world invisible to most. I wondered, however, if I'd ever be free of the things they'd done in homage to that world. I shook my head at the notion and admitted that for all the healing I'd done this day afield, I was not ready to face the bloody issues of the past.

Instead, I forced myself to dwell on the woods before me, to be Little Crow again, as if that sort of limited awareness were therapy. The snow had picked up. The wind, too. The color of the tree trunks had changed toward a darker pewter as the light began its first fade toward darkness. I came upon the yellow flagging tape and then my own faint, almost snowed-over boot tracks from the morning. I slung the rifle and ambled down the trail, seeing it fresh. And it was. The falling snow had weighted the branches even more, making the trail almost tubular. Inside, the gray light made it difficult for me to judge depth. I moved slower, unsure of my footing. I ducked under a pine sapling bent almost in two. My shoulder nudged it. The tree sprang upright, showering snow around me. I took a couple of steps forward, wiping the bitter flakes from my face, and stopped short.

Blurred by an inch of new powder were other boot tracks bisecting the trail. I knelt to look at them. They were much larger than my own and I tried to remember the size of Patterson's boots. The guide was of average build. The boots that had made these tracks were at least a size eleven, bigger than what one would associate with someone five-foot-ten. Then again, how strong was the relationship between height and foot size? These tracks could very well be Patterson's. There was also the possibility that one of the other hunters had abandoned his stand and worked his way this far east.

I was about to walk on when I noticed snowed-over deer tracks that the boots had obscured. They were big tracks. Buck tracks. And beyond that, difficult to see at first because of the light, a dark splotch of color under the snow. I brushed aside the top inch to find blood. I dipped my finger under it and brought it up for a closer inspection. Dark blood. Liver shot. A liver-shot deer is a dead deer. But he can run far before expiring.

Ten minutes to four. Forty minutes until last light. I decided to follow, to see if I could help find the wounded deer. My father and Mitchell had taught me to never leave a wounded animal in the woods. It was worse than unethical, it was a sacrilege. The deer gave its life so that I might live. To leave the deer to waste would ensure the fruitlessness of future hunts.

So I pushed my way through the thick poplar, finding more blood and more tracks. I climbed a small ridge, heading due east toward the Dream, and down the other side into a broad ravine. There was a creek bed underneath the snow and I worked my way across it, mindful of the ice-covered boulders below.

On the other side, the tracks angled south toward the lake for a hundred yards, then climbed east again toward a second small ridge. It was steep. The snow had piled deep against the embankment. I waded forward to grab hold of exposed root systems and used them as a ladder. Inch by inch, I hauled myself higher, seeing more blood where the deer had fallen, until the land leveled.

I stood on the rim of an open depression perhaps twenty-five yards across. Tall larch trees, like sentinels, hemmed the clearing. The snow in the first third of the shallow bowl remained pristine. Blood stained the middle of the next third, then mushroomed to paint the entire rear of the depression the tint of rain-soaked apples. Steam rose from the gut pile at the crown of the mushroom, though the falling snow was cooling the sack rapidly. Soon the scavengers would come for the offal. A few more inches of snow and the blood color would turn rose, pink and finally white again. Purified.

Reflexively, I bowed my head. I gave thanks to the forest for having offered up the animal. There was a trough in the snow running out of the bowl where the hunter had dragged the gutted deer. If I hurried, I could be of help.

I frowned as I ran. There was deer hair in the drag mark, but strangely little blood. No matter, it was easy going in the shallow snow under the thick conifers. And then the ridge angled downhill and the going was easier still. Here in the thicket, it was hard to believe there was a storm intensifying, that anything could be wrong with the world.

Around me, the retracting daylight calmed the forest until all was a deep, almost funereal silence. My pace quickened; I slipped farther and farther down the slope with every stride. I remember thinking that no one had a chance of catching me when I felt like this.

Eventually I emerged into a section where the trees had been thinned by fire. Blackened stumps crested the snowbanks. There were no branches on the standing trees for the first thirty feet, just charred nubs. Far out in the blasted landscape, a white owl launched from behind one of the stumps. It held a red squirrel in its talons. The owl cut the air with quick punches that broadened into sweeping strokes. The raptor angled between the charred trees, melting with every wingbeat until its body was indistinguishable from the storm. And then there was just the dark speck of the squirrel floating in the sky. And then nothing.

The drag trail skirted the edge of the burn and passed back into enormous timber. I had gone perhaps two hundred and fifty yards beyond the burn when far down the slope I made out another opening, the log landing, and in it the orange Piston Bully snowcat. I peered down, looking for Patterson. No movement. No sound.

I followed the drag marks another seventy feet as they wound through the thick tree trunks, and then they stopped and went no farther. No tracks, no beaten-down trough. Nothing.

It was gusty here, some kind of funnel that constricted the wind and gave it bursts of abnormal speed. The snow swirled in miniature white cyclones, then died, then lived and spun again. I looked all around me. Downhill to my right I could see the snowcat plainly. But there were no tracks going toward it. I walked a wide circle around the last tracks. Nothing. And now the wind had blown in so much snow that my own prints, made just seconds ago, were almost gone.

I was about to head down to the Piston Bully when out of the corner of my eye I noticed a fresh daub of blood. I squatted. Another blood spot appeared suddenly, perfectly round at first, then the sharp edge giving way to red gnarled fingers as the blood ran into the veins of the snow surface.

Something heavy made a splat noise on the bill of my wool cap. A third spot appeared on the snow. I looked up in wonderment and the whole of my center wrenched sideways like a fault line giving way, the shock waves roaring outward, knocking me backward and flat.

Headlights sliced at the gloom. The snowcat lurched from my control. I sideswiped a tree before getting the machine back on track. I jammed down on the accelerator, using the scream of the diesel engine the way my daughter, Emily, used her baby blanket, as a buffer against all the fears in the darkness. *Where was Griff!* I had to be close to where we'd dropped him off in the morning. *Where was he?!*

A fawn appeared in the middle of the road, frozen by

the oncoming headlights. I slammed on the brakes, expecting her to run. Instead, the young deer peered lovingly at me. For an instant it seemed that she had been waiting for me. Pressure built behind my eyes. My stomach twisted. I lurched from the driver's seat out into the snow. I vomited.

I crouched outside the headlight glare, unable to shake the terrible scene that had just unfolded before me on the ridge above the log landing. I'd lain in the snow for several minutes, staring at the base of the tree trunk, unwilling to look skyward again, holding tight to disbelief, holding tight to a vision of the forest as beautifully ordered, not brutally arbitrary like this. And then cutting through the haze was the unreality of the cold blue cast of Patterson's eyes gazing, unseeing, at me. His expression, even behind the blood that matted his fine blond beard, was at once comical and unbelieving. The young guide had been scalped, gutted and hung from the tree like a deer.

I knew I had to cut him down, as if taking him from the branches would somehow make what had happened endurable. I went to the tree robotically and searched with my flashlight until I found where the yellow nylon rope had been lashed to a lower branch on the back side of the tree trunk. The knot freed and Patterson's weight shifted to my arms. The insistent pull of the other end of the rope opened me wholly to the horror, and I heard a moan roll from my chest.

Patterson settled on his side in the snow, naked from the waist up, bootless. The flesh on his head was raw and bleeding. A stick lodged between the two sides of his rib cage held his chest cavity open. The tail feather of a red hawk had been lodged between his upper front teeth. There was an agony and a loneliness and a hatred in the wind around me I had not felt since my mother died. I wrenched the feather free. I threw it in the snow. I kicked at it, hearing Patterson talk of his baby earlier that day, and I kicked at the feather again. I saw Emily and Patrick before me. I wanted to hold them until all of it—the guide, the blood, the flayed flesh—disappeared.

Then the state of shock that had allowed me to do all this evaporated. Panic embraced me. I'd lurched from the body, grabbed my gun and fell down the hill toward the snowcat, feeling the sickness swell in me.

The fawn was gone by the time I'd gotten back to my feet. I threw the machine in gear, telling myself if I could get to Griff or the lodge, I'd make it back home to my babies, back to where I belonged, the near past and the long past buried where it belonged.

No more than a quarter mile down the trail, Griff stepped out of the darkness. He had his hat in his hand. His thick white hair was matted with sweat. He squinted and waved his hat at me when I stopped. I jumped from the cabin and rushed to him sobbing. "Oh, God. Oh, God, Griff, they hung him from a tree . . ."

I collapsed, shaking in his arms. He pushed me back. "Who's hung? What tree?"

"Patterson. He's dead . . ."

My throat closed. The arms and chest of Griff's white camouflage suit were smeared with fresh blood. I struggled free of him. I ran.

Griff was right behind me, calling, "Diana! What the hell . . . ?"

My fingers closed on the rifle in the passenger seat and I swung the muzzle toward him, thumbing the safety off. "Don't take another step, Griff. I swear I'll shoot."

The gun trader's jaw dropped. His hands went up. "Calm down, now. No one's gonna get shot here, least of all me. I don't know what you think I've done, but . . ."

"The blood on you," I said. "It's fresh."

His attention shifted briefly to his chest, then back to me. He attempted a smile. "Well, I hope so! Just over there is a giant nontypical whitetail that I arrowed about two o'clock this afternoon. It took me hours to drag him out here. Look at me, I'm soaked."

I studied him uncertainly. "You could have run to get here. It's less than three miles from where I found Patterson."

"Run?" He chortled. "I'm pushing sixty. Young lady, I don't run three miles through snow for anything or anyone."

I couldn't reply; I could still smell Patterson.

Griff lowered his right hand. "Let me get my flashlight. I'll show you the buck."

I hesitated, then said, "Slow."

He fished around in his pants pocket, brought out a flashlight and flicked it on, then played it over the ground toward an opening in the brush line. I caught the glint of thick antler. Griff's bow lay on top of the animal. "Only shot once today," he said. "You can check the quiver."

I engaged the safety. I lowered the gun. "No, I think we should get Cantrell."

A half hour later, the outfitter knelt by the body, scratching at his beard, his baseball cap pushed back so it stuck almost straight up in the air. He touched where the rope had been threaded behind the guide's Achilles tendons. He jerked his hand back as if the rope were razorsharp. "Well, then," he said, rising from the body and twisting his leather glove violently with both hands. "What do you know about that? What do you know about that?"

We'd run into Cantrell halfway back to the lodge. We were so late he'd gotten worried and come looking for us. Cantrell blew out his breath several times as if to control himself. At last, he lifted Patterson's arm. Our flashlight beams crisscrossed on the slender wound in the guide's lower back. Cantrell's expression got hard and I knew what he was thinking; a hunting bullet made a small hole entering, then it mushroomed and created a much bigger hole exiting. It killed by impact and shock. This was different.

Cantrell rolled Patterson over. A similar slit showed just above his right hipbone. Hemorrhage wounds. Patterson had been shot with an arrow. I pointed my gun at Griff.

"I never left my stand except to track my deer," he protested.

Cantrell had a pistol out now. "We'll be checking on that."

"Do it. And quick with the snow falling, or my tracks will be memory," Griff urged. "Besides, who's to say it wasn't you, or you? He was scalped—that's what Indians do to their enemies, Little Crow. Wasn't it?"

"It's also what white soldiers did to Indian women and children," I snapped. "Not to mention the soldiers who used our women's breasts for hats and our boy's scrotums for change purses!"

Griff's lips quivered. "I'm sorry. I didn't mean . . . it must be someone from outside."

Cantrell had been watching us. "Too far to come in from outside. So I figure it's still you."

"Why?" Griff demanded. "I've got nothing against this kid. And if I did want to kill him, why would I hang him in a tree where Diana could find him?"

" 'Cause maybe you wanted her to find him," Cantrell said. " 'Cause maybe you're a nutcase."

Griff retorted, "Just go check my tracks. Check my bow."

"I'll need all your arrows," Cantrell said.

"Done," Griffin said. He handed the outfitter the quiver. "That's deer blood, for your information."

Cantrell took the quiver. One arrow had dried bubbles of blood on it. I watched every blink, every hand movement, every muscle in Griff's face as if my life depended on it. Which at that moment it did.

Cantrell said at last, "I'll be keeping these a while."

Griff nodded, but I could see he wasn't happy.

"Mike," I said, "I want to get out of here. Now."

Cantrell chewed on his mustache. "Not till we check those tracks and get our story straight."

"What story?" Griff asked. "For Christ's sake, Patterson's been murdered, scalped, gutted and hung from a tree."

"More to it than that, I'd say," Cantrell said, his voice rising. "The Mounties investigate killings up here. We don't tell no one, especially the other clients, till I can radio them in."

"Why not?" I demanded.

"I got two reasons. One: could be one of the other guests, and by telling we found a body, we let 'em know that we're

watching before the Mounties can fly in. Two: because me
and Sheila risked everything to lease this property; if we go
back now and tell 'em without a cop standing there, they'll
panic and there goes our dream."

"Or maybe there's a third reason," Griff said. "Maybe you
killed your guide."

Cantrell's features hardened, but his voice remained
steady. "I won't honor that with a response. My wife's been
through some damn hard times the past ten years because
of me. She deserves more than to have it end like this.
What's it gonna be?"

Griff and I glanced at each other.

"You don't have to make your decision 'cause of me,"
Cantrell said. "Do it for Sheila."

I hesitated, then said, "I'll give you the benefit of the
doubt. Which is more than you're giving Griff."

Griff said, "My conscience is clear. If yours is, you'll call
the Mounties the second we get back to the lodge."

"You got my word," Cantrell said.

"What about Patterson?" Griff asked. "They'll notice
him missing."

"Already figured that out. Last week, when we flew out
to get supplies, there was a bad stomach bug in town.
Sheila got sicker than a hound after we got back. Three
days of fever, puking, the trots. I'm gonna say Patterson got
it and is laying low in his cabin so none of the clients get
sick. No one'll go near him."

"What took us so long to get into camp?" I asked.

Cantrell gestured to Griffin's buck on the back of the snowcat. "Griff and Patterson were tracking that deer when the kid
came down sick. Took us a spell to get him and the buck

back to the machines. And you couldn't figure out how to drive it. I came to your rescue."

"We're not leaving his body here," I said, remembering my father. "There are coyotes."

"Wolves, more like it," Cantrell said. "We'll get him into the icehouse. We don't use it this time of year and it'll keep his body cold until the Mounties can take a look. We'll wait until morning time to check your area, Mr. Griffin."

Two hours later, Arnie was on his feet in the dining room. The pediatrician's arms and hands mimed a rifle in action. "About noon, two doe stepped out where I could see them, just feeding along, and then a third, but her tail's out straight and she's acting real nervous, you know, kind of glancing back at the thick stuff they'd come from."

"Buck behind her, my man," Butch said. The recording-equipment salesman had tied his long hair back in a pony-tail. He had a thick gold hoop in his ear I hadn't noticed before and was wearing a colorful embroidered denim shirt.

"You know it." Arnie grinned. "Only the fourth to come by my stand this morning. But the second I see this one, I know he's a shooter. Long tines. That two-foot spread be-tween the beams. And the size of his body! My old man never would have believed it."

Phil bunched up his massive shoulders and shook his shiny black head as if he couldn't believe his misfortune. "And you saw him first through the binoculars I lent you?"

Arnie grinned again. "Clear as day, thanks, Philly boy."

"Don't mention it," he grunted morosely. "Guy comes

unprepared. I got to lend him everything. And he shoots the big one. Man, the world's against me today."

"Hey, I said thanks didn't I?" Arnie protested. "Anyway, I'm getting the gun up on him, praying I don't miss, and . . ."

Dinner was like one of those hallucinations that bubble up during a high fever, discordant and random. I heard the conversation at the table, but my mind jarred under the clash of distant voices and strange, contorted images. Look at them all celebrating their deer, I thought, oblivious to the darkness outside. Or, worse, one of them rejoices in the darkness. I studied each as a psychiatrist would, searching for any hint that one—and I still had not wholly ruled out Cantrell or Griff—was a killer. Griff had acted strange this morning. What was that he'd said to me just before leaving the cat? *The woods can be an unforgiving place.* And Cantrell. I knew he was a hunter. He'd seen death. But the way he'd come up with that plan to explain away Patterson's absence—so quick, so cold. The body right there beside him.

We'd parked at the edge of the lodge grounds and sneaked Patterson into the icehouse before returning to the cats to drive them in with the headlights blazing and Cantrell hitting the air horns. Two huge whitetail bucks hung from a crossbar behind the lodge. We parked in front of the dead animals and made a show of working the iron gambrel into the hocks of Griff's deer before hoisting it up alongside the others.

The rest of the hunters as well as Sheila, Nelson and Theresa straggled out to see what had taken us so long and to pay their respects to Griff and his deer. Cantrell's performance was flawless in explaining our late return and Patterson's sickness. He delivered the story with equal doses of drama and humor. And never blinked.

Earl Addison acted the tycoon and ordered, "Just keep the kid away from us until he's done being sick. Last thing I want is a bug when deer like this are being harvested."

"Don't you worry," the outfitter replied cheerily. "He's already in his cabin. Sheila will take of him, seeing how she's already beaten the flu."

While Griff's buck was substantial, it paled in comparison to the deer Arnie and Lenore Addison had shot. Arnie's six-by-six typical appeared to make the Boone & Crockett record book with very few deductions for asymmetrical points. Lenore's had just missed the book, but was bigger in body than either Arnie's or Griffs, close to three hundred pounds dressed.

At the dinner table, Lenore was saying, "You know, Earl, if you'd just shower before each hunt, maybe you'd see a good buck."

"I did see one," Earl said. "He just wouldn't step out."

She rolled her eyes to the rest of the table.

"He wouldn't step out," Earl insisted.

"Whatever you say, hon."

Kurant took notes as fast as he could while wolfing down his meal. He claimed to have taken several photographs of large deer with his telephoto lens. "They came out of no-where," he said in awe. "One second they weren't there, next they were. Never heard a thing."

"That's how they are," Phil said. "Like they come from a different world."

I'd been toying with my food and suddenly lost all appetite. I caught the journalist looking in my direction and decided I'd better get him talking. "So you enjoyed your first day out?"

"Got a bit cold, sitting there," he admitted. "But yes. What I'd really like to do, if you wouldn't mind, is tag along behind you tomorrow. See how a tracker works."

I caught Cantrell's quick headshake at the far end of the table. Why was he so obsessed with keeping this a secret? Then I saw him glance at Sheila, desperation in his expression. If he was hiding a more evil motivation, he was doing it perfectly. I'd have to give him the benefit of the doubt one more time.

"Maybe later in the week," I said to the writer. "I worked a big buck today and was just starting to figure him out when I lost light. I want to get right back in there tomorrow. It won't be the time for a beginner."

Kurant took the rejection good-naturedly. He had a nice way about him that made you want to talk. "Fair enough, but I'm holding you to your promise."

I wanted to get up from the table and go to my cabin, but I feared leaving early would raise suspicions. As the dinner progressed, I noticed Earl, who sat to my right, becoming increasingly drunk. We had moved back to the great room for coffee. Lenore had left to use the rest room, I was standing next to the bar and I felt Earl's hand brush my fanny. He leered at me. "Must be something, running after those deer the way you do, sugar. Get to know your quarry up close and personal, I bet."

I put my hand on his hand. Emboldened, Earl tried to start a circular motion. Before he got halfway through the first arc, I dug my thumb between the knuckles of his middle and index fingers. At the same time I grasped the blade of his hand and twisted it out and away, a self-defense move I once learned. I batted my eyelashes demurely. "I just think sitting on your *butt* all day like you do, Earl, must be a bit boorish."

Earl winced and struggled to get his hand back. I would not let him. "But yes," I went on, "when tracking you have to know when to push and when to lay off."

I wrenched his hand and released it. Red-faced, he massaged his wrist and smiled wolfishly. "You're a spunky one, aren't you?"

Lenore returned and picked up the tension immediately. "What's going . . . ?"

"Your husband thought we might get in a little after-hours hunt," I said. "I wouldn't play along."

For a split second Lenore's cool demeanor cracked and the sort of helpless pain you witness in the children of alcoholic parents was revealed, only to be masked again with that chiseled, arch expression she habitually wore. The rest of the room fell silent.

"Little man, I think we better have that discussion again about how Texas regards division of property," she said stonily. "It ain't pretty."

Earl glared at me, then at his wife. Then he laughed. "Hell, I didn't mean nothing by it. You know I was born a flirt, sweet thing. Can't do nothing about it, no matter how hard I try."

"Let's go to the cabin, Earl, before she breaks your wrist," Lenore said. "Or I do."

Earl looked at the rest of the crew sheepishly. "Boys, have pity on me, I'm in the doghouse for sure."

Nobody responded. And after the Addisons departed, Butch mumbled something to me about "jerkdom appearing at every economic level." The others yawned nervously and filtered out the front door. I lingered until it was only me and Cantrell.

"Called yet?" I asked.

"Waiting until it cleared out," he whispered. He glanced through the doorway to the dining room toward the swinging kitchen doors. "First I gotta figure a way to tell Sheila."

"You just tell her and get those Mounties in here!" I insisted.

Cantrell's eyes flashed. "I know my business, Ms. Jackman. I'm doing the right thing here in my own way."

"I just wanted to make sure," I said. I did not yield my gaze.

We remained that way for several moments until Cantrell mumbled, "Taking care of it, right now." He disappeared into the kitchen.

Out on the porch of the lodge, I peered up at the moonlit sky. Here and there I could make out the forms of elliptical clouds driven east by high-altitude winds. A troubled sky, resounding against the nothing at all of the infinite night beyond. My great-uncle Mitchell used to stare at the clouds on such nights for hours.

"Night clouds show us the presence of Power," he once told me. "Power moves across the mind like the shadows of clouds cast on the peaks and the ravines of a mountain. We see ourselves and the shapes of our other worlds in them."

Mitchell. He was past seventy by the time I was aware

of him, with skin like old boot leather and a Mona Lisa smile and long silver hair that took forever to dry after he'd been caught outside in the rain, which was often. He had tobacco breath and a soft, gravelly voice. He loved beech trees, waterfalls, snow geese, moose calves, the Cabela's catalog, unfiltered Pall Mall cigarettes, strong coffee, cheese doodles, televised wrestling matches and Bugs Bunny, whom he considered wise.

Mitchell's mother was a Micmac from up near Cape Breton, Nova Scotia. As a young woman, she'd fallen in love with a Penobscot from Old Town, Maine. She'd come south for love and lived among the Penobscots until her death. But she taught her oldest son, Mitchell, much about the Micmac view of the world. As such, he believed that there was not one level of existence, but six: the World Beneath the Earth, the World Beneath the Water, Earth World, Ghost World, the World Above the Earth, the World Above the Sky. But underlying and permeating those worlds was a single life force called Power. He believed that everything he could see and touch and taste and smell and hold was a manifestation of Power. We were Power. The trees were Power, as were the stars and the moss and the wind. Because of that, he referred to the birches and the fish and the deer and even mountains as living things like us.

In the Micmac language, my great-uncle Mitchell was a *Puoin,* or shaman. Mitchell was my baby-sitter and my first teacher.

To be honest, I had always thought about Power as a concept rather than a reality, much in the way I imagine some Christians must regard God. They've had no personal experience with God and so think of Him as a construct.

Mitchell and my father tried to teach me to actually sense Power, but tragedy struck just as the real lessons were beginning, and I left home forever.

Long before that, however, when I was a little girl skipping after Mitchell, the lessons were much simpler. We picked blackberries and blueberries and gathered acorns and butternuts. Soon after that, the old man made me help Katherine clean her fish so I would understand that meat comes from flesh, that it does not just appear in grocery stores by magic. We always put the bones of the fish back into the rivers so more fish would come to our lines, which had been the Micmac belief for generations.

I served an apprenticeship in Mitchell's vegetable garden on the flat near the trout pond. There he taught me to sow seeds and tend plants as if they were part of our family. Which, to his mind, they were. Once, when I was six, I forgot to water the garden during a drought. I'd never seen Mitchell so angry; he puffed so hard on one of his Pall Malls that it ran and scorched his lips.

"Plant's no different than any other living thing, you care for them with respect," he scolded. "Tonight you go to bed without dinner so you understand their needs."

I never, ever forgot again.

In the fall when I was too young to accompany my father and Mitchell on their hunts, Katherine became my guide. She returned every evening to be with me, no matter how busy her schedule in Augusta. She cooked my dinner and read to me before bed. On Saturday mornings she took me on long hikes along rivers. It was on these walks that I learned how beavers built their dams and how the rabbit population lifted and fell in a seven-year rotation and why squirrels hoarded for the winter. I learned to build box nests for wood ducks so their young would be safe from snapping turtles. I learned where the otters were likely to make their slides in winter.

The October I turned five, I found a crow's egg nestled in the pine needles during one of those hikes. I brought the egg to Katherine, who had wondered over it, saying it was a remarkable thing that the egg could have survived the summer in the rookery without breaking. On the way home I dropped the egg and the mess inside dribbled out onto the rocks. I wept. She gathered my face into the crook of her neck and she rocked me until I slept in the warm autumn sun. We did not get back to the house until twilight. My father and Mitchell were waiting for us on the porch. When they heard the story, they seemed prouder of my reaction to the loss of the egg than its discovery.

"That egg was a gift," Mitchell told me that night before I slept. "The crow is a seer. She sees things from the sky that others do not. She feels things others do not."

"Just like you, a little crow," my father said.

"And so I was named," I whispered to myself on the lodge porch. Down near the dock, the shadows moved and my hand flew to my throat. I was alone, silhouetted, vulnerable. Then a whistle came out of the darkness and Grover shuffled toward me.

"Hello, Miss Diana," he said softly.

I lowered my hand deliberately and smiled at the gentle soul. "Hi, Grover."

"Miss Sheila feeds you good after a long day in the woods, I think. Mr. Jimmy always said if you hunt you gotta eat. Miss Theresa says that, too, but she got that from Mr. Jimmy, eh?"

"Do you miss Mr. Jimmy?" I asked.

"Every day," he said.

It was suddenly important to me to know how he would be cared for in the long run.

"None of his daughters or his son comes to see you here?"

Grover scratched at his lip, saddened by my question. "They never likes Grover, 'specially Ronny, that's Mr. Jimmy's real son."

"Aren't you his real son?"

Grover shook his head. "No, miss. Not like he married my momma or nothing. I'm not a real son."

"Mr. Jimmy said that?"

"No, miss."

"Ronny, then?"

He scuffed at the snow and wiped at his nose with his sleeves. "But Ronny don't come to the lodge in I can't remember when, so it doesn't matter, eh? I eat now. Been down to my rock to listen to the loons, but didn't hear none tonight. Probably all gone south by now. But Momma always says I lose time when I'm on the rock, so I eat now, long as Miss Sheila's still in the kitchen."

"I think so." I patted him on the shoulder as he passed. "Eat and sleep well, Grover."

"You, too, miss."

I waited until he'd gone inside, then hurried back to my cabin. I latched the door shut behind me, then shoved one of the table chairs under the knob. I drew the drapes and immediately regretted the caged feeling.

I stripped, and without understanding exactly why, I took the photograph of Emily and Patrick to the bathroom. I set it on the sink. I stepped into the shower, leaving the curtain parted slightly so I could see them.

I leaned against the back wall of the stall and turned on the water as hot as I could tolerate. The steam created a veil between me and the photograph, but I could still make out their almond-shaped brown eyes, Kevin's eyes.

I stayed in the shower so long the water cooled. I tried to tell myself I'd made the right decision in coming here— that events beyond my control had made my relationship with Kevin impossible and that only here, in the forest, could I come to grips with all that had happened before we met.

I had loved Kevin. I still loved him in a way. But the seeds of our connection were based on my need for escape from worlds he could not fathom. Kevin had gone from urban white knight to child stealer in my eyes. I'd gone from stable partner to albatross in his. There was nothing I could do to change that.

But the children. I realized it had been three weeks since I'd held them. I began to cry and I promised their photograph I would figure out a safe and sane way back into their lives.

Overriding my affirmations, however, was the vision of Patterson, a dead young father hanging from a tree, and I stayed in the shower until the water turned to icy nettles.

NOVEMBER EIGHTEENTH

"WIND MUST HAVE blown away the tracks, unless the guy was Tarzan and swung from tree to tree," Griff was saying.

Cantrell was using his binoculars to study the rope marks on the tree limb. "Got to be a strong son of a bitch to hoist someone Patterson's size up there alone with no block or tackle."

I shifted my rifle from one shoulder to the other, noticing in the process how the pale sunlight bore through the forest canopy, dappling the snow and the laden branches, which shed their weight in the light breeze. Three willow ptarmigan flushed from beneath the snow off to my left, cackling before disappearing between two large spruces. I squatted to test the snow consistency, most of it heavy with moisture, some wind-packed, all of it friable. I could not help thinking that it was radiant and peaceful here, a place of beauty.

Only to immediately regret romanticizing what sixteen hours before had been a nightmare. Must have been some kind of reverse psychology at work. I was highlighting the agreeable aspects of this place, rather than face the issue head-on. Not that this wasn't an unusual tactic for me.

At breakfast, Cantrell announced that after dropping off Kurant and Butch, he'd cover for Patterson and take Griff and me out to our hunting grounds. When he returned for us, he'd reported grimly that the radiophone was acting up and Grover, who was something of a savant when it came to electronics, had gone to check the antenna up in the woods behind the lodge. He assured us that Sheila, who was "sacred out of her wits," would call the Mounties as soon as the rig was operable. In the meantime, he wanted to check the tracks around Griff's stand, then return to where I'd found the guide's body before the sign got too old.

The situation made me uncomfortable. But I'd agreed if only to see if I could help determine what had happened. In a strange way, I felt responsible. Patterson wouldn't have been out there if I hadn't requested tracking terrain.

The tracks near the winter rye field all supported Griff's version of his hunt the day before; we found no footprints beyond a hundred-yard radius around his tree stand. Which relieved some of the tension among us. Now we were trying to figure out how the killer had gotten away from Patterson without leaving any sign.

"I think the killer walked backward out of here in his own tracks," Cantrell said. "That's why they seem to disappear."

I straightened and brushed the snow from my pants.

"Definitely not. Either the wind blew his tracks away or he used a branch to sweep them away. Or both. I vote for both."

Cantrell scowled and crossed his arms. "I been guiding in the woods my whole life and I say he walked out backward."

Cantrell was the outfitter. He needed to assert control, any level of control, over circumstances that were disintegrating and threatened his business. The last thing he wanted was to cede authority to a client, especially a woman client. Still, there was no denying that he was wrong.

I gestured to the clearest set of tracks. "If he walked out backward, the heel portion of the track would be deeper. He'd set his toe first, then rock his weight to the rear. It isn't like that. The weight's rolled forward to the toe in all these prints."

"She's right, Mike," Griff said.

"What makes you an expert?" Cantrell demanded.

"I'm not," Griff said. "But I can see something that makes sense."

Cantrell fumed for a second, then said, "Why'd he use a branch, then?"

"He chose this place because of the wind, but he couldn't be sure that the wind was strong enough to fill in his tracks before I found it."

Griff said, "You make it sound as if he knew you'd find the body."

I told them how, twice the day before, I'd had the sensation of being observed. Cantrell made a distasteful expression with his lips. "What are you, one of them New Age touchy-feely types?"

"It was real," I insisted.

"Yeah, sure, and I'm Elmer Fudd," Cantrell said. He walked away.

"How far could he have swept his tracks?" Griff asked.

"Depends on how fanatical he is, I suppose. But if I'm right, we'll pick up boot prints somewhere within a quarter mile."

Cantrell had climbed up the ridge twenty yards. He was next to what remained of the drag trail. He called out, "There's deer hair here. Explain that. I don't see any damned deer carcass or blood."

We climbed to him, taking care to give the remaining tracks a wide berth. I leaned over and plucked several hairs from the shallow trough. "I noticed this yesterday and thought about it last night. I think he laid Patterson's body on a deer skin, or a couple of them, and used them like a sled to drag him down here."

"Why?"

"I don't know. To confuse us? Because it was easier to move a human body that way? I don't know."

"What's this, then?" Griff asked. He reached out to one side of my tracks and plucked a tuft of thick, grayish-black hair. "It's not deer hair."

I took the fur. I rolled it between my fingers, then sniffed at it. I shrugged and handed it to Cantrell, whose expression changed. "Timber wolf," he said. "Probably a gray-phase Canadian."

"But no wolf tracks," I said.

We all fell silent, considering the possibilities. Overhead, a hawk shriek-whistled. I watched both men. Cantrell had a semiautomatic, open-sighted .223 with him. Griff was carrying a pump-action .30-06 taken from Metcalfe's collection.

We were out here together, but there was no sense that we were in this together.

"We're all watching each other," Griff announced. "I don't like it."

"Man's been killed," said Cantrell. "No amount of goodwill's gonna change that."

"I'll show you where it happened," I said. I led them up the ridge to the burn, skirting the edge as I had the day before, then upslope again into the tight circle of trees where I'd found the gut pile.

I froze when I saw what had happened.

"Jesus," Griff said, turning very pale.

"Wolves been at it," Cantrell said, grimacing at the fury of paw prints in the snow.

I looked up into the sky. It seemed more terrible than anything that had happened so far. I thought of my father. I had to fight to keep down the ball that swelled in my throat.

Cantrell and Griff had already moved off toward the ravine I'd climbed yesterday. "It isn't right to leave it like this," I called. I leaned my gun against a tree. I used my hands as a shovel to throw snow over what was left of Patterson, abandoned so cold and maligned. Wordlessly they joined me until the rest was buried.

When it was done, I led them down the steep embankment, up the streambed and through the poplar thicket to where I'd first picked up the tracks. I was able to study the footprints better in the full light. I took off my glove and touched the bottom where the treads had molded the snow. The front of the track, where the ball of the foot should have been pronounced, was light. I pursed my lips and touched the track again to make sure.

"He's wearing boots that are too big for him," I said. "And he was stepping very carefully in Patterson's tracks the entire time. That's why I thought I was following one person yesterday."

Cantrell asked sharply, "If you made that mistake, who's to say he didn't walk backward up that hill?"

"He didn't," I insisted. "And yesterday I wasn't looking right because I didn't have to."

Griff interrupted. "Why the big boots?"

"I don't know."

Cantrell pointed out beyond the snowberry thicket. "He shot Don somewhere out there. I want to see where."

He went first, weaving around the clumps, fending off the low branches and climbing along a rising shelf. Where the shelf met a bank next to a pile of blowdown tree trunks, we found the place Patterson had taken the arrow. It was dim and thick, just the sort of place you'd expect to jump a big buck. And from the sign, there'd been one here and Patterson had been preparing to shoot at it when he himself was shot. He'd lurched sideways after being hit and crawled on his knees for several feet, then gotten up and stumbled forward. In shock, he'd left his muzzle-loading rifle in the snow, still cocked, ready to shoot, and followed the escaping figure of the deer.

I flashed on the image of Patterson using the deer as his guide, trusting the animal's instincts to lead him away from whoever had inflicted this torment. I fought off the desire to sink inside myself.

"This is at least four hundred yards from where he finally dropped," Griff remarked softly.

Cantrell rubbed his sleeve across his chin. "One tough kid."

Cantrell was standing over Patterson's rifle. He picked the musket up finally, squeezed the trigger with his thumb on the hammer and lowered the striker until it was safe to carry. Tears welled in his eyes. He recocked the hammer suddenly, pointed the gun up in the direction of where the arrow must have come from and pulled the trigger. The muzzle-loader went off with a delayed hush and boom. A pine bough fell. He threw the gun. He flailed at one of the tree trunks until Griff took him by the shoulder and led him out of the black-powder haze that lingered in the air.

I climbed the bank and worked the top in semicircles until I found where the killer had stood, then backtracked him. He had stopped several times behind trees, then moved slowly forward on tiptoes. When Griff and Cantrell came up to me, I said: "Patterson was stalked."

Cantrell, who had gotten himself together, threatened to unravel again. "Bastard's got to be quiet and smooth to get up on Don; that kid's woods skills were sharp."

We followed the tracks back along the bank for nearly eighty yards, then out to the edge of an old clear-cut Patterson had passed through and on into a wetland where it appeared the killer had first followed the guide. We left Patterson's track then, focusing on the other. The further into the forest we traveled, the more I wrestled against the urge to turn back; the old-growth trees that had comforted me not twenty-four hours before, were now menacing. After nearly forty minutes of hiking, we came to a stream. Many human tracks trampled the snow there. No footprints sullied the other bank.

"There was somebody else meeting him here," Cantrell said.

Indeed, close inspection revealed two different sets of boot prints: one the killer's with those too-big boots and the air-bob soles. And then these ripple-sole boots, a smaller size.

"Where'd the second guy come from?" Griff asked.

"Upstream," I said. "Met up with the archer and then left together. Where does this stream lead?"

Cantrell got out his map, studied it for a second, then showed us. "It forks up here a half mile or so. One fork heads toward the Sticks, which is pure wilderness. The other, out toward the base of Wolverine Ridge and the fields."

"Where the others are hunting?" Griff asked.

"That's right."

"How long a hike is it in here downstream from their stands?"

Cantrell thought about it. "Four miles to the closest; that would be Earl or Butch. Seven miles to the furthest—the pinko writer there."

"Butch is a bow hunter," Griff offered.

"Yeah, he is," Cantrell said. He looked directly at the older man. "But this stream also runs no more'n six hundred yards back of your stand."

"We've been all around where I spent the day!" Griff protested. "Don't you think you would have found my tracks heading out there?"

"You could have swept the snow clean like he did back there near the body," Cantrell said.

"Well, then, you better go look again!" Griff said. His shoulders had risen under the heavy parka he wore.

"The Mounties will," Cantrell said.

"Good," Griff said. "I've got nothing to hide."

They stood there facing off against each other until I stepped in between them. "Mike, think about it. These tracks are coming into this area, not leaving. We know the killer came in this way, probably with someone else. For Griff or anyone in our camp to have done it, we'd have to find the tracks leading back in this direction."

Cantrell saw what I was saying. We needed to find the killer's escape trail. It was nearly noon by the time we made it back to where I'd discovered Patterson's body. The wind had picked up. Clouds threatened.

"We'd better find his exit trail fast," Griff said. "Or it's going to snow and we're going to lose it all."

Cantrell suggested a trick he used for locating wounded deer. We spread out fifteen yards apart. We walked parallel arcs through the woods west of the tree where Patterson had been hung. At the completion of each arc, we moved farther east and expanded the semicircle. On the third set of arcs, perhaps one hundred and seventy-five yards from the tree, Griff cut the big-boot track and we ran it all the way east to the Dream, where, to our astonishment, we came upon the same set of rippled-sole boots we'd seen earlier that morning exiting the tributary of the Sticks.

We decided to go north along the bank to see if either man had exited the water to cut cross-country toward the other clients. We spread out again, Cantrell at the riverbank,

Griff in another seventy-five yards and me another seventy-five yards west still.

We moved north through the same country I'd traversed a day and a lifetime before. We communicated with hand signals to keep us in a parallel march. I became conscious of the snow. It pushed up the bottoms of my pants and into the tops of my boots. It sloughed off tree limbs, melted at the nape of my neck and trickled like a spring snail down my back. It lifted on the wind and pricked my face.

For many minutes I had only the awareness of snow and sweat and the demands of scanning the forest floor for fresh tracks. I checked my back trail, squatted every now and then to peer forward through the understory of spruce and larch, hoping to glimpse movement—a man, a wolf, I don't know.

We traveled half an hour this way and I dropped fully within the ebb and flow of skirting stumps and slipping over logs. The air in the woods seemed strangely electric after yesterday's storm and in anticipation of the one to come. Yet there was very little sound save for the flitting of chickadees and the raucous cry of scrub jays, and several times the snort-wheeze of deer I pushed from beds. I felt an unreasonable happiness that I suppose came from doing something I knew how to do. It occurred to me that my father would have had a different explanation: he used to say that in each hunt there were moments when the hunter's sensitivity was so acute that time seemed to stand still and the secrets of the forest were revealed.

For my father and Mitchell, the deer hunt was a drama of Power. Not power in the political sense of hunter and prey, but Power in the Micmac sense; that is, the deer hunt was an act of creation, a reflection of the fluid, continuous state of transformation between life and death in which we lived. The Micmac stories I heard over the years always took place here, deep in the forest, for in the real forest and in the forest of our minds we encounter Power. The old Micmacs hunted moose. But Mitchell and my father found the whitetail to be a much more challenging manifestation of Power. The deer and its tracks were but shadows of the spirit we stalked, but by learning to engage with the deer, we learned how to conduct ourselves correctly in the presence of Power.

"Don't fall into the trap of having a purpose in the woods, Little Crow," Mitchell once told me. "Having a purpose says you are making the woods yours, which is foolish. The woods are the woods. What you have to do is find a way to *just be* in the woods so the woods accept you. When you do, you'll be like a mirror, reflecting everything around you. You'll sense worlds that are invisible to most people these days."

I was wondering whether I was "just being" when it seized me again, the sensation that I was under observation. I stopped on the back side of the trunk of a big ponderosa. I took up my binoculars and investigated the sidehill. I cradled the gun. My thumb came to the safety.

I swept the field glasses back and forth, too quick to be of much use. I dropped them to my breast. I closed my eyes to see if I might enter into just being and so better understand where the watcher's energy was coming from. It took a few moments, then a dull, not-unpleasant throb appeared at the nape of my neck. The throb moved around and up the side of my face. I saw clearly the hillside off to my left. I opened my eyes and turned slowly, looking angularly up the hill through the glasses toward a stand of poplar.

"Unbelievable," I said to myself. "Absolutely unbelievable."

Two huge animals, their bodies so cylindrical and heavy that their legs appeared stunted. Their necks were one and the same as their shoulders, swollen all the way to the flesh where ears met heads. Unmoving on the hillside. Breath came in pillows from their muzzles, melting like blown fog among the treelike branches of their upswept horns.

The gun came from its cradle of its own accord; and I had in the scope the high shoulder of the biggest one, the one with the myriad boss of antlers, the one that had just taken two plunging bounds up the hill before turning statue again. I aligned the crosshairs and was squeezing the trigger when I had the sudden, awful thought that maybe these were not the source of my unease.

A fear unlike any I have ever known came over me then. It was a pressurized thing, steady, unfolding and insistent at the back of my knees and around my shoulder blades. It squeezed my ribs until I thought I had lost the capacity to breathe. I felt surrounded and gnawed at and stranded. I wanted to sprint, to clamber up a tree and hide. I wanted to lie down in the snow and bury myself. I wanted to shoot the rifle, run the bolt and shoot again. At anything that moved. At anything that didn't.

For the first time, I knew what it was to be hunted.

I was pinned so completely in the arms of that thought that I barely noticed the two bucks flag their tails and high-step toward the ridge, puffing as they went. I lowered the gun. I leaned my back against the tree and slid down the bark until I was in the gray-shadowed snow. I stared at the silver trees before me as if they were part of a dream that could teach me something. Which, of course, they could.

"Dreams and hunting are windows into other worlds," Mitchell and my father used to say. "They are how we see and respect the lives of our ancestors."

I was a girl, but I was the last of our line. It had seemed preordained that I would learn to hunt.

The process began shortly after my eighth birthday with a series of exercises Mitchell and my father called "my initiation into dirt time." One or both of them would take me into the woods near our house every few days. We raked away leaves, then poured water on the earth and returned the next day to study the tacks that had been left in the mud. Periodically we would return to see how they changed over time and under the influence of weather and the accumulation of debris. Soon I could tell the age of tracks at a glance.

Where there were no visible tracks, Mitchell taught me to lie on my belly to see disturbances in the leaves that marked an animal's passing. "Anything that has Power leaves sign of its passing," he said. "You just have to learn how to see it."

Mitchell showed me how to look at tree trunks to tell where antlers had struck them as the deer and moose went by. My father taught me how to gauge the activity of squirrels and birds for clues to what the larger animals were doing.

"Everything is connected," they would say. "What happens out here is like guitar strings vibrating. The smaller the animal, the more the big vibrations move them. Watch the small animals; they tell you what the woods are feeling."

Once, after school, Mitchell took me to a swampy place and told me to keep my eye on the edge where the open woods met a bog. The edge where two such different environments met, he said, was where the influence of Power was most easily witnessed. He hid me behind two logs and left, telling me he'd return at dark. I watched for hours, trying to see what he was talking about. I saw chipmunks and squirrels and songbirds, but they seemed to be acting out their own lives. Then it began to drizzle and grow dark. I kept looking for Mitchell to appear, but he didn't and I became afraid. A band of chickadees filtered into the pines at the edge of the swamp and I suddenly knew that they were being moved by something big. I expected a deer to step out in the twilight behind the birds, but not the bear. It ambled out onto a log, snuffling the air for scent. Perhaps it was only my imagination, but the bear seemed electric in the drizzle, and that current pulsed outward until it sheathed me and my vision went telescopic; and all there was, was the bear at the end of a glowing tunnel.

"He's a big boar," Mitchell whispered in my ear and the tunnel collapsed and I nearly screamed from fright. But he had clapped his hand over my mouth before the sound could scare the animal. He hugged me and we watched the bear root for insects until it was too dark to see anymore and we could only hear him. When the animal was gone, we made our way back to the trails that led home. I held his hand and watched his Pall Mall glow hot. When he brought it to his mouth, it cast red iron arcs in the darkness. He told me it was a good sign that the bear had come to me. It showed that I had the potential to have animal allies, that I had the sensitivity to become a *Puoin*.

I honestly don't remember how I reacted to this news. I was only eight and a half and did not know there was anything strange about this. But at the very least, it gave me strength to know that Mitchell believed in me, a young girl.

Sadly, the encounter with the bear was his last gift to me. He'd been a three-pack-a-day cigarette smoker since his youth and it caught up with him. Within weeks he became too feeble to go with me into the woods. He became this figure on our front porch, rocking in his chair, telling me about the six worlds beyond our yard.

My parents did not believe in sheltering me from death and I helped care for Mitchell in his last days. Despite the fact that he was proud of my father being a doctor, he despised the idea of a hospital. Mitchell died when I was ten and a half, in our upstairs bedroom with all of us gathered around his bed. For many months afterward, my father did not go to the woods, as if it would be too heartbreaking to endure. I'd find him on the porch staring off. I'd crawl up in his lap and he'd stroke my back.

"I miss Mitchell," I'd say. "But sometimes I feel like he's here."

"He is," my father would reply. "I'm just waiting for him to move off a little so I can breathe."

In many ways my father never fully recovered from Mitchell's death. The man who'd been his anchor was gone. But he knew that his uncle would want him to continue to teach me, so at the end of summer we began again.

My father taught me how to be still in the woods for

hours until I literally became part of the scene and the forest accepted me and revealed itself. Part of me hated the bugs and the cold and the rain. But then there'd be a moment so miraculous—like the time the two beaver cubs played in the pond I'd been assigned to watch, or the day the grouse stood on my outstretched leg and drummed—that all of the discomfort was forgotten.

"Is this how Mitchell taught you, too?" I asked one day as we walked home.

"Yes."

"Do most people know this stuff?"

"They used to, and because of it, they looked at the world as a magical place, which it is," he replied. "Now they see only themselves. They have no respect for nature or their place in it. They kill without respect or reverence. They feel no shame."

In my eleventh year, I began a lengthy study of what my father called "proper woods behavior." Despite his love of the hunt, he had no illusions about it; he understood there was no real reason to pursue game in the mid-twentieth century. Certainly not to fill our stomachs. A trip to the supermarket was more efficient. To my father, the hunt was largely ceremonial, a ritual through which he could reestablish and pay homage to his genetic predatory role as well as to his Micmac and Penobscot roots.

"The hunt reminds us that all life requires death to sustain itself," he once told me. "The key is to have an abiding respect for the death that supports you."

As such, behavior, my behavior, during the hunt had to be meticulous. I was bound by a code of conduct based on a love of the animal and the forest and myself. Be sure of your quarry. Never shoot unless you believe you can kill cleanly and humanely. Never leave a wounded animal in the woods. Never kill anything you would not eat.

Sitting there in the snow, I wondered if any of those rules applied now that I was hunted as well as hunter. I did not have an answer, and when Griff came down the hill toward me, I was shivering and hiccuping.

"This may be more than I can deal with," I said.

Griff lifted me up by my elbow and said, "This is no time to give up. We need your tracking skills too much."

"Whoever is out here is part of the woods," I said. "He was watching me just now, but he didn't disturb the animals. It's as if they accept him."

Griff looked at me strangely. He didn't understand what I was talking about, but he didn't want to upset me more than I was. He brushed the snow and bark off my jacket and handed me back my rifle. "Cantrell cut your tracks way up ahead. There's no others. He's circling back this way, says we're losing light and with the storm coming we should head back."

"I'm telling you I'm scared," I said.

Dusk was upon us when we arrived in the lodge yard. The Mounties I'd prayed to see all the way back were not among the crowd gathered at the meat pole.

"Where are they, Mike?" I asked, annoyed at the edge in my voice. "You said they'd be here."

"Don't know," he grumbled.

"That's not good enough," Griff replied.

"Well, it's gonna have to be!" He punched the dashboard. "Maybe they couldn't get in with the winds picking up this way. Maybe they're already out looking around."

When I climbed out from the cab, Arnie was taking pictures of Butch, who was holding the antlers of a big deer.

"Damn, he's got to be twenty-four inches between the horns," Phil was saying.

"More like twenty-six. Good, good buck, eh?" Nelson replied. "The bases are six inches around. He'll score up there in the Pope and Young, don't you worry."

"I'm not worried." Butch grinned. His eyes looked so glassy and happy that I thought for a minute he was stoned. "I got what I came for."

"Still more than a week of hunting left," said Arnie in a delirious manner. "Who knows what will happen?"

"I still haven't seen a shooter, or anything close," Phil complained.

Nelson patted the wall of Phil's back. "It's gonna happen. Rut's not fully on us yet. Bucks aren't running wild. You're in a good spot. Give it time."

A couple of feet away, Earl stared at the young deer he had killed. Lenore turned her back on him and walked away.

Cantrell made a show of congratulating both men, then slipped across the yard toward the lodge. I started toward my cabin, watching as Sheila came out, backlit at the kitchen door, wringing her hands in her apron. She took off her wire-rimmed glasses and worked at them as they fell into a muffled conversation. Her side of it was tense. I thought, Sheila and I need to talk.

I'd almost made it to my cabin when Kurant caught up

to me. He was huffing from running. Icicles hung from the writer's red mustache. "Any luck today?"

"That buck's too smart for me," I lied. "And the photography?"

"I had a real nice deer step out and when I tried to snap it, the camera wouldn't go. Too cold."

"I have hand-heaters you might wrap around the camera body," I said. "I'll bring them to dinner."

"That would be great!" he said cheerfully. He smiled that smile and went off through the snow. I decided that even if he had sneaked in here, he wasn't such a bad guy. Compared with Earl and Lenore, he was downright pleasant. It is also worth stating, because I'd be less than honest if I didn't, that at that instant I decided I liked the way he moved. His almost delicate walk made me think of Kevin.

Looking back, I realize what I had found initially attractive in Kevin Walker was his otherness. We met at a party the spring of my freshman year at MIT. I was lonely; I had not been home or spoken to my father since Katherine died the previous fall. Kevin was a year older, an English major at Harvard, the son of a prominent Boston investment banker. As I've said, he had lank blond hair and a long, slender, almost feminine build that allowed him to indulge in fashionable clothes. He boasted to me in our first conversation to have no needs save those of the city.

"Anything outside Boston or Manhattan is positively camping," he announced.

"An asinine statement if there ever was one," I replied.

Kevin's eyebrows shot up. He was so used to women fawning over him because of his *GQ* looks that any challenge was intriguing.

"You don't like the metro scene, then?" he asked.

"It's wilderness to me," I said. "I'm from Maine."

"Maine? You poor woman," he said. "Then I'll just have to be your guide. There's no one with a better understanding of the wilds of Boston than me."

"I think you're just trying to get into my pants," I said.

He laughed out loud. "Well, that, too."

I almost walked away right then. But Kevin had this way about him, a studied nonchalance, the sense that he did understand. He was different from the Maine boys I'd held in the front seat of pickups. More important, he had a wildly different view of the world from my parents. And I needed that kind of different. Desperately.

"You're hired to teach me the territory," I said. "But my clothes stay on."

In the months that followed, Kevin introduced me to symphonies, the ballet and foreign films. He read me Borges out loud just to hear the language. We stayed up until dawn in jazz clubs, then took long walks as the city awoke, flushing clouds of pigeons in Copley Square.

We all erect walls around ourselves. Kevin's was built carefully from years in prep schools and summers on Nantucket. But I was to discover that behind the cultivated facade, he was funny, loved books and art and was obsessed with the Boston Red Sox. During that first summer we were at a game—Yankees–Red Sox, of course—and he'd gone to get us some hot dogs during the fifth inning and hadn't returned, so I went looking for him. I found him sitting on the cement staircase with a five-year-old boy named Noel who'd gotten separated from his parents. Kevin was telling Noel stories about Carl Yastrzemski and the

Green Monster while the security guards looked for his parents. Noel was trying hard to be brave, but a single tear rolled down his cheek. Another man might have tightened up. But Kevin never broke the train of his story. He just reached out gently and wiped the tear away and said that was how Yastrzemski used to swipe balls off the Green Monster. I suppose that simple gesture was the seed of my love for him.

He was surprisingly shy when I finally did let him undress me. He knew I had Indian blood in me, and I think that both attracted and intimidated him. He brought me breakfast in bed the next morning and the morning after that.

"You don't talk about your mom and dad," he said, propped up on one elbow. "I mean, they can't be any worse than the ones I've got. Dad's more at home in his office. Mom's a charity shrew."

I looked at him for the longest time, not wanting to wreck this feeling that was growing in me, this feeling that his arms were the safe haven I needed in which to form a new identity. The lies began there. "My mother died when I was young. My father was one of those cold, tyrant types who didn't want kids anyway. When he died last year, I swore I'd never look back."

"But why?"

I pressed my finger to his lips. "It was a promise I made to myself. Please don't make me talk about him."

He wanted me to tell him, but he could see the pain. Kevin smiled and kissed my finger. "I won't. I figure if you're ever ready, you'll tell me about it."

I never did. And like all lies, it returned to haunt me. I was still wondering if I ever would be ready to tell Kevin or anyone else the circumstances of my childhood, of my mother's death, when I opened the kitchen door at Metcalfe. Theresa had her long braid pinned up in a bun. She spooned portions of a tossed salad from a metal mixing basin to wooden table bowls. Sheila stood on tiptoes, peering out the window above the sink. They hadn't heard me come in.

"It's pitch-black out there. I don't know what you expect to see," Theresa said to her.

"Grover's still out there," Sheila replied.

"Grover's never on time for dinner. He's always down at his rock, talking to the birds or the ghost of his mommy or whatever it is he does."

"Don't make fun of him!"

"Hey, hey, take it easy, eh? I'm not making fun of him. He's just . . . weird, that's all."

"He's not weird," Sheila said. "He just don't know any better. I think he goes down to the rock because he's lonely. Don't you ever feel that way?"

"I guess."

Sheila noticed me. Her hands disappeared inside the folds of her apron. "Dinner's not for another ten minutes," she said. "The others are out by the bar, telling stories."

"That's okay," I said. "I was never much for boasting."

Theresa's breasts jiggled when she laughed. "Came to the wrong place, then, I'd guess. Deer camps are worse than fishing camps for boasting, eh?"

Sheila glanced at Theresa and then at me. "The hunting was good . . . today?"

"Second day in a row I saw big, big deer and couldn't get a shot."

"What a shame," Sheila said.

"Shame nothing," Theresa said. "Wish you had got a shot just so I could have seen that guy Earl's face, eh? Imagine two women tagging big deer while he's bringing in a little skipper like that on the Metcalfe Estate."

"Theresa!" Sheila complained.

"C'mon, that deer was puny. And I get the feeling Diana's not easily shocked."

"Lately you'd be surprised," I said evenly.

Sheila laughed nervously and retied her apron. "Well, lasagna for dinner. I hope you like lasagna and salad and lots of garlic bread."

I was about to say I did when Cantrell came through the swinging doors. He looked at me, then at Sheila and then at me again. He brought out his best forced smile. "Dinner ready, hon?"

"Yes, but Grover's not back yet," Sheila blurted out.

"She's tighter than a bird that's found a cat peering in the nest," Theresa said. "Grover's just out at his rock longer than usual."

"Mike?" Sheila said. "I think someone should go look for him."

"He'll be fine," Cantrell said.

"Mike, please?"

Cantrell threw up his hands. "I'm gonna lose my mind in this place. I'll see if Tim'll go down to the rock and take a look."

Theresa scowled as she slid by the outfitter with a tray of salads balanced on her tremendous breasts. "That's nice. You take my husband's dream job and now you want to make him your gofer to boot."

"Don't start, Theresa," Cantrell warned. "I'm not in the mood."

"You may pay me, buster," she said coldly, "but you don't own me or my Timmy. Got it?"

Cantrell pursed his lips. "I've got guests who want to change hunting locations. I need to see to their wishes. If you don't want Tim to go, who would you suggest: Patterson?"

Sheila turned away, scratching at her throat. Her eyes watered. God, he's cold, I thought. Theresa adjusted the weight of the tray. Reluctantly she said, "I'll ask Tim if he'd mind taking a walk to Loon Rock."

"Much appreciated," Cantrell said. He waited until Theresa had exited, then turned to me. "I need to talk with my wife. Alone."

"I just wanted to know . . ."

"Later, Ms. Jackman." His tone threatened. I bowed my head and hurried through the doors, passed Theresa and went out into the lounge, where the other hunters were making merry.

During dinner I dutifully listened to Butch prattle on about the circumstances of his day, all the while wanting to tell him to shut up, to tell the others about the terrible things that were happening in the woods. And then I'd think: But maybe it's him. He's a bow hunter. And I'd bite my tongue.

Just before dessert was served, Earl, who'd been silently drinking most of the evening, announced to no one in particular. "I kind of like my deer. I really do."

The table fell silent and he said it again.

Lenore regarded him sidelong. "Yeah, you're a real woodsman."

"That deer was running with a monster, only they must have shifted positions as they passed behind that clump of trees," Earl insisted. "I saw horns and a shoulder and I shot. It's an okay buck."

"Bamcicide's what it is." Lenore sniffed.

"Aren't you the sweet thing, saying sweet things," Earl snapped. "Maybe I'll start in on some things that aren't so sweet 'bout you, you keep this up."

I saw something go out of Lenore for a second, the way it had the night before when she'd caught Earl groping me. Then she got strong again. "You've got a second tag, hon. There's always tomorrow."

Earl smiled. "That's more like it."

An abominable spell came over the rest of us. I looked at Cantrell, who glanced away, and then at Griff, who stared at the ceiling. Finally Theresa broke the hex, barging through the swinging doors with plates of strawberry short-cake. I didn't know if I could stay awake much longer; my head was foggy from the long day and lack of sleep. I relaxed into the nether state that says go to bed or you'll collapse. As if from far away, I heard Cantrell explain to Phil and Earl the topography of their new hunting locations. I yawned and started to get up from the table.

That was when the screams cut loose. Sheila and Theresa in grinding wails that sucked us all from our seats. Nelson side-slammed through the kitchen doors into the dining hall. He was deathly pale. "G-Grover . . ." he stammered. "The deer pole . . . I . . ."

Cantrell was by him and through the kitchen, shouting

to Nelson to keep us back. But Nelson was in no condition to restrain anybody.

My next recollection is that I had traveled fifty yards outside the lodge and it was spit-snowing and there was a powerful flashlight playing in the darkness, resting finally and awfully on the inverted form of Grover, who had been suspended between the deer. Like Patterson, he had been gutted, scalped and suspended by a rope passed behind his Achilles tendons. A white owl feather jutted from his doughy lips.

Theresa collapsed. Nelson tried to pick her up, but she shrugged him off and dragged herself with bare hands through the snow. She opened her mouth and, as I had done the evening before, relieved her mortal awareness.

"Oh, no," Kurant was moaning to himself. "No."

Sheila sank to her knees behind her husband. She coughed up sounds like choked burps when he played the torch over Grover's body, then focused the beam on the slicing wounds on either side of his rib cage.

The rest of us slouched mute before this apparition, forced penitents unwilling to believe in the sacrificial form tossing ever so perceptibly in the breeze. My first impulse upon breaching from that miserable first wave of shock was to flee. Instead, I turned barbarous and screeched at Cantrell. "Where are they, Mike? You said you'd call the Mounties! Instead, you tried to cover it all up, and now there are two bodies!"

They were all looking at me now and I realized my whole body was racked with tremors. I heard myself screech at Cantrell again. "Where are the Mounties, Mike?"

"What's she talking about—bodies?" Nelson demanded numbly.

Cantrell tried to speak, but no words would come.

"Patterson," Griff said sadly. "Diana found him last night way out at the end of the property—just like Grover. Mike wanted us to put him in the icehouse so you all wouldn't lose control. We lied about him having the flu."

Nelson took that revelation like a slap. "Don just had a baby," he mumbled.

"I want to go home, Earl," Lenore whined. "I want to leave right now."

Earl nodded blankly, then suddenly came alert, the businessman responding in a crisis. "I want me and my wife on that plane going out of here, ASAP. They're coming, the Mounties, right?"

Cantrell shook his head as if he couldn't believe it himself.

Arnie took a step forward, his hands balled into fists. "What do you mean, no? This is a slaughter!"

Sheila's burps slurred into halting phrases. "We . . . we tried all night . . . but the radiophone . . . something's wrong . . . I, I told Grover to go check the antenna this morning . . . he never came back . . . and . . . and . . ." She couldn't manage any more.

"Oh, Jesus," Butch croaked. "Who's doing this?"

"Who?" Phil cried. "We're in the middle of fucking nowhere! There's no one else in here but us!"

I could see it now in the way we all slivered our glances and arched our backs and bent our knees: we were turning on one another, pressing backward into the invisible corners

of our minds, an instinctive response so far inside our genes
we couldn't have controlled it even had we wished to.

"You think it's one of us?" the magazine writer asked in
a slow, detached manner that I interpreted as shock.

"One of the bow hunters," Hill announced. "See? That's
an arrow wound."

"Through and through," Nelson agreed.

"Then it's you," Earl said, jabbing his finger Griff's way.
"Or Butch."

Arnie took a step away from his friend. "Hey, I didn't kill
anyone," Butch protested.

Lenore went walleyed and edged toward her husband.
"We should lock the both of them up until the police get
here, just to make sure."

"Absolutely," Earl said. "One of them's a psycho."

They were arguing among themselves now. No trust, no
camaraderie, only the response of animals threatened with
attack. Suddenly, for some reason, the shaking left me. I
felt apart from it, able to act.

"No one's locking anyone up yet!" I yelled. They quieted,
expecting me to flip out again. But I was serene. I told
them how we had discovered two sets of boot prints far
out near the Dream leading away from Patterson's body,
and how it was impossible for either Butch or Griff to have
hiked all that way in one day. They chewed on my information for several moments, the theories and suspicions it
conjured vying for dominance.

"So there are two people hunting us. That what you're
saying?" Butch asked.

"Yes," I said.

"But why?" Theresa blubbered.

Arnie stared out into the darkness. "Who cares why? If it's true, we're sitting ducks out here!"

"He's right, Mike," Griff said. "We should get everyone inside."

Earl, Lenore, Arnie and Theresa hurried toward the lodge. Phil and Kurant seemed torn between staying and leaving. Sheila looked to safety and then to her husband. "Mike? What are we going to do?"

Wordlessly Cantrell handed his wife his flashlight. He unwound the cord from the cleat on the stanchion. Griff and Nelson got hold of the rope, too.

"Wait!" Kurant said. "We should take a picture."

Nelson looked like he wanted to clobber the writer. But Kurant insisted: "They're going to need photographs of the scene, aren't they? The Mounties, I mean."

"This better not end up in some story," Nelson warned.

Kurant didn't answer him. He just ran back to the lodge and returned with his camera. The flash burst three times, throwing long shadows toward the forest.

At last they let the rope run through the pulley on the crossbeam. The weight on the gambrel descended toward earth. Phil and I laid Grover on his back in the snow. Kurant took another picture. I leaned forward, swallowed, then plucked the white owl feather. I did not destroy it the way I had the raven's quill in Patterson's mouth. I wanted it.

They took Grover by his wrists and ankles and dragged him to the icehouse. They wrapped him in burlap, then laid him on the floor next to the similarly wrapped body of Patterson. Cantrell squeezed shut the hasp on the lock to the icehouse and turned to face us. I remember thinking that he appeared to be watching something move at a great distance.

"We need to fix that radio antenna," Nelson said.

The outfitter ignored his guide. He said, more to Sheila than to the rest of us, "I'm sorry."

"We'll go on," his wife replied firmly. "We always have."

Cantrell regarded her lovingly for several seconds. "Okay," he said finally. "Griff, Phil and Nelson, I want you armed. Diana, you and I will carry tools and flashlights. Kurant, you go inside."

"No way," Kurant said.

"Inside," Cantrell growled. "Now."

Kurant crossed his arms. "Sorry, this is the story now and I intend to be there."

Cantrell stepped forward. "The hell you will. You reporters are all alike. You'll turn it into something worse than it is."

"Can it get worse than it is?" Kurant snarled.

Sheila put her hand on Cantrell's arm. "He's right, eh?" she said. "Let him take his photographs. Maybe it will help."

"I was just trying to save some of our life from the vultures."

"I know."

"What are going to do, Cantrell?" Earl demanded for the fifth time in as many minutes.

"I'm thinking on it," the outfitter responded.

We were back in the lodge, had been for close to an hour since inspecting the antenna. The gravity of our situation pressed down on us like some brooding and malignant hand. I kept thinking about the radiophone and how much I wanted to call Emily and Patrick and even Kevin, to tell them I was okay, even if I wasn't. And yet that world, or what had been my world for so many years, now seemed like one in which I was no longer a welcome resident. I was taut and jumpy and questioning my sanity. Who wouldn't have? I had been the last person to see Patterson alive and one of the last to see Grover. I couldn't help asking if I might be the next to go. And the second I did, I understood that was what was going through everybody else's mind, too. Especially after what we'd found at the antenna tower.

Nelson had led the way through pines to the bare knob of rock three hundred and fifty yards behind the camp where the transmitter stood. We moved single file, with flashlights blazing. Easy targets. I spent the entire march fighting off the same claustrophobic reaction to being hunted that I'd suffered in the woods near the Dream earlier that day.

Miraculously, we reached the antenna without incident. Nelson and the others stood guard while Cantrell and I climbed the knob. In the frigid air, the snow had become a driven talcum dust that abraded our exposed flesh. I cast my light on the snow. "He's been here," I said. "The one with boots too big for him."

"I see 'em," Cantrell said grimly. "Those there are Grover's. He's been wearing them chain-tread pac boots since Sheila bought 'em for him a few weeks back."

We called the others up. Griff and Nelson went to a green metal box at the rear of the superstructure. I shone the light on the tracks for Kurant, who took a couple of photographs but didn't know if they'd be sharp because of the snow glare.

"Sonofabitch!" Griff groaned from around the other side of the tower. "The repeater's smashed!"

Cantrell's flashlight arced up the side of the antenna. "Got the coaxial, too. Cut the whole thing out."

Nelson leaned his head against the tower.

"What's going on?" Kurant demanded. "What does that mean?"

Cantrell's shoulders sank. "It means they've cut us off. We have no way to talk to the outside world until the floatplane comes back on the twenty-sixth."

"Cut off!" Kurant cried. "For how long? Don't you have a cellular phone, anything?"

Cantrell shook his head. "One of the things we were gonna do after the season. We're in this alone until the plane returns. Eight days."

Which is what Cantrell had to tell the others upon returning to the lodge. As a group, we were used to being alone in the woods, self-reliant, able to tolerate physical and mental hardships. Everyone in the room listened to the outfitter with a stoic expression, but there was an unmistakable odor in the air. The faint, burning-wire scent of panic.

"Is that all you're going to say?" Lenore said shrilly. " 'I'm thinking on it'?"

"That's what I said," Cantrell snapped.

"Great," Lenore announced. "Our leader is frozen, unable to act. Earl, honey, for all your faults, you do know how to assemble facts, see what needs to be done and make a decision. Take over for these rubes."

Nelson pointed at Lenore. "You, rich bitch, shut your

mouth or I'll shut it for you. No one's taking over here, least of all some computer twerp and his catalog wife."

Lenore couldn't believe it. "Well . . . well . . ." she sputtered. "I guess we know who isn't going to get a tip on this trip, don't we?"

Earl looked at his wife incredulously. "Ahh, stow it for once, will you?"

For a moment Lenore lost all color, then regained her composure, turned and poured herself a drink. A big drink.

"How about barricading the doors?" Arnie asked.

"Barricade?" Phil responded. "You think I'm staying in here for the next eight days, you're out of your mind. I don't like being inside."

"You'll be where you're told to be," Cantrell said. "The only way we're going to survive is to stick together."

"What about the snowcats?" Butch asked. His ponytail had come undone and his hair hung in his eyes. "Couldn't we ride out to the nearest town?"

"The trail's too narrow heading out," Cantrell said. "It's meant for snowmobiles or ATVs."

"I saw some snowmobiles in that utility shed," Butch said.

"They're old and town's eighty-five miles," Theresa said.

"There's nothing closer?" Griff asked.

She shook her head morosely. "No town for eighty-five miles."

Her husband snapped his fingers. "Maybe we don't need to get to town."

Nelson crossed the room to the big aerial photograph and pointed to a blur of gray. "There's an abandoned logging camp outside the northwest boundary of the estate. I haven't been there, but I remember someone saying there's a radiophone."

"You're sure?" Cantrell asked.

"Yes!" Theresa said, excited now. "I heard old man Metcalfe mention it a couple of times."

"Then we go for it," Griff said.

"First thing in the morning," Cantrell said.

"Thank God," Sheila said.

I wasn't sure who to thank. Griff walked me to my cabin, where I loaded the rifle and set it against the wall. I propped the back of one of the chairs under the door handle and hung an extra blanket over the window to prevent any light from showing outside. I sat in the overstuffed chair facing the deer head. I twirled the owl feather in my fingers and thought of Patrick and Emily. I started to cry, wondering if Kevin would use this time away to turn them against me. I asked myself how our marriage could have gotten so tangled, and I had to admit the knots were fashioned by my hands.

We were married the summer I graduated with degrees in chemistry and computer engineering. He was already working as a publicist with Krauss. I thrived in my new life, rising quickly at the start-up software company that gave me my first job. Writing computer programs was like setting off into new country; I approached each project as a forest to be scouted and understood. But more important, I was happy in my new self, and by our third anniversary I thought I'd put the hunt, Power, my parents and Mitchell behind me forever.

We bought a town house in the Back Bay. Saturdays

were extended shopping sprees on Newbury Street, dinner and the latest film at the Nickelodeon. Sundays were brunch and lazy days reading the *Globe* and the *Times*. At parties during the early years, Kevin liked to tell our friends that I was a wild Maine savage he'd found wandering in the city and tamed. I'd always smile and correct him: "Civilized," I'd say. We'd both laugh.

We rarely left Boston except for weeklong vacations to Nantucket and Key West, which, because we usually took holidays at the same time as our urban friends, were for all intents and purposes Boston with a whaling theme and a palm tree, respectively.

There were moments in these vacation spots, however, usually at sunset, when I would find myself at the water's edge within earshot of the latest cocktail gathering. The waves would froth at my ankles and I'd be taken by an obscure longing to be more alone and yet more involved than I was. Invariably, Kevin would approach at that point and hand me a Sea Breeze and we'd walk together back to the party.

Patrick was born in the fifth year of our marriage, Emily in the eighth. My children raised in me the idea that I was connected to the future—if no longer to the past—and I adored them for it. Of course, our marriage had suffered the usual pressures that accompany the raising of young children, and by the time of my father's suicide, we had lapsed into the routine of kids, work and once-a-week sex.

So perhaps I was ready for the dreams that came to me after my father's death. My ancestors believed that dreams are windows to the other worlds and that the animals we meet in dreams can tell us of the future, or force us on journeys we are reluctant to take.

After the dreams began, and after I had chased the buck through the snows of southern Maine, my behavior became more erratic, much to Kevin's dismay.

Several times later that winter and into early spring, I slipped out of bed in the middle of the night. I drove the ninety minutes to Maine and entered the woods in the darkness. I got to the point where I could crawl into a thicket from downwind and flash my penlight into a deer's eyes and revel in its snort and the way it crashed away.

By late April the forest was heavy with pollen. Tree frogs peeped in a soprano chorus. And the briars at the edges of fields were thick with new growth. One night, under the soothing light of a full moon, I stripped and lay in a deer's musky bed until dawn came. I listened as the hoots of barred owls irritated roosting male turkeys. The toms raked the dawn with furious gobbles.

When I arrived home that morning caked in mud, reeking of animal musk, I suggested to Kevin that we send the children off to school and spend the day in bed. He demanded I seek help. I refused, saying there was nothing to be helped. He slept in the guest room after that night.

Nineteen months after my father's death, I received some of his forwarded mail. In the package was a letter describing the opening of the Metcalfe Estate. I read the letter a dozen times, especially the passages that described the remoteness of the forests. It called to me in a way I find difficult to explain. Looking back, I believe that my mind demanded a retreat into the chaotic reality of the wilderness, the unconscious, unknown place where the roads end and we begin; otherwise I would surely go mad. The next morning, with no word to Kevin, I took seven thousand dollars out of the savings account and booked the hunt. I took another two thousand for airfare and to outfit myself with the necessary equipment.

Kevin had our accounts frozen after he discovered the withdrawals.

"How could you take that kind of money without asking me?" he demanded.

"I knew you wouldn't let me have it," I replied. "And I needed it. You wouldn't understand."

"You could have at least tried," he said. "Diana, I feel like I don't even know you anymore."

I hesitated at his sad expression. "Maybe you don't, Kevin. Maybe that's the problem. But before I can tell you who I am, I need to go hunting."

"Hunting? That's what you spent nine thousand dollars on?" he cried. "Absolutely not. I hate hunting. You'll just have to call them and get the money back."

"And if I don't?"

Kevin looked at me icily. "Diana, you told me once that if I loved you, I wouldn't ask you questions about your father. I didn't want to, but I respected your wishes. Now I'm telling you, if you love me, you'll get the money back. That's what it comes down to—do you love me?"

I twirled the owl's feather in my hand, admitting that what had once been so clear had turned cloudy. I had loved him once. Now I didn't know anymore.

To get my mind off him, I studied the owl's feather in the gaslight glow. The white down filigreed out from the quill. I raised it and blew. The feather lofted and swirled to my knee. A soft, gentle thing.

Why feathers? I asked myself. Why feathers from ravens and owls? The killers were sending a message. But what? The raven was a scavenger. The owl, a bird of prey. I couldn't see the connection.

I took the feather and placed it under a tumbler turned upside down on the table. It was close to midnight now. I remember suddenly feeling more tired than I had ever been before. I lay down on the bed in my long underwear, then brought the loaded rifle in bed with me.

I did not fall asleep for a long time. I did not want to sleep because I did want to close my eyes and hear the creaking of the building in the wind and the flick of snow against the windowpanes. But despite my efforts I heard sleep coming, and as hard as I tried to fight, I couldn't. The talons of it came over me and I passed like a shadow into the night.

NOVEMBER NINETEENTH

THE NEXT MORNING, the sky had barely flattened toward sunrise when, against the dove whistle of the wind outside, the floorboards on the cabin porch creaked.

I had been up for nearly an hour, huddling under the blankets, waiting in the cold for the light to come because I forgot to bank the stove the night before. Dawn would give me courage. Until it came, I told myself, I would not open the door to get kindling. Who knew what might wait in the darkness?

The boards protested weight again. Chewing at my lip, I slipped from the bed with the rifle and padded across the cold floor to the curtained window. I peeked out, trying to see the porch, but all I could make out were the butt-ends of the log pile.

A moment passed, then two. The boards groaned a third

time. I turned down the gas lamp until it sputtered and died, then eased the chair out from under the doorknob. My heart felt ready to stop forever, but, gun in my right hand, I took the latch with my left and yanked the door open.

Kurant scrambled backward on his heels, dropped his flashlight and skidded onto his fanny when he found my gun barrel thrust in his face.

"What are you, crazy?" I squeaked. I had gone fluffy inside.

He crabbed backward on his elbows through the snow that had welled behind the woodpile, sputtering, "I was trying to figure out if you were awake yet! I wanted to talk. I'm . . . I'm . . . I couldn't sleep and . . . I wanted to talk."

"No, you're scared."

"I am not." He brought his legs under him. He wiped at the icicles that clung to his mustache. "I mean, aren't you?"

"Of course."

"Well, then . . . ?"

"Bring some kindling," I said, actually glad for the company. "My stove's out."

I built a tepee with the sticks over the embers buried in the ashes. I put some scraps of paper in below and blew. It smoked, then flamed, and I added more sticks until the interior of the stove crackled. Kurant intently studied the feather.

"What do you think it means?" I asked.

Kurant started. "I don't know. Why? Why would I know?"

"I didn't say you would. I just figured somebody like you, a writer, would have a theory."

"I hadn't thought of it," he said quickly. He glanced away

and made a whisking motion in the air with his hand. "I mean, I did, but mostly I just thought of the way Grover hung there. All night I thought about it . . . and I kept asking myself—what makes a human want to hunt another human? What makes a human want to hunt anything?"

There was a passion in his voice I hadn't heard before.

"So you weren't being honest when we got here, were you? You are against hunting."

He shrugged. "Let's say I don't understand the impulse."

"I think there's more to it than that. You're a vegetarian?"

"When I can be," he admitted. "Here it's impossible, so I do what I have to do. It's my job. But that's besides the point. What's your take on the feathers?"

"Maybe they're meant to answer your question: what makes a human want to hunt?" I said. And then I had a thought that chilled me more than the dank cold inside the cabin. "Or maybe the feathers are not what we're supposed to be seeing at all. Maybe they're just a calling card. Maybe it's who's being hunted that's the message."

"I don't get what you're . . ."

"Hunters," I said. "The hunters are being hunted."

Kurant dropped down hard in the leather chair. He chewed at his mustache, then murmured, more to himself than to me, "This is worse than anything I could have come up with. I thought I'd looked at it from every angle, but I didn't consider brutal irony."

I was about to ask him what that meant when a knock came at the door.

"Diana?" Griff called out. "Cantrell wants us. Now!"

"Give me five minutes," I called back. I turned to Kurant. "If you don't mind, I need to shower and dress."

*   *   *

The writer left. And as I got into the shower, I couldn't help remark again that he reminded me of Kevin in his mannerisms, sure of himself and yet, in some ways, weak.

After Kevin had given me the ultimatum to get back the money, I stayed out of the woods for a week and acted the dutiful wife. I told myself to call Cantrell, to cancel my slot. But I kept having the dream of the buck running and I put it off. That weekend I made plans to take Patrick and Emily to the Arboretum in Brookline, a safe alternative, I thought, to the big woods that beckoned.

But nature's canvas and woman's design are often at odds. In the car, I felt myself drawn out of the city, out past the densely inhabited suburbs toward the more rural areas, all the way to the Quobbin Reservoir northwest of Springfield. We parked near a logging road and I led the kids into the woods. They had never been in a real forest before and I could see their discomfort: Emily sucked hard on her thumb and Patrick held my pants leg even when I told him to run ahead. But after a couple of hours, the woods worked their magic on them. They dashed up the trails to show me a mushroom growing in the black soil or a trout darting in the shallows of a brook. They froze in amazement when a doe and her fawns crossed a ridge in front of us.

"Can we follow them?" Patrick asked.

"Go ahead," I said. "As long as you're downwind, they won't smell you."

Patrick ran after the deer, only to catch his foot on a root and fall. He squirmed on the ground, crying and holding his ankle. We were miles from the road and it took me hours to carry him out, especially with Emily crying that she was tired and hungry. I hadn't brought enough food or water. Then she fell and cut her chin.

I'd told Kevin we'd be home from the Arboretum by noon. We returned long after dark, after a two-hour trip to the emergency room to get stitches in Emily's chin and a cast on Patrick's ankle. Kevin was wild with worry and demanded to know how it had happened. I told him simply that we'd been out for a walk and they'd both fallen.

"I was chasing a deer way out in the woods," Patrick said.

"I was hungry and slipped on a rock," Emily said.

"They'll both be fine," I asserted cheerfully.

"Have you gotten the money back?" he asked.

"Tomorrow," I promised.

Two days later, without warning, he went to see an attorney. He painted me as a troubled woman whose behavior constituted a threat to the kids and used the hospital reports and the withdrawals from our savings account as evidence. He filed for divorce and a restraining order.

I got the order in the parking lot outside my office. I raced home, furious, but by the time I got there, the locks had been changed. My clothes were boxed in the garage. I demanded and got a hearing in family court. The judge asked me all about the money I'd spent and the late-night disappearances and taking my kids to the woods unprepared. I explained as best I could without bringing up the dreams.

He must have sensed that I was telling much less than I knew.

"I'm not convinced you are as much a threat to your

children as your husband has alleged, Ms. Jackman," he said. "But I'm concerned enough, based on some of the things you've done recently, to ask you to undergo a psychological evaluation. If everything comes back okay, we'll talk joint custody."

I could see what was going to happen, what a psychologist might find out about me, about my past and how it was worming its way through my mind, how it could be construed as something destructive—to me, to the people around me. I'd lose Emily and Patrick for sure. It sickened me, but I understood that getting custody in the long run meant possibly losing them for now.

"I don't think I need to talk to a psychologist," I told the judge. "I'm their mother and I love them and that should be enough."

"Then I'm going to have to limit your access," the judge replied. "One hour every two weeks until such time as you agree to an evaluation. Next case?"

The months living alone in the apartment before flying out for the hunt had been the longest of my life. I tried to make each visit and telephone conversation last, to imagine for myself and the kids that the situation was only temporary. It seemed to work with Emily, who was still young and has always possessed my mother's unfailing optimism. Patrick, however, knew. And because he is so sensitive and introspective, I could hear his pain every time we spoke, every time he asked, "When are you coming home, Mommy?"

"Soon, honey," I said to myself as I dressed. "I promise you, soon."

*   *   *

"Two of the snowmobiles run okay enough to make the trip," Cantrell announced. "But no one's worked the trail out of here in three years. I don't know what we'll face between here and Camp Four."

We had come outside on the back porch of the lodge facing the game pole. The snow flew sideways in sheets. The hanging deer were rimmed in ice crystals. They twisted and swung in the wind like dancers frozen in attitudes of free flight. Gray, nameless birds braved the gale to alight archly between the outstretched legs of the stags and peck at the ruby meat. The faces around me were haggard with exhaustion.

"I need three volunteers," Cantrell said.

I raised my hand. So did Griff, Nelson, Phil, Kurant and, to my surprise, Arnie. I wanted to use the phone to call home, to talk to Patrick and Emily. It seemed very important to hear their voices, as if that music alone could keep me safe until the plane returned.

Cantrell looked us over, then pointed to Griff, me and Arnie. "Griff will drive the second machine. Arnie and Diana will ride shotgun, watching our backs."

Phil jumped forward. "You're taking a woman and a guy who falls apart on a bumpy airplane ride over me? Listen, man, I was in 'Nam."

" 'Nam!" Butch laughed. "Phil, you talk as if you walked rice-paddy hamlets in the Mekong Delta. You were a supply sergeant at the Army auto works in Saigon."

"I was still there, man. You and Arnie were smoking pot, protesting and hiding from the world at Penn State. But I was there."

"I didn't smoke pot," Arnie said.

"I did," Butch said. "But so what, Phil. It's still not like you had combat experience or anything."

Kurant began his protest before Phil could respond. "You're trying to keep me away from the story, Cantrell. I won't stand for it."

Nelson stood there shaking his head as if he couldn't believe he wasn't going.

Cantrell gestured at his lead guide first. "Tim, I need someone with a head on his shoulders to be in charge here. And, Phil, I'm sorry, 'Nam or no 'Nam, the last thing I need on this trip is someone who flares up like you do."

Cantrell jerked his head in Kurant's direction. "As for you, I don't give a rat's ass about the press's 'right to know.' Arnie goes because he's a doctor and will follow orders. Diana, because she . . . well . . . she says she has some feel for whoever's doing this."

"Feel? What the fuck does that mean?" Phil cried.

I said, "It means I've tracked them, and that gives me some understanding of how they move. And at least three times in the past couple of days, one of them has been watching me. I felt it. They could have killed me if they wanted, but for some reason they didn't."

"Uh-huh." Phil snorted. "And there's a lady on television back home can give you the million-dollar lotto number if you stay on her nine hundred line long enough."

Kurant was staring at me. "How did you feel it? Them watching you, I mean."

"A feeling, a hunch, you know?" I said, not wanting to open that door any further than I had to. "Let's leave it at that."

"What does your crystal ball say, Madame Diana—women aren't in season?" Earl asked snidely.

"I don't know," I said. "I haven't studied their regulations."

"Hey, little man, I don't see you volunteering," Lenore snapped.

"I hate snowmobiles," the tycoon sniffed. "The things are a menace."

Lenore scoffed, "What he doesn't want to tell you is that he broke his ass bone falling off one during a hunt in Manitoba last year. Earl, you've got the balls for business and women, but when it comes right down to life and death, you got no spine."

"Why, you . . ."

"Shut up, the both of you!" Cantrell commanded. "I'm sick of listening to your constant bickering."

Earl paused, then looked at Lenore. "We bicker?"

Meanwhile, Phil's shoulders seemed to become part of his ears. "So she's got a feeling for him, so what?" he said. "Seems to me you want someone along who can shoot, not talk New Age crap."

Cantrell glanced from me to Phil and back again. Doubt had taken hold. Phil wasn't protesting Arnie. He was protesting me. Because I was a woman. Because I was in a man's terrain. We face this our entire lives. Having to prove that we are worthy, that we can stand in the forest. But Katherine had taught me never to back down. Men, she constantly reminded me, are convinced more by action than by word.

In one motion, I swung the .257 off my shoulder, dropped to one knee, sighted in on a bird feeder barely visible through the storm on the farthest edge of the compound's clearing, perhaps one hundred and twenty-five yards away, and touched off. The bottom of the feeder shattered. I ran the bolt, sighted and fired again, taking away the top: all in five seconds. I stood, glanced at Phil, whose mouth hung limply open. "Maine high school biathlon champion. Two years running. Your turn, Supply Sergeant."

Phil looked from me to the feeder and back to me again. "Shit."

I slung the gun and walked by Cantrell toward the snow-mobiles. "Shall we go?"

By the maps, Logging Camp Four was about twenty-seven miles away, a two-hour ride if the trails were clear. But to Nelson's knowledge, no one had maintained the trails in several years. It would be a slower trek.

I sat backward on the machine against Griff. We rode out of the lodge yard, uneasy at the vacuum created by the speed of the machine and of the storm, a vacuum swallowing the familiarity of the estate in gaping chunks of white and wind, casting us in fits and starts deep into the forest, deep into the unknown. Pucker brush, hawthorn and other dull-colored thorn vegetation clawed at us. I had trouble keeping my balance as Griff wrestled the snowmobile through drifts and under overhanging limbs.

For a while, however, we maintained a steady clip. I tucked my chin inside the lapels of the heavy fleece parka I'd gotten out for the trip. The straight trunks of the pines and the larch became blips in my side vision. The snowmobile treads kicked spinning clouds of snow behind us. The clouds eddied and ran and came back on themselves. This motion, which seemed foreign one moment and familiar the next, reminded me of Mitchell watching the night clouds against the full moon.

I decided that the movements of snow in the wind were probably about as close as I would ever come to an appreciation of the cosmic vision my ancestors had of this world. And yet, watching the swirls in the snow, I had the idea that I was in danger, that the invisible clouds around and within me were rotating on themselves, threatening me with a descent into the eye of a storm.

My father liked to say that understanding is the unsteady child of confusion. Whether that was something he came up with or another of Mitchell's sayings, I couldn't tell you. But at the time, it seemed as fitting a thing to dwell on as any. My father's point being, I suppose, that chaos reduces us to the instinctual rather than to the patterned. Groping for purchase, relying on our most primitive skills, we find new handholds to who we are and what we are capable of.

A mile out from camp, the windshield touched a branch, sending a shower of icy snow down my back. I shook it off and told myself to stop the introspection, to do my job and protect Griff. I gripped the gun tighter. At every curve and streambed, whenever the white-on-white landscape forced us to slow, I'd scrutinize the woods. Like that of a little girl out in dim light for the first time, my imagination played tricks on me: rocks became human backs, tree limbs turned to arms, and logs mutated into the prone forms of waiting archers. Mitchell used to tell me that the forest was filled with shape-changers who could manipulate the form of Power for their own ends. I'd never believed that was true. Now I didn't know what to believe in.

It struck me then that no matter what shape the killers appeared in, I was unlikely to see them at ground level. They were bow hunters by training; they would wait from above. I was about to tap Griff, to tell him to stop so I could turn around to watch over his shoulder for danger above and ahead, when the snowmobile lurched and slowed.

Cantrell and Arnie were already off their machine. I went forward in front of Griff. A tree trunk blocked the trail. Off to the left, the yellow of a newly hewn stump showed through the snow.

"That didn't come down in a wind," the pediatrician said anxiously. "It's been dropped."

"Fuck it all to hell," Cantrell growled.

"I don't like this," Arnie said. His cheek twitched. His gun barrel began a tight little dance in the air. "I don't like this at all. They're trying to trap us in here. That's what they're doing, you know. They're trying to trap us in here!"

Griff came by me unhurriedly and slipped the gun from the young doctor's hands before he knew it had happened. Griff clicked the safety back on. "It's time to be straight now, Doc. We don't want to hurt each other accidentally."

Arnie gazed at him blankly. Then he dropped onto the tree trunk. He kneaded his knee with his left hand. He cleared his throat, then did it again. When he raised his head, he had come back from inside. "It won't happen again."

There was no chance of moving the tree and no chance of going forward the way things stood. I crossed through the deep snow to the stump. No new tracks around it. Weather had discolored the wood. I figured it was at least a week or two since the tree had been felled. It bore the chip and gouge marks of an ax. "They don't believe in chain saws," I remarked.

Cantrell, who had been sitting on the angular hood of the snowmobile, brightened. "But we do!"

Cantrell insisted he'd make better time alone returning the six miles to the lodge for the chain saw and left before we could stop him. Griff, Arnie and I waited by the downed tree. We said nothing to each other for several minutes. Then Griff handed Arnie back his rifle.

"Thanks," the doctor said.

"Don't mention it," Griff replied.

We took positions with our backs to one another, blinking away the driving snow, watching the woods for movement, telling each other stories to keep the worry at bay.

Arnie had met his wife in high school. She had supported him through medical school by working as a court reporter. They had three girls. The oldest, Michelle, was nine and had asked him to take her hunting sometime. He'd been considering it, but now he didn't know if he would. Griff's son, Jack, was a graduate student in electrical engineering at Georgia Tech. He rarely hunted anymore. "His generation doesn't have the attention span for it," Griff said sadly. "It's all quick images and information digested and spit out."

I told them how Kevin had tried to keep Patrick sheltered from the idea of hunting after my interest had been reawakened. Even after I'd left the house, Patrick was pretending his crutch was a gun. Much to Kevin's dismay.

Griff laughed. "Doesn't your husband know it's in the genes? Something that goes back tens of thousands of

years? You can't wash away the innate desire to hunt in a
generation or two."

"People who live in cities are disconnected," I agreed.

"Yeah," said Arnie miserably. "Well, at least people in
the cities aren't being hunted."

"Do we watch the same evening news?" Griff asked.

Before Arnie could respond, we heard the distant pule
of Cantrell's snowmobile returning and then, through the
driving snow, saw the headlight. With the long-bladed chain
saw, the outfitter made short work of the trunk.

When we got on our way again, it was ten o'clock. We
would not reach Logging Camp Four until nearly two. Over
the course of the next seventeen miles, we encountered
eight dropped trees. And the planks on the rude bridge that
spanned the Sticks had been hacked away.

In silence, we cut young aspens to lay across the bridge
supports that remained. But I could tell that the level of
effort the killers had gone to in order to trap us inside the
estate was on our minds, fragmenting our concentration.
The ninth tree blocked the trail about a mile and a half
from the logging camp.

"I'm beat," Arnie complained. "I don't know if I can
move another log."

"We can't," Cantrell said. "We're out of chain saw fuel.
We'll walk it from here."

"I can't," the pediatrician whined.

"You have to," Griff said. "It's all of us or none of us."

My back ached. My long underwear was chilly and
clammy against my skin from wrestling the logs free of the
trail. I was fighting off the chatters. But I had come this far.
I wasn't turning back. "I want to use that phone."

"Me, too," Griff said.

Arnie surrendered. "All right, let's get it over with."

Cantrell broke trail. I followed, with Arnie and Griff bringing up the rear. There was now eight new inches of fluffy snow on top of the fifteen inches that had fallen since our arrival three days ago. I tried to focus on what was ahead of me, not behind, to embrace the idea that the future was still a possibility and the past a ballast to be dropped. But as we marched through that chalky world, I found myself unable to shake the memories that the storm had spurred.

My father lived in two worlds, maybe more. He was a physician in public. But his private life was dominated by the teachings he'd learned as a boy from Mitchell. He did not consider himself a full-fledged *Puoin,* or Micmac shaman, as Mitchell did. But my father was, in every sense of the word, a medicine man.

I was probably twelve when that fact fully struck home, when I realized how well he managed to bridge the worlds of traditional and modern medicine man. It was two days before Thanksgiving. We were at the cabin outside Baxter. Katherine was due to arrive for the holiday the next afternoon. It had been snowing on and off for several days— good tracking conditions—and we had had a run on one nice deer that left me nodding off at the dinner table. There was a knock at the door. A man from a camp about two miles from ours. His son was running a high fever and complained of stomach pain.

Their tar-papered cabin was a single-room affair with a potbellied stove in the center. Kerosene lanterns hung from nails in the rafters. A half-dozen men milled about. The tops of their union suits ballooned out from green wool pants. They regarded me as if I were some kind of invader in their inner sanctum. Which I was. I could tell some of them looked at my father the same way. He was a doctor, but he was also an Indian. If my father sensed their prejudice, he did not show it. He went straight to the boy, curled up on one of the lower bunks sweating and groaning. Frank was three years older than I, beautiful really, with reddish hair, freckles and thick hands. But the fever had washed out his skin and made it claylike.

I stood near the door with my hands behind my back, breathing through my mouth so I would not have to smell the thick odor of men who had not bathed in more than a week. My father knelt by Frank and examined him for several minutes. The boy kept moaning. I remember his moans. Thinking about them while I was walking into Logging Camp Four reminded me of my own moans when Patrick and Emily were born. I've come to believe that the threat of entering this world and the threat of going out elicits the same response, a gibberish spoken in some primordial language we all understand yet loathe.

Anyway, my father stood up suddenly and said, "Frank needs a hospital, but it's too far in this storm. We'll have to do it here."

He motioned to Frank's father and a couple of the other men to clear off the wooden picnic table. They found a sheet that wasn't badly soiled and they stripped Frank, which made me stare; I was twelve, after all. They laid him on the sheet on the table. My father called me forward and told me I'd help. I shook my head no, but he had a way about him that let me know that I would have to do it. I helped him boil the instruments. He put some liquid on a gauze and told Frank's father to hold it over his boy's mouth. Frank stopped moaning.

As my father worked, I watched his face for signs. He offered none save a wink toward me now and then, and a word of support to Frank's father, who was sweating profusely. I handed my father the instruments he called for. I did not want to look down. When I had to hold gauze on the wound, I looked away quickly and studied Frank's penis for want of anything else to focus on. It was all over in an hour. The appendix had been minutes from rupturing. We stayed all night until the boy's fever ebbed. At dawn, my father told them they should get Frank to a hospital as soon as they could, but that he would be fine with rest.

It takes a crisis to question the characteristics of our lives. On the drive back to our camp I drowsed, watching the truck's windshield wipers slap at the thick, falling flakes in the early-morning light. In that hypnotic state, it was suddenly important to know why my father had become a doctor, and I asked him. He didn't say anything for a long time, then told me it was probably for a lot of reasons, but only one stood out: he had been taught from an early age that to live a full and truthful life, one must achieve balance.

"It is said that if you would be a hunter, a taker of life, you must also be a healer, a giver of life," he said. "There are many kinds of people who can manipulate Power. In the old stories there are the *Kinapaq,* who use Power for their own ends, to run fast as the wind, to dive deep into water, to carry trees on their backs. But we are descended from *Puoins,* who use Power to cure. I saw becoming a doctor as a way to be modern and yet be whole."

An ironic response, of course, when you consider what happened six years later. But I get ahead of myself, because at that moment in my reverie, we spooked a bull elk from its bed not twenty-five yards off the trail to Logging Camp Four. If you have never heard a frightened elk sprint away through the woods—and until then, I never had—think of the skittering crash of football linemen. Think of that unexpected din in a silent forest.

It was a full five minutes before any of us could take another step. And another five before the adrenaline drained from the back of my throat. We were all that way in the last part of the hike: jagged and raw from hours under the pressure, real or imagined, of being toyed with, of being game.

Suddenly, when even I was beginning to think it might be better to turn back, the woods broke into a slash of whip trees I could not identify, but wondered at; they were blood-red and thorned and rimmed the clearing and the snow-buried buildings of Logging Camp Four. Cantrell waved us all into a crouch behind a large boulder. He brought out his binoculars and swept them back and forth across the clearing. After several moments, he whispered to me to stay there and cover the clearing while he, Arnie and Griff went for the phone. I started to protest, but then stopped; I had set myself up as the markswoman. I would act the part.

They skirted the edge of the slash to reach the rear of the closest of the outbuildings. The wind blew due out of the north, directly in my face. I squinted while they crept along the south side of the building, where there was very little snow.

Arnie slid up behind Cantrell. Even from one hundred and fifty yards away I could see the pediatrician's rifle shake as the outfitter drew a pistol, hesitated, then bolted toward the Quonset hut, only to bog down in drifts of wind-blown snow. He foundered, but managed to keep his feet under him and made it to the stoop and the door. Griff followed. Arnie was last. There was a moment of indecision at the door; then they all disappeared inside, leaving me alone in the storm.

Isolation can be a fortifying or dispiriting experience. My parents enjoyed the former; they always returned from the woods invigorated. But kneeling in the snow behind the boulder, I felt submerged in my own powerlessness. I couldn't shake the overwhelming sense that something was wrong here. I kept looking over my shoulder and up into the trees, craning my head in every direction, then forced myself to stop. What good would worry do? My father used to say that death springs from every angle of the compass; the key to living is to remain calm at the center.

The door to the Quonset hut crashed open.

Arnie tore headlong off the porch into the snow, stumbled, tried to rise and stumbled again. I swung my rifle toward Arnie, then the door, then back to Arnie. The powder snow clung to his eyebrows and around his nostrils. His mouth, pinked by the wet snow, arched open. He tried to scream, but made no noise.

I was up and running, foolishly trying to zigzag across the clearing. But after fifty yards in that white quicksand, I was too tired to do anything but plow on in a straight line, exposed, vulnerable. By the time I reached the Quonset hut, Arnie had dragged himself over next to the storage shed, where he cowered.

I went up the front steps slowly, then ducked into the murky interior with the gun before me. It was colder inside than out. Breath came like clouds from Griff and Cantrell, floated and disappeared in the rafters. The outfitter slouched on a broken couch. His eyes were closed. His pistol was tossed beside him. Griff was on the floor, his back to the wall, his head in his hands.

There was a third man inside, a man with a splotchy gray beard looking at me with open, filmy eyes. He was rocked back on his knees in the far corner, hands gripping the vanes and nock of a cedar arrow which showed at his throat. The broadhead was lodged behind his neck in the wall. Hoar coated his skin. Made him perfectly white. Except for the dull red crystals frozen in a downward stream from the corners of his lips.

I was unable to let my attention wander from the dead man, unable even to shiver. It occurred to me that if my children were to know what I was facing at this moment, they would never sleep again. I suppose this is the terror we all eventually confront. With luck, it does not occur until we are past caring. What frightened me more than the dead man was the fact that I was nowhere near as horrified as I'd been finding Patterson and Grover. Was I approaching the point of being past caring?

"Who is he?" I asked weakly.

Cantrell didn't open his eyes. "Must be Pawlett, the trapper that Barney, the floatplane pilot, said was missing."

"How long's he been like that?"

"Cold as it is, two, maybe three weeks."

"Radiophone?"

"Smashed. Looks like he was going for it when they caught up to him."

Griff picked his head up. He'd aged in the past half hour. "We don't know if it was them. I mean, he's not scalped. And there's no feather in his mouth."

"Because he's not a hunter, not one of us," I said. I told them the theory that Kurant and I had come up with earlier that morning. "I think this guy may have just gotten in the way."

Cantrell rubbed his sleeve along his beard. "Then they've been in here, in the forest here, for a long time, planning this."

"Not planning," I said. "Scouting."

I regretted saying that the moment the words passed my lips. The idea that two, maybe more, people had been roaming the woods looking for places they might kill us was as debilitating a thought as I'd ever had.

A floorboard grumbled behind me. Cantrell lunged for his pistol. Griff scrambled to stand. I spun, my gun rising toward the silhouetted figure in the doorway. Arnie dropped his rifle on the stoop and threw his hands up. "Don't shoot! Jesus, don't!"

My throat choked with heat. And I knew I wasn't past caring. Not yet anyway. I let down my rifle. "Don't ever do that again, Doctor," I whispered.

Arnie didn't move for a second. He blinked several times, groping at control. He stared down at his pants. "I pissed myself," he said meekly.

I saw his humiliation and said, "Who wouldn't with three guns pointing at them?"

The pediatrician attempted a weak smile. "I want to go back. We're going back, right?"

"Soon," Cantrell said.

"It will be dark in a couple of hours," Arnie said.

"I know," Cantrell said.

"But . . ."

"Soon."

"What about him?" Griff asked, gesturing toward Pawlett.

"Leave him," Cantrell said. "We've got nowhere to put him and I don't think he minds."

"I mind," Griff said. He walked over to the trapper and, grimacing, reached behind Pawlett's head to take hold of the arrow shaft below the broadhead. Griff gave a tremendous tug that freed the steel from the wood. He put Pawlett, still in that praying position, on his side. "There a blanket or a tarp or something we can cover him with?"

Cantrell looked around, then headed off toward a door in the corner. Without prompting, we all followed.

In the kitchen, rancid grease coated the cast-iron skillet on the cookstove. Griff tugged on a heavy door across from the sink. The carcass of a spike buck stripped of meat hung from a rafter inside the cold-storage locker.

"They were living here for a while if they ate all of that," Griff said.

Cantrell knelt, reached into the corner beyond the deer and brought out what looked like a dog's leg. He studied it, his nostrils flaring. "Timber wolf," he said. "Gray phase."

Without another word, Cantrell tossed the leg back inside the locker. He went out into the main room and crossed to a latched door next to the entryway. I was right behind him. The others lagged. Narrow beams of light, barely enough to let us know this was the bunkroom, shone through canvas that had been nailed about the window frames.

In the darkness I kicked something. It fell and there was a flash of phosphorescent light and a ringing explosion. I dove to the ground expecting more gunfire, frantically trying to get my safety off and figure out where it had come from. Now Arnie and Griff were shouting outside the door. I boxed at my ears, trying to get the ringing to stop. We lay there for what seemed a long time.

"Diana, you all right?" Cantrell whispered at last.

"Yes; you?"

"Still breathing. Where is he?"

"I don't know. I couldn't see where the shot came from."

Behind me, the door cracked open and I cringed. A shaft of light cut into the room. Cantrell squirmed forward on his belly to get behind a bunk bed. I was scrambling back into the shadows when I saw what it was that I'd kicked: a lever-action rifle still smoking from discharge.

"It's all right," I called to Cantrell. I pointed at the gun.

He shut his eyes. "I thought I was a goner."

I yelled to Griff and Arnie. "C'mon, I kicked over a loaded gun."

Griff had a flashlight in his hand. Arnie came in behind him, pale and shaking. "I want to go," he said. "Right now."

Griff patted him on the shoulder. "Let me get a blanket and we're out of here."

Griff stepped inside. He cast the beam around the room. He found a blanket on the nearest bunk and went out. I had Arnie train his flashlight on the gun, a model 94 with a chipped stock and faded bluing. And next to it, a pack stained with tobacco juice and other grimes. There was little in the pack: a mess kit, a knife, .30–.30 shells, some jerky, dried fruit and a rain poncho.

"Probably Pawlett's," I said.

"Why would he leave his gun in here?" Arnie asked, gripping his own rifle a little tighter.

"I don't know," I said. I took the flashlight from Arnie and shone it deep into the room. The dust had been disturbed back there and I walked over to a heavy oak table against the wall. Several pools of white candle wax caked the tabletop. And between them, quivering in the wind blowing through the open door, were bits of bird down.

"It's them, all right," I said. I squinted at a chunk of something black lying on the table against the wall.

I set my gun against the table and reached out to it, immediately recoiling at the thin, soft bristle that brushed my palm. I turned with realization and, choking, I elbowed my way past Cantrell and Arnie. I ran now toward the kitchen, holding my hand before me as if I'd burned it on hot embers. The hand pump in the sink was rusty and it shrieked when I worked it, even after the icy water erupted over my skin.

Griff found me there. My hand was turning a purplish color from the frigid bath and the scrubbing I was giving it with the coarse dishcloth. He took the cloth and drew me away from the sink. My knees threatened to buckle and he grabbed me.

"That was human hair, a scalp . . ." I whimpered.

"I know," Griff said. "There was blood on the table, too."

The implication set in and I held tighter to him and closed my eyes. I wanted to be anywhere but British Columbia. I wanted to be home, normal, listening to Kevin prattle about his latest publishing coup.

"Hour of daylight left," Cantrell called grimly. "Better we start hoofing for the snowmobiles or we'll get caught out here."

They say time accelerates in the presence of danger, but for me the opposite was true; the three-hour trip back to the Metcalfe Estate plodded. I could not shake the sensation of the hair and dried flesh against my skin. It had awakened something in me, something I didn't know I could feel. I knew that no matter what happened, I would not allow myself to be disfigured like that. It was that realization that made me understand for the first time that I might have to kill a human to survive this ordeal. I wondered if I could.

The creeping effect of this confrontation was a winding of my intestines and a knot at my scapula. On the phone one night about a month after my forced exile from our home, Kevin and I had had a vicious argument about the trip to Metcalfe. He accused me of barbarism. I told him the hunt was an ancient tradition with a stiff moral under-pinning; unlike him, a commercial carnivore, I accepted the moral weight of my canine teeth. Kevin claimed it was a savage act, no different from killing a human, maybe worse, in fact, because the motivations were so suspect in this day and age.

But killing a human was different. I knew it was true and yet I couldn't tell Kevin why I knew it was true; that wound, scabbed over for nearly fifteen years, was still festering and continued to fester on the ride back to the estate.

Overlying all of that was the knowledge that we were

trapped in here, that my life might no longer be measured in decades, but in days. For an instant I allowed myself to consider how Patrick and Emily would deal with my dying out here. The idea so sickened me that I quashed it immediately; such thinking could corrode resolve, make me less than the woman I would have to be to survive the coming days.

Whether it was emotional fatigue or an instinctual need to retreat, I somehow slept on the back of the snowmobile for the last ten miles to the lodge. Griff nudged me awake as we entered the yard. A single light glowed through the stained-glass window of the stags on the second floor of the lodge. The lower windows were dark.

The kitchen door opened and now we could see them all crowded at it. Our faces said enough.

"They're not coming, are they?" Theresa said.

Cantrell shook his head. "Radio's smashed."

"Phil's been shot," Butch said.

"What?" Arnie cried. "Is he okay? Don't tell me he's not okay!"

"Flesh wound," Butch said. "He's upstairs, locked in the middle bedroom."

The pediatrician bulled his way inside. The others pressed in around us, jabbing the air with questions. Sheila forced her way to the front and told the others to let us in out of the cold. I stepped inside the kitchen, instantly surrounded by the odor of frying onions and garlic. I'd forgotten how enveloping warmth and scent can be. I soaked in it, oblivious to the anxious chatter about me. I limped forward into the great room and slumped into one of the overstuffed chairs by the fire. The others trickled in.

In turns, Griff, Arnie and Cantrell laid out what had happened. Kurant peppered them with questions. I was so tired I couldn't speak.

When Griff described Pawlett's fate, they became visibly shaken. Even Nelson reached out to the wall for support. After it had sunk in, Butch slapped his hand on his thigh. "Philly was shot at with a cedar arrow, too."

"What happened?" Cantrell demanded of his guide.

Nelson held his palms up. "I ordered everyone to stay here in the lodge for the day. But the guy's got his own mind. He managed to slip out around midmorning. He says he just meant to hunt around the camp—"

"Where is he?" Cantrell jumped in. "I want to hear it from him."

Nelson motioned up the staircase toward the second floor. "He's a stubborn bastard, eh? Couldn't be sure he wouldn't try to go out again, especially after what happened. Took his gun away and locked him up there in the old man's bedroom."

"Get him," Cantrell said.

While we waited, Kurant slipped over next to me. "Sounded rough."

I smiled, thankful for his concern. "I'm alive."

He patted me on the leg. "I'm glad you are. I was worried."

"I can take care of myself."

"Yes and no, I think."

That made me uncomfortable, so I was somewhat relieved to see a very annoyed Phil following Nelson and Arnie down the stairs. "Your guide locked me up like I was some street gangster or something!" he yelled at Cantrell. "I want my fucking cash back!"

The outfitter was having none of it. "You disobeyed my guide's orders. You almost got killed because of it. Now knock off the bull and tell us what happened."

Phil glowered.

"Philly, c'mon. Who else can tell it?" Arnie asked.

Phil nodded, but his tone was defiant. "I went out 'cause I was thinking it was dumb to stay inside. Still do. This week's the peak of the rut, and, damn it, I put down some righteous cash for this hunt and, killings or no killings, I was gonna get my deer."

"Brilliant," Arnie said. "The guy's just brilliant. Been this way since childhood."

"Hey, don't diss me, Doc," Phil snarled. "You got your trophy buck."

"Aw, Phil, don't you get it?" Butch demanded. "The big-buck contest is over. Just tell 'em what happened."

Phil clenched his teeth, but began. "I went east along the lakefront, then cut north, figuring to make a nice loop, not too far from camp. I'd been out about an hour, working through the pines, you know, figuring that the deer would be waiting out the storm in the thick stuff. I came to a nice little clearing with a lot of browse in it and I spotted a couple of deer feeding on the other side. I stopped to see if a good one might be following. I got in the middle of three pine trees where the wind couldn't get at me, rested my Browning automatic rifle against one of them and started to glass the deer. Man, I hadn't been there two min-utes when I hear this *thwack!* noise and my right arm gets yanked sideways, pinned against one of the trees. There's an arrow, one of them cedar fuckers, right through the bottom of my new camo jacket. I snapped my head left and—hard to find the mother at first—but then I see this arrow come up around thirty-five yards away. And behind it is this fucking clown in snow camouflage, boots to face mask. And he's got this gray wolf cape on for a hat. He's drawing down on me."

Lenore got up and headed for the bar. "I've heard it twice and it still gives me the shivers."

"Recurve or a longbow?" Griff asked.

"How the fuck would I know?" Phil complained. "I mean, some crazed asshole with a wolf hat's gonna stick me, who's gonna look at his bow? But I'll tell you what, man: I wasn't dying that way. I learned not to die in the 'Nam."

"C'mon, Phil," Arnie groaned. "Not 'Nam again."

"Hey, hey," Phil said, wagging a muscular finger at the pediatrician. "There were snipers and bombers everywhere in that country. The auto works got hit a bunch of times while I was there."

"Just tell them what happened," Butch insisted.

"I reached down left-handed and got the autoloader up, flipped the safety, stuck the butt against the tree behind me and started blazing! Barrel on that mag was jumping all over the goddamned place."

Phil nodded his shiny head with satisfaction. "I'll tell you, that chickenshit bastard didn't have the guts to hang in there and stick me, ha! ha! After my second shot, he put his ass in overdrive. With that snow gear on, he wasn't twenty feet into the thick shit and—poof!—he just went invisible."

"Did you track him?" I asked.

"Nah, I was bleeding pretty good. The broadhead got an inch of my triceps. So I got my arm freed and came in. Theresa patched me up; then her man here threw me in stir when I said I wanted to go back out after the mother."

"For your own good, eh?" Nelson insisted.

"Sounds it," Cantrell agreed. "From now until the float-plane comes back, we're not leaving the lodge yard."

"Another week!" Lenore protested. "Why don't you just cut that last tree on the trail and go to the nearest town?"

"It's too far, how many times you got to hear it?" Theresa asked sourly. "I grew up in Barna. It's sixty miles beyond the logging camp, thirty-five of it by two-track. And it's a snowbelt up there, gets hit hard in these storms, eh? Those old machines aren't worth a damn. They'd bog down."

"So we stick it out, no problem," Butch said hopefully.

Phil took a step forward. "Maybe you, Abbie Hoffman, but not me."

"Pal, you're pissing me off," Cantrell said.

"Hey, hey, hey," Phil said, wagging that beefy finger at the outfitter now. "I'm the only one here who's seen Mr. Screw Loose *mano a mano*, and I'm telling you he was on top of me before I knew it. He's that good. Sure enough, I think he'd rather stay in the trees, but who's to say he won't just come in here after us? Man, he pulled Grover's body right in here and hung him on the pole while we ate dinner. If you think he's gonna stop there, you're outta your mind."

Before Cantrell or Nelson could break in, Phil barged on. "We're all good hunters or we wouldn't be here. Now this fucker's tryin' to kill us using deer-hunting tactics. I say we turn it on him, do the same to him and whoever else is with him. I'd rather die trying to cover my ass than sit in front of a fire spanking my monkey, not knowing when the shot's coming."

"We're staying inside," Cantrell said again.

"Hey, who elected you Pol Pot? This is my life you're talking about," Phil retorted. "At least put it to a vote. Majority rules, this is America, right? Well, Canada, sorta the same thing, am I fucking right?"

Cantrell glanced at his wife, who nodded. "Okay, we vote. I vote inside."

"Me, too," said Nelson.

"Make that three," Earl added.

Lenore looked at him with utter disgust. "So predictable."

"I'm not looking to die, sweet thing," Earl snapped. "We got business at home, remember?"

"What's her name, this business?" Lenore taunted. "Does she tell you you're a big, brave hombre? Or does she know how little you are?"

The Texan's fingers dug into the leather chair. "At least everything I got works, Lenore. For all that talk that body of yours does, I'm the one who knows you're all bait and switch."

Lenore's expression did not change, but her fingernails trembled. "How dare you! In public like this!"

"What's the matter, sweet thing?" Earl grinned. "Am I getting too close to the enchilada?"

She threw her drink in his face and snarled at him: "I'm sorry God screwed up my plumbing and I can't give the little man a little man to leave his computer company to. But I'm still the best thing that ever walked into your sorry-ass life. Don't you forget it."

Lenore laughed at Earl's expression as the Bloody Mary ran down Earl's face. She threaded her fingers through that thick mane of exquisitely dyed hair. Then she took us all in at a glance, and pointed at Phil. "Anyone wants to take my scalp for a trophy will have to fight for it. I'm with you, Muscles."

"You bitch," Earl said as he walked toward the bathroom.

No one said anything for the longest time after he left. Lenore fluffed her hair again and looked at us. "Don't worry about it. Earl and I . . . every now and then . . . we need to tell each other how much we . . . love each other. Finish the vote."

"Butch?" Phil said.

"Outside," he replied without hesitation, but he did not look happy.

Arnie struggled to control his voice. "I don't want to go out there again. Not after today. But I'm not waiting in here to die on my knees like that guy Pawlett. I'll hunt."

"Arnie, my man," Phil said. "All right."

Griff pursed his lips and gestured to the outfitter. "I hate to say it, Mike, but I think they're right. We have a better chance if we go after them."

Cantrell was stone-faced. "Sheila?"

"I'll stay inside."

"Guess I got to be a team player sometime," Theresa said, rolling her eyes. "Inside."

"Five for, five against," Phil said, looking at me and Kurant.

"I'm going to abstain," Kurant said. "I'm a journalist. I'm supposed to be covering this."

"Up to you, Diana."

I felt a sour giddiness low in my chest. This is what women must have suffered thousands of years ago when they gathered their children to break camp and head after their mates into unexplored terrain. Men had their hunting cults to prepare them for such upheaval. Women had no such institutions. We have always been relied upon to negotiate the vagaries of life with an instinctive optimism. A return to security in such instances often seems impossible. As it did at that moment for me.

I realized I had spent the previous fifteen years telling myself I could remain encamped in the Back Bay of Boston, sheltered from the savage issues of a life. The thinness of my philosophy now struck me as ludicrous. The hearth would have to be abandoned. "I'm going out."

"I knew she would!" Phil cried.

"But on two conditions," I added. "We try to capture, not kill, them. And neither you nor Cantrell is in charge once we begin."

"What? Who the fuck, then?" Phil demanded. "You?"

"No," I said. I pointed at the guide. "Nelson."

There was a lot of grumbling on the outfitter's part over putting Nelson in charge. But Cantrell came to see my position. The guide had worked on the estate for three years. He knew the land better than anyone. If we were to have a chance at capturing the killers, we needed a strategist who could adapt instantly as the hunt evolved.

When it was agreed upon, there appeared among us a new strength. We were taking action. We were asserting control, acting less like potential victims.

While Sheila finished up with dinner, we pored over the map. We put red pins where we'd found the intruders' footprints. White pins where we'd discovered secondary evidence, such as the felled trees. Green pins for the bodies. A blue pin for Phil's encounter.

A fragmented pattern emerged. They had killed Pawlett, then moved south toward the estate sometime in early November, felling the trees to trap us. The freshest sign was located east and north of the lodge, this side of the Dream and south of the Sticks. We would focus our efforts in that nine-by-nine-mile quadrant.

"Hundred and ten square miles is a lot to cover," Nelson was saying at dinner.

"We don't try to cover it," countered Griff. "We try to predict their movements based on the travel corridors they're using. People are creatures of habit, just like animals."

"Yeah, but don't we need to know where their camp is, where they sleep, where they eat?" Lenore asked.

"Sure would help," Cantrell agreed. "But we got no idea where that is."

"Not exactly, maybe," I said. "But if the tracks we found leading to and from Patterson are an indication, it's somewhere north of the Sticks."

"And within a few hours' hike," Butch said.

"They'll come south tomorrow," Nelson said, nodding. "If we can get them moving on our terms, we should be able to backtrack them to their camp."

"Let's not forget we know a lot about them already," Griff said.

"Like what?" Theresa asked.

"Like those cedar arrows. It means he, or they, shoot traditional recurves or longbows."

Kurant's face screwed up. "Sort of bow-hunting fundamentalists, then?"

"I think we're talking fanatics, not fundamentalists," Arnie said. "But so what?"

Griff waved his fork in the air. "The method they're using is as important to them as the end result. If they just wanted to kill us, they'd use a gun. A longbow has an effective range of maybe twenty-five yards. It forces them to be more methodical, restricts them to thick cover, says that they've hunted for a long, long time."

"You all think I'm so friggin' stupid, don't you?" Earl interjected.

No one replied. He'd been drinking hard since his verbal brawl with Lenore. She smiled grimly at us and then at her husband. "I think it's someone's bedtime."

Earl laughed and slapped the edge of the table. "You think because I let her get on me like she does that I'm a stupid shit, don't you? I see it. The way you look at me."

He didn't wait for an answer. "But, folks, I'm no stupid shit. I've made forty million bucks in my life. Earl Addison. He's a little eccentric, sure. But stupid, no, no, no."

"Little man . . ."

"Shaddup, will you for just once?!" he roared, rolling his bloodshot eyes. He waved both hands at us like a preacher. "You're the ones who're stupid. Stupid and blind."

"You got a theory about what's happening here?" Griff asked.

"You betcha, bub," Earl slurred. "You think about it.

They drag Grover into the lodge yard and hang him. Why? To scare us? Sure, I believe that."

"Tell us something we don't know, little man," Lenore said.

"Ah, sweet thing . . . that's what I love about you—you never change. They ain't coming in here with Grover just to scare us; they're doing it, or rather *he's* doing it—the one with the air-bob soles—because he feels at home doing it."

"You're drunk," Lenore said, dismissing him with a flick of her long fingernails.

"That so?" Earl said, gesturing up at the longbow and the quiver of cedar arrows hanging below the big nontypical buck above the fireplace. "Now, who's drunk, or stupid, or crazy? Not me, sweet thing. Not old Earl Addison."

"But Metcalfe's—" Kurant began.

"Who says so?" Earl interrupted. "I heard they never found the body."

My head began to thrum. And the semblance of control our decision to hunt had instilled in us now threatened to unravel.

NOVEMBER TWENTIETH

THAT THOUGHT ALMOST destroyed our little community. If James Metcalfe was alive, why was he hunting us? Could his purpose be so twisted that he'd kill his beloved illegitimate son, Grover? And who was hunting with him? I jerked in and out of sleep under these burdens and the conflicting emotions Kurant had provoked in me.

Cantrell had ordered us not to travel anywhere alone. At least one person in each group had to be armed. He gave guns to Sheila and Theresa, to Butch and to Kurant. The writer had blanched when accepting the .12-gauge shotgun.

"Carrying this goes against everything I believe in," he said as we trudged through the snow back toward our cabins. Griff had remained behind with Nelson to plot our tactics for the morning.

"The gun's just for self-defense," I said. "Anyway, we're trying to capture them."

"C'mon—it's self-defense if we stay here in the compound. Otherwise it's murder. And you know as well as I do that the way this is going, we're not capturing anybody."

I said softly, "I can't think like that."

"I'm paid to think like that."

"So you're not going in the morning?"

"I have to go," Kurant said. "It's my job. But I never saw it coming to this. I guess I have a vision of man as more sophisticated and civilized than the tribesman or . . ."

"Or the hunter?"

He stuck his chin out. "Yes."

"Well, what are you going to do out there tomorrow if you come face-to-face with Metcalfe or whoever it is? Say, 'I think the human being is above this sort of thing, so don't kill me'?"

"Don't patronize me."

"I wasn't."

"You were," he insisted.

I took in his dim form in the darkness. I wanted things, for once, to be cut-and-dried. "I didn't mean to be."

We reached my cabin. He stood on the porch while I got the door open and one of the lamps lit. I could tell he wanted to come in. Despite my exhaustion, I wanted him to come in. In the soft, flickering glow, he reminded me of Kevin, or at least what Kevin used to be. I was frightened of everything that had happened. And I needed to retreat into something that was familiar. I needed to hang onto a warm body in the night, to take hope. That's what making love is, isn't it—primal hope?

Finally I said, "Come in."

"I'd like that," he said.

He took off his coat and hung it on a peg over the wood-stove. He rested the shotgun in the corner. He took a seat in the chair underneath the buck. "You surprise me."

"Why?"

"Because you're a woman. And still you don't reject all this."

"Reject what?"

"This way of life. The killings just go hand in hand with it."

"As far as I'm concerned," I said, "this is the work of two people who are mentally ill."

"Is it? Or is it just the natural progression of the throw-back, barbaric culture in which they were raised?"

"Already developing the themes of your article, I see."

"I have to think ahead."

"So do I," I said, cooling quickly to the idea of him spending the rest of the night in my cabin, then describing it in his chronicle of our nightmare. "I'm tired now. I think you'd better go."

"Something I said?"

"Yes."

"Don't hold it against me," he said gently.

I nodded. "Whatever. You'd better go."

I shut the door behind him and sighed. I might have found a few moments of physical refuge with him, but spiri-tually I was in this alone.

I locked the door, then braced it with the chair. I turned down the lights and brought the loaded rifle into the bed-room and stood it against the wall where I could reach it.

I got into bed and tried to sleep. I kept asking myself, was he right? Was my childhood a barbaric throwback? Was my soul damned by my supplications within a pagan religion?

In fits and starts I drowsed into a troubled sleep. I cried in my dreams. Katherine appeared as she was when I was fifteen. She laid my head in her lap and stroked my hair. I understood that this was the day that I'd lost my first boyfriend, a soccer player named Stan with remarkable green eyes and powerful legs who'd also taken my virginity on a dusty bearskin rug at his father's fishing cabin. In the addled reason of the hormonal teen, I was certain I'd been cheated out of my one chance at a soul mate. I snuffled a more base description of my convictions to Katherine, who, incredibly, responded with giggles.

I'd stormed to my bedroom, not believing that she could be so callous.

"Now calm down," she soothed, coming after me. "I was laughing because I had the same breakdown after losing my first boyfriend. You'll learn that life rarely hands out soul mates on the first go-round. For the most part, we get boys posing as wise men who appear to see the whole world, but who are really fumblers who can't see past the ends of their penises."

She said this with such charity that I couldn't help but laugh.

She reached out to stroke my face. "The rough edge of each fumbler rubs you toward who you will be. When life thinks you've been disappointed enough, your soul mate will appear and you'll know immediately."

"Did you know when you met Dad?"

"Even before I met him," she replied. "I was running for

a second term, giving a speech at a garden party thrown by one of my father's cronies. Your father wandered among the delphiniums at the rear of the crowd. He was the handsomest man I'd ever seen. But it was the way that he stared off into space that got to me. For some reason it was important to me that he listen to what I had to say. I gave the speech directly to him, but he never looked at me. I went up to him later and asked him why he didn't listen to my speech. He said he did. I said he didn't, that he was looking off into the sky. He assured me he'd been watching hummingbirds feed in the tulip trees, but had used my voice as music to narrate their flight."

It was a story I'd heard countless times, but I asked as I had countless times: "You fell in love with him right then?"

"Wouldn't you?" She laughed as she always did.

I stirred in my dreams and came awake for a moment. I grimaced at the knowledge that I might have spent years with a man who would never have thought to tell me my voice was the melodic counterpoint to nature's drama. It was then that I realized that perhaps we are granted several kinds of soul mates in life; Katherine was the one I can point to with certainty.

Which is what made the winter of my fifteenth year so difficult. It was swearing-in day at the statehouse in Augusta. My father and I always went to watch her take the oath. I loved seeing her on the floor of the Senate, among all those men, standing tall.

Afterward she hosted a get-together in her office. Katherine got up on her desk. She talked about the legislation she hoped to push in the coming session.

"Maine's rivers, as much as her forests, are her spirit,"

she began. "For too long we have ignored the fact that the spirit is being slowly squeezed out of our waters by paper-mill chemicals and efforts to develop the banks of our wildest rivers.

"The legislation we'll push for will ensure that . . ." She stopped. A puzzled expression spread across her face. She looked around for my father, found him and smiled. "The legislation we'll push for will ensure that Maine and Mainers will . . ."

She tried a third time. And when that failed, she brushed back a lock of hair that had fallen across her eye. "Excuse me, won't you, everyone? I'm not feeling very well . . . the excitement . . . I'm fatigued."

Fatigued was a word one did not associate with my mother; she was one of those people who never needed more than four hours of sleep a night. My father eased his way through the crowd and helped her down. The two of us and her chief of staff got her into her office, where she could lie down on the couch. My father asked her questions, all of which she answered coherently. Fifteen minutes later she was back on her feet, ignoring my father's orders that we go to the hospital for some tests, attending to the business of legislating. But in my eyes much had changed; until that day, I'd always regarded my mother as a still water incapable of being riffled by unseen currents.

The second episode took place three months later. I came home from school on a Thursday afternoon. The legislature was on its Easter break. Katherine was at the fly-tying table my father had built for her for Christmas.

"Hi," I said.

"Hi there," she said, distracted. That same puzzled expression on her face. She held up the incomplete fly. "For the life of me, I can't remember what hackle to use."

My mother had been tying the Catskill version of the Elk Hair Caddis for as long as I could remember. "You all right?" I asked.

Katherine set the fly down on the table and stared through the magnifying glass at it. "I've been forgetting things," she said simply. My mother was forty-seven. She was renowned for her ability to cite the details of a dozen pieces of pending legislation off the top of her head. She should not have been forgetting things.

After several inconclusive tests in Bangor, we trooped south to Portland and finally to the Leahy Clinic in Boston. Three days later, they returned a verdict: Katherine exhibited all the signs of early-onset Alzheimer's. My mother was losing her mind on a daily basis.

I came awake in the cabin at 4 A.M. Tears rolled down my cheeks as I remembered how stoically she'd taken the news. She'd even managed to make a joke about how the newspaper columnists could now rightly describe activity at the statehouse as "immemorable." A month later, though, I found Katherine in her bedroom gazing at the rain-splattered window as if from a great distance.

"What's the matter?" I asked, choking at the sight.

"Oh, nothing," she replied. She bunched up the fabric of the bedspread with her fingers. "I was just thinking that I don't want to forget you or your father or this world of ours, ever."

It was my turn to draw her into the crook of my neck.

*   *   *

I got up from the bed in the cabin, lit the gas lamp and showered. Under the steaming water I wondered whether I was, in some way, the opposite of my mother. She feared that the drain of thoughts, memories and emotions would leave her a helpless fawn, lost in the forest. I feared that the overload of thoughts, memories and emotions would render me not ignorant, but frozen by the spotlight of greater awareness.

An hour later, Nelson struck his spoon against his oatmeal bowl. "The storm, thank God, has let up somewhat," he began. "We have to assume that whoever is out there will see that and come close to camp, hoping to catch us flat-footed like he did Phil."

Nelson wore a suit of brown-and-white camouflage and a green kerchief tied around his neck. He went on. "What I want to do is use a circle drive. We push him to the middle, squeezing closer and closer until we jump him."

"How big a circle?" Griff asked.

"That's the problem, eh? Mike says no matter what, we don't travel solo. Everyone works in teams. Each team carries a two-way radio. We found six of them upstairs. They have about a three-mile limit, so we'll stick to that range. If we don't sight him or cut his track in the first drive, we'll move and try again."

He brought us all to the map and pointed out the quadrant northeast of where Phil had been shot at and southwest of the skidder landing where I'd found Patterson.

The plan was this: Phil and Arnie would leave directly from the lodge, work their way along the edge of the lake for a mile, then cut north. Earl and Lenore would be dropped off about a half mile directly north of the lodge; they'd work due east. Cantrell, Sheila and Butch would drop in off the old skidder road. Nelson and Theresa would move in from just west of the skidder landing. And Griff, Kurant and I would march south along the Dream for half a mile, then work west toward a huge beaver pond, which would be our rendezvous point.

Fear is a smoldering fire in the quarter light of a rainy dawn. As we gathered our gear to head out into the pre-dawn, its sick-sweet odor wafted around us.

"How long will it take to reach the pond?" Earl asked dully. He was fighting a big hangover.

"Two and a half, maybe three hours," Nelson said. "But take your time. And each team must call me on the radio every fifteen minutes. If you have a sighting or cut a track, call immediately, eh?"

Laden with fourteen inches of new powder, the tag alders at the Dream's bank were filigreed jewelry of silver and ivory photographed in black and white. Where the water was inky and swift, ice had not yet formed. But about the boulders, the fluid had crystallized and run out blue and translucent like a winter cloud trailing a front.

As the snowcat carrying Nelson and Theresa chugged back to their set-in point, Griff walked off by himself. He stared at the river. Praying, probably. I had made my own acts of devotion before leaving the cabin.

We'd come slow up the logging road. I sat in the front seat, my head out the window looking for sign. Aside from those of deer and moose, I'd seen no man tracks that would indicate that Metcalfe, or whoever it was hunting us, had entered this section. Part of me—the part that cherished the idea of surviving all this until I held Emily and Patrick again—was happy we'd seen nothing.

Kurant put his hand on my arm. "I'm sorry I upset you last night. I felt there was something between us."

"I didn't," I said. "We're just two people thrust into a barbaric situation. Those kinds of false feelings are bound to come up."

"That's not fair."

"Nothing is," I said. "We've got something hard to do now. I don't want it to be made foggy by some romantic notion you might be carrying around."

He looked at me as if I were a stranger he'd met on a plane. Which I was. "Okay, then. Good luck."

"You, too."

The walkie-talkie on my belt squawked. Griff came toward us slowly. Heavy bags hung under his eyes. I was about to say something when the radio squawked again.

"Everybody ready and in position?" Nelson asked.

One by one, the voices came over the radio: Earl, Phil, Cantrell, me.

"Okay, then," Nelson went on. "Take your compass readings. Keep each other in sight. Move slowly. Stay in contact."

We skulked parallel to the river for about twenty minutes. We were three abreast, about fifty yards apart. I was in the middle. Kurant walked on my left, Griff on my right. Overhead there were breaks in the clouds and an eerie blue sky shone through. Replaced by a squall and then more blue.

The gusting breeze dislodged snow from the thick brush. Clumps of it fell at our slightest touch. The movement and the soft thumps as it struck the drifts kept me alert. Kurant quaked at each snowfall. He held the shotgun before him as if it were alive and feral. Until now, he'd been an observer. Now he was a participant.

The radio buzzed. "This is Cantrell. Nothing so far."

"Hard to see in here," Earl came back. "Everything's weighed down by the snow. Jumping a lot of deer, though."

"Phil?" Nelson asked.

The radio went to static for a moment, then he came back. "Not yet."

I took the radio from the holster. "We're almost as far south along the Dream as we want to be. No tracks. We're going to turn east in about five minutes."

I whistled to Kurant and Griff. I pulled out the topographical map. "We're about two miles from that beaver pond. We'll get on either side of this feeder stream and work our way along it."

"It's going to be tight in there. A lot of red willow and rushes," Griff said.

"I can't see a better way to do it, though," I responded.

He took the map and pored over it, finally nodding. "Okay, but let's close ranks to stay in sight."

Kurant motioned to a thin slide behind the tang on the shotgun. "I push this to shoot, right?"

"The safety," I said. "Then just point and pull the trigger. It's a semiautomatic. Five shots."

We moved on then, down the slope toward the feeder stream. As Griff feared, the tangle of alder and red willow in the drainage slowed our progress to a crawl. To keep in visual contact, we were forced to walk no more than fifteen yards apart. The deer had come into this slough heavy during the storm; shoots and buds of the past summer's growth had been gently nipped off; and the deer tracks and poop were everywhere. Several times we pushed them from their beds and the brush in front of us erupted with snort-wheezes and grunts and the rifle-shot cracking of branches.

An hour went by in that manner. The muscles in my forearms and upper back ached from gripping the gun stock at each invisible pop and crunch. Sweat pooled around the backstrap of my bra and at the waistband of my long underwear. A headache took shape between my eyes from trying to peer ahead through the frozen jungle.

I glanced at my companions as we passed through an opening. Kurant's face had gone ashen. Griff's cheeks sagged like those of a man in his seventies. I was worried about them.

We had just come out of that opening, and I was working right along the stream bank, when I saw them, deeply cut into the snow, emerging half frozen at the water's edge. Ahead of me, the accumulation on the puckerberry had been brushed off. I whistled softly. Griff and Kurant stopped. I pointed downward. I took the radio and hit the transmitter button twice to alert the others.

"I've got his tracks," I whispered into the radio, fighting against the pressure forming like deep water around me.

Nelson came back immediately. "Where?"

I could see them all staring at their radios, waiting for my response. The killer was ahead of us somewhere in the broad loop of the lasso Nelson had laid out. They were waiting to hear how close he was, how close confrontation might be.

"We're less than a mile from the pond," I said. "He came

THE PURIFICATION CEREMONY

THE PURIFICATION CEREMONY   187
THE PURIFICATION CEREMONY 187

in by this feeder stream. It's the one wearing the wave-sole boots. He's heading almost due east."

"Get in behind him, Diana," Nelson said. "Keep Kurant and Griff close. And I want to hear what he's doing every two minutes."

"Okay."

Cantrell came on. "First chance is our best chance. After this, he'll know we're hunting him."

I got on the track, paralleling it so as not to disturb his sign. I noted with grudging admiration the way he threaded himself, calculated and soft, between the tendril trunks of the streamside growth. I found where his wolf-skin hat had brushed through snow clinging to limbs and left hairs when he'd looked left and right. I found where he'd knelt to scout the terrain ahead. I found three holes where his fingers had probed the snow. He was examining everything, even the consistency of the surface below him. He was a good hunter, no doubt about it. The next thought turned me jittery, bloated and cramped inside; he was stalking us, even as we stalked him. Any mistake meant . . .

I shook it off. I could not think of him as a hunter. That could dull resolve. I thought of him as game. Game to be respected. Even feared. But game nonetheless.

The trick to writing a good piece of computer software is to anticipate the pitfalls and snafus that might thwart a user, leaving her frozen at the keyboard, wondering where she went wrong in the electronic wilderness. The same is true of executing a hunt. I thought ahead as I moved on the track, allowing my memory of the topographical map and my general knowledge of how the killers had moved in the past to draft scenarios as to how this one might act as he approached the beaver pond. The watercourse was his ally as well as his path. But soon he'd have to abandon it. Maybe he'd circle the pond to the north and run into Nelson or Cantrell. Or maybe he'd leave the stream bottom to cut crosswind toward the lake and those who pressed at us from the south.

We were now no more than four hundred yards from the beaver pond. The wind died. The forest took on a deep and abiding stillness that closed in around me.

The radio crackled with voices. Where was he? they were asking. Our noose was tightening. He had to be right up ahead. But there'd been no sightings. Against the back wall of all of this played the image of a nocked arrow.

I was racking my brain to devise new scenarios, when he did something I didn't expect. The track in front of me stopped. Completely. Just as it had the night I found Patterson.

I stared at the last footprint, unbelieving. It came in around me then, the same sort of electric pressure I'd felt anticipating the appearance of the bear so many years ago. I snapped my head and my gun skyward, looking into the gaps between the tree limbs around us. I felt exposed, vulnerable, trapped. "He's here!" I hissed to Kurant and Griff. "Get down!"

They threw themselves in the snow. They backed up against the trunks of larch trees, searching the forest canopy. No movement. No sound. Just our throttled breath struggling through clenched teeth. And the flicker of snowflakes. And the call of scrub jays and magpies.

The radio buzzed. I reached to turn down the squelch.

My hand was halfway to my hip when a branch high in a towering jack pine to Kurant's left wavered. Fourteen inches of snow poured off. The reporter swung his shotgun and fired at the white cascade. Three times the roar plugged off all other sound. More snow fell. A severed branch plunged to earth. I swung my rifle to the spot where Kurant had shot, safety off, fighting to see the man shape.

But there was no man. There was only the collapsing comprehension that our emotions and our will were being sucked off into the black hole created by the shotgun blast, by the loss of the track and by the knowledge that the killer had heard the shot and now had our position plotted.

The radio chattered. Earl. Then Phil and Cantrell, followed by Nelson ordering everyone to be silent.

"Diana?" he demanded. "Diana Jackman, please call in. Diana?"

I could not reach for the radio. I had become a squirrel in the shadow of a hawk, turned to stone in the conviction that wings had been trimmed to dive. A minute passed. And then another.

"Diana?" Nelson called.

"C'mon, woman," Phil said. "Just hit the transmit button if you're okay."

Finally my fingers moved. I struck the button.

"How about that!" Cantrell said. "Tell us where you are. Tell us if you need help."

Kurant's head turned. Blood trickled down his chin. His lip was split. And glowing across his cheek was a great red welt from where the butt of the ill-shouldered gun had smacked him.

"He's not here," Kurant said dully.

"Don't be so sure," Griff called back. "He could be play-ing with us."

"Oh, he's toying with us," I said.

I got the radio finally and managed to give Nelson our position and tell him we were all right. He barked orders to the rest of them to move in our direction.

I slipped the radio back into the holster, then whispered to Kurant and Griff to cover me. I wanted another look at that last track before the others arrived and obliterated the sign.

I crawled to the footprint and studied it from six inches away. He had remarkable skills. Ordinarily when an animal sets its feet back in its own track, there is a stark indication of a rolling weight in the imprint and a brushing at the edges that enlarges the volume of the sign. Here, there was the barest reflection of his rearward movement. He'd gone backward in his tracks in this nearly perfect manner for fourteen paces. It dawned on me that he was acting just like a mature white-tailed buck would when it figures out it's being pursued. My stomach went to cramps again.

I circled toward the stream and found crust from splashed water forming on the powder snow; he must have jumped sideways a good eight feet and landed in the shal-lows. I leaned out into the stream to study the overhanging branches. About fifteen feet ahead was a limb devoid of snow where he'd passed and bumped his shoulder.

I frowned.

"What's going on?" Griff asked behind me.

"He knows we're after him," I said, more to myself than to Griff. "Yet he's going forward in a situation where a deer would probably have circled to the rear. It doesn't make sense."

And then it hit me. He wasn't acting like a deer. He was acting like a big cat or a wolf, like a predator. He'd wanted us to freeze like squirrels when the track suddenly ended. He was hoping for a panicked response like Kurant's shot to give away our position and perhaps the positions of the others.

I yanked at the radio in the holster. The antenna caught in my belt. I tore at it, jerking it free finally. I fumbled with the squelch and brought it to my mouth.

"Nelson. Nelson, this is Diana. Tell everyone to—"

I jumped nearly a foot at the deafening explosion of the large-bore rifle somewhere ahead of me in the forest. Another shot, followed immediately by the unmistakable flat punch of metal striking flesh.

I was running forward now. Earl's high-toned voice came over the radio. "I got him! Hound dogs! I finally got him!"

Nelson came on. "Where? Earl, where are you?"

"I'm down below the . . ."

The transmission stopped. There was a split second of silence. I waited for him to finish.

Instead, I heard a sound burst from deep inside a man accustomed to being in control, to having things go his way. It came from three hundred yards off to my left. But the way the forest carried the sound, it changed its shape and appeared before me like a cornered animal. It pulsated, baritone and guttural at first, then broke over into a savage falsetto wail that could have shattered crystal . . . only to be cut off by a third rifle shot.

Another long silence. And then Lenore's trembling voice

crackled. "Please . . . oh, please, help us . . . don't let it be like this . . . please don't let it be like this . . .".

Lenore Addison sat in the snow in a weed patch in an old burn of perhaps half an acre. The browned seed crowns of the buck brush wafted in the bitter wind and brushed her face. She had her husband's head in her lap. Her expression had never seemed so loving. Earl gazed in the direction of the crumpled form of the biggest white-tailed buck I've ever seen in any magazine or book.

Earl was moaning: "It burns. It burns, Lenore. But look at him, sweet thing. Just look at my Booner."

Lenore stroked his face and cooed to him: "He's the prince of the forest, my little man. You did real good."

"But my legs won't move. How can I drag him to camp if my legs won't move?"

She looked up at us, tears streaming down her face. Her tough, manicured facade was gone. She was that dusty unsure girl from some backwater in Texas brush country now. "He's all I've got. What am I gonna do?"

Arnie and Phil emerged through thick spruces that rimmed the south side of the burn. Arnie took one look and rushed to Earl. "Hold him still," he told Lenore. "We don't want more damage than has already been done."

Phil took off his orange knit cap. His skull glistened with sweat. "What the fuck? I thought he shot the dude."

"That's not important right now, man," Arnie snapped.

Phil kicked at a stump. "We had him!"

"My father was a doctor," I said, kneeling next to Arnie. "I've helped in emergencies before."

Arnie nodded. "Hold him while I cut away his clothes."

The cedar shaft and the exquisite turkey-feather fletching jutted from Earl's parka low in the center of his back, just above his pelvis. Arnie drew out his hunting knife and sliced at the clothing around the shaft. The fabric tugged at the arrow once and a shudder went up through Earl and he screamed and then retched. I held Earl tighter while Arnie trimmed away the last of the wool shirt. The arrow was exposed now, and from the length of the shaft showing above his flesh, the broadhead had not penetrated deeply. There was very little blood, but it had obviously struck spine and done its work.

"Earl," Arnie said after a few minutes of palpating the area. "You've been hit bad, but not as bad as it could have been. The arrow looks to be just above the first lumbar vertebra, which means your legs may not move right now, but, depending on the damage, they may in time. And you won't lose your bowel or bladder control. The important thing right now is to get you stabilized and back to the camp. Do you understand?"

Earl let out a muffled "yes." By then, Cantrell, Butch and Sheila, and Theresa and Nelson had come into the burn.

Cantrell took one look and cried: "I knew this was a dumb idea. I knew it."

"It's my fault," Lenore whimpered.

"What happened?" Kurant asked. He had a notebook out of his pocket.

"Can't you give it a rest?" I asked. "Her husband's wounded."

"No!" Lenore said. "I want to tell him . . . I want to tell him what I did. There's a big knob back there in the woods and we were coming up to it when we heard the shot . . .

and Diana said she'd lost the track. But then we jumped this deer on the face of the knob and I knew it was a record-book buck, what Earl's been after his whole life. I told him we'd have to split up, and I'd try to drive the deer to him."

"I wanted to, sweet thing," Earl whispered. "Not your fault. I wanted to."

"I cut to my right about seventy-five yards and let him out of my sight," she continued. "I found the deer's tracks again about a hundred yards further on. He was trying to circle the far end of the knob, pushing crosswind toward Earl. I'd gone only another fifty feet when I came on a man's footprints alongside the buck's. I guess he'd seen the deer, too, and decided to run with it. I sprinted, trying to find Earl . . . to warn him . . . but before I could yell, he shot. And I thought, It's all right. Earl's shot the killer. It's all right . . ."

She paused, her lower lip quivering. "And then Earl, he screamed that awful scream. And when I could see through the brush into this opening, Earl was facedown next to the deer and that bastard was running toward him with a knife out, the wolf skin trailing off his shoulders like wings. I knew what he wanted and I was not going to let him have it. I went right at him. He heard me breaking branches coming in and he changed directions so fast, you know . . . going inside out on himself like he wasn't human, but . . . I don't know . . . an animal or something . . . I got one shot at him and I missed . . . I . . . I never miss."

She broke down and sobbed. Theresa went and put her arms around Lenore's quaking shoulders. Earl's gloved hand stroked at her leg.

"Lenore, I—"

"Clippers," Arnie said, interrupting him. "Anybody got pruning clippers in their packs?"

"My leatherman tool's got a little saw," Nelson offered.

"It'll have to do," Arnie said. He took the tool from the guide and opened it to the saw. He got some alcohol from a first-aid kit in his pack and drenched the saw and the wound.

Cantrell and Nelson held Earl's legs. Kurant and Griff got him by the shoulders. Lenore cradled her husband's head. Phil walked to the west fifty yards or so, unable to watch. Butch looked off into the snowflakes falling. Sheila knelt next to me and at Arnie's direction helped pack snow around the wound. I gripped the shaft. I tried to let my hand float with Earl's breath. When he was convinced the flesh was numb, Arnie set the saw's teeth into the arrow about a half inch above Earl's back. The saw made a grinding noise at the first bite. Earl went white, dry-heaved, then passed out.

Arnie worked in time with Earl's breathing, too. He let the teeth bite on the exhale and free on the inhale. Bits of red wood flared into the air. I watched the saw work in a failed attempt to keep my mind off the fact that I hadn't read the sign clearly. We'd had our best chance and one of us had been crippled. The killer was putting ground between us. If we were to go after him, it would have to be soon, or the wind and snow would obliterate his tracks and leave us as ignorant and as vulnerable as we'd been setting out this morning. In any case, he knew clearly he was being hunted now. And he'd tell his partner. And that made them even more dangerous than before.

The shaft broke free. Now there was just a nub of wood showing from Earl's back. The snow had reduced the swelling. The three blades of the broadhead were visible against the purpling flesh. I stared at the blades and the way they formed a Y under Earl's skin. An intersection of pain and mad purpose that I couldn't begin to comprehend.

Arnie had Phil and Butch cut saplings to form the braces and support limbs for the ribwork of a stretcher. Cantrell took drag ropes and articles of clothing from each of us. He lashed the limbs to the saplings, then cut holes in the clothes and tied them in the gaps. Arnie got smaller saplings and strapped them lengthwise along Earl's body to keep it ridged, to minimize the damage.

When the litter was complete, we all slid our hands under Earl and lifted him onto the stretcher.

"We're going to have to hurry," Arnie said. "He's going into shock."

"Can that broadhead stay in there until the plane comes?" Sheila asked.

Arnie didn't respond.

"Arnie?" Butch said. "That's six days."

"Operating could open him to more infection," Arnie said, "but depending on how he responds to the medicine, we might have to."

"You gonna cut him out here?" Phil cried. "Damn."

Lenore crossed her arms across her chest. "You're no surgeon. I want a second opinion."

Arnie shook his head. "There are no second opinions here. Just me. And I'm not going to do it unless I have to."

"Arnie, you can't . . ." Butch began.

"Shut up, Butch." Arnie cut him off. "I may be a small-

time pediatrician to you, but I'm the only doctor you got.
I'll make the call on this one."

We all looked at Earl for a moment.

"Well, what about the mother who did this?" Phil demanded. "We've got to go after him now, before he gets
away."

"No!" Cantrell said. "We tried that and look what's
happened."

Kurant said, "We probably would have had him if Earl
hadn't gotten horny to kill some innocent animal and forgotten we were out here to capture a murderer."

"You asshole!" Lenore screamed. She raced at the journalist and pummeled at his head.

Nelson grabbed her and pulled her away. Cantrell got in
the writer's face. "I've had enough of you and your smart-
guy remarks. All you've done since you've been here is do
your best to stir up trouble."

Kurant sort of smirked. "Am I wrong? If I'm getting the
facts wrong, tell me."

Cantrell gritted his teeth so hard I thought he'd break
enamel. "Fuck you!"

"Anybody ever compliment you on your agile command
of the language?"

The outfitter's punch caught Kurant square in the solar
plexus. He made an *ooomph* noise in disbelief, then reared
backward into the snow. No one moved to help him.

"C'mon!" Arnie cried. "We need to get Earl back to the
lodge. He's going into shock."

Cantrell was all business now. He pointed at Phil and
Butch. "You guys get the front. Griff and Nelson are at
the back."

Nelson cleared his throat. "Mike . . . Phil's got a point, eh? Now, hold on before you get crazy on me. This killer has made big mistakes the last couple days, missing Phil and wounding Earl. He's losing control. He'll make more mistakes. I want to take Diana and track him out of here."

"No way," Cantrell said. "I can't have any more clients wounded or dead."

I stepped forward. "We won't try to close in on him, Mike. It's only a scouting mission, try to figure out where he goes when he leaves. If we don't go after him now, the snow's going to fill his tracks and we'll be right back where we were."

Phil nodded. "Even if we don't go after him again, we can tell the Mounties where to start looking."

"Mike!" Arnie pleaded. "Earl's fading."

Cantrell threw his arm at me and Nelson. "You've got three hours," he said. "Then you turn back."

Nelson was a hunter my father would have respected. He moved surefooted, steady and aware through the tangle beyond the beaver pond. He'd taken Kurant's 12-gauge in case we jumped the killer at short range. Though it was unsaid, I understood capture was no longer an option.

We each took one side of the sign and worked it north. The killer had gone out from the burn in sprinting strides; the toes of his boots dug troughs as they exited each print; his knees dragged out hollows between the tracks. Incredibly, he'd kept this pace up for almost a half mile, then slowed and leaned against a tree and urinated. I found more wolf hairs clinging to the branch above his spoor. A quarter mile later, Nelson found a place where he'd stooped. A linear slash in the snow marked where he'd rested his bow.

Beside it was a clear print of his bare hand. Seeing it, strangely, I could see him, checking his back trail, plotting his escape. My own right hand seemed to tingle. The tingle turned to the stinging of snow robbing flesh of warmth. And that degenerated into the itch of gradual numbness and the trickle of melting snow on my wrist. I stared at my hand, not quite believing. It occurred to me that had this happened a few days before—before Patterson, Grover, Pawlett and now Earl—if it had happened when I'd been tracking a deer and not a man, I would have taken heart from the sensation; it marked, in no insignificant way, that my skills were returning to that level at which I'd abandoned them in my late teens. But I was scared of the feeling.

"You don't look so good, eh?" Nelson said.

I looked at him dumbly, then stammered, "I-I haven't eaten or h-had anything t-to drink since before dawn."

He fished in his pack and brought out a peanut butter sandwich and a water bottle. We split the sandwich and shared the bottle. He got out a cigarette.

"Can't shake the habit," he apologized. "And this doesn't seem the time to quit."

I blurted, "I know. I . . . I can feel him all around me sometimes."

Nelson gave me a queer look. "I guess."

I decided not to mention it again. We moved on. The tracks went almost due north. We climbed with them two thousand vertical feet up the central ridge. Every few hundred yards he'd loop and watch his back trail, then loop again and set out. I figured we were half an hour behind him. On the ridge top he took to the dense softwood thickets. He coursed through the jade maze with the fluid purpose of a bear that has scented dogs.

The more we followed the track, the more I found myself able to predict where he would turn, where he would circle, where he would flank and where he would run. For a while there, I thought I understood him.

"He's going to break through that saddle up ahead, then angle back about a quarter of the way down the slope on the other side," I announced.

Nelson grinned sourly. "Thinks he's a deer, eh?"

"At times he acts that way."

But when we got in the saddle, he had not crossed through. Halfway between the two knobs, he'd walked backward in his tracks, then jumped west and accelerated uphill for thirty-five yards. There he'd tucked himself inside a large blowdown spruce, then bolted, cutting cross-grain to the slope almost to the break-off point before weaving down through the saddle and up the other side. I felt sick.

Nelson scratched his head. "Guy doesn't know where he's going or why, eh? I think he's losing his marbles, that's what that shows."

I shook my head, trying to quell the nausea. "I wish it did."

I explained that I believed he was jeering at us, showing us that we could not predict his moves, that, in fact, he was predicting ours. He'd crouched in the blowdown to demonstrate he could have killed us as we advanced on the false trail.

"But one of us would have gotten him, eh?"

"Maybe," I said. "If we'd gotten over the shock."

"I don't get shocked so easy," Nelson said. "I say we push him some more."

The tracks took us to the very top of the eastern knob. He'd trotted to the edge of a rimrock, then taken a narrow game trail off the rock that forced us to face the cliff, use our hands for support and edge our way down. The sign suggested that he'd used his hands very little in his descent, which made me wonder whether he was more animal than man.

By the time I reached the bottom, I was soaked from the effort. It was nearly two-thirty. We'd been on his track almost three hours. "Cantrell said . . ."

"I know what he said," Nelson said testily. "But we're gonna give it another half hour. Up till now he's been running wild. He's got to do something we can pattern sooner or later."

We continued to drop in altitude in an easterly direction. The eerie blue sky of the morning was but memory. Clouds had returned, cold steel in color and pregnant with new moisture. The first snowflakes of the week's fourth storm fell.

"We're going to lose him if this keeps up," I said.

"Not if I can help it, eh?" Nelson snapped.

He lengthened his stride and I struggled to keep pace. On the downslope the killer's gait opened as well. I imagined him loping, a rising sea of powder snow billowing behind him. His irises were jaundiced, his pupils diamond in shape. With my gathering fatigue came questions: did his tongue ever loll from the corner of his mouth? Did his belly ever bark in emptiness? Did his throat parch? Or did he defy such human conditions?

"Bugger's a beast," Nelson cried when we reached the flat and we both stopped, bent double, gasping for breath. "He knew we'd run that slope!"

"He doesn't move like a seventy-year-old man," I said.

"Who said Metcalfe was seventy?" Nelson asked, surprised. "James was in his late fifties and hard as a rock."

"You think it's him?" I asked.

"I don't know, eh? A strange man, that James, but I never thought he'd go in for something like this. Then again, he got damned weird after Annie, Grover's mom, died. They were lovers, going way back. The old man loved her more than his real wife, that's for certain. Nancy Metcalfe was a shrew. Kids weren't much better, especially the boy, Ronny."

"Grover told me Ronny was mean to him."

"That was Grover being kind. Ronny was a sadistic little shit. You know, the kind of kid who'd blow up a frog with a firecracker. There's a story that when they were kids, he smashed Grover's pet loon over the head with a rock while Grover was watching."

"Ronny a hunter?"

Nelson thought about that for a second. "Yeah, but not as good as his father. Not by a long shot."

"But it's possible. That it's Ronny, I mean."

"At this point anything's possible, eh?"

I took it in, trying to figure out what would make James Metcalfe, a man grieving for his lost love, turn madman. Or, if it was Ronny, what would make the son of a famous hunter turn murderer. I could come up with no answers that satisfied me.

"Where are we?" I asked, changing the subject.

"About a quarter of a mile from where Griff had his stand the first day," Nelson said.

Something clicked deep inside me and I stared at him in disbelief. "We've got to move! He's going to lose us in the water!"

And then we were racing over fallen logs, through poplar whips, over hummocks swept clean of snow by the wind, slipping on the long-forgotten frozen red earth that did not offer solace, only a covenant of the unknown. The brush grew thick in the drainage bottom. We crashed into it. Thorns snagged at our clothing. We were close targets in the brake, but dread did not accompany me; I was the sudden welcome sister of a harpy, praying for conflict.

I beat Nelson to the stream bank, sliding up to it on my knees, my safety off, my index finger poised at the trigger. Earl's attacker had gone to the rushing water cleanly and not exited the other side. I looked for silt in the streambed. I peered at the snow on the overhanging brush for clues to the direction he'd taken. There was nothing but the patina of new snow on old snow and, under it, dead branches and, under them, the aerated fury of water.

I sat cross-legged, leaned my head against my gun and cried; it was my vote that had brought us out here today, my vote that had put an arrow in a man's back. And when it counted, my skills had failed me. Water travel was part of his pattern, his willful use of Power, but I had not anticipated his using the stream again.

Nelson came in behind me, huffing and choking with

exertion. He glanced at me and then at the last track. He watched the stream for a very long time while I composed myself.

"Must have gone on his hands and knees out of here, eh?" he said at last. "Got to want to leave a place something fierce to crawl in ice water."

I got out some tissues from my pocket and blew my nose. I pressed snow to my eyes to reduce the puffiness. "I don't think physical pain enters into his reasoning," I said. "He's beyond it."

That idea bounced around me during the hike south in the unfulfilled hope we'd find his exit trail this side of the Sticks. It sat on my shoulder on the long trudge out to the logging road in the twilight and in the pitch-darkness and driving snow while waiting for Cantrell. It would not leave me, even when we'd reached the lodge and I'd slumped in a chair to drink the steaming-hot cup of coffee Sheila gave me while Theresa bustled around her man. If Earl's attacker was beyond pain, death did not matter; he'd already experienced it in some manner and been reborn as this monster hunting us.

Arnie had moved a bed down into the great hall, where Earl could be cared for. He'd shot the businessman full of Demerol, then opened the wound enough to lay in a shunt he'd fashioned from the trimmed finger of a rubber glove to drain off the fluids that pooled around the broadhead. He had Lenore spoon-feeding Earl mass dosages of antibiotics he'd crushed and dissolved in boiled water. Still, the pediatrician looked worried.

"We've got to keep a close eye on the shunt for evidence of spinal fluid," I heard him tell Cantrell. "If we find it, it means his spinal column would be open to infection, which threatens his brain."

"Jesus." The outfitter ran his stubby fingers through his beard. He looked haggard and beaten and in need of a deep sleep.

"We're not there yet," Arnie said. "I just wanted you to understand what we're up against here. I've got him on antibiotics, but I don't know if I have enough for six days."

"What about cutting the broadhead out?" Cantrell asked.

Arnie grimaced. "If the tip of the broadhead is just touching the spine, then we're better off leaving it as it is and trying to make him comfortable. I try to cut it out, I run the risk of opening a spinal column that was intact."

"And what if the broadhead's in the spine and there is fluid coming out?"

Arnie rubbed at his forehead. "A close call. Maybe you try to cut it out, irrigate it and provide drainage. Maybe you don't. It's a no-win situation. Either way, he's going to get much worse before we get him out of here."

"So what do you want from me, Doc?"

"A watch schedule," Arnie said. "Someone must be with him around the clock. I'll be here, too. But I'll need sleep in case he crashes and I have to operate."

"Done. No one's leaving the compound anymore anyway."

I'd been listening to it all with my eyes shut. I opened them to find Kurant listening to the conversation and taking notes. I closed my eyes. I couldn't believe I'd considered sleeping with him. Then again, I thought, no man is an island. No woman for that matter, either, though I can believe that a woman must at some level be an atoll, a ring of islands connected by reefs. Our outer shores take terrible beatings, but we offer shelter in the lagoons we create at our center.

I allowed myself a wry smile at the thought. And then, whirling out of my subconscious, it hit me. And I sat up straight and looked over at the enlarged topographical map of the Metcalfe Estate. I walked over to the map and stared at the little sliver of brown in the thick swath of blue. I shivered in understanding, knowing for certain now where the killer was camped.

NOVEMBER TWENTY-FIRST

I WENT OUT from the cabin three hours before dawn, skirting the pines on the lakefront. Six new inches of snow had fallen. The air had warmed. The snow was wet. I kept to the shadows thrown by the gas-lights mounted on the corners of the porch of the main lodge and headed for the storage shed next to the icehouse, where the bodies of Patterson and Grover lay.

The corroded bolt to the shed wailed when I drew it. I waited five minutes after the noise cut the night. No movement in the house. No sounds but the whispers of snow. I got inside and flipped on my flashlight. Rubber chest waders hung on a nail above the snowmobiles. I took them and lashed them across the top of my knapsack. I would need them where I was going.

The knapsack rode awkwardly now with the top-heavy

weight of the waders, but I shrugged off the discomfort and went out into the stormy night. I shut the door and drove the bolt home with a second cry. A baton of light flared in my eyes. I held up my hand to block the blaze. "Who's there?"

The light dropped toward my waist. Lenore stood on the bottom step of the back porch, a blanket wrapped around her shoulders. She was still in her hunting clothes from the day before. Her features had retreated, leaving her bone-exposed like an animal after a severe winter.

"I can't sleep. I saw you come by the window. Where are you going?"

"To find the killer's camp."

Lenore took several steps toward me. Her expression was grim, her color unnaturally pale. "Earl's stoned on those drugs Arnie gave him. He moans and sweats."

She paused and the faintest smile crossed her trembling lips. "He calls my name. Not the others'. Mine. Lenore. But he can't hear me and I can't help him."

I didn't know what to say. I was beyond her now, already going deep into the forest of my mind. "Please don't tell them where I've gone."

"I don't know where you're going," she replied honestly. "But if you do find it and they are sleeping, remember my husband and . . . cut their throats."

There are women who believe they have suffered so much they have inured themselves to suffering. Lenore seemed one of those women. I wanted to tell her that if you live long enough, however, you find that the tapestry of this existence is composed of knots of wracking seizures and recoveries. Lenore did not realize the jumbled perceptions that accompany ruthless pain had only just begun to weave themselves around her. That she would have to discover for herself.

I walked away from her, head down into the storm. I passed the dim frozen forms of the hanging deer on the pole. Their carcasses shifted in the wind. The racks of the biggest ones clacked against each other—it is the sound you hear deep in the woods when the rut comes on and the bucks, driven by forces beyond their control, enter the annual rites of madness. I shivered at the clacking and hurried to get beyond the noise.

I took a straight route out the logging road to the east-west road. I figured I had at least a three-hour head start before my absence would be discovered. They would not find my tracks because I would take my cue from the killer; I would go to water and move forward into the end of something, leaving no trail behind me.

The darkness embraced me. There is a resonance to moving with only a thin shaft of light to guide you in such darkness. The night presses and pulses around you. It threatens and soothes, turns the snow under you to pumping mottled cream, like the wings of hawks at dusk. I kept my sanity under the pressure of the darkness the way I'd been keeping it since I'd arrived. For years I'd stood outside myself, able to live with what I'd become by watching Little Crow as if she were separate, a creature in a cage to be studied and, at times, pitied. But in these past few days, and certainly within the past twelve hours, I'd moved within Little Crow, not in retreat, but in exploration, searching for the sign of who I'd been before my mother died.

In the months after I'd comforted her in her bedroom,

Katherine had a stable period. By early spring of the following year, however, it was apparent that she was sliding by inches into a state of alternating realities, of clarity and then of murkiness. We'd find her running her fingers over framed family photographs in the den. She called Bert the postman "Charley." She asked why Mitchell, dead nearly six years, hadn't come down to dinner.

And she got lost on opening day of trout season. I'd gone south along the riverbank that morning, while she said she was going to one of her favorite pools. We'd agreed to meet at ten and move to another section of the river. Ten came and passed. I walked upstream toward her pool. In one of the last patches of snow beside the bank, I discovered her prize six-weight bamboo fly rod and her wicker creel. The water above the pool was high and frothy. I ran along the bank, looking for her tracks. I found none.

"Katherine!" I screamed. "Mom!"

There was no sound but the rushing water. I was sixteen years old. I panicked and jumped into the river and crossed to the other side. I ran frantic like a bird dog in cover. A half hour later, I found her on her knees in a shallow, turning over rocks to see what sort of nymphs she could find. When she heard me, she looked up and smiled.

"Honey, I didn't know you were coming to fish today."

"It's opening morning, Katherine," I said, kneeling beside her. "I'm always with you opening morning."

"Opening morning?" she said. "Imagine that! It feels like I was fishing here just yesterday."

I reached out and touched her hair. Her scent and the river's mixed and swirled around me. "Let's go home now," I said.

My father was the one who had to tell her. He took her down to her gazebo in early June. I watched from the window. She fought at first. Her arms flailed and she took on that imperious pose I'd seen her use with visiting lobbyists standing in the muck of her casting pond. But my father had delivered bad news to a thousand families. He held firm. I could see a brownout of the energy that always seemed to render her skin electric. Her knees buckled and she fell into his arms. I went to the bathroom and threw up.

Two weeks later, just as the summer began, Katherine resigned her seat in the State Senate. She made light of the event, but it was apparent in her carriage that jettisoning her position had blurred the edges of her being.

She fished most every day that season. Each morning I awoke to the whip and ring of her fly line extending out over the pond. It was as if she believed that the constant attention to the mechanics that had been her personal Tai Chi since childhood could give her a grappling hook on the shale slope she now lived on.

And surprisingly, for almost a year, it did. When Katherine took to waters, she assumed the lucidity of a spring-fed stream. Sporadically, when she was doing well, she spoke of writing books or teaching a course at the university in Orono. But by the fall of my seventeenth year, the number of days when her mind turned muddy rivaled the clear ones.

The day before my father and I left for deer camp that November was one of her bad days. A friend had offered to stay with her. I went to kiss her good-bye and she grasped my hand as if she'd never hold it that way again.

As I made my way through the darkness, leaving the

Metcalfe lodge far behind, I admitted that in many ways she never did hold my hand like that again. It was our first good-bye.

Funny, I could feel her fingers when I left the east-west road after two miles. They stroked my palm and became the fingers of Emily and Patrick: Emily's reaching for me the day I moved out of the house under court order, Patrick's waving slowly from his bedroom window.

I took a compass reading. I headed true north toward the ridge I'd climbed with Nelson the afternoon before. Another half hour and I reached the stream where we'd lost the track. I lay on my back in the gloom before dawn, tugged off my boots with the snow pelting my face and wriggled into the chest waders. I repacked my knapsack. I entered the stream, breaking through the ice that had formed at the edges, working my way into the flow. The water squeezed at the waders, numbed my feet and created in the furious manner of its passing the sense that I was abandoned now by the worlds within and behind me.

I sloshed forward with my heart pressed into every rib in my chest. In the gathering light, I held the gun in front of me, barrel ahead, to part the branches that overhung the stream. I believed that at last I understood what pattern there was to the killer's movement. The ripple prints and the air-bob prints were made not by two people, but by the same person shedding hunting boots for waders. In the chest-high waders, he could use the watershed to travel without leaving sign, then switch to the air-bob soles to make his stalks.

The Sticks and this stream were routes of entry into his hunting ground; the Dream and its tributaries were his escape routes. Unless the wind was out of the west, as it was now. Then the pattern was reversed. If I was right, I would not encounter the killer on the way to his camp; he would head south along the Dream, his nose into the wind. I would have the chance to invade his camp while he set about his crazed purpose miles away.

Full daylight had come by the time I reached the Sticks River. The swift current nearly spun me around several times in the first hundred yards and I moved to the shallows despite the difficulty I had cracking through ice to make headway. I slid my feet around the submerged slick rocks and over driftwood that jutted from the ice like gnarled hands. The roar of the river covered any noise I made.

Where I could, I hugged the bank so I might peer down-stream unnoticed. Twice, deer broke from the flat in front of me, startled to scent and then witness my half-drowned form. At nine-thirty the water went white; I was approaching the confluence of the Sticks and the Dream.

I had almost been within sight of the killer's camp the very first day of the hunt, when I'd tracked the monster buck and failed to get a shot. On the map, the island where the rivers joined appeared to be no more than ten acres. Nelson had described it as piece of rock. But when at last the island came into view, it was thick with young poplar. At its center was a granite outcropping, jutting from the pale-trunked trees like a man's bald pate appearing from thick side hair and a beard. I swallowed at the sense it all made now. According to Micmac tradition, the joining of rivers is a place of tremendous Power. I could feel the mixing of energies, but beyond what the waters generated there was something more, something unstable, something deadly.

The cold had penetrated deep into my muscles, and my knees ached so badly I was almost in tears. But I dared not leave the security the water afforded me. I hid myself in the roots of a tree washed sideways and lodged between two boulders at the point where the Sticks collided with the Dream. I laid my rifle in the branches. I used my binoculars to peer the sixty yards across to the island. There were footprints in the snow coming down to the far shoreline.

Slipping from my hiding place, I waded along the bank until I found his tracks exiting the water. They were fresh, maybe a half hour old and heading south. I was safe. I took a step and immediately tripped and floundered in the shallows. My right foot was tangled in something below the waterline. I reached down, doing my best to ignore the way the freezing water numbed my bones all the way to my shoulder, and tugged at the rope until it freed itself from my foot. A heavy-duty yellow nylon rope connected to a grappling hook. I looked around and found where the hook had scarred the thick exposed roots of a big pine on the bank. I had to lean with all my weight to get the hook set. The rope stretched taut above the water all the way to the island.

Now it was as if the island were some great magnetic center and I was being pulled to it; I wanted to invade his camp, understand his Power and leave without him knowing I'd been there. I dug in my pack and got out my drag line and tied a loop about three feet in diameter around the yellow nylon rope. I strapped my gun to the top of the knapsack and shouldered it, then passed my head and arms through the loop; if the current managed to tug me from the lifeline and the river flooded the waders, it would keep my body attached and my head above water.

That never happened. Through some strange coincidence, the collision of the rivers had, over time, piled up a series of boulders and a sandbar between the shore and the island. I was able to cross in about fifteen minutes without the white water ever reaching the top of the chest waders. But by the time I made the far shoreline, my fingers were so cold they barely moved and my feet felt as if they were encased in shattered glass.

From the water I stared at the ripple footprints he'd made. I turned backward and slipped my ripple-soled boot into his tracks and retreated into the thicket, my mind as alert as it has ever been. There were no smells here save the iron scent of snow, no taste but aluminum at the back of my throat, no noise except the river and the faint rush of blood at my temples. And none of that thick, watching presence I'd sensed twice in the woods.

The track circled the hill to the east and climbed. I grimaced at the effort required to ease my boots into his prints without altering them and prayed for a skiff of snow to obscure whatever minor changes I'd surely made in his tracks. But for only the second time this week, the air was void of snowflakes. About forty yards up the hill the footprints abruptly stopped before a pile of branches. I tugged at the pile and it slid away to reveal the mouth of a cave about waist-high.

I'd like to say that I was brave at that moment, but I was not. I made up reasons not to go inside. I made up reasons to go back to the river and to the lodge and, in retrospect,

I should have. But a voice inside me kept saying I had to go in. I had to see the lair.

Peering inside, I was surprised to discover that after a tube of perhaps eight feet, there was a cavern into which a weak shaft of light streamed. I crawled down the tunnel, pushing my pack and gun before me. I stood up inside a rock room about fifteen feet wide by twenty feet long and ten feet high. There was a cleanly broken fissure two feet long and six inches wide on the right wall where it met the roof. A plastic tarp had been fixed over the hole to keep the snow out yet let the light in. Below the fissure lay a fire ring; he could pull the tarp, light his fire and let the smoke escape after dark. From my calculations, the fissure faced east; the smoke and whatever other light source he used would not be seen from the shore of the estate.

Despite the fissure, the room was dim. I got out my flashlight and shone it around. I suppose I expected to find the place stinking of death and in total disarray, a reflection of the terrible mental disorder I had come to believe was behind the killings. Metcalfe, possibly. Or Ronny, his son, the one who'd returned only once. Or something more twisted, someone who was in here hunting us solely for sport.

But there was nothing ghoulish about the room. I took a quick inventory. Spruce boughs had been hung to give the air the pleasant odor of the forest. Cooking utensils were piled neatly in a corner. A sleeping bag rolled and stored on end. Clothes and boots arranged inside the sort of rubberized duffel bag canoers use. Firewood and kindling split and stacked near the fire ring. Much of the cave floor was covered with deer skins, some new, some old, all of them laid out in a manner I understood was based on some logical system but failed to fully grasp. The effect was that of the mysteriously austere, regimented, yet distinctly hallowed feeling of photographs I'd seen of the interiors of Zen monasteries.

I went over to the duffel bag and dug through the clothes and odd gear, looking for some clue to the killer's identity. He had money, no doubt. Everything about the equipment—from the miniature propane stove to the mess kit to the insoles to his boots—was state-of-the-art and expensive. But there was nothing that spoke to his character. I was digging around in the bottom of the duffel when my fingers closed on a flat piece of canvas. The green khaki billfold had a stiff backing and was strapped shut with Velcro. Inside there were three photographs.

The first showed a dark-featured man wearing sparkling-white cotton pants and shirt embroidered with brilliant red thread and adorned with equally brilliant blue, yellow and red tassels at the waist and wrists. He sported an umbrella-shaped hat with similar tassels and a crest of bright orange and blue feathers on top. The man was balanced on one foot—arms outstretched—on the edge of a cliff high above an arid plain. Two women with long black hair and cotton skirts and shawls watched. The effect was chromatic and haunting.

There was an adobe house in the second photograph. The picture was shot in the early morning. A golden light warmed the blue door and the massive oak tree in the yard. Peacocks and guinea hens mingled in the foreground.

The last snapshot was a portrait of a woman. Brown-eyed, brunette, an oval face, soft, pleasant features, a loving smile turned toward whoever held the camera. My first thought was: She's beautiful. My second: She was familiar. I'd seen her before or someone who looked just like her. But where? I racked my brain, but came up with nothing.

I put the other two photographs back in the billfold and stuffed it in the bottom of the duffel bag. Her picture I put in the map pouch around my neck, then stood and turned, taken aback to discover that there was an opening about a foot wide in the corner of the far wall of the cavern.

There are places in this world that are undeniably saturated with dark energies—city alleys, the rookeries of ravens, empty old houses—and I could feel that whatever lay around the corner in the next cavern was one of those places, only more threatening.

Go ahead, I told myself, *you've come this far. Finish it.* I had to will myself across, careful not to disturb any of the meticulously arranged possessions. I stood before the black space for several minutes until I could goad myself to step forward one last time.

I was struck first by the scent of candle wax and then by a sick-sweet smoky odor I couldn't identify, and then, unmistakably, by the smell of decaying meat.

I flipped on the flashlight to behold a shrine. There was the fresh cape of a deer turned hair side out, stretched in an oval of ash saplings and hung flush to the wall above a rock outcropping. The rack of a ten-point buck hung at the top of the shrine. Below the horns, the feathers of hawks, or owls and of ravens linked together in a half-moon-shaped fan by animal sinew and by tiny wooden beads, black and blood-red and forest green. There were three arrows, the shafts of which were painted bright yellow. The feathers, however, were not fletched in a traditional manner; rather, they appeared to be bunches of eagle feathers loosely bound to the cedar just below the nock. And below the arrows, the skull of what had to be a wolf, boiled free of flesh, dull white. Bright red candle wax ran from the skull's sockets like tears. Wax from a dozen or more white candles caked each end of the out-cropping in thick slabs and had dripped down the face of the rock.

I shivered and looked over my shoulder, knowing I should leave. Within the empty cavern behind me grew the unmistakable sense of danger. I tried to get my legs to move, but my attention was drawn back toward the shrine. There, below the wolf's skull, at the center of the out-cropping, stood a larger, framed version of the snapshot of the pretty brunette. I took two steps toward the picture, saw more, froze and fought off a rising nausea. Arrayed around the photograph were four human scalps. *Patterson's. Grover's. Pawlett's. And one other. An altar. A trophy room. Both.*

Without warning, my heart seized the way it had in the forest the day of the hunt when I suspected someone was watching me.

"Kauyumari said you'd be the one who'd come," a deep voice behind me growled.

I started and screamed. My gun, which had been resting against my hip, fell and struck hollowly on the stone floor. I stared at the gun, my escape, gone.

"Know my name? Know my name?" the voice asked.

"James Metcalfe?" I said.

He laughed and said again, "Know my name?"

"No."

"Turn," he said, satisfied at my answer. "Slowly, or I will deliver you to Tatewari now."

I was seeing it all now—her photograph, the shrine, the scalps, the cavern walls, my gun on the floor, my gloved hands—as though I were looking through the wrong end of a set of binoculars; the world appeared far away, small and curved. Trembling, I pivoted to find a cedar arrow straining against a taut string and the flared arms of a long-bow, all pointed dead at my chest. The illusion was that a pale gray wolf held the bow; the animal's pelt had been meticulously cut and sewn so that it clung to the top of his head and over his brow down to his nose like a second skin. The cape hung around his shoulders and melded into a silver-flecked beard and from the beard into a suit of white fleece camouflage. I had the sudden and horrible realization this must have been the last thing seen by Paw-lett and Grover and Patterson and whoever had lived below that fourth scalp.

He motioned for me to move by him into the main cavern, and in that motion I understood he possessed tremendous, fluid strength. As a child, I had heard Mitchell tell stories of people he called *Kinapaq*. Unlike the *Puoin*, the *Kinapaq* manipulated Power for their own ends. In Micmac myths, the *Kinapaq* could run like the wind, toss boulders across rivers, hold their breath for hours under water. I'd always laughed at the idea; despite the fact that at times I'd had inexplicable experiences that Mitchell and my father attributed to Power, at a certain level I still did not fully believe in it. Power and the six worlds were the stuff of legends, legends that gave meaning and a sense of ancient history to our way of life. But they weren't real.

Now I didn't know. I got a feeling about him that I had never experienced before; I knew that if I tried to fight or flee now, he would kill me instantly.

"Kneel," he commanded when I'd reached the middle of the cave. "Hands behind your back."

I swallowed hard, but did as he asked.

He slipped behind me. The bow limbs squeaked in protest. The tip of the broadhead pricked me at the back of neck, and it was all I could do to keep from crying out. He took hold of my wrists with one hand and quickly tied them together with wide strips of deer hide. He gagged me with a red handkerchief.

He forced me facedown on the deer skins and tore the waders off me, then tied my ankles together with longer strips before sitting me upright against the wall of the cave. He threw a tanned deer cape over my legs, turned without a word and went into the alcove. He come out immediately, carrying my rifle and one of the yellow-shafted arrows.

"Kauyumari said you'd be the one to come," he said again, unloading the gun. "He says you are the only one with a true sense of the forest. I left the island this morning so you would enter of your own will."

Don't whine. Don't struggle, I thought. Let him talk. Let him reveal himself. Know the deer, my father used to say.

He retracted the bolt to retrieve the bullet in the chamber. He knelt in front of me and checked the lashes around my ankles. "Don't try to escape," he said. "I will know where you run before you do."

I nodded, knowing somehow that what he said was true. He crawled out the tunnel with my gun.

Until then I'd been relatively calm. It was as if it were all happening to someone else and I was standing there watching. Now, alone in the dim confines of the cave, the weight of the situation bore down and I began to shake. I summoned up every ounce of mental energy to stop it. I knew he knew I was frightened, but I didn't want him to see it. He had not made any untoward movements so far and I was afraid that any physical demonstration of weakness would provoke an attack, as it would if he were a predator and I a crippled forest animal. I had to show him I was strong.

Several minutes of deep, controlled breathing managed to quell the tremors, only to give way to a profound sense of weakness as the adrenaline left my system. I struggled feebly against the lashes. Who was he? He had an ageless quality about him. He could have been Metcalfe or his son, Ronny. I realized I had no idea what either man looked like; there were no pictures or paintings of any of the Metcalfes in the lodge. That was more than strange, and yet I hadn't thought of it before. Questions raced through my head. Were the pictures of the Metcalfe family removed on purpose? Who was this person—Kauyumari—who'd said I'd come? What was the significance of the other photographs I'd found in his gear—the one of the man balancing on the cliff and the other of the adobe house? Who was the fourth person who'd given a scalp? Why hadn't I felt him coming the way I had in the woods? My mind raced in circles, considering and discarding theories, until all was a jumble and I felt terribly tired.

*   *   *

I must have dozed, because when I opened my eyes again, he was sitting cross-legged on one of the deer skins about six feet away, studying me. There were two yellow arrows before him in a cross formation and beside them a gourd of water and beside it the wolf skin that had been removed from his head to reveal a thick shock of steel-gray hair. He must have been remarkably handsome once, but that seemed to have been drained from him, leaving a gaunt, bony face above the beard line and thin, almost blue lips. I could see his eyes clearly now—the irises were a willow green, the pupils hugely dilated and black, the whites filmy and bloodshot. The most tortured eyes I've ever seen.

He reached out and untied the gag, then sat back.

We held each other's gazes for several minutes. My heart caught again. It was as if he actually had the ability to reach inside and read me. I turned away, sickened by the sensation, but it did not cease.

Finally I blurted, "Are you Ronny Metcalfe?"

He said nothing.

"If you won't tell me who you are, at least tell me why you're doing this sick thing."

His body squeezed up tight, hinting at something unfathomable simmering below his tranquil outward surface. For a second I feared it would boil over and I would be swept away. Instead, his eyes became glassier, heavier, and he said thickly, "I've seen the pouch around your neck. You have Indian blood in you, don't you?"

"Micmac and Penobscot," I replied.

"Northern Woodland, Algonquin." He nodded. "What is your name?"

"Diana," I answered. "Diana Jackman."

"No, your Indian name."

I hesitated. "Little Crow."

That seemed to satisfy him. "Little Crow, I watched you in the woods. You are a fine hunter. You come to it with reverence. Very rare. And yet trailing behind you, like a shadow, is a sadness, a confusion that you are unwilling to face."

I started at that. "I . . . I'm just here to hunt."

He laughed, but there was no feeling in it. "I see things others do not. We are kindred spirits, I think."

In spite of myself, I snapped, "We have nothing in common. I don't kill people for sport."

"Sport!" he roared. "This is no sport! I'm here to cleanse the filth that has defiled the hunt, to purge the evil liquid that now festers within the great ceremony, to render balance where there is none!"

He was on his feet now, raving, kicking over pots and pans. He held a wicked-looking knife with a black stone blade and a deer-antler handle. I scooched back against the wall, cowering from his rage.

"Kauyumari and Tatewari have commanded me to come here," he fumed. "Here there is no sacrifice and thanksgiving for brother deer. There is just the pursuit of trophies and all of it . . . all of it orchestrated by him, the one who corrupted the sanctity of the hunt to begin with. Him! Sanctioned in his evil deeds by the laws of *civilized* man, making his money from it!"

He yanked at his hair, then coiled himself down to pluck the two yellow arrows from the floor of the cave. He held one in each hand and closed his eyes halfway and began to shuffle, almost a dance really, in slow, purposeful circles around the firs. As he moved, I could sense the frenzy draining from him.

Tears streamed down my face. I could not help it. Finally he stopped before me. "Can you understand?" he asked softly.

I shook my head, snuffling.

He knelt in front of me. "I've scared you, haven't I? I'm so sorry. Do you know you remind me of someone I loved?" And he reached out to stroke my face.

I jerked away from his touch, but he smiled. "You think I'm a barbarian, but I'm not. I am an educated man. I did my doctoral thesis on the Huichol peoples of the Sierra Madre. Do you know the Huichol? I've been living among them again since the abomination."

"I've never heard of them," I said, trying to keep him talking about something that seemed to soothe him.

"We worship the deer," he announced. "Deer is Kauyumari, the messenger between man and God, whom we call Tatewari. Deer also brings Peyote to earth. Peyote is as sacred to the Huichol as the deer. Peyote and other plants in the desert bring visions of Tatewari to the taker."

If he caught my befuddlement, he did not show it. Instead, he looked out into a distant place and spoke tenderly. "Once, a long, long time ago, the Huichol lived in Wikuta, the hallowed high desert. We were a hunting society and the deer was our brother. Even now, when a Huichol hunts a deer, he does not try to chase it as you or I might do here. Instead, we look for a deer that will stand and face us and not run. Then we set snares where he lives and catch him so that we might talk to the deer as our brother, to tell him why he must die so we may live. It is difficult because before he dies, the deer talks to us with his eyes and breaks our hearts.

"When a Huichol kills the deer in the sacred way, he finishes by offering prayers to Tatewari and to Maxa Kwaxi, elder brother deer," he continued. "When all is consumed, the bones are buried in the forest so that deer may regrow from his bones."

He laughed. His face radiated with animation. He touched the side of his nose. "We hunt Peyote the same way in the same place, the Wikuta, the sacred desert. Kauyumari is there, too. We believe, in fact, that deer comes from the sky and where he lands, Peyote is found. Therefore Peyote must be tracked and shot with an arrow like deer."

He fell silent and sighed at the memory. I was trying desperately to understand him, to figure out what the murders had to do with it all. "Do you see yourself as a Huichol?"

He laughed, this time a real laugh. "I am more than a Huichol," he said. "I have trained these past few years to become a *Mara'akame*, what you might call a shaman. I lead the hunts for deer and for Peyote and Kieli, which also brings great visions. In my visions I am one of the wolf people who came before all of us. Wolf is my animal ally. He has led me here to purify that which has been desecrated."

"Why us?" I demanded. "We've done nothing illegal, nothing to hurt you."

He ignored me. He stood suddenly and ran back into the alcove, returning immediately with a small drum, the deer horns, the third yellow arrow and a buckskin pouch about eight inches long. He sat across from me a third time. He reached into the pouch and brought out what appeared to be a short length of animal intestine filled with blood.

"This is deer's spirit," he informed me, unwrapping a piece of sinew he'd used to tie the intestine shut. He smeared some of the blood on his fingers and then, before I could react, smeared the blood on my face in long streaks.

"Don't. Please," I begged, recoiling from the moisture on my skin.

"I can tell that in your way you worship the deer, too, Little Crow," he went on. "But you have unfinished business with deer. Because I have respect for you, I will help you complete your business before I have to go."

"No," I said. "Please, I don't want to—"

"In some ways, you know," he interjected, "the Huichol are children. They hunt only Peyote and deer and Keili and raise corn and believe these are the ways to know God.

"But I have learned that there are other paths into the spirit world. There are some *Mara'akame* among the Huichol who disapprove of the men I have sought out in the far reaches of the Sierra, the men who have taught me other ways to talk with Tatewari."

His face screwed up and he hissed through his teeth, "They cursed me for following these men and learning these paths. They said ingestion of the Datura plant would lead to madness. But I wanted answers Peyote would not give me. Datura has given me the wolf as an ally, has given me the vision."

He cocked his head. "Do you think I was wrong?"

He said this last with such intensity that even though I

had no idea what he was talking about, I shook my head. "No," I said. "I believe knowledge is a good thing."

He nodded, but said nothing more. He arranged the arrows in a splayed pattern around the drum, tips pointed outward like the points on a compass. He dripped blood on the yellow arrows, smeared blood on his own cheeks and started to chant, low at first, then gradually increasing the volume until the sound echoed off the roof of the cavern. Despite a hoarse, hollow voice, the singing was beautiful, and though I knew not the language, I understood he was talking to his Tatewari, the God of the Sierra Madre.

Now his every action turned gesture, precise, ritualistic, layered with meaning I felt but did not comprehend. He reached into the buckskin pouch again and removed a stout wooden pipe with a short stem and then another, smaller pouch. He unwrapped the pouch, still singing, and a stench, acrid and fungal, filled the space between us. He plucked a wad of a dark, stringy mixture from the pouch and thumbed it into the bowl of the pipe, then set the pipe on the drum.

He stood and placed the wolf's cape back over his head, then bowed in four directions before padding once more clockwise around the fire ring, all the while singing in that hoarse, hollow voice.

After completing the circle three times, he knelt, got stick matches from the pouch, lit one and held the flame to the bowl. The sick-sweet smoke I'd smelled in the alcove belched forth from the pipe. He sucked on it and held his breath before releasing a cloud of gray. His eyes fluttered and threatened to close, but he shook this off.

"An old wise man of the Sierra taught me the mixture,"

he said, holding the pipe stem toward me. "Datura, Keili—
the tree of the wind—Peyote, cannabis and the mushroom.
He called it the path to past visions. I call it memory smoke.
Memory is how I see Tatewari's purpose for me. What is
God's purpose for you, Little Crow?"

He gestured for me to take the pipe in my mouth. I shook
my head violently and gritted my teeth. "No, I don't want
any."

He reached around the back of my head and took hold
of my hair. I struggled, but he held me in a vicious grip,
wrapped his lips around the pipe bowl and blew smoke
back out the stem into my face. I held my breath as long
as I could; then he took his other hand and pinched my
nose shut and he shook my head as if he were disciplining
a dog. I screamed and gulped air and the smoke that now
surrounded us like fog.

He retreated after seeing that I had made several great
inhalations of the smoke. He returned to his singing, which
now seemed to hang around me like a warm blanket. I
delighted in his voice. I focused on him and on the plumed
arrows he waved about him as if he were sweeping the air.
The plumes left contrails of glittering red and yellow floating in the space between us.

The cave wall beyond him sparkled and pulsated, and
my ears rang and I felt a heaviness at the base of my skull
that quickly spread down my spine and up over the top of
my head, pooling like a hot, comforting liquid behind my
eyes. My head seemed to separate from my body and ex-
pand and become its own distinct being, capable of hearing and touching and seeing everything. The pattern of the
green lichen on the walls of the cave came alive, swelled

and ebbed with each of my breaths, mutating into a thousand distinct designs.

I stared at the wall for what seemed an eternity; and then I was aware of him again. His eyes were closed, he rocked back and forth and he was still singing, but it was different from what I had heard before. His voice, passionate and longing, bounced off the cavern walls and came deep inside me and mixed with the drugs to stir brilliant, hallucinatory colors in my mind. My eyelids grew heavy and I shut them, to find myself swimming in rivers of ruby and pearl and emerald.

All went to blackness suddenly and I was very afraid. Then, as if in a night sky, a first star appeared from behind windblown clouds. The star shimmered and turned red and grew. I went into the star, blinded by a crimson light that settled into a woodland landscape at dawn. I was in snow, snow that drifted in a stiff wind. And there I saw myself impaled upside down on the branches of a massive pine tree, its roots descending far below the snow and the earth, its limbs rising impossibly high into the sky. I stared at myself, unbelieving. My lips moved, but I heard no words.

There was the night and the clouds again and another star, which darted about the sky and became a bird of a thousand colors. The bird hovered in the night sky and sang a lullaby.

The bird arched high into the blackness, exploded and became a huge circular painting composed of many colored yarns and bird feathers. Women with electric azure hair gave birth in the painting. Men fished with boys on an emerald stream. Dogs howled at the moon. At the center of the painting a crow held a mirrorlike orb in its beak, and for a split second the faces of my children appeared in the orb, calling to me. I wanted desperately to hold the orb, to talk with them, when in the upper right-hand corner a deer with flaming fur took a step. I tried to stay focused on the orb and Emily and Patrick and the crow, but the deer compelled me to follow and I did, surprised that the deer was a fawn going to the emerald stream to drink. I entered the stream alongside the fawn. The river was not water, but many iridescent streams of odors I'd long forgotten—the wet leaves that used to blow up alongside my mother's gazebo in October, my father's bay-leaf aftershave, Mitchell's Pall Malls, the oven in our kitchen, the hospital smell that seemed to linger in the air near Katherine in her last years.

That last scent was like a powerful current that bore unceasingly at my legs until they gave way and I slipped under the surface of the river of odors into a blackness. I turned and swirled in the blackness until a silver bubble came at me. I grasped the bubble and looked into it, shocked to see the front hall of our home outside Bangor and a much-younger version of myself walking in wool socks on the wood floors, feeling the uneven surface through the bottoms of my feet, seeing the photographs of us all on the wall. Mitchell hoeing the garden. Katherine and me on a fishing trip to Labrador. My father with one of his biggest deer. Wedding pictures. Baby photos. A family. A lifetime.

I watched myself turn into my father's office and Katherine was sitting there on his lap in her flannel nightgown, and my father asked me to shut the door. It was February inside the bubble, my senior year in high school. I knew what my father was about to say even before he said it, and I didn't want to hear those words repeated. I had never wanted to hear those words. But the things occurring within the bubble were my past, beyond my control.

Now Katherine was looking away from me into the distance. And my father was saying, "Your mother doesn't want to go blank. She doesn't want to fade to a nothingness that haunts us. She knows that if she lived long ago, the forest would treat her as it would any enfeebled animal and end her life long before her mind turned completely dark. She wants us to be the forest for her, Diana. She wants us to help her die while she can still remember us."

I watched my younger self watch Katherine, unbelieving. After she'd resigned from her Senate seat, I had prepared myself for everything—for the loss of her mind, for her slow, lingering descent—but not this.

"I won't let you!" I cried. "I don't care what Mitchell or what the old ones might say; you can't do this."

"It's what she wants," my father replied.

"How do you know what she wants?" I screamed. "She can't tell you where the mailbox is half the time."

Katherine reached for me and said, "I want this, Little Crow."

But I pulled away, sobbing, "No, you don't. He's filled your head and my head with all this stuff about nature and his ancestors and how no one sees the world whole anymore except us. You don't understand what he wants to do."

"Yes, I do," she said.

But I wouldn't listen to her. I turned on my father. "Daddy, I know you think of yourself as a modern *Puoin* or something. But put Mitchell aside for one second. You're a medical doctor. You took an oath. You can't kill her or help her kill herself. They'll take your practice away. It will be the end of you."

My father's face clouded and now he was yelling at me. "I took a far more important oath to her when I married her. Little Crow, you've got to understand . . ."

"No, I don't! And I'm not your Little Crow anymore. I'm Diana Jackman. And she's my mother. And if you do this I'll tell the police. I'll have you thrown in jail for murder!"

I was crying now in the dark river of the hallucination and my hands were crushing the bubble, which developed a waist like an hourglass. I was inside the bottom bubble suddenly, squished inside and frightened. I beat against the sides, but no one heard me. Then a face appeared outside, Mitchell's face. He talked to me about the forest and the shape-changers and the need to cloak myself in Power lest I be harmed. His voice faded and I became aware that the bottom of the bubble was pressing me upward through the neck toward the upper bubble and I screamed, feeling the pressure, not in my head, but in my chest, around my heart. The pressure became excruciating, much, much worse than the racking hour and twenty minutes I had spent in transition during Patrick's birth. My ribs were on the verge of cracking when I burst into the top bubble, which exploded and left me floating again in the darkness of the river.

I was no longer feeling myself as I floated. That is to say, I was still myself, but someone else, too. A second heart beat within me, a second set of lungs took breaths, and I saw visions of things I knew were memory, but not from my experience.

I saw a small house filled with primitive Mexican art:

sculptures of men holding bows and huge yarn paintings like the one I had already seen and entered in my hallucination. I was looking for someone, walking fast through a bedroom with white furniture and then a sewing room and then a room with a great many deer heads on the wall. The rooms were all empty. And then I heard noises outside at the rear of the house.

I walked through a kitchen and opened the door to see a policeman leading two men away from me toward a cruiser. Another policeman approached with this look on his face that told me I was about to be cast to the winds.

My entire body went vacant. I followed the officer toward two ambulance men working with their backs to me. I passed them and focused on the face of the woman in the killer's photograph. She was lying on her back in curled brown leaves. Tiny bubbles of blood shone at her lips. Her eyes swept lazily from the men working over her to the sky and then to me.

Suddenly I was in the darkness again and nearly bent in two, tearing at my scalp to ward off the scorch of disbelief and abandonment and terror writhing within me. I seemed to be propelled forward through the darkness now. Only the darkness had become the first light of day over a vast desert plain that gave way to charcoal mountains. I touched down on the plain in a grove of purple-leafed plants and strange lime-green cacti, the arms of which looked like thorned antlers. One plant before me had no thorns and I sat on it, legs crossed, and I noticed I was naked, but had no definable features as man or woman. Just blank skin.

The sun glowed over the mountain peaks, throwing shadows of the cacti across the desert landscape before me. A huge deer appeared in the sky and floated to earth, only to run zigzag through the cacti. Pale blue flowers bloomed in each of his tracks. And then I was holding the leaves of the plant on which I sat. I squeezed the leaves and they oozed black blood into my palms, through my fingers, gelling in the dust at my feet. In the distance a wolf came down out of the mountains.

I raised the bloody leaves in the wolf's direction, and an indescribable rage pouring from the black blood dripped onto my stomach and burned its way inward. It bore into my veins, hot, tearing at whatever was left of me, and I screamed and screamed a promise of vengeance.

My eyes snapped open and I heard horrible, choking cries. The killer still sat before the drum, body convulsing, drenched in sweat, nostrils flared, his eyes half rolled up in his head. My last thought before I passed out was that I was his mirror image.

I believe the entire hallucinatory experience, from the time he blew the smoke into my face to the time I awoke to find a fire burning in the ring, encompassed five hours. Oddly, I did not feel lethargic or weakened by the drugs, but my senses were dulled, as if the stimulus of the visionary world had dampened the effect of reality.

He was piling his gear near the tunnel entrance.

"I'm thirsty," I croaked.

Wordlessly he took up the gourd next to the fire ring and held it to my lips. He would not look me in the eye.

When I'd finished, I asked, "You're leaving now?"

"The end is near," he announced as he stood. "I must

finish the ceremony before the blackness comes to take me as it did your mother."

I froze for an instant, understanding that somehow we'd passed inside each other in the bubble. We had shared shapes, and now he dimly knew the clouds on the night sky of my heart as I knew his.

"Why here?" I demanded, knowing that if he meant to finish the ceremony, he meant to finish me, too. "You still haven't told me why you had to do this here."

He took me in with a blank, unmoving stare. "In August, at the time when *Tao Jreeku*, Father Sun, was at his most powerful, a messenger came to me in a vision, a messenger with hair like fire. He said her killer was unrepentant for his transgressions. He said he had gone far north into the forests where no one knew of his evil deeds and was hunting again. I asked Tatewari and Kauyumari if what the messenger said was true, and they said it was and this was why the hunting everywhere was so poor. Wolf came to me later. Wolf told me I had to restore the balance, to avenge. I will kill the killer and all who follow him to purify the hunt."

"There's no killer here," I said. "No one except you."

He snorted. "You are blind. He's been here a very long time. I have scented him since my first day in the forest. I have felt his terror grow as I have hunted his brothers. He knows I am coming to inflict on him what he inflicted on me."

"But why the rest of us?"

"You are part of him and by being part of him, you further defile the hunt. I will sacrifice you all."

He said no more, just turned away.

I called after him: "Who did this to you? Who's the woman in the picture?!"

"Silence!" he bellowed, spinning in his tracks to glare at me. "He will suffer! They all will suffer!"

I drew back from the explosion. I dared not say another word for fear he would finally turn on me. He panted and coughed and tore at his hair again and then went through the circular dance that had soothed him earlier. When he was composed, he bundled up his gear inside several of the deer skins. He added wood to the fire, then laid strips of venison on metal skewers and thrust them into the flames. He fed them to me rolled in a tortilla he heated on a rock. He checked my restraints, got into a pair of chest waders, then disappeared out the tunnel into the night. Over the course of two hours he returned repeatedly to take away more bundles. Ice caked his beard. The skin on his face and hands turned scarlet from the cold, but he seemed not to notice.

Each time he left, I tried to free myself from the lashes around my wrists. The knots never gave an inch and I fell into a deep despair, sure now that I would never hold Patrick or Emily again, that I would die at the hands of a madman. I felt the need to pray. I fumbled around in my head, wondering whom or what to pray to, and realized sadly that because Kevin and I had basically lived the agnostic life, I had only the spiritual teachings of my childhood to fall back on.

I thought about the stories I'd heard Mitchell tell so many times, about men and women who camped on lakeshores deep in the forest and had encounters with Power. Nothing I could remember had prepared me for this. Those had just been stories. I was inside a story of Power now and had no guide to lead me.

In desperation I grasped at one of the most cheerful memories I have: when I was seven, we all went on a picnic in early May to a beaver pond far out in the woods. Beaver ponds are strong places, Mitchell always said. He took water from the pond in a birch bark bowl and stared at the reflection. My mother held me in her arms, and she and my father sang a song to the world waking up from winter.

I remembered some of the words and closed my eyes and sang them. The more I sang, the more I could smell the succulent new grass and the peeper frogs calling from the river's edge; and I found myself comforted by the idea that even though my kids might have to endure the winter of my passing, they would endure and find spring again.

When I stopped singing, I opened my eyes to find him squatting at the tunnel entrance watching me. He had my gun. "We're leaving now, Little Crow," he said.

"Where?" I asked, encouraged that I was not to remain behind in the cave.

"Not far," he said.

I hummed the spring song to myself. It was a good way to prepare to die.

He came behind me with that Stone Age knife and cut away the lashes at my wrists and then again at my ankles. As the blood returned to my feet and hands, it made my skin itch painfully. He told me to get my waders on. My limbs had gone numb from so many hours of inactivity and I had to wriggle my entire body to get my legs down into the rubber sheaths. He handed me my gloves and hat. When I put them on, I saw by my watch that it was a quarter to eleven in the evening; I'd been in the cave almost an entire day. He motioned with the gun toward the tunnel and I crawled through the passageway. I emerged into a stiff wind under a sky where clouds fractured the moonlight.

"Move away from the tunnel entrance and face downhill," he commanded.

I took two gingerly steps away from the tunnel. He scrambled out immediately and nudged me down the hill with the gun barrel. I grasped at tree branches to help me slide on wobbly legs down the rock face until I'd reached the maze of poplars I'd passed through that morning.

He flashed the light so I might see his path. We walked together until we got to the bank of the Dream, on the far side of which I could see the faint glow of a fire burning. He motioned to me to move into the water and raise my hands. He gave me a piece of rope to loop around the one that stretched back to land. Before I went out onto the sandbar, he loosened the strap around my chest, making sure that if I let go of the rope and tried to float away, the waders would fill quickly and take me to the bottom.

Then he slung the gun across his chest, shoved the thin flashlight between his teeth and looped his own safety line around the cable. "Go," he ordered.

A cloud passed in front of the moon just as I entered the water, immediately spurring in me the memory of the river of odors in my hallucination. His flashlight flickered like a strobe on the white water, chopping everything into rapid snapshots of information: the raging ice water buffeting me, my slithering movements across the submerged boulders, the dim outline of the far shore and the possibility of living a little while longer. Twice I came off the boulders and was suspended nearly horizontal by the current, only to have him pull me back to the center. I finally staggered into the shallows and fell on the bank, panting.

He drew that ugly knife again. He cut the rope that had linked him to his sanctuary, then ordered me to move. About fifty yards back from the bank, he'd erected a shelter of sorts by lashing the deer hides between several saplings to form rear and side walls as well as a shallow roof, and more hides on the ground for a floor. The fire burned brightly in front of the shelter. I knelt next to it and warmed my hands.

"Take off the wader and the rest of your clothes," he commanded.

"M-my clothes?" I stammered.

"All of them," he said and he pointed the rifle at me.

"Why?"

"It's not what you think," he replied.

"Then why?" I insisted. From his expression I could tell he was within another level of existence, in the world of hallucinogens and visions. I fought against a rising hysteria. "You're going to kill me, aren't you?"

"No, I have more respect for you than that."

"Then what—" I began.

He cut me off. "Don't talk. Just do it."

My eyes watered as I lay down on my back on the deer hides and wrenched myself free of the waders. He took them and walked back toward the river and flung them into the darkness.

He returned and watched without emotion as I stripped

off my jacket, pants, vest, shirt and long underwear. I placed each article in front of me until there was a pile.

"Finish," he said.

I slipped out of my panties and bra, but did not remove the leather-and-quillwork pouch around my neck.

"Finish," he said.

"It's the only thing I have of my family," I said, shivering despite the intense heat coming from the fire. "I won't take it off."

He threatened to explode, then went the other way and grinned. "You are very much like her," he said.

"Like who?" I asked, knowing already. "Was she your wife?"

He stiffened. "She was more than my wife, she was my mate." He walked around behind me, knelt and put his hands on my shoulders.

I said nothing. I looked into the fire, tensing, waiting for the assault to begin. Instead, he bound my hands behind me with a thong of deer hide.

"Do not fret," he said. "During sacred rituals, the *Mara'akame* is forbidden from any sexual act, though I long to."

He crawled in front of me and looked at my body with obvious hunger. I glanced away, humiliated, as he tied my ankles together. When he was positive I couldn't escape, he draped a hide around my shoulders and another over my legs.

He stood back to admire his handiwork, then picked up the pile of my clothing and threw it into the fire. The gun was thrown in the river. Coming back, he turned over the charred remains of my clothes so they would burn completely, then added more wood until it sparked and shot flames toward the branches above. I turned my face away from the heat. There, protruding from the snow five feet from the edge of my shelter, was the broken femur bone of a deer. This must have been where he butchered the deer he had killed before taking the meat and the hides to the island, I thought.

Meanwhile, he was fishing in his pack. He turned around with a smaller pipe than before, a second leather pouch with a strange blue design on it and three feathers: one black, one whitish, one copper. These he tucked into my hair.

He sat next to me and watched the fire as he packed the pipe bowl. "This is a different mixture, Little Crow," he announced, taking a burning stick from the fire and applying it to the bowl. "No visions. But all your senses will become razor-sharp, like a mirror reflecting perfectly all that is around you. The breath of the wolf, the hunting smoke."

I knew from past experience there was no fighting him, so I took the stem in my mouth and drew in a deep inhalation of the concoction. Inside, the smoke expanded and pressed out hot against my lungs. I coughed and hacked and teared, but took a second drag of it at his command. As he had predicted, there were none of the overpowering sensations I'd experienced earlier in the day, but the smoke had an almost immediate effect: my ears, eyes, nose, tongue and skin hummed. I could smell the river beyond the fire, and the poplar saplings on the island beyond that. I could see the shapes of trees out in what had been darkness. And then, to the west, I could hear the faint howling of wolves.

He seemed to hear it, too, for he stood and crossed straight to his backpack. He brought out two more sacs of the deer blood. He bit at one with his teeth, then dripped some of it on the deer hide that covered my lap and continued dripping it in a diagonal line to a point about forty feet beyond the fire ring. He did the same thing in a second direction with the other sac. He threw the sacs into the fire, then hoisted the pack on his shoulder, picked up his bow and tied his quiver to his hip and leg. Even from twenty feet away I could hear his breath, shallow and quick now, the kind of breath you get when you have sighted game you wish to take.

"You said you would not kill me."

"And I will not," he answered, jerking his head west toward the Sticks River. "They will. They are my allies. They come every night and I feed them deer meat. Now they will feed on you, a sacrifice to my allies."

I struggled against the lashes. "You are crazy! She would think so, too!"

Two huge strides and he was before me, his knife raised over my head. I bowed, awaiting the inevitable, preferring it to the prospect of the wolf pack.

Instead, he knelt and said earnestly, as if he had to make me understand, as if I was the only one capable of understanding, "She loves me for what I am doing. For us the hunt was a divine ritual, a way of meeting God through the pattern of life and death that makes up this life. I am making the ritual clean again, as it was before her loss."

"No, you're making it evil."

His expression hardened. "You don't see, then, do you?"

"I see a man gone mad from his wounds."

"Well, so be it," he grunted. He stood. "I misjudged you. They are coming now. I must go to the camp of my enemy to complete the purification ceremony."

And then he was a form flowing into the shadow world beyond the fire and gone. The flames, leaping and sawing at the night sky just minutes ago, had waned, leaving just a crackling fire. Within minutes it would linger to embers. I twisted my arms and legs against the knots he had tied. But all I achieved was a dislodging of the deer robe from my shoulders; it sloughed off and settled around my waist. I gazed down at the ivory-and-black quills so tightly woven on the surface of my pouch and I wanted to cry.

The wind picked up and clawed at my breasts like icy, sharp fingernails. I looked down at them in the firelight and was overcome with the vision of those late nights at home in Boston when I had held my babies and felt them draw milk from me; and all had been right and good and possible. I closed my eyes and let that sensation calm me for a few precious moments.

I heard the first one padding toward me from my left. She traversed the drifts like coiled force, panting and lolling her tongue in anticipation. The thick hollow hairs of her winter coat caressed the willow whips along the riverbank. I smelled the blood he had dripped on me and the snow and the different, almost copper smell of the dried blood around the wolf's muzzle from an earlier hunt. She did not come in close enough for me to see her at first. She waited until five others had joined her.

A chunk of wood on the fire burned through and collapsed and the circle of light diminished. I sensed her advance, the others fanning out behind her. The clouds overhead broke and the moon shone through, bathing the crescent of land around me in a pale light.

Two of the wolves growled and nosed the blood trail to my right. The other three sat on stumps about forty yards away, their topaz eyes reflecting the dying flames that offered my only protection.

NOVEMBER TWENTY-SECOND

A STRANGE QUIET swept over the midnight woods. It settled around me, raising bumps on my flesh, made me understand it was not a true quiet, more a white noise composed of monotonous rhythms, like chants or drumbeats heard from afar. The gentle din became the veil through which I watched the wolf closest to me drop its head and its center so its shoulder blades spiked above its spine, tail out straight. A hunting posture.

I dug my heels into the deer skin and kicked back toward the rear wall of the shelter.

The wolf growled and took two quick steps forward. The second wolf trailed the scout and stood at its hip, intent on me. Another step and suddenly a gust of wind bellowed the fire until it popped and sparked with renewed life. The smoke billowed out along the ground, grating at the eyes of the hunters. They sneezed, choked and retreated toward the rest of the pack. They would wait until the fire died before they attacked.

I was suddenly weaker than I'd ever been in my life, surprised I could even remain sitting upright. The vague forms watched me and I wondered if I'd have the will to die with dignity. Mitchell always maintained that death was just a passage to one of the other worlds, and what we leave behind becomes a new source of life. He buried the bones of his deer because he believed the animals would reenflesh themselves for future hunters. Would my flesh give Power to these wolves and so to the killer?

The fire ebbed again. And in the shadows the she-wolf took a cautious stride to the right. I knew what she was doing from a story my father had told me years ago, after he'd witnessed a wolf pack take down a cow moose during a hunt he was on in northern Minnesota. She and her pack would try to flank me, to get behind me so they could tear at my back before going for my throat.

She took another step and I flashed on my father's body worried by scavengers and then on the bloody snow where this pack had torn at what was left of Patterson. The quiet started to envelop me again. Only to change its shape into seething anger when I thought of Patrick and Emily. I would not pass from this world meekly.

I wrenched my arms and legs against the lashes, but they did not budge. The pack leader took three more steps, sinking into herself even as she moved. And the rest of them began to slowly fan out around me.

The fire was perishing. I rolled to my side and got my feet under one of the deer hides and kicked it into the flames. The tallow and the hair sizzled, flared and sent forth an acrid, sickening smoke that forced the animals back several yards. I rolled around some more and tried to get my hands into the fire, to burn away the knots. The flames seared my palms. I screamed and threw myself forward away from the fire, facedown in the deer skins, sweating with effort despite my nakedness.

The wolves growled behind me. My back was exposed. They wanted to attack, but the fire and the horrible smoke kept them at bay. I was struggling to get myself turned around when I saw the sharp femur bone sticking out of the snow five feet from my sanctuary.

The killer's smoke became my ally. I saw my escape, but the way was fraught with danger; to get to the broken bone I'd have to go away from the fire out into the snow. But there was no recourse, so I got to my knees without further thought and hopped forward to the edge of the deer skins. I sensed a wolf to my left take two steps in my direction.

"Live or die," I told myself. "Live or die."

With one great effort I thrust my body up and out. I came facedown on the side of the bone, feeling the jagged edge slice into my cheek. The scent of the sudden burst of my blood was blown to the wolves. They snarled. One howled. It was her, the alpha bitch; she knew I was wounded. She didn't know how. She didn't care. All she knew was that I was bleeding in the snow outside the heat of the dreaded fire.

I got hold of the bone with my teeth even as the first wolf attacked from my right, then jackknifed my body, swinging my bound feet at it, feeling my heels thud against fur and the animal manage one rip at me before darting back to safety. No time now. I bent in two again, barely aware of the snow numbing my exposed skin. I rolled over and over and got back onto the deer hides.

I spit out the bone and worked myself around to get it into my hands. I set the jagged edge into the rawhide and began sawing, only to slip and gash my left arm above the wrist. The blood ran freely down my arms, but I held tight to the bone, repositioning it on the lashes even as the increased volume of the blood scent reached the pack and the she-wolf howled as if to say time was on her side.

"You believe I'm dying today, bitch, but I'm not," I said, grinning wildly into the darkness. "You, on the other hand, might want to think about it."

The fire retreated to the tip of a single branch as thick as my wrist.

Twenty-five yards behind me, there was a scratching noise in the snow. I glanced over my shoulder to see the beta animal—a scrawnier, meaner version of the pack leader—gather his legs and charge. Frantic, I sawed one last time at the hide, feeling it catch, cut and break through. I rolled over and toward the wolf even as he leapt, teeth bared. I drove the tip of the broken bone into his throat.

The impact blew me back and down. The wolf bit at my arm reflexively, not understanding what I'd done. His teeth tore a ragged gouge below my elbow before he entered his death throes and released me. He squirmed and bucked and whined. His nails scored my stomach before he flipped over between me and the fire. He clawed furiously at the white bone showing at his throat. His muzzle, now peppered with bright, frothy blood, jawed at the air and then stilled.

I got to my knees in time to witness the alpha bitch utter a low-toned growl, then race forward from about fifty yards away. The others spread out and came on, too. I grabbed the closest deer hide to me with my left hand and threw myself forward across the dead wolf toward the fire. The dried fat on the back side of the hide exploded into flames even as I grabbed the last remaining burning branch. I tried to stand but couldn't; my ankles were still tightly bound. I would fight on my knees.

She dashed in at me from an angle. And I waited until she dipped her head, preparing for her attack bound. When she did, I stabbed forward with the glowing branch. She came up fast and hard and into the burning tip with her eye. Her screams as she writhed away into the darkness were from another realm.

I turned and slashed with the branch at the first of the three subordinate wolves coming in behind me, then flung the flaming deer hide onto its back. It howled and spun in circles, trying to rid itself of the fire that now fed on its fur. The other two wolves jumped back at the apparition of their burning brother and turned tail after him when he fled, smoking, into the night.

I froze next to the dead wolf, listening, looking, waiting for the forms to attack again. But the strange quiet was gone. There was only the normal sounds of the woods at night: the soft bumping of branches in the stiffening breeze, the hoot of the owl, the rush of the river, the rustle of dead leaves. Above me, the clouds had broken fully. The full moon bathed the forest in a gentle light. It was all familiar and comforting. Yet against and within all of this I noticed something that had the quality of a déjà vu; it was an insistent, oscillating force that seemed to permeate everything around me and contained both good and evil in equal measure. I understood that it had always been there, but that I had never noticed it before.

I broke down then, sobbing at all that I'd been through. A trembling took hold of me. My stomach contracted and I threw up the food I'd eaten in the cave not more than an hour before.

The convulsions finally stopped, but the shuddering went on. It became more violent, and I realized I was chattering, too, and probably going into shock from exposure. I needed to warm myself or I'd die.

I set my feet against the dead wolf and freed the femur bone and cut my ankles free. Needlelike pain shot through my feet when I stood, but I accepted it. I wrapped one of the deer hides around my waist as I would a bath towel and caped a second about my shoulders. The lower trunks of the pines around the shelter were thick with dead limbs, and within minutes I had the fire roaring again and my toes were returning to life.

For several moments I considered trying to ride out the five hours until dawn beside the fire, but the madman's vow to kill everyone on the estate demanded that I move. I tended to my wounds first, pressing snow into the gash on my cheek until the bleeding stopped, and then binding my left forearm with a charred strip of my shirt that had been blown clear of the fire. The teeth wounds on my shin and shoulder were superficial, but oozed. With luck they would not infect before I could get to Arnie.

I took a rock and cracked it against the bone until a piece broke free, exposing a sharper edge. With it I sliced some of the hide into six long strips about a foot wide. These I wrapped in double thicknesses around my feet, then lashed them to just below my knee with narrower strips of hide. From there to mid-thigh I similarly fastened a single thickness of the hide. I cut in two the deer skin I'd been using for a skirt. I rewrapped one of the pieces around my waist—a short skirt I could run in. I hacked a slit in the center of the second piece and put my head into it. It fit like a smock. From a third hide I fashioned a long, hooded robe that I cinched at my neck and girded at my waist. I cut two smaller pieces of hide and secured them to my hands for mittens. I broke off the back portion of the deer bone, then set a pine branch up into the marrow channel and wrapped the connection tight with hide. A flimsy spear, but better than nothing.

I was about to leave when I noticed my leather-and-quill-work pouch lying in the snow, torn from me during the fight. The woman's photograph lay beside it, scratched and bloodied. I wanted to despise her, but I couldn't; I'd felt the love he had for her and understood that somehow she'd been transformed from innocent victim to talisman in a psychotic's twisted scheme of vengeance. I tucked the photo back inside the pouch, then retied it around my neck.

I looked at the wolf already going rigid in the charcoal-colored melt by the fire ring, knowing well that wolves tend to avoid humans and only in rare instances attack them. I wondered at the swirl of pulsing energy I'd sensed after the rest of the wolves had fled. What dark corner of what plane of existence had this man tapped into with his bastardized ceremonies and the hallucinogens in his pipe? And what were the other forces he commanded that I had not yet witnessed?

I stopped to stroke the wolf's dense fur. "Watch over me," I whispered.

Then I stood, took a bearing on the log-landing where Patterson had dropped me off that first day and set off.

The drugs that the killer had made me smoke no longer ruled my head; they had settled and become the lenses through which I viewed the world. The moonlight filtered angularly through the forest canopy and bounced off the snow of yesterday's storm now firming in the frigid air, now casting the landscape before me in a troubled glow. The dark jade and hammered-iron shapes of the trees clawed at the light, broke it, made it their own.

But I ran through that fractured terrain, a rising sea of snow billowing about knees, with a growing sense of my place in it. My ancestors believed that nearly everything could change both its shape and its mind. From my per-spective—a 1990s woman with an MIT degree in computer engineering—their universe was unpredictable, unreliable, frightening. They had survived in what must have been a psychologically brutal environment, where nothing was as it seemed, by becoming equally unpredictable, able to change mind and intent at a moment's notice. I was learning.

By the time I reached the log-landing, frost from my breath and my sweat caked my eyebrows and lashes and rimmed the hood of the deer-skin cape. I paused in the light of the setting moon to study the tracks there. Man prints and the metal tread of the snowcat. They'd been out here looking for me yesterday afternoon, leaving just as the storm passed.

I got water from the little stream to quench my thirst; then I heard gunshots far in the distance. My heart sank. He'd had at least an hour, maybe an hour-and-a-half, head start. Could he already be at the lodge? I sprinted forward into the dark hours, feeling my way toward the estate by the ribbed, frozen track the machine had left under my feet.

It was four in the morning by the time I trudged into the yard of the estate. Every light in the lodge blazed. Left on for me, I supposed, a beacon calling to the lost hunter in the night. I smiled, thinking of a good meal and a hot shower, of being safe within the closest thing I had now to a family. I had barely taken ten steps into the yard when I heard the action of a pump shotgun.

"One mo' step and it's your last," came an edgy voice in the shadows to my right.

"Phil?" I called. "Is that you? It's me, Diana."

"No shit," the auto-parts man said, coming out of the darkness. "Woman, you're damn lucky I didn't pull the trigger. Where the hell have you been? And what the hell are you wearing?"

"I'll explain later. I heard gunfire an hour ago."

Phil sighed, the sigh becoming a shudder. His lip quivered. "He's been here, done his dirty work and gone. It's crazy in there."

"He told me he was going to kill us all," I murmured to myself, not wanting to ask the next question.

Phil was ahead of me. "Butch," he said, and the tears rolled down his cheeks.

The strength I'd been feeling since escaping from the wolves evaporated. "I'm sorry," I said.

Phil stared at his feet. "He was my man since the fourth grade, you know? We changed a lot when we got older. Kind of a hippie freak there in the early seventies, against the war and all that shit. I went Army, but I still loved him, and that fucker with the wolf hat just butchered him."

I put my hand on his powerful shoulder and for a second he leaned against it. Then he looked away from me, embarrassed. He wiped his nose with the sleeve of his wool jacket. He didn't seem to know where he was. He didn't seem interested in where I'd been.

"Phil, I talked to the killer."

He looked at me with bleary eyes. "He talked to us, too. Go on in, tell 'em all about it. I can't go in there now. It feels better being out here on patrol."

Shouts and moans of disbelief echoed from the main lodge as I crossed the yard. I was so tired I couldn't figure out where they were coming from at first. The doors stood shut. The windows, too. Then I raised my head toward the second floor, toward the stained-glass windows. The central window, the one that had depicted two stags fighting, was no more. Just tangled branches of lead and broad petals of busted panes, a giant flower of many dark colors.

I went inside through the kitchen door. The lights were all on, but the room was empty. I opened the door to a room saturated with the aftermath of what must have been pandemonium. Arnie, Griff and Cantrell were on the first landing of the staircase, wrapping Butch's body in a white sheet. Lenore loomed over Earl on the far side of the room, supporting his head while he sipped from a cup. Theresa and Sheila held each other on the couch in front of the fire. They had the dazed look of survivors five minutes after the car crash.

"It's my fault," Theresa sobbed. "It's all my fault."

"No, it wasn't, honey," Sheila choked out. "You made a mistake. That's all."

Kurant and Nelson were upstairs on the landing in front of the shattered window. The guide punched the wall as the writer took photographs.

"How could he live through that jump?" Nelson demanded.

Kurant shrugged. Nelson turned, yelling the same question this time, looking for some kind of reply from below, when he caught sight of me in my deer-skin suit. I took another step and the room began to whirl. Nelson started toward me in slow motion. Kurant came at me, too, the both of them pointing, talking in a garbled language I couldn't understand. Blood-red dots appeared before my eyes and I felt myself collapsing inward and down into a comforting blackness.

I remember my eyes fluttering open to see a blurred image of Griff sitting beside me. He managed a weak smile and told me to go back to sleep, that I'd be all right. And I sank again into that warm blackness, which gave way into a creamy existence the color of the strange quiet that had embraced the woods after I'd driven off the wolves. There Griff became my father, a silent, determined figure passing me in the halls of our home in Bangor to check on my mother, even as I braved the springtime of my senior year in high school. It should have been a joyous time of college-acceptance letters, of proms and confidence.

But I lived a secret life.

I spent every morning before school with Katherine, helping her dress for her day, talking with her in her lucid moments about the insects that were likely hatching on the rivers, talking to her in her addled moments like a toddler. Every conversation was tinged with the fear that this could be the last, that I would return to find my mother murdered by a father clinging to a vision of life that had been all but extinguished a century or more ago.

I never warned my father again about my feelings. I didn't need to. He could see them in the clouds that passed over my face when he'd come to say good-bye to Katherine before departing for rounds at the hospital and the clinic.

I'd leave Katherine slowly, envisioning all that might happen and praying it would not.

I must have been calling out in my sleep, because suddenly I jerked awake and Griff was pressing an ice pack to the nasty swelling on my cheek, saying, "Your daddy's not here, Little Crow. It's just me, and you're going to be all right."

I stared at him for a long time before asking, "What time is it?"

"Quarter to six in the evening," he said. "Arnie says you were suffering from hypothermia and exhaustion. It's a miracle you got back here at all considering you had just those deer skins for clothes. He's already sewed your cheek and your forearm up. And he cleaned out those nasty dog bites, though he's worried about rabies. We found the bloodied picture of a woman in your pouch. Is she part of this? Phil said you talked to the killer! What happened?"

Woozily, I sat up on the couch they'd laid me down on in the great room of the lodge. I was dressed in somebody's thick flannel robe. The room spun before settling. Arnie was checking on Earl across the room. Lenore hovered nearby. "Tell me what happened to Butch first."

Griff's expression tightened. "A nightmare. Cantrell and Nelson and I tried to backtrack you yesterday morning, but we lost your footprints in the storm around nine. Every two hours we drove the cat along the logging roads hoping to find you coming in. But by this time yesterday, I thought we'd lost you for sure."

"What about Butch, Griff?"

"We were pretty low last night at dinner, but I'd made up my mind to go back out at first light and look until I found you," he went on in a strained voice. "Arnie had Earl's vital signs stabilized, and no loss of spinal fluid, thank God. But he still had us on shifts around the clock. Butch had midnight to three. Here's the awful thing: Theresa left a window cracked in the kitchen to air out the fish smell from dinner."

"He came in an open window?"

Griff nodded, chagrined. "Yeah, she's taking it hard, figures she's to blame. Way I see it, he would have gotten in somehow. Anyway, Theresa said when she finished her shift at midnight, Butch was lying on the couch by the fireplace, reading a book. We figure the killer came in around a quarter to two. Earl says the painkillers were wearing off by then and he couldn't sleep. He saw the guy coming through the kitchen door with a weird black knife out and that wolf cape on, heading straight for him.

"Earl yelled for Butch," Griff continued, "and Butch woke up and went for his gun. But Earl says he never saw anyone move that fast in his life. Before Butch could swing the shotgun around, the killer had the fireplace poker in his hand and was clubbing Butch's wrist. The gun went off before Butch dropped it, and that woke up Phil and Arnie in the next cabin and Cantrell and Sheila in their cabin.

"Then Earl says the killer hit Butch on the side of the neck with the poker and he dropped. By now Phil and Arnie were banging on the front door. And the killer knew he was getting closed in on and he started to run. Only Butch wouldn't give up. He got the ash shovel and chased the sonofabitch. Cantrell was working at the kitchen door, trying to get it open.

"Well, the killer went up the stairs and Butch followed, right on his heels. Only Butch tripped and the killer—" Griff shook his head, not believing it. "He spun and cut Butch's throat before he could even get his feet under him. Cut his throat and slashed off part of his ear and the right side of his scalp in one motion. Took it with him."

My mind reeled with the image of the shrine in the cave. "What about the stained-glass window?"

"I'm coming to that," Griff said. "Just as he cut Butch, Phil threw one of the porch chairs through the front window and jumped through right when Cantrell got the kitchen door open. They both shot at the guy as he went up the last flight to the landing."

Arnie had left Earl's bedside to come up behind Griff. There was a bleak cast to his skin. "I've never seen anything like it," the doctor said quietly. "Phil and Mike shooting at him from two different angles and neither of them hits him. He had that hunk of Butch's long brown hair in one hand and the knife in the other and he went straight at the stained-glass window and dove through it. He landed on the porch roof in the snow, rolled off and kept on running. Butch was dead by the time I got to him."

He hung his head.

Griff said to me, "But what happened to you?"

"You better get the others," I said.

An hour later, I'd gotten into real clothes. Arnie had cleaned and redressed the bite wound on my arm. He'd given me a mouthful of antibiotics and some painkillers. My back and leg muscles were stiff and my left arm and cheek throbbed, but I was clear-headed.

They were gathered around me in the great room, silent. The chaotic despair I'd stumbled into was gone, replaced by a new and jaundiced view of the world, a view shaded by a nervous vigilance; and I knew they knew that nothing I would say would change that. It would likely make it worse, for they would be thinking—why did she live and the others die? And I would not have an explanation.

I told them how I'd come to guess at the position of the camp on the island at the confluence of the Sticks and the Dream, how I'd gone upstream to the Sticks in the waders, how I'd crossed to the island, entered the cave and found this photograph and another like it on a macabre altar. Before I could continue, Lenore interrupted. "Who is she?"

"Who cares?" Phil snorted. "Who's the motherfucker in the wolf's hat?"

"He wouldn't tell me who he was," I replied. "He just kept asking me, 'Know my name? Know my name?' When I asked him if he was James or Ronny Metcalfe, he just laughed."

Theresa's head turned into Nelson's shoulder and she whimpered. "He's crazy. He's going to kill us all. And we don't even know why."

Beside her on the couch, Sheila was rocking gently back and forth, a handkerchief pressed to her mouth, her eyes shifting from me to the photograph and back. Cantrell leaned against the fieldstone mantelpiece, his body stiff, his expression narrow and hard. Kurant was watching both of them, but especially Sheila. The fire in the hearth flared for a second and illuminated the writer's red hair, which had the sudden and terrifying effect of triggering in me the memory of the cave and the killer's rants. And the horror of the cause of these murders was laid out before me in broad stroke and sickening detail.

"Diana?" Griff said, gently shaking my shoulder. "What's the matter? Arnie was asking you what happened in the cave after you found the photograph."

Stunned, I stammered, "I-I know who t-the killer is and w-why he's here."

Phil's head shot forward like a snapping turtle's after a frog. "You know who . . . ? I thought you said . . . fuck it . . . who?"

I gestured at Cantrell, "Ask Mike."

The outfitter came off the mantelpiece braced for a fight. "How in the hell would I know?"

"I think you do," I said. "Their faces must haunt you every night."

"Don't know what you're talking about, lady," he said. His gaze was a shell built of many layers around a cruel secret.

I met that cold glare and matched it for almost a minute until Sheila cracked and tore the handkerchief from her mouth. "Stop it, Mike, just stop it! It's over. I won't go on living a lie anymore!"

She was on her feet, no longer the little, mousy woman. She was red-faced and strung out and nasty.

"You'll sit down, Sheila," Cantrell growled. "And you'll shut up if you know what's good for you."

"I won't shut up, eh? Can't shut up anymore. And I won't cover for you neither!" she screamed. She turned to me. "That's Lizzy Ryan in that picture—I'd know her face anywhere. It's been eating at me the past six hours. It's him, then, isn't it? Devlin Ryan out there?"

"I didn't know it when I was in the cave. But I think so now."

"Then God have mercy on our souls," Sheila wailed, and she collapsed into her chair and wept. Her husband did not move to comfort her. No one moved to comfort her.

"Devlin? Lizzy? Someone gonna explain what's going on?" Earl demanded blearily from his cot.

I said to Cantrell. "Are you going to be a man and tell them, or will I?"

For a moment the outfitter hesitated; then Phil stepped up in front of him, his massive paws balled into a fist. "My man Butch is on ice out there. I been shot through the arm. You don't start talking soon, I'll know why not."

Cantrell shot a look of pure hatred at me, then said stiffly, "My name's not Cantrell. That's Sheila's maiden name. My real name's Teague, Mike Teague. The woman in the picture is Lizzy Ryan."

Griff gasped. "Teague? You mean like the guide Teague? The one who was with the hunter in Michigan who shot . . ."

"Yeah, the one who shot Lizzy Ryan in her backyard while she was hanging clothes," Cantrell said, finishing his thought. "Not guilty as charged."

"You fucking loser," Phil said. He turned and flung his arm out in disgust.

There was a moment of stunned silence, then Nelson demanded, "How could you?"

"How could I what?" Cantrell snarled. "How could I have let Dilton shoot her? I see it in my head ten, twenty, sometimes a hundred times a day, and I'm telling you it was a deer's tail flickering in the sunlight. Not a mitten. It was a mistake! An accident! Jury said so."

Cantrell slammed his fist into his palm. "But I was still branded. Dilton, he goes back to his job in Chicago, says he won't hunt again, no problem. But for me it's a big problem. The state took my guide's license. I couldn't make payments on our lodge. We lost it. We moved up to Ontario and lived with Sheila's sister. I pushed a broom at night for five long years, waiting for my Canadian citizenship to clear. Then this deal come up through one of Sheila's cousins and we bid on it, because guiding deer is what I know how to do, what I love to do, because it was my last hope of getting myself free of that one mistake. That one stinking mistake in the woods."

His voice trailed off and he slumped into a chair and held his face in his hands. He began to shake. Sheila went over to him and held him around the shoulders. He whimpered to her, "You don't know how much I wished I'd thought it was a mitten and not a deer's tail. You just don't know, Sheila."

"Yes, I do, Mike. 'Course I do."

I gazed into the fire, could not watch them, because I knew how they felt; I understood what it was to be empty and alone and tormented by a terrible secret.

I shook myself from my trance, only to notice that Kurant had been taking notes. His face was flushed and his eyes darted around the room. He saw me watching him, scratched his head and said, "Still doesn't explain how this guy Ryan got here."

"You think you're so clever," I said sharply. "You're as much at fault for this as the Cantrells."

"What's that supposed to mean?"

"You know just what I mean," I snapped. I explained how Ryan had captured me and made me smoke from his pipe. I told them everything that he'd said in the cave. "In one of his crazed moments he said he'd been visited by a messenger, a messenger *with hair like fire*."

"Yeah," Kurant said warily. "So?"

"So at first I thought it was just ravings. But just now, when I saw the fire light up your hair, I thought: What if he was telling the truth? What if someone did track him to the high desert of northern Mexico, someone who knew that the Teagues were back in business, someone who might goad him to come north, an *ironic antagonist* for a dramatic story he was working on about the culture of trophy hunting."

Every eye in the room was focused on the reporter.

"What about it, man?" Phil threatened.

Kurant tried to remain stoic, but the corner of his mouth twitched.

"You lousy piece of dung!" Arnie said.

"Four people are dead!" Griff cried.

"My husband's paralyzed!" Lenore seethed.

"And Don's wife's a widow with a little baby and she don't even know it yet," Theresa added. The loathing in her voice was liquid.

"I'm not the one who's at fault here!" Kurant yelled, leaping to his feet. He pointed at Cantrell. "He's the one who helped kill a defenseless woman. Not me. He's the one who got off scot-free. He's the one who made a mockery of that woman's death. Did you know she was pregnant—Lizzy Ryan?"

"No!" Sheila cried. "No, that's not true."

"It *is* true," Kurant said. "Only six weeks. And the evidence was suppressed at the trial. But I got hold of the autopsy report. I know how brutal this was."

"It was an accident," Cantrell moaned. "It was all an accident."

"Yeah, sure it was, Mike," Kurant went on, the passion in his voice rising with each word. "All you hunters are alike, gun-happy nuts who don't give a damn about the rest of us who have to witness your blood sport."

"That's not true," I said.

"It *is* true!" Kurant yelled. "The whole thing's barbaric."

I looked at Kurant in a new light. "You think you're righting some wrong here, don't you?"

Kurant adopted an imperious attitude. "I intend to tell the story as it should have been told in the first place.

Dilton and Teague walked away from a senseless killing and left behind a shattered man."

"Who's now killing people!" I screamed.

"I'm not responsible for that," Kurant said flatly. "I just went and talked to Ryan, that's all. I was doing my job, getting his side of the story."

"His side!" Phil shouted. "You fucknut, I should bust your ass right here, right now."

"Hoping to dominate me, to feel like you're king of the jungle?" Kurant asked snidely. "I don't think so, Phil."

My laugh was coarse. "You set him in motion as sure as I'm sitting here."

Kurant shook his head. "I'll never believe that. I'm not responsible."

Nelson got up from the couch. "What about when we started finding the bodies, eh? You must have known then. You could have warned us."

Kurant's expression, so arrogant, so sure, wavered. "I didn't know."

"Bullshit," said Arnie. "You had to have."

"I didn't."

"Not even when we started finding feathers and scalps?" I demanded.

"No, no, I . . . that is . . ." A cold sweat had formed on his upper lip. "I mean, I was afraid. I was afraid . . . the feathers and everything, 'cause I'd seen that kind of thing before in Mexico . . . but I told myself it was impossible. I mean, it is almost five thousand miles. Impossible, right? You know, I—"

The flat of Phil's beefy hand caught the reporter flush on the side of the face, sending him crashing to the floor. "You

lying sack of shit! You knew and you didn't say nothin'!"
he roared. "You helped kill my man Butch just so your
story'd be juicier. In 'Nam we would have fragged you for
this. You'd already be in the body bag. Fuck it! I'll do ya
right now."

Phil went for the Buck knife in the sheath on his belt.
Nelson and Arnie tackled the huge man high and low. The
pediatrician sat on Phil's chest while he struggled. "Don't,
Philly, the scumbag's not worth it."

"Get off me, Doc," Phil pleaded. "For Butch. For Vinny.
The hunter would have wanted me to do him."

"No, he wouldn't have," Arnie said softly. "Vinny was
better than that. Your dad was better than that."

Phil glowered, but finally stopped struggling and dropped
the tension from his barrel chest. "Keep him away from
me. That's all I'll say."

Kurant got to his knees. A trickle of blood showed in the
corner of his mouth and his cheek was purpled from the
blow. He looked warily at Phil. And for a fleeting moment
I caught something in that action, a sense of dismay, of
knowing deep down that his noble intentions had turned
foul and deadly. But the regret was gone in an instant.

"What do you want from me?" Kurant asked sullenly.

I wanted an admission of complicity, but I knew we'd
never get it. Instead, I said, "If we're to have any hope of
stopping him and surviving, we need to know everything
about Ryan. Tell us what happened in Mexico."

Kurant hesitated.

"Talk," Griff ordered. "Or we'll let Phil have a few minutes with you alone."

Kurant moved his jaw and swallowed several times, then

resigned himself to our demands. He said thickly, "I'd been on this story a couple of weeks and I got a tip that the Teagues were getting back in the business up in Canada under a different name. I went after the story."

"Couldn't leave us alone, could you?" Cantrell said.

"I didn't ask you to go back into guiding," Kurant said, the hatred pure and open now. "You did and I followed."

"Get to Ryan," Arnie commanded.

"It didn't take long to figure out through court records that they'd changed their name to Cantrell, and from there it took some digging, but I found out they'd leased this estate. I got the history on it and knew the place was a rich vein of story material. So I booked a slot."

Kurant shifted uncomfortably in the chair and rubbed at the swelling in his lips. "I could use some ice."

"Forget about it," Phil said. "Keep talkin' or I'm goin' for my blade."

"All right, all right, no need to prove what a man you are," Kurant sniped. "I tracked Ryan through the Anthropology Department at Michigan State and they said he'd quit the year after the trial and gone back to live with the Huichol Indians in northern Mexico. I guess from the insurance settlement he could afford to do that. Can't cost anything to live down there.

"I speak pretty good Spanish, so I went down in June as a kind of whatever-happened-to-Ryan sort of thing. Took me about a week, but I finally found the village where he'd lived in the Sierra for the first couple of years after Lizzy's murder."

"Her accidental death," Sheila said, glaring.

"Her murder," Kurant replied.

"What did the people say about Ryan?" I asked, remembering how upset he had become when he talked about being thrown out of the community.

"That's the thing," Kurant said. "The Huichol were incredibly friendly, welcomed me into their homes, fed me, but when I mentioned Ryan, they got these clouds on their faces and they'd politely ask me to leave. I finally got one old woman to open up. I'd read Ryan's dissertation on the Huichol, so I understood some of what she was talking about, but a lot of it went over my head. Basically, they have this religion based on deer, corn and Peyote."

"Some religion," Theresa sniffed.

"It's very ritualistic," Kurant went on, ignoring her. "The deer is one of their gods and the Peyote allows them to talk to their gods and obtain visions. It's real weird, complex stuff, like I said, and I don't claim to understand it all. But from what I can gather, Ryan had gone native and was training to become what they call a *Mara'akame* in the religion."

"Like a witch doctor or something?" Lenore asked.

"No, not like a witch doctor, like a shaman," Kurant said condescendingly. "These shamans are more spiritual guides and leaders than voodoo men, from what I could gather. Becoming one's not easy. Takes years, according to the old woman, and most of the people who try aren't up to the training."

"Was that what happened to Ryan, he wasn't up to the training?" Griff asked.

Kurant nodded. "The old woman said he was willing enough, but there was something about 'his heart being spoiled for it.' She said the shaman who was teaching him refused to continue after Ryan started screwing around with Datura. That's what they call Jimsonweed, a real powerful psychotropic that has some bad side effects. Ryan left all pissed off and moved to a settlement higher in the Sierra, a community of what the old lady called 'sorcerers.' "

"Give me a break," Arnie scoffed.

"I'm just telling you what she said," Kurant replied in a huff. "To the Huichol this stuff is real. They believe sorcerers are failed shamans, people who have acquired some powers but who haven't demonstrated the strength and knowledge to control that power for good. They're like a kid whose father gives him a Corvette for his first car. An accident waiting to happen."

I shuddered at that last statement. I hadn't told them about my encounter with the wolves yet. I wanted to hear everything before I did.

"Did you see Devlin in the mountains?" Sheila asked.

Kurant's expression turned grim. "Took me two days to get up there on horseback with this kid Ramon that the old woman had set me up with. Ramon didn't like the idea of going up there, but I paid him enough, so he did it. It was real wild, jumbled terrain, you know? Boulders and walls of red clay and flats choked with purple cholla cactus. What you'd expect in the desert, not the mountains. Two days of riding and we came to this ruin of a town. Dusty. Mangy dogs ruling the streets. Fifteen, maybe twenty people living in it. Ryan had set up house in the wreckage of a two-room mud hovel set flush against the bottom of a cliff, just beyond an abandoned adobe church. There were a couple of chickens roosting in the thorn brush and they flushed when Ryan came out."

Kurant hesitated. "He wasn't what I expected."

"How's that?" It was the first time Cantrell had looked up from his hands or spoken since Kurant began his story.

"Well, he'd . . . he'd aged a lot from the pictures I'd seen of him at the time of your trial. Grayer certainly. Skin blasted by the sun. His eyes were almost opaque. And he was dressed in this ceremonial outfit, what the Huichol call the dress of the *Peyoteros*, the pilgrims who travel on sacred missions in search of Peyote: bleached baggy pants and a shirt made out of flour-sack cloth, sandals and a bright red blanket around his shoulders and this domed straw hat with brilliant yarn tassels of blue and yellow and red hanging down from the brim."

I said, "There was a photograph in the cave of a man dressed like that, but it wasn't Ryan."

Kurant nodded and went on: "Probably one of the *Mara'-akame* who taught him. Anyway, I got down from the horse and introduced myself, said I was working on a story about what had happened to him and I'd come a long way and would appreciate it if we could talk. He didn't say anything at first, just motioned to me and Ramon to come inside. Ramon was freaked just being there in the sorcerers' village. He said he'd stay in the yard with the horses. Inside, it was actually very tidy. There was a rough table and a couple of chairs, a straw mat for a bed and lots of books and local artifacts—earthenware bowls and pitchers and stuff. Kind of what you'd expect . . . except for the . . ."

Kurant hesitated, as if he were groping for words.

"Except for what?" I asked.

He stood up, his arms crossed. "This is where you're gonna get pissed off, say I should have known it was him here, but, damn it, I didn't think it was possible! The Sierra's thousands of miles from here."

"Spit it out," Phil said.

"There was a . . . shrine in the corner," he said, giving me this chagrined look. "Not as ornate as the one you described in the cave, but a hoop of feathers and some candles and . . . that, that picture of Lizzy there."

"There were feathers and you didn't put it together?" I cried.

Kurant hung his head. "I know. By the time we found Grover, I was thinking it, but, you know, I just didn't want to believe it was true."

"Or you did, and you didn't want it to stop," Arnie said.

"Why the hell would I do that?" Kurant shouted.

"For a better story," Arnie said.

"Fuckin' bastard," Phil said.

"No!" Kurant fought back. "He was so calm when I was there that I couldn't believe he'd be this psychopath. Ryan was this lonely guy who liked to talk about the kind people he was living with. He asked me about what was going on in the world, but he didn't seem to care much about any of it, though he seemed amused that we had a president from Arkansas."

"What about when you talked about Lizzy?" Lenore asked.

Kurant got this puzzled expression on his face. "He said he'd put that life behind him."

"But the picture . . ." Earl said.

"I know," Kurant said. "Looking back, I see it doesn't make sense. I think he was playing me. From what Diana says, he was probably drugged up, and I didn't realize how well he was masking what he wanted out of me."

There was a moment of silence; then Sheila asked, "And when you told him about me and Mike?"

Kurant wouldn't look at her. He didn't say anything.

"Kurant?" I said.

"Well, he didn't go batshit and drool, if that's what you're asking!"

"What did he do, then?" Cantrell demanded.

Kurant stuffed his hands in his back pockets. "He . . . he wanted to know everything about the deal. Where you were going to be. What you'd been doing. And I told him . . . you know, 'cause I needed his reaction for the story. And when I said you were getting back into guiding, he seemed to drift off for a while; then he started to speak in this language, Huichol, I guess. I don't know. I guess he thought I was someone else, because then he started chanting and then dancing around with this yellow arrow in his hand, kind of like you described him in the cave. And I got this sick, closed-in feeling, like he was gonna lose it and I was the one he was gonna lose it on, but he didn't. He just kept singing and dancing like I wasn't even there.

"The kid, Ramon, must have heard the singing, because all of a sudden he came in the door wide-eyed and sweating and shook me by the collar and said we'd better get out of there. I tried to say good-bye to Ryan, but he just kept dancing and chanting that chant over and over and over again."

Kurant stared off into space.

"That's it, eh?" Nelson asked.

Kurant went on as if we weren't there. "Ramon made us

gallop out of the town. A wind had come up and there was dust blowing everywhere. A couple of miles out, I asked Ramon what Ryan'd been chanting back in his hut. Ramon didn't want to answer, but I made him. He said he'd only heard it once before a long time ago, after his uncle's mistress had been murdered by her jealous husband. He said it was a chant to call animal allies . . . a chant to invoke devastation and revenge in the wake of a lost love."

We all fell silent, each of us grinding on his or her thoughts. Phil looked around at us and started to laugh. "Bunch of bullshit, that's what it is. Sorcerer bullshit. This guy's just a fruitcake."

I looked at Phil sadly. "I wish he were."

"You know something you aren't telling us?" Griff asked.

"He has the power to call wolves," I said, and I told them what had happened after Ryan had taken me from the cave.

"Oh, c'mon," Arnie said. "It's a coincidence. He'd just been feeding the wolves there every day. They came."

"Wolves don't like to go near anything with the slightest scent of man on it," I said. "No, there was something much more powerful at work than just a behavioral response."

Theresa whined, "You're saying he can't be killed! That there's nothing that will stop him?"

"I'm saying I don't know how to stop him."

"What does he want?" Phil asked.

"He wants to purify the hunt," I said. "He sees this as a purification ceremony."

"By killing us all?" Lenore asked.

"Yes."

The room fell quiet, each of us absorbing and turning over Ryan's story. I now knew more than the bare facts, but it still wasn't enough. I'd seen the man face-to-face. I'd felt his pain in the hallucination. But there was more to this than revenge. And until I figured that out, I would not understand him. Without understanding, I couldn't hunt him correctly.

Cantrell cleared his throat. His eyes were glassy and his hands were trembling slightly. "I think I know how to get him."

Sheila lifted her head from her husband's shoulder. "How?"

Cantrell stared at the floor. "He says he wants to kill us all, but I don't believe it."

"That's what he told me."

Cantrell shook his head. "It's me he wants to kill. It's my presence he wants to wipe out from the woods. If we're gonna kill him, we'll have to use me as bait."

"No!" Sheila cried, stunned. "No, I won't let you, Mike!"

He grabbed her by the wrists and shook her. "I started all this, Sheila. Now I've got to be the one to end it."

NOVEMBER TWENTY-THIRD

"ANY SIGN YET?" came Nelson's whispered voice.

"Nothing," I radioed back.

"Be his shadow, eh?" the guide said. "His life depends on it."

Beads of snow and frozen rain pelted the thicket around me in pale curtains that drew and opened at the whim of the southwest wind. Brief gusts snaked along the forest floor and crawled up my pant legs, making me shiver. I was wearing a set of Griff's snow camouflage. I was as close to invisible as you can become in this world and yet I felt naked, exposed, though not as starkly as Cantrell.

Sixty yards in front of me, the outfitter stuttered over downed trees and limped through brambles of black branches with an arthritic gait that hadn't been there yester-day. Part of it was show; he was making enough noise and

awkward movement to attract attention. Part of it was the
weight of playing decoy in a hunt for a madman.

Cantrell stopped in mid-stride at the base of a west-facing
slope. He crouched to peer through the underbrush that
bearded the rise. I knew what he was doing; somewhere
just ahead, Arnie was perched in a tree stand where he
could see one hundred and fifty yards in one direction and
two hundred in another. Arnie was carrying a .300 Winchester magnum with a high-powered scope, ready for a long-
distance shot should Ryan bust out and run.

I knew Arnie was there, but seeing Cantrell stop made
me jumpy. I slid the safety off the .35 Whelan pump I'd
taken from the Metcalfe collection and brought the rifle to
my shoulder. The Whelan was a brush-cutting gun with a
heavy bullet that created a lot of killing energy in close. In
close was where I, the shadow hunter, was likely to have
an encounter with Ryan. I got up tight against a tree for
stability and looked down the iron sights at Cantrell, reas-
sured by the familiar heft of the gun; my father had used
a Whelan for his hunts in the cedar swamps near our cabin
near Baxter Park. It was not my perfect little .257 Roberts,
but I had shot a rifle like this many times as a girl and that
was comforting.

To my relief, Cantrell continued his jerky, weakened animal stride up the slope. I eased the safety on and trailed,
craning my neck to all sides, alert for any motion, any
noise, any whiff of attack.

I straddled a log, cracking a branch. With a cackling that
almost stopped my heart, a flock of willow ptarmigan burst
from beneath the snow between my legs and flushed cra-
zily through the trees toward the outfitter. He spun in his

tracks, a long-barreled pistol thrust before him, the terror of anticipation plastered across his face. One of the birds tore by him at eight feet. Instinctively he swung the muzzle of the pistol at the bird before letting his right arm and the gun drop wearily to his thigh.

The echo of the cackling birds died. Cantrell and I ogled each other across the seventy yards that separated us. There were no words between us, but I could feel the overwhelming pressure that had gathered around him in the past few hours; he and I were playing a game with infinitely high stakes, a game where there would only be losers. Who would lose? A question chanted by Cantrell and me and everyone else in the woods that dreary morning.

This hunt had been Cantrell's idea. A simple variation off a tactic used by deer hunters everywhere. He and Nelson had decided to limit our options and so Ryan's. On the map in the great room of the lodge, Cantrell had used a grease pencil to highlight a mile-long by half-mile-wide corridor north of the beaver-pond flat where Ryan had wounded Earl and south of the high ridges Nelson and I had chased him across before losing him in the feeder stream of the Sticks. The terrain was marked by four interconnected razor-backed slopes, no more than three hundred vertical feet in elevation, each no more than two hundred yards apart, all feeding onto the flat-topped rise where Arnie waited. On the map, the razor-backs looked like the gnarled, bony hand of an old man. On each of the fingers, high in a tree stand like Arnie's, a hunter waited. Theresa sat in a hemlock about a quarter of a mile east of me, on the knuckle of the first finger. Kurant's position was on the same finger, but well out toward the nail. Kurant hated being there, hunting, but he knew he had no choice; Ryan was unlikely to make distinctions as to who would live or die. Griff covered the first joint beyond the knuckle of the second finger, Phil the second joint of the ring finger. Nelson was west of me on the knuckle of the pinkie. Cantrell had put his wife on the nail of the shortest finger, the place he felt was strategically the safest location, the stand least likely to see action.

Once Sheila had accepted that her husband was determined to go out as bait, she demanded to be out in the woods, too.

"No," Cantrell said. "I can't let you go."

But Sheila had stood her ground, showing the inner toughness that had enabled her to stand by her man even in the wake of Lizzy Ryan's killing. "If you think I'm sitting in this lodge while you go out and try to get yourself killed, you're out of your mind, eh?"

As it was, there was very little sleep in the hours between the planning of the hunt and the execution. Long before dawn we moved Earl and Lenore to a room on the second floor of the lodge. Arnie had changed the dressing on Earl's back, dosed him again with antibiotics and painkillers, then handed Lenore a shotgun. As she'd closed the door behind her, I thought of her sitting in the hard wooden chair next to her husband, facing the door alone for the rest of the day, wondering at any noise in the floorboards beyond. I could not have stood it. Better to be out in the elements, moving.

We'd left the estate an hour before daylight, all of us on foot, Cantrell and I walking each stander to his tree. There we screwed in metal foot pegs to take us twenty-five feet

up, then attached metal stands to the trees with chains.
The shooters were in place by 8 A.M., fighting the dank
cold, trying to remain motionless in the trees while Cantrell
and I wandered between the finger ridges, hoping to draw
Ryan into our trap.

The strategy was sound. Ryan had demonstrated with his
attack on the lodge that he was willing to take almost any
chance to complete his twisted ceremony. But instead of
trying to cut his track and deal with him in the chaos of
the open woods, the outfitter wanted to control the parame-
ters of the hunt by restricting our setup to this small chunk
of terrain. Our goal was to lure Ryan into one of the funnels
between the fingers where either I or the standers could
get a shot before he got to Cantrell.

Now, however, I had my first pangs of doubt. I'd been
dogging the outfitter for nearly three hours and completed
three loops in and around the razor-backs without sign of
Ryan. On the radio there was an increase in the volume of
whispered, desperate chatter: "Seen anything?" "No, you?"
"Nothing." "I don't like this."

Cantrell slid the pistol into his shoulder holster. He took
off his baseball cap and wiped his brow with his sleeve.
He got out a water bottle from his fanny pack and drank
from it. Then he nodded to me and gestured toward the
ridge where Arnie waited. I signaled back that I'd be right
behind him. I checked my watch 11:31 A.M.

The first shot was a flat cracking explosion behind me,
over my left shoulder. And then a second and a third, all
of them from the far side of the first finger, midway down
the shelf.

"Theresa!" I despaired. One of the two standers we'd

believed least likely to encounter Ryan had shot first. I sprinted back toward her position along the trail we'd gouged in the snow. As I ran I tugged the radio from my belt and shouted into it, "That's Theresa shooting! Stay off the radio until I call you. Cantrell! Cantrell! Listen to me: if she's missed, he's going to loop. Move toward her south-southeast. I'll go straight at her."

"Okay," came the outfitter's hoarse reply. I didn't turn to see where he'd gone. He was on his own now. I couldn't be the shadow anymore.

"Theresa?" I huffed into the radio. "Theresa, answer me!"

"Get down here!" she whined in return. "I think I hit him, but I can't see him anymore. Hurry!"

Theresa hugged the trunk of the fir we'd selected for her earlier that morning. Her face, barely visible under a green wool cap, had an anxious sheen to it. She tottered in the tree stand upon seeing me, then got her balance and shakily pointed the barrel of her rifle south toward the ridgeline.

"Down there, eh?" she panted. "Just on the edge of the last shelf near that blowdown larch tree I heard this god-awful screaming, like a baby with colic or something. And then on the other side of the larch I see this white blob moving. You said he'd be wearing white camouflage, so I figured he was crawling along out there and I shot until I couldn't see him moving anymore."

She hugged the tree tighter, flattening her enormous breasts. "You don't think I've killed him?"

"I don't know, Theresa. We'll have to go see."

Theresa shook her head, her mouth slack and open. "I can't go down there not knowing. If he's dead I don't want to see what I've done, no matter what he's done to us. I . . . I was never much of a hunter."

"Okay," I said. "But I need you to cover me."

She nodded uncertainly, then got her arm free of the tree trunk and faced south.

Forty yards beyond Theresa's stand, the clearing gave way to scrub spruces. Tufts of pale weeds poked through the surface of the windblown snow. I went from tree to tree, pausing behind each to scan the terrain below me.

"Diana?" Cantrell called on the radio. "I can see Theresa in her tree and you about three hundred yards east of me."

"Anyone else?"

"No."

"Then come in slow toward that shelf about fifty yards south of me. That's where she saw him before she shot."

I edged closer, the butt of the Whelan an inch from my shoulder. I dissected the grid around the larch for any hint of motion, the barest speck of sound. Cantrell came into my field of vision, slow, rolling his toe into the snow before settling on his heel. He braced the pistol with both hands. As he came in line with the larch, he gestured to me to stop.

"There's blood ahead of me, other side of the tree," he whispered into the radio.

Everything changed. I searched for a crumpled figure on the forest floor. But there was only snow and ice-clad branches clawing through snow. I made it to the tree trunk and peered over, instantly sickened by the blood and the decapitated form of a giant snowshoe hare. I swallowed, got across the log and picked up the headless animal. Its back leg dangled at an obtuse angle, broken not by the

impact of a rifle bullet, but by the bending force of powerful human hands.

My mind raced, trying to decide why Ryan would break
the animal's leg before throwing it onto the shelf, only to
have my weakened train of thought shattered by a fourth
gunshot, this one full and blasting and close. I threw myself
flat behind the log, then scrambled around to see where
Theresa was aiming.

"It's not her!" Cantrell yelled. "That's Kurant!" He ran
forward, caught sight of me still holding the rabbit, hesitated, then took off to the east, calling over his shoulder,
"Ryan's looped the other way!"

I sprinted after the outfitter, the Whelan in my left hand,
the radio in my right. "Kurant? Kurant?"

"He screamed and I shot!" Kurant came back. "He's still
screaming, but I can't see him. What should I do?"

"Don't shoot again unless you're sure it's him!" I called
back. "No one shoot unless you're sure it's him. He's
using—"

I tripped over a log in mid-stride. The radio flew from
my hand and disappeared in the snow.

I didn't have time to search for it now. I had to keep up
with Cantrell. He was a possessed man, sure that he was
close, that the end of his nightmare was at hand. One way
or another. I got up and went after him, driven by the
notion that I could save Cantrell from Ryan, or at least from
himself. We endure times of crisis by telling ourselves the
prettiest lies we can imagine.

The rabbit was still screaming when we came upon it in
a shallow depression one hundred and ten yards east of

Kurant's stand. The rabbit writhed and squalled and spun on its side, unable to comprehend that its back leg was shattered and no good anymore. Kurant's shot had struck two feet high, debarking a stump.

Cantrell leaned against a big boulder, kneading at his side, his breaths coming in great gasps. "What's he doing with this rabbit shit?" Cantrell demanded. His skin was gray. His head swiveled in one direction and then another, sure that at any moment an arrow would fly at his chest.

The stitches in my palm and forearm ached. My head pounded from the exertion. But I forced out the only explanation I could come up with: "Decoy. He's using them to figure out where we are and where we're weakest. The rabbits scream and hobble around. We shoot and he knows where we are and what we're capable of."

Cantrell squinted in thought, followed immediately by a look of pure exultation. "Then he's gonna go north toward the next finger! At Griff and then Nelson!"

Cantrell took off again, quickly finding the deep trough of a path we'd all tramped down from Kurant's stand to Griff's earlier that morning. I tried my best to stay with him as he poured downhill toward the swale that separated the two razor-backed ridges, but Cantrell was mad with adrenaline, sure that he was a step ahead of Ryan. By the time we reached the bottom, he was more than a hundred yards ahead of me, a ghost of a figure in the sleet and the wet snow falling. And then gone.

The pain in my hand and forearm had gotten worse. I suppose I had not physically or mentally recovered yet from my ordeals in the cave and with the wolf pack. I stopped, doubled over, trying to catch my breath. I reached for the radio to warn Griff of what was coming and then cursed; the radio was back there in the snow below Kurant's stand. Cantrell's carefully thought out funnel hunt was dissolving into exactly the chaotic scene he'd hoped to avoid.

I had taken only two steps down the trail Cantrell had followed when a blip of information registered in my peripheral vision. The faint shadow of a track heading not northwest toward Griff, but true north. Toward Sheila.

"Cantrell!" I screamed. "Cantrell!"

But the wind had picked up, and with it the suffocating din of pelting snow and sleet. He would not have heard me at eighty yards, much less the two or three hundred that now separated us.

I turned, a growing knot pressing in my stomach. We'd mistaken Ryan's ultimate goal. He didn't want Cantrell to die more than the rest of us. He wanted the outfitter to feel the same absolute sucking vacuum of emotion he'd endured witnessing Lizzy's last breath. He didn't just want Cantrell to die. He wanted Cantrell to suffer before he died.

And then I was running again, true north, my stride matching the long, loping, purposeful gait echoed in the snow before me. For an instant I saw myself racing down the front lawn of my parents' home toward the gazebo and the prone figure of my mother. Tears flowed down my cheeks and the knot moved from my stomach to my throat as I babbled, "Don't do it, Ryan. She's innocent. Please don't do it!"

By the time I made it around the tip of the third finger, I was grasping at hope, telling myself that somehow Sheila would see Ryan first, that any moment now gunfire would break the evil spell that embraced these woods. I broke away from Ryan's track halfway across the brief dip between the third and fourth fingers and cut diagonally at Sheila's stand. If he held to the manner of approach he'd used with Theresa and Kurant, Ryan would circle Sheila and come at her from the north.

I might have time.

The snow on the south face of Sheila's razor-back was deep and dense with moisture. I flailed my way up the slope, frantically scanning between the trees for the open hardwood glen in which we'd placed her stand before dawn.

I couldn't find it. I was on top now, but still surrounded by thick softwoods. And then it dawned on me: I'd misjudged my position by a good twenty degrees; I was west of Sheila by at least two hundred yards. I held the stock of the Whelan before me like a battering ram and snapped dead branches and snow-laden limbs out of my way in a pell-mell rush east.

Ryan must have heard me coming. For as I broke from the fir trees his legs and arms were already spinning in space, gyrating to keep his body vertical as he dropped the twenty feet from the metal pegs we'd screwed into Sheila's tree. Her body swung a few feet below the base of the portable tree stand, supported and bowed by the nylon-webbing safety strap Cantrell had insisted she lash around her waist. A cedar arrow jutted from her rib cage.

I slid to one knee as Ryan landed, casting the Whelan to my shoulder, trying to find his chest in the peep sight as he struggled for footing. He had the bow in one hand

and a knife in the other. He'd been trying to cut her down when I appeared.

Ryan's head came up then and he looked right at me, comprehension followed by disbelief, followed in turn by a screwing of his gaze into a penetrating concentration. And in that instant, that instant when I should have squeezed the trigger, I felt my heart seize and I was back in the cave with him, overwhelmed by sorrow and the primitive chants and the hallucinogenic smoke. I saw Lizzy Ryan die. I saw my mother worry the hem of her nightgown on the last morning of her life. Both images melted into a shifting kaleidoscope of refracting and reflecting images: my mother dead on the grass near the gazebo, Lizzy plucking wet clothes from a wicker basket.

"No!" I shouted, understanding suddenly that he'd used his power over me to cause the moment of hesitation. But that was all he needed. Ryan dove sideways and rolled toward the bank even as I swung with him shotgun-style, fired, pumped the action and fired again.

"I missed him," I said numbly. "I had a clear sight picture, Griff, and I missed him . . . twice."

Griff had his arms around me. Cantrell knelt below the snow-coated body of his wife, which swung in the gusty wind like a weather vane. He had not uttered a sound since his arrival in the clearing. He had gone vacant, dropped to his knees and stared up at Sheila with the resigned look of the doomed.

Phil was climbing up the pegs to get her down. Arnie was helping. Kurant was off at the edge of the clearing. After he'd vomited, he'd gotten out his camera and was

taking photos. Theresa would come no closer than the edge
of the clearing. As if drawing near would make her suscepti-
ble to Sheila's fate. She kept her back turned to us, holding
tight to Nelson.

"You said she was dead when you got here," Griff
soothed. "There was nothing you could do."

I pushed back out of his grasp, seeing not Griff through
my tears but a blurred, white-haired man. "I'm always late,
aren't I? Aren't I?"

"I don't know, Little Crow," Griff said, confused. "Are
you?"

"You know I am!" I cried. He reached for me, but I
swung my arms violently as if to strike him and Sheila and
everything churning in my mind. My shoulders became
heavy and I wanted more than anything to lie down in the
snow and sleep forever. But overriding it all was the desperate need to explain to Cantrell why I'd been unable to save
his wife.

I knelt next to the outfitter. Phil had swung her body
around the side of the tree. Arnie was reaching for her.
Cantrell still stared upward, unseeing.

"Mike, I . . . I tried to get to her, but I got lost."

He gave no indication he'd heard me and I said it again.

He turned his head and looked through me. He spoke
in a flat, terrible voice. "I been losing myself since the day
I helped murder Lizzy Ryan. Only thing that kept me from
disappearing from this world was Sheila. Lost? It's all lost
now. All lost."

Arnie had hold of the safety strap above Sheila's waist.
Griff waited below with his arms raised. Phil severed the
line at the tree trunk and she settled into Griff's arms and

then into the snow. Cantrell went to her, took off his glove and brushed the slush from her cheeks. Whatever was left of him vanished in that simple gesture.

It took us almost three hours to get Sheila's body back to the lodge. I wish I could tell you what went through my mind during all that time, but I can't recall any of it, only that we all seemed to be pushing on through an infinite darkness because there was nothing else we could do. We tried to put Sheila in the icehouse with the others, but Cantrell had pushed us aside and lifted her and taken her to their bed in his cabin. He put her under the blankets and sat by her side holding her hand, his head bowed. Arnie slipped the pistol from Cantrell's holster without the outfitter noticing and we left him alone with her.

Theresa had managed the hike back in a stoic silence. But when we were at last in the great room of the lodge and had brought Earl and Lenore down and told them all that had happened, she broke down. "So now we wait to die, eh? All of us? We've tried everything and he just keeps coming. That's what's going to happen. He's just going to keep coming."

"Theresa," Nelson said, walking toward her. "Enough."

She swung her beefy arm at him and caught him square on the jaw. "It's not enough. Not for him! He can come in here and kill Butch and we all shoot at him and no one hits him. We can lay traps for him and he knows what we're doing before we do. He's inside us. Inside me with that Indian voodoo. I feel it!"

She pointed at me. "You know it's true. You said he can do things you don't understand."

I nodded, that sleepy, heavy sensation hovering around me again. "It's true."

"Then we're gonna die, all of us, before the plane comes back."

"I don't know," I said, and I didn't. The last shred of certainty I'd clung to had evaporated with Sheila's death. I no longer saw the world in the same way and I was groping desperately for purchase.

"Three days," Lenore said hopefully. "We can make it."

"Can we?" Theresa asked. "Can we really?" She sank into the sofa and sobbed.

I stood and walked by the hollow men that had once been Griff and Kurant. "I'm going to my cabin."

Outside, the bellies of the clouds roiled in shades of blue and steel gray, spitting out half-dollar-sized flakes as the wind shifted to the north again and the temperature fell. The ice at the lakeshore had buckled and heaved in the past two days, only to refreeze into threatening pale blocks like tombstones. I climbed out onto the frozen cemetery, moving toward the black line where open water still defied winter's advance. I stopped five yards from the ebony mirror and looked into it, seeing the driving snow reflected on the surface, now mutating into relentless memories: Ryan blowing the Datura smoke into my lungs, Cantrell imploding at the touch of his dead wife's skin, my own fingers touching my mother's chill, damp cheeks.

I balked at that image, an image I'd buried deeper than any other. But it would not stay buried. There was no escape from it now. In the end, what other choice did I have than to face who I'd been? In the end, what was there to follow but the fleeting mental images of me, of my children, of

my husband, of Mitchell, of my father, of Katherine? I have
come to believe, like my Micmac and Penobscot ancestors,
that we live more than the sum of the present moments in
this visible world; we exist within layers of reincarnated,
reinvented memories that shape-change and prod us across
invisible boundaries into the many worlds of the mind.
Until we gather unto us the Power to navigate there with
confidence, we are lost and alone, savages in a dark forest.

As it was with Pawlett, I cannot tell you exactly how my
mother died. My father told the police that he had been
working in his office in the basement that morning, going
over a billing problem with his surgical practice; that he
had left Katherine sleeping in her bedroom; that when he
had gone to check in on her, he had found her gone. He
had flown through the house calling for her. It wasn't until
he noticed that the case to her favorite bamboo fly rod lay
open and empty on the kitchen table that he had checked
the pond.

I was taking a chemistry final. And by the time the princi-
pal had found me and driven me home, Katherine's body
was almost dry. My father had tried to get between me and
her. I looked into his eyes and saw a window into a world
that frightened me to my core. He was a stranger. I pushed
him aside and went to the bank of the pond and knelt next
to her. Her color had faded; the rose-and-speckled hue of
the rainbow trout had gone to plastic. I touched her cheeks,
stunned to find her so cold and damp. I held her and cried
until my father came and tried to pull me away. I stood
and whispered in as vicious a tone as I could manage,
"Don't you touch me. Don't ever touch me again, you sick,
fanatical bastard."

I knew what he had done and I hated him for it with every ounce of my being.

When they had taken her body away at last, I sat in the glider in the gazebo and watched the surface of the pond mirror the lime, immature leaves of the birch trees blooming. A detective from the sheriff's department, a pudgy man with an unruly mustache and garlic breath, came over and asked me if it made sense. Would my mother have gone to her pond in her nightgown to fly-fish? Would she have fallen and drowned as my father had theorized?

I glanced back at my father, who was standing on the hill talking to another detective. I despised the very sight of him. But for reasons I still do not fully fathom, I simply nodded and said, "My mother had been terribly sick for years, Detective. I don't think she even knew where she was the last six or seven months. The only thing she seemed to remember at all was fly-fishing."

I kept appearances up, played the dutiful daughter during the wake and the funeral, but I rebuffed my father's efforts to get me to talk. When it was done and she was buried, I told him that I'd be leaving for Boston. I would not attend my graduation ceremonies. He tried to contact me several times, but I never responded. I buried my past behind me, never allowing myself to speculate what might have happened that morning. Katherine was dead, and that part of my life was dead, too.

But now, shivering in the storm by the shore of Metcalfe's lake, I could not stop myself from gathering the shards of that awful day and, together with the suspect clay of my imagination, reassembling them into an explainable vessel of meaning.

The final days of May are a glorious time in Maine. The lilacs and crab apples have bloomed, ripened and begun to fall in the southern breezes, tinting the air with the sweet perfume of promise. The rivers have settled after the engorgement of winter's runoff and the nymphs have begun to hatch; the world above the water flutters with the gossamer wings of mayflies in their mating dances, diving and spiraling before sacrificing themselves on the river's surface to sate the trout's hunger. These days were Katherine's favorites.

She had dwindled to an echo of herself by the spring of my senior year in high school. Her mind had stiffened under the relentless assault of the disease to the point where she rarely spoke with ease; her thoughts were like a jigsaw puzzle tipped off a card table.

The last time I saw her alive it was early morning, the time of the hatch, and she was sitting in a wicker chair by the window in her bedroom, gazing out toward the gazebo and her casting pond. The dew on the grass glittered under the rising warm sun. My father had already been in to see her. Her hair had been brushed and her makeup applied with care. She hummed an old song and her fingers busied themselves worrying at the hem of her white cotton nightgown.

"It's a morning to remember, isn't it, Little Crow?" she asked when I came in to bring her breakfast.

I smiled. When she called me Little Crow, it usually meant her mind would be flexible for much of the day.

"The brookies are rising to meet it in the pond," I said.

"I've been watching the ripples," she agreed dreamily.

Now her wrist and shoulder act on muscle memory. The line loops gracefully in the warm May air. She spots the kiss of a trout on the water, false-casts once, twice, three times before laying the dry fly perfectly on the spot. For a moment all is still—the trout, the fly, the water, my mother, my father—and then the trout darts and the fly disappears and Katherine raises her arms to set the hook just as my father slips in behind her. The water below them ripples with his movement, warping the reflection so her face becomes his and, in my mind, his became the homicidal countenance of Ryan peering at me across the clearing that morning.

Out on the frozen lake the storm howled, a blizzard, a whiteout around me. It clawed at my skin and beat at my eyes until I feared I would go blind. It came from beneath me then, from deep under the snow-covered ice. It wrapped itself around me, crushing my stomach and rib-cage until I choked for air. I heard the wind's tone turn to tortured moans. I doubled over, knowing that the god-awful noise came not from the north, but from me. I collapsed under the blizzard's assault, holding tight to my stomach, wanting more than anything to give myself over to the storm's Power, to lie there until the snow shaped-changed me forever. No pain. No suffering. No haunting dreams of years gone by. And when the spring came, I would shape-change again and join James Metcalfe at the depths of the lake.

I took off my coat and laid it on the ice. I forced myself not to hold my arms tight to me. The cold would work better if I exposed myself wholly to it. I lay down and

"That old fat one that lies near the spring, he rolled over and slapped a couple of minutes ago."

"When was the last time you caught him?" I asked. Talking about fishing usually kept her on track.

She shrugged and smiled and drew her fingers through the air in a lazy arc. "Oh, I don't know. Does it matter?"

"No, I guess not."

Katherine stopped talking and drank the orange juice I'd given her and absently bit at the rye toast with the honey she adored. I watched her eat in silence, wondering for at least the thousandth time that spring how it was that she could remain so ethereally beautiful outside despite the ravages within.

"I've got to go to school now, Mom." I said to her at last. "Chemistry final this morning. Last one before graduation."

She did not reply. She was watching a great blue heron that had landed in the shallows on the far side of her pond. I took the tray from her lap and made to leave. I was at the door when she called to me. "Little Crow?"

I turned and Katherine held her hand out to me. I put the tray down and went to her. She gathered me in her arms and brought my face into the crook of her neck and I smelled wild hyacinth and I could have been six again, it made me feel so warm and secure. She kissed me on my forehead when I pulled away.

"I'll see you this afternoon," I said and I went out without looking back. My thoughts were of the test to come.

I imagined then that my father had been waiting for just such a day, when the red-winged blackbirds called from the willows, when the bullfrogs roared in the reeds, when the heady spice of the viburnum gave way to the delicate

scents of the lilac. It was a fitting setting in which to carry
out his deed. It cohered with his vision of the world, a
world imbued with invisible, mysterious Power, where nature ruled and to live in union with it was the blessed way.

I could see him, intoxicated with the certainty that this
was how nature would have wanted it. Nature culled the
weak. Its power was indiscriminate, arbitrary and ruthless,
yet beautiful. My mother should die in beauty before she
became a shell, a mockery of nature.

Now he leads her down the hill, telling himself that this
is the right thing to do. *She has forgotten everything,* he tells
himself. *She should have her last clear moment in the waters
before her mind turns permanently black.*

Katherine has long forgotten her decision to die with
dignity. She believes only that he is taking her to the pond
to practice her cast. Halfway down the lawn, she looks
down at herself and asks him, bewildered, why she is outside in her nightgown.

My father is not thinking of her now. He is not thinking
of the oath he took as a doctor. He is thinking only of
Mitchell and the rituals and legends he has used to define
a lifetime. He is taking the ceremonies far beyond what his
uncle taught him; he is taking them to their extreme, making the ultimate devotion.

He says, "You look so beautiful in your nightgown, I
didn't want to change you."

And because she can still remember that she loves my
father, Katherine smiles and enters the water with him. He
watches as she draws the tippet and the leader and the
first few feet of green floating line through the ferules. The
line lies on the water.

turned my face into the drifting snow, and within moments I felt the first sense that my body was retreating, shutting down blood flow to my arms and legs. My hands and feet numbed. I felt drowsy, the first signs of hypothermia. *I will become sleepier,* I told myself, *and then there will be nothing but the blackness of the river in my hallucinations in the cave.*

It came for me, slinking along the ice, an oily thing, the presence of which I felt, not saw; and I was preparing myself to greet it when, from far away, I heard the sounds of children laughing and giggling. A pleasant thing to imagine when you are about to die, I thought. But the laughter came again, more insistent, and now I recognized the laughs as those of my own children. I lifted my head from the snow. I saw them before me in the swirling white: they were at the dinner table, much younger than they actually were, Patrick maybe five and Emily two. She was sitting in her booster chair, eating and painting herself in spaghetti. Patrick was making faces at her and she was laughing, the noodles and tomato sauce spraying from her mouth, so abandoned in her glee that it went straight to my heart and warmed me, made me want desperately to live. If I died, I could not teach them how to survive in a world of shifting, vicious Powers—some physical, some emotional. My death here would be a curse they might spend a lifetime trying to hide from or trying to explain to themselves.

I stood up shakily and faced the blizzard. I ignored the burning cold and turned into the face of it and vowed, "I will not doom them to that."

I got my coat back on and crawled through the white on white for almost an hour until I found a tree and then another, and the trees gave me a frame of reference from which I could navigate. I found my cabin at last and went into it, dazed and nearly numb.

I looked around the room, at the furniture, at the walls, at the gas lamps, at the oil painting and finally at the buck. Hatred welled inside me at all that the deer seemed to embody and I tore it from the wall and raised it over my head by its antlers. I gazed up at the buck, wanting to remember its shape before I dashed it against the wall. In its glass eyes I saw myself looking back.

I stared through the deer and into myself for a very long time. I lowered the buck finally, frightened at and yet resigned to my sudden understanding that stopping Ryan would demand that I follow one of Mitchell's and my father's tenants of hunting—to hunt the deer well, you must become the deer. To hunt Ryan, I would have to be willing to enter a world where nothing was as it seemed, where turbulent Powers ghosted through animal and rock and sky. I would have to give myself completely to the forest of the mind and risk madness.

As a girl, I had listened to Mitchell recite the legends of our people, how the *Puoin* prepared for their rituals and their travels within the six worlds by erecting a pole or a tree branch outside their lodges. These they hung with gifts. It was the visible manifestation of the tree that connected the world we see, touch, taste, smell and hear with those ephemeral realms below, above and beyond. Warming myself before the stove in my cabin, I admitted that I did not comprehend an eighth of all I needed to know to perform this ceremony, but I did not have a choice. I would remember as best I could the shadows of my early life.

I opened the door and let the blizzard inhale me again. I fought my way to one of the trees and broke off a big limb. I brought it into the cabin room and propped it up between two chairs. On it I hung the deer-skin robes I had worn the night I escaped from the wolves. On the skins I hung the picture of Emily and Patrick and beside it the picture of Lizzy Ryan. Around both photographs I draped the bloodied bandage I'd taken from my forearm. Above that I placed a small mirror from my cosmetic compact. Below, I affixed the raven's feather I'd taken from Grover's mouth and a lock of hair cut from my bangs.

When I was satisfied I went into the bathroom, stripped and showered. I came out and rubbed myself with crushed, fragrant needles from the crown of the tree limb that had become the centerpiece in the altar of my shrine.

I turned down the gaslights then, wrapped myself in one of the deer robes and sat cross-legged facing the shrine, warmed by the fire behind me. I forced myself to recall every detail of the last hunting lesson my father had begun to teach me before he had announced his decision to let Katherine kill herself.

I was sixteen and a half that fall, a veteran hunter who had tracked and taken seven big whitetails. It was nine o'clock one early November morning. Overnight the first three-inch storm had swept over Katahdin. We had criss-crossed the forest since dawn, but found no tracks.

"The first storm makes the deer nervous, unwilling to move and show us where they've been," my father said.

"So we go home, wait until afternoon?"

"No," he said, smiling. "You are going to learn to track them with your heart."

I frowned.

He said, "There are energies in the forest that, with concentration, you have already learned to sense. Energies that give evidence of an animal's passing. This is just a new way to sense that energy."

"I don't understand."

"Think of how I taught you to look at which way a fern had been twisted to tell a buck's travel direction."

I nodded. "Yes."

"Now, remember how I trained you to open your ears to all sound and how you have learned that the volume of small animal chatter changes with the approach of a big animal."

I nodded again.

"All these exercises were just getting you ready to let your heart be a sense," he went on. "It's only with your heart that you can feel Power, invisible but real and living around us in the trees and the cliffs and the rivers and the sky and the wind."

The "heart hunt," as my father described it, involved abandoning control of your heart until it adopted the rhythms of the energies that pulsed around it. He claimed it was at once a way of truly joining spirits with the deer during the hunt as well as a cloudy window that allowed a first glimpse into the world of Power.

I had not been very successful in my lessons that fall. Twice I had achieved a fluttering in my heart in anticipation of a buck's appearance in the woods, but I had never been able to wipe away the frost that clouded my vision and look into the other world my father claimed he could see.

Now, sitting before my shrine, my life seemed to depend on it. I tried to slow my breathing as he had taught me and after a while I got my respiration to even out until I could feel my heart beating. But no matter how hard I tried, I could not get my heart to feel anything but my own sorrow.

"I can't do this!" I screamed at the deer head on the wall. "I'm not strong enough. Maybe I should just die."

The deer stared back at me. So I tried again. I calmed myself and focused, soon feeling my heart once more driving the rush and flow of blood at my temples.

I closed my eyes to the deer and imagined myself the way my father and Mitchell had described the oldest of the old ones in our legends: a woman draped in leaves and moss, living in a hole beneath a tree where the dead are buried. In my mind it became the deepest, stillest part of the night and I dwelled on every breath, easing the pace down, expanding the volume and length of each inhalation and exhalation until my brain glowed and then sparked with an oxygen-fired sensitivity, until, at last, I felt the troubled rhythms of my heart steady and become gentle probing waves that left me, bounced off the ceilings and walls and returned so that even with my eyes closed I could see.

It was late when I knocked at the front door to the lodge.

"Who's there?" Phil asked.

"Little Crow."

I must have been a sight, for when the door opened, Phil looked away, embarrassed the way I used to be encountering the addled street people who lived around Copley

Square. I had taken soot from the woodstove and smeared black ribbons on my skin to break up my profile. I was dressed in Griff's white camouflage outfit. On the wool shirt I wore underneath, I had pinned a piece of deer skin and my children's photograph over my left breast, and over my right I had affixed the picture of Lizzy Ryan. In my hair I wore the raven's feather.

"Woman, where the hell do you think you're going, looking like that?" he demanded.

"Hunting," I said, pushing by him. The lights in the great room had been dimmed. The fire in the hearth had gone to coals. Theresa slept on one of the couches under a red-and-black wool blanket. A shotgun lay on the floor beside her. Lenore was curled up in a chair across from her. Nelson paced on the landing before the shattered stained-glass window, a rifle held at port arms. Kurant sat one floor below, studying through the window the broad oval of light that banished the darkness of the lodge yard. Arnie was tending to Earl, who seemed to have taken a turn for the worse in the hours since I'd left the lodge; the tycoon was shifting and groaning on the bed in the corner. Griff was nowhere to be seen.

"What d'you mean, hunting?" Phil snapped. "We all took a vote. None of us are leaving this room until the plane comes. Round-the-clock watches. We all make it or none of us do."

"I don't know if the plane is coming any time soon," I said. "The ice is too thick and broken up around the dock. They're going to have to wait until a smooth section freezes, or they're going to have to come in after us by land, which could take days. So you die your way, Phil. I'll die mine."

I kept moving as I talked, padding by Theresa and Lenore into the dining room, where I pulled up a chair and was standing on it when Griff came out of the kitchen with a pot of coffee and a plate of sandwiches. He saw Phil first and then me and then Metcalf's bow and the quiver of cedar arrows which I now had in my hands.

"Diana, I hope you're not thinking of—"

But I was already down off the chair, moving toward the door to the great room. "The only chance to stop him is to go after him alone," I said.

Griff put the coffee and sandwiches on the table and ran after me. He caught me as I was about to go out the front door.

"You can't do this," he said.

"I have to do this," I said sadly.

"Give me one good reason."

I thought for a moment about telling him everything, then decided he couldn't possibly understand all of it, so I gave him the piece of it he could grasp: "I was taught as a child never to leave a wounded animal in the woods."

THANKSGIVING DAY

IN THE LEGENDS I remember from childhood, the shaman encounters Power after becoming lost deep in the forest. One story in particular accompanied me as I walked east toward the dawn. It was the tale of a young boy who wanted to run away from his cruel older brother. He loses himself to his former life by shooting his arrow into the woods and running as fast as he can to catch it before it falls to the ground. His mind is on each flight of the arrow, not the familiar world of home and parents. Soon he finds himself in alien terrain, disoriented, relying on his senses to survive.

I walked far out along the logging roads toward that eastern quadrant of the estate where Ryan seemed most comfortable. I drew one of the six cedar arrows from the quiver on my back, spun myself in circles, then loosed the arrow into the stillest, darkest moments of the night. As soon as I let the arrow go, I ran after it.

The snow under the new snow, the snow that had been wet yesterday, had frozen to create a firm, even floor beneath my feet. I ran without fear of being tripped by an unseen log or stump or rock; they had been buried, changed by the Power of the storm.

The blizzard weakened and finally stopped. And the clouds broke overhead and the darkness around me gave way to the light of the waning moon.

I told myself as I ran after my arrow that Ryan had embraced the chaos of the forest of the mind. To kill him, I would have to do the same. Ryan believed he was a *Mara'a-kame*. To survive the final clash certain to come, I, despite all my education and training in the visible world, would have to become a *Puoin*, the last of a line of Micmac shamans that stretched back through my father to my great-uncle and his mother beyond to the old ones who once had lived in the forests of Nova Scotia.

I ran until I felt the first pangs of uncertainty and fear that well up in the understanding that you are lost. I slowed, sweating, letting my eyes roam in the forest heart, casting back and forth through the dimness to catalog the weird relief of gray-and-black gnarled shapes against the snow-pack. My mind played games with me. The black triangle off to my right, probably a chunk of unexposed rock, became the face of the alpha-bitch wolf, intent on revenging her lost eye. A mosaic of thin dark lines—a branch? two saplings intertwined?—became Ryan's arms supporting bow and arrow.

The evidence was mounting; I could not trust anything I

could sense here in the ordinary meaning of the word. So
I closed my eyes and repeated the sequence of memory
and rhythmic breathing I had followed the evening before.
Soon I could feel my heart beating outward, striking objects
and reflecting back to me the energies within the predawn.

I opened my eyes and crept through the gloom, all the
while continuing to probe the mutating shapes around me
with my heart. A deer browsed into the wind on the bench
above me. Two more steps and she caught my scent,
snorted and bounded away. At dawn I sensed a ponderous
force buried under the snow in a thicket of pine and knew
a bear slept there. A half mile more and the sun cleared
the ridges on the other side of the Dream, sending brilliant
shafts of light and Power through the woods.

Above me and to my left, hidden in the boughs of a
majestic ponderosa, I felt a small, troubled being that had
the peculiar ability to look at the world both as vast landscapes and as specific blades of grass. The young crow
cawed loudly as it left the tree. And, for a moment, I closed
my eyes and left with it, soaring on an updraft until I looked
down upon the forest as I had eight days ago in the
floatplane.

When I opened my eyes again, I was frightened to see
that even though the sun still shone magnificent and bright,
what appeared to be a fine crystalline snow filled the air.
I raised my face to the crackling blue-and-white mist, expecting brief cold stings. Instead, my cheeks, nose, mouth
and eyelashes were caressed as if by warm feathers. There
was a grain in the pattern of this precipitation; it seemed
to run, then break around and over invisible objects, and
then retract almost the way a waxing tide will inhale and

exhale boulders on the seashore. And yet I could still see clearly through the feather snow to the sunlit trees and the drifts over boulders and the crow that had circled back into the glen, heading for its rookery. The crow flapped and glided in on the current of the feather snow as a kayaker would. I realized in awe that I was seeing as the crow saw, that for the first time in the nightmare, I had an ally.

When the warm crystals passed by my body, they blew outward and swirled. Standing still, I created an eddy in the current of the feather snow. I took a step. The swirl expanded, a minor wave in front of me. Ahead some hundred yards, there appeared the suggestion of a swell in the pattern of the snowfall. There was no wind, and I watched the swell grow before a doe and a fawn stepped out.

This is what it's like to lose your mind.

For much of the morning I crept through the forest, the bow in my left hand, an arrow in my right, teaching myself to interpret the billows and wafts that appeared in the grain of the snowfall much the way I had learned to track deer so many years before. An animal's passage would be preceded by a bulge in the pattern. If the animal stood still, the ripples were smaller. Birds in flight caused the ripples to curve.

Near midday I believed I was beginning to understand the limits and permutations of my madness, that I could navigate in this world and, when my task was finished, leave it behind. We cling to such fallacies in times of crisis out of ignorance. And yet it is only during times of crisis, under increasing levels of stress, that we strip away the veils that separate us from deeper levels of existence, self-knowledge and pain.

My wanderings had taken me along a shelf above one of the small clear-cuts that dotted this part of the estate. Suddenly, I was confused to notice, at the far left of my peripheral vision, the feather snow not bulging, but being sucked away suddenly as if by a tremendous vacuum. I turned and stared at the phenomenon, at the way the snow now spun inward and retreated like a whirlpool.

Then I sensed a rapid reversal in the maelstrom and a hot, piercing energy flew straight at me from the center of the cone. It was like one of those times when you touch something terribly hot and you react by pulling away your finger even though you have not yet experienced the hurt. I dove forward and down, hitting snow even as I heard the smack of the arrow striking soft wood above me.

I rolled over twice and got up tight behind a blowdown tree. Ryan was here, close enough to shoot at me. I nocked an arrow onto the bowstring and brought the whole contraption into a position where I could draw fast and release.

Ryan must have taken the way I dove forward as sign of a hit. For he came close to giving me the perfect shot; when I caught sight of him, he was sprinting diagonally through logging slash at about forty yards. The gray wolf's cape fluttered behind him. He was trying to get above me to see whether I was down for good.

There was an opening in the brush about fifteen feet ahead of the religion professor, and I drew and swung the arrow at the opening and released a fraction of a second before he entered my line of fire.

Admittedly, my experience with a bow was limited; as a girl, I'd learned the art at summer camps and continued in my backyard on a target Mitchell built for me out of hay bales. And I had hunted for two seasons with a recurve, but had never taken a shot at an animal because I wasn't sure of the distance.

Still, there's no doubt in my mind that the release was good and the arrow flew true. But in the middle of a full sprint, Ryan changed direction by a few degrees of angle and made a flicking motion with his left hand, his bow hand, even as he crashed to the ground and rolled from my sight. My arrow clattered harmlessly into the saplings beyond him.

A sickening feeling came over me. It was one thing for me to have ducked at some extrasensory warning I did not fully understand. It was quite another to have such a high degree of awareness that redirecting a speeding arrow was part of your Power. I was not up to this challenge. My mind turned hazy with the thought that sooner or later today I would die.

But before that thought could hamstring my will, I heard a guttural whine on the flank opposite Ryan. The feather snow there bulged, the swell becoming tubular just before she stepped into view. A thick crust of blackened blood had formed over her left eye. The flesh below it was pink and worried free of fur. She cocked her head in my direction, slunk forward two steps and growled. Then I sensed Ryan sneaking through the slash to my left, both of them pinching toward me, sure that the steep rock face at my back would prevent me from fleeing. My throat constricted and I fought against the squeezing off of breath that seemed to slow the flow of the feather snow around me.

I felt, but never saw, the crow pass over the opening. I only knew that I was suddenly certain of all of the features of the landscape around me, and just as certain of my escape route.

About twenty yards to my left, hidden by a curve in the shelf on which I hid, was a steep-banked old streambed that cut down-ridge. I drew, raised up and fired an arrow at the wolf. It crashed into the dry deadwood right beside her. She turned tail at the racket and loped into the thicket. She was not frightened. She would merely try another angle of attack.

But I was already up and dashing toward the streambed. It looked like a ten foot-wide frozen staircase, in places denuded of vegetation, in others choked with shoulder-high cedars. The streambed went straight up for twenty yards, then began a snake dance of curves to a spring at the ridge top. The footing was good and I bounded up the stairs, anticipating the curves and the openings in the cedars even before I saw them. I had gained about four hundred vertical feet in elevation before I felt Ryan and his ally below and behind me in the streambed. Accelerating, I burst through several openings and over a series of downed logs before flashing on the crow's perspective again. The streambed changed course just ahead of me. The bank rose sharply on the left side. There were downed tamaracks there in which I could hide and shoot. A place of Power. An ambush.

What followed seemed to unfold in slow motion.

Long before I saw her, the feather snow emanating from the cedar jungle below me jetted and swirled. I craned my head forward, waiting. The snow swirled again.

And then I heard the snarl and snapped my head over my shoulder upstream to the opposite bank. She had circled me! In one leap, the wolf carried herself over and down and halfway across the stream. I could not turn to get the shot. I was trapped.

In a low crouch she came up the bank, wary, her shoulder blades popping with controlled effort. She bared her teeth and flicked her tongue even as I made a futile effort to get myself turned around with the bow, even as I knew it was over.

There are moments in a life that are inexplicable. This was one of mine. In the streambed below me, exactly where the feather snow had swirled moments before, a ten-point buck stepped from the cedars and paused in the opening. Flecks of bright, frothy blood, lung blood, shone at his muzzle. I do not know if Ryan had shot the animal as he'd followed me up the streambed and that was what had caused the bizarre patterns in the feather snow prior to the wolf appearing. Perhaps it was just the energy being given off by a wounded animal fighting for its life. I do not know.

I only know that the buck was there and that I believe it was the oxygen-saturated scent of his lung blood that saved me; the Power of the liquid life force draining from the deer seemed to sever whatever hold Ryan had on the wolf. She stopped cold in her tracks and responded to an instinct ingrained over thousands of generations. She turned her head so the blind eye faced me and sniffed the air. Sinking inside herself, she made ready her attack and took two catlike steps toward the deer.

The wolf never knew that my arrow split her lungs and heart and passed out behind her opposite shoulder and buried itself in the snow. Instead, she leapt away on a dead run, confident of an easy kill on wounded prey.

The buck faced her, his rack down and swinging to and fro. Ten yards from him, the wolf's front legs buckled and she plowed face-first into the snow, twitched and died. The buck came up walleyed in terror at the sight. In two bounds he was gone.

I made it to the ridge top in time to hear, far below me, an explosion of hatred when Ryan found his ally dead. The feather snow behind me reacted as if blown by a hurricane.

For the first time that morning, I smiled. For more than a week we had used tactics that had us acting as hunter while Ryan played the deer. And he had foiled us, crippled us, killed us by adopting that strategy.

Now the deer and the crow occupied my mind. I would set the pace. I would choose the terrain. I would let him hunt me until I could lay some kind of trap for him again. I would try until one of us was dead.

I ran across the ridge top, then looped backward, cutting my own tracks and those of Ryan in pursuit before retreating back down the streambed, taking the frozen stairs three at a time. Halfway to the bottom, I spun backward into my own tracks of a half hour earlier, tracing them with care for ten paces before jumping far to one side and breaking up the bank and then traversing a shelf.

Here the wind of the previous night's storm had blown the snowpack as hard and smooth as a billiard table. I flew across it as if I no longer had feet, but wings. My head was up, aware, culling the information flowing into my brain the way my computers do running data. I had confidence that I was in control, that I had Power.

Ahead, the shelf narrowed to a bottleneck. I ran through the funnel, noting how steeply the land fell away to my left toward the flat and the clear-cut where not an hour ago Ryan and I had attempted to shape-change each other forever. A cluster of thirty-foot pines had grown up in the bottleneck. Where the funnel drained into a broad, long hardwood glen, I jumped downslope and crabbed back just under the shelf lip before stopping in a tangle below the tightest part of the bottleneck. I got an arrow, my second to last arrow, nocked it tight and held the bow loosely in the direction from which I expected him to come. I knew he'd sensed my arrow in flight before, but I hoped the death of the wolf would be enough to disturb his focus.

There was no noise or movement in the woods around me for the longest time. Then the feather snow wafted and fluttered right along the surface of the shelf above me like the hem of a thin curtain brushed by a meandering summer breeze.

My chest tightened at the sight of it. The shift in the pattern of the snow was so subtle, so gentle, yet so intentional that I knew that he knew I was inside his world now. Surely not as honed in my abilities as he, but inside it nonetheless; and he was coming after me with respect, hunting slow and methodical.

The sound of my heart had been a comforting presence all morning. Now my nerves rose and began to clash with the consistent beat of my heart. The feather snow tapered almost to flurries. I drew back the bow and held it. I struggled to remain clear, to see him before he saw me. But from deep inside me a gnawing sadness wormed its way toward my heart and clouded me with regret. The gauntness of my father's face in the morgue. Patrick begging me to come home. Phil crying for Butch. Lizzy Ryan gazing into the last blue sky of her life. All these things whirled about me, then slowed.

Ryan was kneeling between two boulders thirty-five yards away. He was at full draw, too.

I don't remember releasing my arrow. That memory was swallowed whole by the slicing punch of his arrow through the fleshy part of my right breast. It glanced off my rib cage and continued through the muscles at my armpit before leaving me. My numb arm trembled and contracted. Heavy dark spots appeared before me. I shook my head, trying to free myself from the shock of the wound. But nothing prepares you for this. You actually feel the Power seeping from you.

I heard a cry and the spots shrank and my vision cleared. My arrow had caught Ryan in the thigh. With both hands he had hold of the broadhead, which thrust out a good four inches from the side of his leg. He was staring at me and I knew that he had caused the sadness that destroyed my concentration as a way of masking his movements. I tried to get my dying hand to react, to take my last arrow and finish him, but it would not answer my call. It had curled up like a claw.

"You will die for Lizzy!" he screamed at me. "You will die for her and Kauyumari and Tatewari!"

I knew what Ryan was going to do even before he did. The Datura smoke had anesthetized him to pain that would have finished another man. It had turned him to animal. The sudden knowledge that I had brushed only the surface of his insane world spurred in me an abject, blind terror. I ran downhill toward the Dream, my arm flopping uselessly beside me.

I cannot describe the sound he made in the woods behind me as he wrenched the arrow shaft from his leg, only that it seemed like thunder clapping after lightning and that the lightning followed me the way it would a metal boat on open water.

I had a head start of maybe a hundred yards while he cut a length from the wolf cape sufficient to stem the flow of blood from his leg. I kept reaching inside my coat to gauge the extent of my own wounds from the wet, sticky feeling under my arm. Nerve damage for sure. To the muscles and tendons as well. But, miraculously, his arrow had not sliced a major artery. I slipped my dead arm between the string and the arm of the bow and pulled it tight to my body. The cross-pressure would limit my blood loss and keep my arm from swinging as I ran. The happy effect of that improvement fled when I turned after another hundred yards to see that I was leaving not only tracks, but bright red evidence of my passing in the snow.

Ryan would find it and it would trigger bloodlust and he would come after me as the wolf had come after the wounded buck in the streambed. I ran on, trying to call up my heart as a sense and the crow as my ally. But I was a novice at entering the other worlds, a novice who required a still forest, a still mind, a still body to slide open the curtains and peer through the window. All around me now was chaos. I'd lost my heart.

The faint gurgle of the Dream reached me and I realized I'd be trapped ahead on the flat along the river. It would end there. I would end there.

I thought of Patrick and Emily and even Kevin, and I began to sob, the tears clouding my vision, and I tripped passing through a choke of serviceberry and crashed onto my wounded shoulder.

The pain shot up and through me, firing my brain to a white coil. And in that superheated state I saw my father standing before me, telling me not to give up, to hunt in the way I knew best. "Know the deer," I heard him say, and then he was gone and the pain with him.

Now I studied the terrain before me as any good deer hunter would, as an evolving situation that with finesse could be worked in my favor. I went straight to the bank of the Dream, wrenching myself free of the camouflaged anorak and hanging it over a piece of driftwood on the bank. I put my hat there, too. From thirty yards back, it all might suggest a slumped woman. Letting my right arm dangle free again, swallowing hard at the broadening red circle on the right side of my chest, I walked in circles to encourage the thick drops of blood to paint the snow, to tell the story of an animal wandering deranged in the shadow of death.

I glanced at the piece of deer skin and the photographs of Emily and Patrick pinned to my shirt. Lizzy Ryan's face in the photograph was smeared with my blood. Then I jumped down the bank and trotted north twenty yards along the river's edge, mindful not to step on the weak ice that masked the furious current. I clawed my way up the bank and slipped through the jack pines toward my back trail. Ryan would be coming slow again, especially with a wounded leg. I had time.

I got my left foot between the bowstring and the tip of

the bottom bow limb. I grasped the tip of the top bow limb with my good hand and pressed downward, reaching with my teeth for the groove in which the loop of the string had been set. It freed on the third try. I laid the bow on the other side of, and perpendicular to, a pair of saplings growing about six inches apart, then brought the string around the back side and, after thirty seconds of struggle, got the string looped back on the opposite bow limb.

Panting now, murmuring directions to myself to keep my mind off the predator sneaking my blood trail, I got my last arrow on the string and laid it between the saplings. I sat behind the bow, then shimmied the weapon to about knee height, hooked three fingers around the arrow nock, got my feet against the saplings and pulled back. The riser of the bow held tight to the saplings and the limbs flexed toward me.

I had to scrunch down to look across the plane of the arrow and through the V of the three-bladed broadhead. I aimed at a point thirty yards back from the bank from where I felt sure Ryan would see the concentration of my blood in the snow as well as the anorak and the hat. If that caused the slightest shift in his attention, I had him.

I had no time to think about anything. He was suddenly there, limping his way through the choke of serviceberry, kneeling where I'd fallen to look at the blood swatch, to make his own assessment of my physical condition. He smiled, stood and took an awkward step forward out of the thicket.

"Keep coming," I whispered to myself. "Ten more feet, you sick bastard."

Ryan stopped after another step and let his eyes trail my

trail across the flat to the heavy splash of blood I'd left on the bank. And finally to my anorak and hat.

If I'd been able to support the bow with both arms, I could have shot him then. But the way it was, with the riser against the tree, I could not move the bow in his direction at all. I had one shooting lane and he was still five feet from entering it.

Ryan swiveled his head, taking in the woods around him. I hunkered down, praying the saplings and the brilliant sunlight in his face would protect me. He paused for a fraction of a second as he turned to face my direction, and I felt his awareness pass just over me, return and pass again toward my anorak and hat.

He stayed still, looking at the anorak and the hat and the blood. I had been holding the bowstring and the arrow nock with three fingers for close to four minutes now and my fingers began to quiver.

"Come on," I whispered. And then he moved.

Whether it was the trembling in my fingers or the sudden release of pressure against the riser that affected my shot, I'll never know. But I'm positive that when Ryan grinned and moved into my shooting lane, I had the broadhead locked on his chest. I let the arrow go. It flailed sideways, a reddish flash in the late-morning air, then straightened and struck him low with the sound of a fist plumping a pillow. He humped up and dropped his bow and grabbed his stomach. He looked at his stomach as if he couldn't believe it.

"Gut-shot," Ryan said, shaking his head. "She gut-shot me."

I had gotten up by now and stepped out from behind the saplings, expecting him to fall at any moment.

Instead, he raised up and turned toward me. I shivered as the shadow of something evil and powerful surrounded me.

Ryan's eyes flared and he reached to his waist and brought out that wicked stone-bladed knife he'd had in the cave. "I'll destroy you!" he threatened, seething, and he came at me, no limping, no sign of the arrow that had just passed through his paunch.

I ran toward the river, hysterically thinking that maybe Theresa had been right; in the Datura state, he could not be killed in any conventional sense.

Ryan caught me the first time ten feet from the riverbank. He threw himself forward and got his hand around my ankle. I crumbled through the dead branches of a blowdown with my bad shoulder. The agony seared through me again.

But my own Power surged, reacting, feeding off and against his. I lashed out with my free leg, catching him on the ear with the toe of my steel-shanked boot. His hold on me wavered and I kicked again, knocking the knife from his other hand. I struggled forward on my knees, slipping and falling as I tried to get back on my feet.

He caught me the second time right at the edge of the river. He hit me hard with both fists between the shoulder blades, knocking the wind from me. I collapsed forward and he went with me, pinning me on the shore next to the thin ice.

"Know my name?" he chanted in that hoarse voice. "Know my name?"

He rolled me over and got his hands around my throat; and I stared into his blank eyes and choked out, "Death."

His face glowed in an indescribable rapture. He dug his thumbs into my windpipe.

My Power came up again and I bucked and beat at his side with my one good arm. He never flinched. He just squeezed tighter and began to sing to his god, to Tatewari, and my Power again ebbed away like water in thawing ground. A halo—black at the center, shimmering white along the inside edge—appeared all around him. It was as if I were looking at the negative of a photograph taken of him in direct light.

I stopped trying to hit him and my arm fell to one side and struck something long and cold and cylindrical. The volume of his chanting rose. I heard him invoke Kauyumari, the deer god, and Keili and Peyote. I felt the last of me slip toward his fingers. And with that I felt the coming of night.

I accepted the fall of light and went toward it. And just as I was about to enter the night, far behind me I noticed that the chanting had stopped. Ryan had eased the pressure around my throat.

I choked and coughed and spit. He still knelt on me, his hands resting on my neck. But the homicidal frenzy I'd seen in the face of the mad Huichol sorcerer was gone. This was the devastated, lonely religion professor I'd felt in my hallucination. Ryan was gazing tenderly at the photograph pinned over my wounded right breast. In our struggle the snow had washed my blood from her picture. He took his hands from my throat and stroked the picture and murmured, "Lizzy. Oh, Lizzy. I miss you so much."

I glanced to my left. My good arm rested on a piece of

ice-encased driftwood about eighteen inches long and about as thick as my wrist. I closed my fingers around it and looked back to him, even as I felt him become aware of me again and his face contorted toward rage.

I swung with every bit of strength I had left, stunned at the blast of black electric current that surged through me when the club struck and caved in the side of Devlin Ryan's head. Now I was the one surrounded by the black, shimmering halo. I was the negative. I was Death, changer of shapes, stealer of Power.

Ryan tottered for a second, highlighted in a sudden eclipse. The light faded from eyes still focused on his wife. Then he slumped off me and crashed through the ice into the Dream.

APRIL

I COME OFTEN now to the burial ground of my parents and Mitchell. It is on a knoll on tribal lands, on an island actually in the Penobscot River, ten miles north of Old Town. You must use a canoe to get there, and lately the water has been high and fast with the winter runoff's and the spring rains; I have been forced to launch well upstream and ride the current to reach them.

I have gone six times since ice-out last month, driving the entire way from Boston to Bangor on Friday nights so I can cross at dawn on Saturday mornings. I've never had a problem going to their world and returning. Yet each time I step into the canoe and feel the river's force creep up the paddle into my still-healing shoulder, I fear that this will be the last crossing for me. I have come to understand the silk strings that connect us to this world.

Yesterday I took Emily and Patrick to meet their grand-
parents. It was one of those mid-April Maine days when the
frigid, clear dawn gives way to a day that flirts with sixty.
Nature seducing us with the first inkling of the warmth to
come.

There was fog hovering above the water near shore. The
kids had been yawning in the truck until we'd reached the
river. But once they got outside, the spirit of the waters
invaded them, made them want to be part of it. Patrick
helped me get the canoe down from the roof. He is almost
nine and I see my father in him with each passing day.

We pushed off from shore, instantly sucked into the Penobscot's power. I imagined myself the crow navigating on
the feather snow and I let the craft accept the river's course
until we needed to veer off. There was a moment when
the white water became a roar around us, when Emily and
Patrick turned to me, frightened. Emily said she wanted to
go home. Patrick tried to be brave and said nothing. I just
smiled and told them to ignore what was under them, that
it was a place they need not understand yet. Better to look
instead to the island.

That calmed them. They turned and faced the approaching shoreline with such eagerness that I almost dissolved in the joy that they were once again with me.

For many months after my return from the Metcalf Estate,
I feared I would never have that kind of moment with them,
especially after the publication of Kurant's melodramatic
account of the slayings. He called the ten-thousand-word
article "Revenge of the Hunter," and reduced the complex
forces that had been in play along the border of British
Columbia and Alberta to a simplistic clash of good and evil.

In Kurant's eyes, the victims had been "consumed by the throwback barbarism that underlies the culture of modern hunting." Especially so Cantrell, who committed suicide with a rifle in January.

He even had a quote from Lenore to the effect that she and Earl would never hunt again. The computer tycoon would be forever confined to a wheelchair and reliant on her care. I could not help wondering whether or not Lenore secretly believed that Earl in such a state—unable to chase women and flaunt them in her face—was the greatest trophy she would ever bag anyway.

Griff and Arnie told Kurant that they still supported hunting, but were unsure if they would go the woods again this coming fall. Phil, not surprisingly, refused to talk with Kurant at all. Nelson and Theresa were trying to negotiate a new hunting lease on the estate, but the Metcalfe heirs were balking at the idea.

To the writer, Ryan was driven by vengeance against a system that wrongly valued the rights of the hunter over the rights of his wife. He framed Ryan's story as a failure to embrace the fact that his wife's death proved hunting was wrong. Instead, the professor had retreated further into the primitive, predatory state and gone mad in the process.

As I expected, Kurant took no responsibility for his role in aiming Ryan's homicidal energy north. And he avoided the issue of when he began to suspect that Ryan was the killer. He would have to live with that understanding the rest of his life.

I was portrayed as the heroine determined to save the band of hunters. Even so, Kurant digressed at some length into a discussion of whether or not, in my final effort to kill Ryan, I had crossed the boundary between self-defense and first-degree murder. I had hunted Ryan down and killed him when I could have remained in the camp with the others. Indeed, there were members of the Canadian Mounted Police team that finally arrived on the estate four days after I killed Ryan who seemed intent on getting me indicted on that charge. But the Canadian judge who looked into the case found that the intensity of the situation on the Metcalfe Estate had created "such an overwhelming atmosphere of mortal threat that it is certain that Diana Jackman killed Ryan in self-defense and in defense of the rest of the survivors."

Kurant's story also revealed that the fourth scalp in the cave belonged to J. Wright Dillon, the hunter who had shot Izzy. His body was never found, but the DNA match with the flesh in logging camp four was identical.

When I attempted once again to get joint custody of Patrick and Emily, Kevin's attorney tried to use the events at Metcalfe against me, asking the judge in family court to stick by Kevin's earlier request that I be psychologically evaluated. After all, how could the courts allow two young children to be left with a woman capable of coldly hunting and killing someone?

My attorney had argued that it showed I was capable of protecting the children, that the experience had only made me a better mother. Kevin whispered something to his attorney and it dawned on me this wasn't about the legal process, this was personal. It had to be worked out personally.

Before the judge ruled, I asked him if I might have some time with Kevin alone, no attorneys. Kevin's lawyer objected, but Kevin looked at me and I mouthed the word "please." He hesitated, then nodded. The judge said it was almost lunchtime and we could use a conference room until court reconvened in two hours. I was as nervous as I'd been hunting Ryan when I followed my husband into the book-lined office.

Kevin stood awkwardly in the corner, fiddling with his starched cuff.

"How are you?" I asked.

"Been better," he said. "I don't like courtrooms."

"I don't either," I said. I played with the front page of the *Globe* lying on the table. "Believe it or not, I missed you."

"Uh-huh." He wouldn't look at me. I waited until he did.

"I guess you didn't think about me at all. Even after all that happened in Canada."

Kevin seemed startled by that remark. "No, of course I thought about you. I was . . . worried. How are you?"

I hesitated. "Better. Better than I've been in a long time."

He hesitated. "I wish I could believe it."

"I know," I said. "And I know that it's going to take a long time before you believe it, too. I told you once if you loved me you wouldn't ask me about my life before we met. I was wrong and I'm sorry."

"Diana, I still think—"

"Hear me out," I pleaded, and I told him I'd been unfair to him since the day we'd met, that I'd hidden a huge chunk of my life from him and that was not the sort of foundation on which to build a relationship. Then I told him the high points of it; how I'd been raised, how my mother had died, how I'd run from her death and my father for years, a stranger to myself and, in more ways that I cared to admit, to him.

"The world changes shape and we change shape as we grow older," I said, "but from the time we are born to the time we die, we search for things that are true and constant to cling to. I clung to you for years because you loved me . . . almost without question. And you have to believe me when I say that no matter what I may have hidden from you or done to you, I loved you. And part of me still does.

"But the past came for me, Kevin, and I've had to admit who I am and what I am. I know it doesn't make much sense right now. But I'll do my best to explain all the details if you give me half a chance."

Kevin shook his head. "I don't know if knowing the real you will help, Diana. I'm afraid I'm always going to look at you and see this person who lived a secret life. This didn't happen to someone in a newspaper story. It happened to me! I don't know if that can ever be repaired."

I fought the tears to no avail. They streamed out and I sobbed, "I know. I've hurt you and I'm so very sorry. I know that you don't think we can ever save this marriage, and maybe we can't. But I'm asking that you think about the happy times we did share. I'm asking you for peace and to share our children. For their sake as well as mine. I need them, Kevin. I need them to be whole again."

He didn't say anything for the longest time. The tears kept coming and I hung my head, sure that he would continue to fight me and that Emily and Patrick might never be part of me. Then I felt his finger brush away the tears on my cheek. "That's how Yastrzemski used to swipe balls off the Green Monster," he said.

I could not stop crying.

We talked for another half hour. In the end, I agreed to

a psychological evaluation. Kevin agreed to a more lenient custody agreement. I have them two weekends a month and every other Monday night. It is a start.

The bow of our canoe ran up on gravel washed down by the spring rains. Patrick jumped out and pulled the canoe onto shore. The burial island is about a half mile long and a third of a mile wide. As a child, I enjoyed coming here because the girth of the island is grassy and peppered with hundreds of paper birches. I led my children south along the deer trails that crisscrossed the meadow grass, still stiff from the dew that had frozen overnight and now shimmered in the morning sun. Emily found a bird's nest in the budded low branches of a birch and cradled the treasure in her arms.

She and Patrick ran ahead toward the southernmost point on the island where the graves are. I felt strangely cleansed in a way I hadn't in a long time, even though I continue to have flashbacks about the death of Ryan and what I did after I killed him.

I lay on the bank of the Dream for a long time after I'd hit him with the log, feeling Ryan's presence beside me, feeling the river trying to tug him toward the other shore. When at last my strength returned, I got up and fashioned a bandage around my wound. Then I pulled him free of the water and stared at the peace in his face. How could a good person like this have gone so far into the night?

I had to know. I put my lips to his and inhaled all that was Ryan in the breath that remained. I closed my eyes and let his head fall into my lap, hearing in my mind the fleeting musical sounds of a woman's voice. I felt her warmth around me, cradling me until there was part of me in her. I caught flashes of their memory, and just before I sensed the dark part of his world coming into me, I sensed something else, an energy I had not thought to examine closely before, and its dominant presence in Ryan shocked me. I blew out the breath, shaking.

I dragged his body up onto the bank, covered it with snow and marked the spot with his bow so the Mounties could come to claim it if the wolves didn't first. When I was done, I was sweaty and my shoulder ached and I was seized by the need to wash.

I built a fire near his body, then stripped and went to the Dream. The ice water on my skin made me cry out, but I forced myself down into it, feeling it numb me, make me aware, reconciled and yet dead to who I was before I'd struck Ryan down. Back at the fire, sitting there, I felt my reawakening skin sting and itch. That feeling has not gone away. And probably never will.

I did not talk about what happened after Ryan's death with the psychologist. Nor did I give more than passing reference to Power or the Micmac legends. She was a too-thin woman in her thirties, given to fashionable clothes, and drove a convertible sports car. What could I have said under the circumstances? That I have come to believe through the horrible events at Metcalfe that there actually are invisible worlds constantly clashing in the air around us? That I have embraced a vision of this life forged centuries ago by primitives living in the Northern Forests? She'd have recommended I be kept from my children and undergo years of therapy.

So I said nothing about the feather snow or the flashes of electric light that passed into me when I killed Ryan. Nor did I tell her that I took Ryan's breath and that he now lives in me. Instead, I just go about my life as best I can, trying to rebuild it as best I can.

The canoe trip yesterday was an important step toward the goal. Mitchell is buried on the point where the Penobscot rejoins itself. Katherine and my father are behind him, a little bit higher on the gradual slope.

"Did you miss your mommy and daddy?" Emily asked when at last we stood before the stones that marked the spots. The warm south wind picked up and blew my hair into my eyes.

"Mommy?"

"Yes," I said. "Every day now."

They asked what my parents and Mitchell were like and I told them some of the stories that always come to my mind when I think of them. I told them how my mother embodied all the colors of the trout, and how on days like today my father sang songs to the spring, and how my great-uncle believed that even the smallest blade of grass and the tiniest pebble were alive.

They looked at me, confused, as they should have been. I laughed and tousled their hair and told them that it would take me a long time to tell them all the stories, and then maybe, just maybe, they'd begin to understand.

We stood there in silence for a long time after that; then Patrick and Emily wandered down by the riverbank to explore. I sat cross-legged among the graves and watched as a kingfisher launched from the top of a hemlock on the eastern shore. The bird bore down quickly on the shallows, angled its wings, then splashed into the water, surfacing almost immediately with a wriggling fish in its beak.

Patrick yelled, "Mommy!" and held up a smooth white rock he'd discovered. Emily still cradled the nest in one hand while stirring the water with a stick. I asked myself whether that rock or the nest or the stick would enter their dreams, form a place in their minds as it would have in the children of my ancestors ten or twenty generations ago. There was no answer to that and I knew it. I could only hope they would find some place in their hearts for such things.

As for me, the deer no longer runs in my dreams. Instead, my trips into the forest of my subconscious are marked by the expression on my father's face that day when I rushed home to find Katherine dead on the bank of her casting pond.

For so many years I had believed his expression was one of satisfaction, that he had taken his vision of the world to its logical conclusion and that he rejoiced in the strength of his faith. But leaving Ryan's body to wander back through the twilight toward the lodge, I had had a different vision of the events leading up to Katherine's death, and it is that vision that revisits me almost every night.

I dream now that my parents were waiting for just such a day, a glorious day of renewal, for my mother to die. It cohered with an ancient understanding of the universe, a universe imbued with invisible, mysterious Power, where nature ruled and to live in union with it was the blessed way.

I dream that my father waited until long after I had left

for school to come for my mother. He led Katherine down the lawn, hearing and smelling and seeing everything around him in a heightened, precise manner—the red-winged blackbirds calling in the willows, the bullfrogs roaring in the reeds, the scent of the lilacs' last blush, the breeze across the pond water. All the crazed bustle of spring.

Only there was no religious frenzy flowing through my father as I once believed. There was only the sense that he was terribly apart from all that surrounded him, aware and yet not aware, his focus Katherine and only Katherine. For she had been his Power, the beating heart through which he made sense of the world.

I dream of them sitting in the white glider in the gazebo, watching the water play with the light and the mayflies dance. They hug each other for the longest time, believing they are doing the right thing, that they are following the precepts of their religion, that they are living and dying in accord with nature. And then I hear my father's deep, gravelly voice singing not the birth song of spring, but the leaving song, the song of autumn.

And when he finishes, he cannot go on. It is Katherine who has the resolve to stand and walk to the water's edge and beckon him. She wades into the pond smiling, her bare feet pressing down into the inch of soft muck that winter and two months of spring have laid over the sand. Her nightgown lifts and floats about her knees.

My father feels sick as he gets to his feet and follows her. He is in agony as he kisses her one last time before she sets herself back into the water, pressing his hands into her chest. He takes over now, because it is what she wants. He holds her below the surface during her brief struggle, watching not the final bubbles of air leave her lungs, but the last of the morning's mayflies flutter and die on the mirror of water above her.

In my dreams the water ripples and I see someone I don't recognize at first. The dawning of awareness comes slowly. It is my father, a much younger version of him. And then the water ripples again and it is me. And out of that comes grief and the racking cries that always awaken me, the cries that signal my understanding that almost fifteen years before my father committed suicide in the woods below Mt. Katahdin, he'd killed himself drowning my mother, just as I have killed myself by killing Ryan.

"Mommy!" Emily cried, shaking me from my thoughts. "Come look."

I went down by the river then and found them crouched around a patch of frozen mud thawing in the strengthening sun. In the mud there was a single, clear track of a big deer probably trapped on the island during the sudden thaw, waiting for the river's fury to subside before it could swim to land.

I squatted next to Emily and Patrick and showed them how to run their fingers along the wall of the track and into its depths to determine the deer's weight, his direction of travel and the time that had passed since he'd been here. They got down on their knees and studied the track, absorbed with what I was telling them.

"Let's follow the tracks," Emily said.

"Let's do that," I replied.

And I took their hands and led them back toward the birches, where I would teach them to hunt as I was taught.

I felt once again that energy within Ryan that had so disturbed me. That energy and the words of my father's suicide note echoed and mixed within me as we walked. And for the first time, I understood that the same thing that had motivated Ryan was what my father was trying to describe in his suicide note. And it was the same thing that fortified and nearly consumed me during the ten days at Metcalfe. All of nature's creatures are murderers. We must murder to live. It's the law of the forest. But unlike the animals, we who are human are aware of this and must suffer each death as a small death within ourselves. We who are human carry the dead within ourselves. As such, we have been imbued with the highest and most complex manifestation of that thing my ancestors called Power. It drives us. It haunts us. It can become twisted and destructive. But it can also heal. It can give us rebirth at every death. It can offer faith, forgiveness and sanity where there seems hope of none. Some of us will spend a lifetime hunting for it.

Emily tugged at my sleeve. "What are you thinking about, Mommy?"

I paused and looked over my shoulder at the graves of my parents and my great-uncle and then back to my children. "Love." Then I took my children into the forest.

Here dies my story. Here lives my story again.

Sunday, May first, nineteen ninety-eight

THE STORM THAT marked the beginning of three of the most brutal weeks on record in Vermont began shortly after midnight. The wind shifted suddenly in direction and intensity from a shrouded breeze out of the southeast to a cruel, irregular gale from the northwest. The temperature dropped into the mid-thirties. A cold rain mixed with graupel snow came slanting across the central Green Mountain like an unexpected demise after the false birth of a serene, warm April.

On the flank of Lawton Mountain the storm filled a bouldered brook that in less than five miles plunged two thousand vertical feet to the valley floor. Other swollen rills disgorged into the brook during its rapid, aerated descent.

By the time the channel widened to become the Bluekill River, one of the most famous brook- and-brown trout streams in the eastern United States, the watercourse raged bronze and whitecapped past the budding sugar maples that edged the fields where cows browsed on spring's first clover.

The river gnawed at the banks in sight of the under-construction second homes of the fly fishing and skiing gentry who were making the Lawton Valley their latest weekend getaway enclave; it boiled past the town's old millworks that housed designer outlets and trendy curio shops. It lashed the stonework of the restored Federalist manors of the town's stately southside before sluicing under a red covered bridge and once again charging through field and into a softwood forest, where mid-morning it passed a bizarre-looking cabin set back in a pine grove fifty yards from the water's edge.

The right side of the cabin had the classic lines of a late nineteenth century post-and-beam farmhouse, complete with wraparound porch. But the left side was unnaturally canted; from ten feet off the peak of the slate roof, the wall plunged abruptly to the ground. No windows, no doors on that side. The clapboards were bare and weather-grayed.

At exactly ten that morning, I was pacing across the porch of that cabin in waders, a tan fishing vest, and a green felt crusher, a cellular phone mashed against my ear.

On the fifth ring: "You got me," a voice said.

I mustered false bravado. "Lucky me!" I replied.

There was a pause on the other end of the line, then my partner, Jerry Matthews, came on aggressive. "I thought we agreed not to talk."

"C'mon, I've been eight days on the water, getting ready for my ninth afternoon rise as we speak."

"Then go to it, pal, because you're no good to me or anyone else this way. Take the month. Hell, take two, because I can't deal with you the way you are."

I cleared my throat. "Are you going to the wedding?"

"Man, don't do this to yourself."

"I'm over it," I said. "Are you going?"

Jerry sighed on the other end of the line. "An old friend asks me to her wedding, I go. By the way, I better cut this short. I'm due at the church at noon."

I stopped talking and slumped into the wooden Adirondack chair on the porch, staring off through the drizzle at the raging river. "She's getting married in a church?"

"Ironic, huh?"

"No, what's ironic is my ex-wife gets remarried and I turn forty all in one day."

Matthews groaned on the other end of the line. "Sorry, I forgot. Happy birthday, buddy. Rotten timing, all of this, I guess. But, hell, shit happens to the best of us. We're born crying, we age disgracefully, we croak."

"And then what?"

"That's the big mystery," Jerry replied. "Go fishing, Pat, it's the only thing you love. Then find a nice mountain babe and invite her to dinner for your birthday."

I hesitated. "What are you telling people?"

"I'm covering for you, if that's what you mean. The story goes you're up in Vermont fishing and researching a priest who is up for sainthood. By the way, I had lunch with Jeanine Kelso at The Discovery Channel yesterday. She's hot on the idea."

"You're not a fibber," I said, gaining strength. "I've got an appointment to talk with the parish priest on Monday. He's supposedly the expert on Father D'Angelo."

"Well, that's a first step, Pat. But promise me a couple of things."

"What's that?"

"Do more fishing than work. And don't let your mid-life crisis kill you."

"I'll try," I promised, then I clicked off the phone. I stood and saw my reflection in the window glass. Six feet two inches tall, two hundred and twenty pounds, reasonably fit. A smirking, high-eyebrowed mug more than a few women have found attractive, marred by wrinkles now and flecks of gray that show plainly along the temples of my receding hairline. Sacks of loose skin under sunken bloodshot eyes. A man who has not slept soundly through the night in nearly four years. A man who has abandoned work on four projects in less than eighteen months and shielded himself from criticism and pressure with overdoses of fly fishing.

I retied my wading shoes, then took up my new graphite six-weight rod and reel and made my way to the river in an effort to fend off the hot point of a migraine now threatening—as if the hypnotic pulse of the rushing water around my lower body could loosen the emotional screws tightening in my head.

I did not pause at the water's edge but used my spiked wading staff to feel my way out into the surging current. Twice I stumbled, barely managing to keep my balance against the insistent water that pummeled the backs of my knees.

I found stable footing on a sandbar and tied on a bright

red streamer, the only hope for a strike in the murky high water. Then I played out line and drew the rod back to one o'clock before stiff-arming the tip forward and halting sharply at ten. In the chill mist left over from the storm, the line straightened on the backcast, looped at the braking action, then unfolded neatly and disappeared into the brown water against the far shore. I stripped line quickly until the streamer reappeared, raised the rod, and cast again. For almost a half hour the repetitive, flowing movement stilled my mind as a mantra might a Buddhist monk.

After a half hour with no strikes, I tied on a big yellow maribou—a lure more suited to western rivers—cast it, then watched my fluorescent orange floating line course rapidly downstream. The spool on the reel began to turn, playing out more line on the frothy water. The line snaked and danced hypnotically on the water. It became every fishing line I have ever cast, a line that arced over my head and landed in the muddy waters of the Ganges River. Nine years ago.

The ghat, the grand stone staircase that formed the river's bank, was packed with men, women, and children waiting to bathe. Goats bleated. A cow lowed in the late afternoon sun. Six half-cremated corpses lay on the stone at the water's edge, waiting to be taken to the center of the holy river and released.

Dressed in my fishing gear, I ignored the looks I got, wading off the ghat toward the current. I wasn't expecting to catch anything, but it had been a long day of travel and I needed to feel a cast or two and the water around me. After a half hour I had fallen under the Ganges' spell.

"Orvis comes to Allahabad," a throaty woman's voice broke the spell. "I've seen it all now!"

I stopped stripping my line and glanced over my shoulder. She was tall and big-boned, with a lion-like mane of auburn hair that framed an angular, freckled face, sparkling green eyes, and marvelous lips. She wore wraparound sunglasses, a Boston Red Sox baseball cap, a red batik skirt she'd hiked up over powerful thighs, and a plain white T-shirt over pendulous breasts. A Leica camera was slung around her neck. A camera bag hung off her shoulder. She waded to within yards, looked me up and down, and laughed.

"Some friends grabbed me in the street up there to tell me a crazy American was throwing red feathers on green string into the Ganges," she said. "Call me crazy, too, but I just had to see it."

"Providing merriment for the locals is just part of the job," I quipped.

Before she could reply a throng of hundreds appeared at the top of the stone staircase. Many of them were singing and carrying purple flowers. I looked far down the bank at the adjoining ghats and saw thousands more. One by one they cast the flowers into the river and then waded in and started bathing. Within minutes we were surrounded by a multitude of half-naked people. The woman was snapping pictures of the bathers surrounded by floating wheels of purple flowers. I felt asinine in my waders and vest.

"Do they come down to take a bath like this every day?" I asked.

"Once a year they come to wash away their sins," she said. "In the next ten days a half-million people will bathe along this half-mile stretch. Hindu scriptures say the festival dates back to the origins of the earth when gods and demons squabbled over who got holy nectar."

I watched as hundreds poured water over their heads. "And the holy nectar does what?"

"A drop guarantees immortality," she said.

"So we're all here scrubbing up for immortality?"

"I suppose you could put it that way," she said.

"Then I have a chance at it, too?" I said, throwing her a smirk.

She shook her head and grinned. "I don't think the waters of immortality penetrate rubber waders."

"Oh," I said, feeling even more foolish.

She snapped another picture. "So who are you? What are you doing here?"

"Patrick Gallagher. I'm filming a documentary on Hinduism using the construction of the ancient temples to tell the story."

"Really?" she said, putting her hands on her hips and shooting me a bemused expression. "I just published a book of photographs on the temples."

"You're Emily Beckworth?" I said, impressed. She was legendary for going native in various cultures around the world, then using her insider status to take intimate portraits. In the past ten years she'd published award-winning books on Japanese Zen monks and their monasteries, aboriginal tribes in Australia's outback, the Yak herdsmen of Outer Mongolia, and the Stone-Age peoples of Papua New Guinea.

"I am," she said.

"You wouldn't be interested in being my guide, would you?"

She cocked her head and gave me an odd smile. "Depends on what the pay is."

A flash on the surface of the Bluekill River startled me from my memory.

It's rare, but during big runoffs, lunker brown trout will sometimes leave their carrying positions behind rocks to flare up to seize mice and other small bait churning at the surface. I cast twenty feet below the flash and stripped line. Instantly, I felt the hook catch and my rod bent nearly in two.

Monster! I thought, my heart pounding. Bluekill monster brown trout. A trout like this could salvage my birthday.

I tried to play him on the six-weight line, but he felt twelve, fifteen pounds. Maybe more. I would have to wait until the invisible beast tired to have any chance at landing him. The spool gyrated. The line screamed through the ferules. The fish headed straight downstream toward a beech tree that had crashed into the river during the previous night's storm. If the fish got into the submerged branches the line would snap. I would lose him. I stumbled after the fish, trying to close the gap between us, twitching the line like some voodoo priest performing an exorcism.

Suddenly there was slack line on the water.

"You've got to be shitting me!" I shouted, figuring he'd shaken free the fly. I slapped the water in disgust. Then slapped it again. "Damn it!"

Dejected, I started reeling the line in. Eight feet of slack and the line tightened and a great weight rolled toward me, catching in the current then tugging away. He was still on! But very sluggish *Had he become tangled?* I wondered.

With the wading stick I eased my way forward, stopping every few yards to reel in the coils of slack line. At a bend in the river I came to the end of the floating line. The butt section of the tapered leader disappeared under the coffee-colored water just in front of the half-submerged beech tree.

I ignored the image of a big brown trout's razor-sharp teeth, put my hand around the leader, and followed it down under the water to where it met the tippet. The line was as taut as a tuned piano string. I found the streamer's thick hackle, then groped forward, searching gingerly for the hook.

My fingers brushed what felt like stiff cloth and I jerked back, startled by the sensation. No big fish, but my heart was beating like I had a blue marlin hook-up. I reached down again to pinch and rub what lay beyond the hook.

It was stiff cloth.

I grabbed a handful of the fabric and pulled, feeling that heavy weight roll toward me, then catch in the current and jamb back into the limbs of the downed beech tree. The cork butt of the flyrod wedged tight among the beech tree's exposed limbs. I dipped deep with both hands and pulled upward with all my might. The weight came toward me and surfaced. I was staring at the face of a dead man.

I was screaming long before I was aware I was screaming.

Explore Uncharted Terrains of Mystery
with Anna Pigeon, Parks Ranger by

NEVADA BARR

TRACK OF THE CAT

72164-3/$6.50 US/$8.50 Can

National parks ranger Anna Pigeon must hunt down the killer of a fellow ranger in the Southwestern wilderness—and it looks as if the trail might lead her to a two-legged beast.

A SUPERIOR DEATH

72362-X/$6.99 US/$8.99 Can

Anna must leave the serene backcountry to investigate a fresh corpse found on a submerged shipwreck at the bottom of Lake Superior.

ILL WIND

72363-8/$6.99 US/$8.99Can

FIRE STORM

72528-7/$6.50 US/$8.50 Can

ENDANGERED SPECIES

72583-5/$6.99 US/$8.99Can

The Joanna Brady Mysteries by
National Bestselling Author

An assassin's bullet shattered Joanna Brady's world,
leaving her policeman husband to die in the Arizona
desert. But the young widow fought back the only way
she knew how: by bringing the killers to justice . . . and
winning herself a job as Cochise County Sheriff.

DESERT HEAT
76545-4/$5.99 US/$7.99 Can

TOMBSTONE COURAGE
76546-2/$6.99 US/$8.99 Can

SHOOT/DON'T SHOOT
76548-9/$6.50 US/$8.50 Can

DEAD TO RIGHTS
72432-4/$6.99 US/$8.99 Can

*And the Newest Sheriff Joanna Brady Mystery
Available in Hardcover*

SKELETON CANYON